Young Adventurers: Heroes, Explorers & Swashbucklers

All rights reserved. No part of this book shall be reproduced or transmitted in any form or by any means, electronic, mechanical, magnetic, photographic including photocopying, recording or by any information storage and retrieval system, without prior written permission of the publisher. No patent liability is assumed with respect to the use of the information contained herein. Although every precaution has been taken in the preparation of this book, the publisher and author assume no responsibility for errors or omissions. Neither is any liability assumed for damages resulting from the use of the information contained herein.

This is a work of fiction. Names, characters, places, and incidents either are the product of the author's imagination or are used fictitiously. Any resemblance to actual events or locales or persons, living or dead, is entirely coincidental.

ISBN-13: 978-1-940758-07-7

Cover Design by Instinctivedesign

Published by:
Intrigue Publishing, LLC
11505 Cherry Tree Crossing Rd. #148
Cheltenham, MD 20623-9998

**Young Adventurers:
Heroes, Explorers & Swashbucklers**
Tales of teens saving the day in the past, the present, the future & other worlds

Table of Contents

PINEY POWER 1
SIDETRACKED 17
AIR AND SPACE AFTER DARK.......................................41
THE MYSTERY OF RAVEN'S HOLLOW 53
THE GIRL WHO SLIPPED THROUGH THE MIRROR 67
PUPPY LOVE AND ZOMBIES 97
FANGIRL, RIP AND THE ALIEN 119
COMING OF AGE 134
WOLF DAWN 153
SISTER GRASS 176
TOORI'S CONSTELLATION 188
THE HACK-JACK PROSPECT..205
THE WRECK OF THE BLUE PLOVER...........................223
RETURN OF THE KNAVE 243
FIRST MISSION..271
THE POWER 284
THE BLUE ORB 292
CONTRIBUTORS..306

Meet the young adventurer who will grow up to be known as Repairman Jack, an underground mercenary who is a fix-it man for your supernatural problems. As you'll see, Jack started fixing things pretty early...

PINEY POWER

F. Paul Wilson

Old Man Foster had the signs posted all over his land.

NO FISHING
NO HUNTING
NO TRAPPING
NO TRESPASSING

No kidding. And no big deal.

Jack never paid them much attention. He figured since he wasn't involved in the first three, he deserved a pass on the last. No, what caught Jack's eye was the bright red object tacked to the bark just below the sign.

"Hey, check it out," he said, hitting the brakes. His tires skidded in the sandy soil as his BMX came to a stop. "Who'd put a reflector way out here?"

Weezy stopped her bike beside his. "Doesn't make sense."

Her birth certificate said "Louise" but no one had called her that since she turned two. She was older than Jack–hit fifteen last week, while Jack still had a few months to go. As usual, she was all in black–sneaks, jeans, Bauhaus T-shirt. She'd wound her dark hair into two braids today, giving her a Wednesday Addams look.

"Never noticed it before."

"Because it wasn't there," she said.

Jack accepted that as fact. They used this firebreak trail a lot when they were cruising the Barrens, and if the reflector had

Young Adventurers

been here before, she'd remember. Weezy never forgot anything. Ever.

He touched the clear sap coating on the head of the nail that fixed it to the tree. His fingertip came away wet. He showed her.

"This is fresh–really fresh."

Weezy touched the goop and nodded. "Like maybe this morning."

Jack checked the ground and saw tire tracks. It had rained last night and these weren't washed out in the slightest.

"Looks like a truck," he said, pointing.

Weezy nodded. "Two sets–coming and going. And one's deeper than the other." She looked at Jack. "Hauled something in or took something out."

"Maybe it was Old Man Foster himself."

"Could be."

Foster had supposedly owned this chunk of the Jersey Pine Barrens forever, but no one had ever seen him. No one had ever seen anyone posting the land, either, but the signs were everywhere.

"Want to follow?"

She glanced at her watch and shook her head. "Got to go to Medford with my mom."

"Again? What's this–an every Wednesday thing?"

She looked away. "No. Just works out that way." When she looked back, disappointment shone in her eyes. "You going without me?"

Jack sensed she wanted them to go together, but he didn't think he could hold off.

"Yeah. Probably nothing to see. If I find anything, we can come back together."

She nodded and offered half a smile. "Sure you won't get lost without me?"

He glanced at the sun sliding down the western sky. Every year, people–mostly hunters–entered the Barrens and were never seen again. Folks assumed they got lost and starved. No big surprise in a million-plus acres of mostly uninhabited pine forest. If a vanilla sky moved in, you could lose all sense of direction and wander in circles for days. But with the sun visible, Jack knew all he had to do was keep heading west and he'd hit civilization.

"I'll manage somehow. See you later."

He watched her turn her Schwinn, straddle the banana seat, and ride off with a wave. After the trees had swallowed her, Jack turned off the fire trail and began following the tire tracks along the narrow passage–little more than two ruts separated by a grassy ridge and flanked by the forty-foot scrub pines that dominated the Barrens. They formed a thick wall, crowding the edges of the path, reaching over him with their crooked, scraggly branches.

The passage forked and the tracks bore to the right. A half dozen feet into the fork he spotted another reflector. At the next fork the tracks bore left, and sure enough, another reflector.

Odd. He'd figured the first had been a marker for the starting point of the trail. Grass and trees could thicken over a growing season and obscure what had once been an obvious opening. But whoever had come along here this morning was marking every turn, placing reflectors where headlights would pick them up as they approached. That meant he was planning to come back in the dark. Maybe tonight. Maybe many nights.

Why?

Jack found the answer a half mile farther on where the tire tracks ended in a clearing with a large, solitary oak in its center. Near its base someone had dumped a dozen or more 55-gallon oil drums–old ones, rusted, banged up, and leaky.

He jumped at the sound of a car engine roaring his way. A few seconds later a weird-looking contraption bounced into the clearing on the far side. It had the frame of a small Jeep, maybe a Wrangler, with no roof, sides, or hood. The engine was exposed, though the firewall was still in place, and instead of a steering wheel, someone had fixed a long-handled wrench to the column. The front and rear seats had been replaced by a pair of ratty-looking sofas occupied by three kids in their mid teens. Jack recognized the driver: Elvin Neolin from his civics class. He'd seen the other boy around school as well, but the white-haired girl was new.

Pineys.

They lived out here in the woods. Some had jobs in the towns around the Pines, and some lived off the land–hunting, fishing, gardening. All were poor and a few were a little scary looking in their mismatched, ill-fitting clothes and odd features. Hard to say why they seemed odd. Not like they had bug eyes and snaggle teeth; more like looking at a reflection in one of those old-time mirrors where the glass wasn't even.

Some folks called them inbreds, talking about brothers and sisters getting together and having kids. Jack didn't know if any of that was true. People liked to talk, and some people just naturally exaggerated as they went along. But no one could deny that some Pineys didn't look quite right.

The kid riding shotgun was Levi Coffin, a sophomore at SRB High. Coffin was an old Quaker name that Jack envied. Jack Coffin...how cool to have a name like that.

Levi jumped out and strode toward Jack. He was tall and lanky, and his clothes were too short in the arms and legs. His mismatched eyes–one blue and one brown–blazed.

"This your doin'?"

Jack tensed. Levi looked a little scary.

"No way. I just got here." He jerked a thumb over his shoulder, north. "Followed tire tracks from back there. They ended here."

Levi glanced over his shoulder at Elvin who was staring his way. Elvin was on the short side with piercing dark eyes, stiff black hair, and high cheekbones. Looked like he might have some Lenape Indian in him.

Their eyes locked, then Levi turned away, muttering, "All right, all right."

What's *that* all about? Jack wondered.

Levi inspected the tire tracks while Elvin hopped out and walked over to the drums. Jack sensed the white-haired girl staring at him from the buggy. He realized with a start that she had pink irises. White hair...milk-white skin...what was that called?

Albino...she was an albino.

"I can't see him, Levi," she said in a high-pitched voice.

Was she blind?

Piney Power

"What?" Levi swiveled to stare at Jack.

Elvin was struggling with the top to one of the drums. He looked toward Levi who turned back, then gave his head a sideways jerk toward Jack.

Elvin nodded, saying, "Hey, Levi. Gimme a hand."

Levi walked over and touched the lid–barely touched it–and it popped loose.

Jack felt a funny sensation ripple down his spine as he remembered an incident in school with Levi. Something way strange here. He hesitated, then started toward the drums as the two boys lifted the lid. They dropped it when they saw what was inside.

"Damn!" Levi said. "Damn them to hell!"

Jack might have quipped about where else you could damn someone to, but the rage in Levi's voice warned him off. He stepped up and saw the thick, cloudy green liquid; his nose stung from the sharp chemical odor.

"What is it?"

"Some sort of toxic crap," Levi said. "They're using this spot as a dumping ground."

"Who?"

"Crooks from upstate. We've found stuff like this before."

Jack said, "Better than dumping it in some river, I guess."

Levi glared at him and pointed to a barrel on its side. The sand near its top was wet with gunk.

"That one's leaking. It sinks into the ground water. And guess who gets their water from wells out here. *We* do. But who cares about Pineys."

Jack understood some of the reaction. Kids at school tended to rag on the Pineys, make fun of their clothes, joke about the brother-sister connections. But Jack wasn't one of those and didn't like being lumped in with them.

"No fair."

Another look passed between Levi and Elvin, and then Levi shrugged. "Forget it. El says you're okay."

Fine, but Jack hadn't heard El say anything.

"We should tell the cops," Jack said. "My sister used to date a deputy and–"

5

Levi and Elvin and the girl were shaking their heads...same direction, same speed, moving as one. Jack was getting creeped.

"Uh-uh," Levi said. "Cops ain't gonna go patrolling the Pines looking for someone they don't know, who might or might not come back."

"Oh, they'll be back."

Levi's eyes narrowed. "How do you know?"

"Because they marked the path with reflectors."

"Yeah? Show us."

As Jack reached for his bike, Elvin pointed to the weird buggy. "With us."

"You're old enough to drive?"

The two boys laughed.

"Plenty old enough to drive," Levi said. Elvin never said much at school and didn't seem to have much more to say out here. "Just not old enough for a license."

"Aren't you af–?" Jack began, then cut himself off. Afraid of being caught? Out here? By what–the Jersey Devil in a sheriff's Stetson? Stupid question.

He spotted a "Piney Power" sticker on the rusted rear bumper.

"What's that mean?"

Levi shrugged. "Some folks hereabouts think Pineys should get organized and vote and all that." He glanced at Elvin. "We just like the sound of it."

Elvin laughed. "Yeah. Sounds cool."

The girl said nothing, simply stared at him.

Jack gave the buggy another once-over. Without sides, a top, or even a roll bar, it had to be the most dangerous car he'd ever seen. He'd be risking his life in that thing.

"Well," Levi said, "you ridin' or not?"

Jack couldn't wait.

"Wouldn't miss it for the world."

As he seated himself on the rear sofa, the albino girl scooched away and squeezed against the far end. Her pink gaze never wavered from his face.

"I can't see him."

"Yeah?" Levi turned in the front sofa and looked at Jack. "El says he's okay."

"But I can't *see* him!"

Jack waved his hand between them and she flinched.

"You can see me."

"That's Saree," Levi said. "She's talking about a different kind of seeing."

Jack was going to ask what he meant but then Elvin started the engine with a roar.

Trying to ignore Saree's unwavering stare, he directed Elvin down the path, following his own bike tracks, till they came to the firebreak trail. Elvin turned around and drove back.

Levi was right. The Burlington County sheriff's department didn't have the manpower to stake out Old Man Foster's land or even this one path. Could be weeks before the dumpers made a return trip. Had to be a way to make them give themselves away. Or better yet...

An idea began to form.

"What's down that way?" Jack said, pointing left as they approached the first fork.

"More of the same," Levi said. "Why?"

"Wondering if there's a spring nearby...the deeper and wetter the better."

"I know a cripple," Saree said, still staring.

Elvin followed her directions through a few more forks that left Jack totally disoriented.

"You know where we are, right?"

Saree rolled her eyes.

Okay, dumb question to ask a Piney. But at least she seemed to be relaxing a little.

A few minutes later, she said, "Right up here."

Elvin rolled to a stop before a thirty-foot-wide cripple–a water-filled depression half-surrounded by white cedars. Without the cedars it would have been called a spring.

Jack couldn't help smiling when he saw it.

"Yeah, this'll do."

"Do what?"

When he told them their eyes lit. Saree even smiled.

"I still can't see you," she said. "But I think you're okay."

Weird. Too weird.

2

"What's wrong with inbreeding?" Jack said as he spooned some niblets into the well he'd made in his mashed potatoes.

His mother gasped. "Not at the dinner table."

"No, really. I want to know."

His father cleared his throat and adjusted his steel-rimmed glasses. "Thinking of marrying Kate?"

Kate laughed as Jack said, "No!"

His folks sat at opposite ends while Jack and his older sister Kate sat across from each other. Only his missing brother Tom kept it from being a full family meal. Jack didn't miss him. Tom was a pain.

"Then where's this coming from?"

Jack shrugged. "Kids at school talk about Pineys..."

He couldn't get those weird kids out of his mind. They seemed so different...like they had their own language...an unspoken one. And that lid on the barrel...Elvin couldn't budge it but Levi just touched it and it popped free. It reminded Jack of the time Levi and Jake Shuett faced off in the cafeteria a couple of weeks ago over some remark Jake had made about Pineys. Suddenly a catsup pack Jake was holding squirted all over him and his lunch plate dumped in his lap. Jack had written it off to a spaz attack. He hadn't given it much thought, but now...

He wasn't expecting much information from his folks, but Kate was home on a laundry run from medical school–it was only in Stratford, barely thirty miles away–and maybe she'd know.

He glanced at her. "Why's it bad?"

Kate was slim with pale blue eyes and faint freckles. After starting med school she'd cut her long blond hair back to a short, almost boyish length. Jack still wasn't used to it.

She paused, then said, "It's bad because we all have defective 'recessive genes' hidden in our DNA that are passed on from parent to child. Now, as long as that defective recessive gene is matched up with a working gene, all is well. But if a mother and a father both have the same recessive gene, and each gives it to a child, that child could have problems."

"I saw an albino girl today—"

She nodded. "Perfect example: Two normal-skinned parents, each carrying an albino gene, have a one-in-four chance of having an albino child. Family members tend to share a lot of the same recessives, and so inbreeding—when close relatives have children—increases the risk of genetic diseases, because the closer you're related, the greater the odds of matching up the same recessives in your kids."

Now the important question: "But are all recessive genes bad? Could there be ones for, like, big muscles or a good memory?"

Kate smiled. "You're thinking. That's good. Yes, plants and animals are bred for drought resistance and giving more milk and the like."

"Well, in that case, inbreeding people could have some good effects, right?"

"Theoretically, yes. But for every Einstein or Muhammad Ali, you could get a number of kids with cystic fibrosis."

Or weird powers?

Or maybe I read too much science fiction, Jack thought.

3

Jack awoke to the sound of someone whispering his name...coming from the window. He hopped out of bed and crossed his darkened room. The high moon lit the grinning face on the far side of the screen.

"Levi?"

"Would you believe they came back again tonight?"

Jack felt his heart rate kick into high gear. "They took the bait?"

"Hook, line, and sinkhole. Figured since it was your idea, you oughta come see. We got the car. Wanna?"

"Be right there."

He pulled on jeans and a rugby shirt, stepped into his Vans, then unlatched the screen and slipped into the night. Levi led him around the corner to where Elvin and Saree were waiting in the buggy, Saree behind the wheel–no, wrench. Her white hair looked silver in the moonlight. They hopped in and Saree took off without a word. At least she couldn't stare at him.

The Pines were practically in Jack's backyard, but she entered along a path he didn't know. She made seemingly random turns through the trees but seemed to know where she was going. Finally she stopped in a small clearing.

"Gotta walk from here," Levi said, "else they'll hear us."

The four of them hopped out and this time Saree led the way, single file, down a deer path.

"They fell for it, Jack," Levi said from behind him. "Just like you said. I never would've thought of that in a million years. You got a twisted mind. I like that."

Jack enjoyed the praise, but thought the solution had been obvious. Whoever had dumped those barrels didn't know the Pines, otherwise he wouldn't have needed to post reflectors. So Jack's idea had been to move the reflectors off the path to the dumping ground and onto a path that led to the cripple instead.

He heard angry voices before he saw anyone. Saree slowed her pace and gradually a glow began to grow through the trunks. They crouched as they neared the treeline. Jack peeked through the underbrush and saw a flatbed truck angled nose down into the cripple. Its headlights were still on and its motor running. A blue tarp covered whatever was stacked in its bed. Its front end sat bumper deep in the water and its rear wheels had dug ruts in the soil from trying to reverse its way out.

One man was cursing and swearing as he stood in the two-foot-deep water and pushed against the front grille while another gunned the engine and spun the tires.

"Now that we've got them," Jack said, "what do we do with them? Call the sheriff?"

Levi shook his head. "No way. We bring in some grownups. They'll take care of them."

"Take care of them how?"

"Piney justice."

Piney justice...Jack had heard about that. He was going to say something, but right then the one in the water gave up pushing

Piney Power

and slammed a hand on the hood.

"Ain't gonna happen, Tony!"

Tony–dark, heavyset with a thick mustache–jumped out and began kicking the water in a rage.

"Save it, man," said the other guy as he splashed past him, heading toward the rim of the cripple. "We're gonna have to offload this stuff to get outa here."

"How'd this happen, Sammy? We marked the trail!"

"Must've made a wrong turn. Or..." He stopped and looked around. "Or somebody moved the markers."

Tony stared at him. "Who?"

"Wise-ass locals, my guess. Probably out there right now having a good laugh."

Uh-oh, Jack thought. Time to leave.

"Yeah?" Tony reached into the truck cab and pulled out a revolver. "Well, laugh at this!"

He began firing wildly. One of the slugs zipped through the brush between Jack and Saree, narrowly missing them. Jack froze in terrified shock while Saree let out a shrill yelp of surprise.

"There!" Sammy shouted, pointing their way.

Levi yanked on Jack's arm. "Run!"

Jack didn't need to be told twice–or even once. The next half minute became a riot of crouched running, snapping brush and branches, darkness ahead, shouting behind, and then a high-pitched scream that brought everything to an abrupt, panting halt.

"Saree?" Levi said, looking back. "I thought she was–aw, man, they got Saree!" He turned to Jack. "Go with El for help!"

"You're staying?"

He nodded. "Can't leave her."

Jack wavered. Why had he come here? He wanted to be home. Then Saree screamed again.

"I'll stay with you."

"No way. You go–"

"Elvin doesn't need help. Saree does."

Elvin was already at the car, starting it up. He wasn't waiting. That settled it.

"I don't get it," Levi said as he turned and started back toward the cripple.

"What's there to get?"

"You don't owe her. She's not kin."

Jack couldn't see what that had to do with anything. He wished he'd stayed in bed, but he was here now.

"We came together, we leave together."

Levi didn't reply. They were almost back to the cripple.

"Come out, come out wherever you are," a voice was singsonging. "We got your ugly girlfriend."

Jack peeked through the brush. The moonlight and backwash from the headlights revealed Tony standing on the rim of the cripple by the rear of the truck. He had his gun in one hand and a fistful of Saree's hair in the other. She looked terrified.

Sammy, standing a few feet to his right, shouted, "The rest of you get out here now. We ain't gonna hurt you. Just put you to work. You got us into this mess, so you're gonna get us out."

Jack saw three options. Help was on the way, so until it arrived they either could do nothing, find ways to distract them, or show themselves and do whatever they wanted.

"Get out here or this could get ugly," Tony said, twisting Saree's hair and making her wince. "You don't wanna see *how* ugly."

Jack winced too, and crossed doing nothing off the list. He decided on distraction. He could always show himself if that didn't work.

"Stay here," he whispered. "Gonna try something."

"Wait–" Levi grabbed for his arm but Jack pulled out of reach.

He moved counterclockwise along the treeline, feeling around the ground until he found a fist-sized hunk of shale.

Perfect.

He backed up, cocked his arm, and let fly toward the truck. The rock bounced off the tarp with a gonging sound, then splashed in the water.

"Son of a bitch!" Sammy yelled, flinching.

"You guys deaf?" Tony shouted. "Remember what I said about things getting ugly?"

Piney Power

Oh no. Jack's gut knotted as he saw Tony yank Saree backward. She lost her balance and fell into the water. Tony stayed with her and held her head under the surface as her arms and legs thrashed and splashed. It was only a couple of feet deep, but plenty enough to drown her.

"She stays under till you come out!" Tony yelled.

Jack couldn't take it. Only option three remained.

"Okay! Okay!"

His bladder ached to empty as he jumped out of the bushes with his hands raised.

To his left Levi also stepped out, hands high, saying, "Let her up!"

As Sammy started toward them, Tony pointed the gun their way and grinned. "When I'm damn good and ready. You kids–*aah!*" He dropped the gun and released Saree as he grabbed his right hand with his left. "She broke my finger!"

Saree sat up, choking and gasping and crying. Jack had seen one of her thrashing arms come near Tony's hand but no way it touched him. She lurched to her feet and staggered away toward dry ground.

Tony started after her. "You little–my gun!" He turned and bent, feeling around underwater.

As Sammy turned to look at his buddy, Jack took off toward Saree. He grabbed her outstretched hand and pulled her up the bank of the cripple.

Sammy started toward them. "Hey–!"

Suddenly he tripped and fell face first into the water. But instead of rebounding to his feet, he stayed down and began kicking and thrashing as Saree had. He couldn't seem to get up.

Tony finally noticed. "What the hell are you doing?"

He started toward Sammy but tripped himself. He went down and stayed down too. Were they stuck in the mud? No, their arms and legs were free. It almost looked like they were being held down. But–

Jack saw Levi on his knees, white-faced, eyes focused on the men in the cripple. As Jack headed for him, Saree grabbed his arm.

"Leave Levi be."

13

Jack pulled free. As he neared he could see the boy's lips pulled back in a snarl. His face and hair dripped sweat, his shirt was soaked, and air hissed between his clenched teeth like he was bench pressing twice his own weight.

"Levi...?"

He glanced at Jack and just then the two men in the cripple got their heads back above water. But not for long. Before they could draw a full breath they plunged their faces back beneath the surface.

And then everything seemed to happen at once. Elvin roared out of the trees in the buggy followed by a pickup full of rough-clothed men with shotguns, Levi let out a breath and slumped forward onto his hands, the two men in the cripple got their heads out of water and sucked air.

When they caught their breath and looked around they found themselves staring into the headlights of the buggy and the pickup, and down the muzzles of half a dozen shotguns. One of the Piney men, tall with a gray beard and features that looked like they'd been taken apart and put back together wrong, had lifted the tarp and was looking at the barrels hidden beneath.

"Not good," he said, shaking his head. "Not good ay-tall."

"You don't wanna mess with us," Tony said, still panting. "We're connected, if you know what I mean."

"I'm right sure of that," the old Piney said. "And we'll want to know who to." He swiveled and his gaze fell on Jack. "Who's this 'un?"

"Friend of ours," Levi said, rising to his feet. He'd caught his breath. "He set the trap."

"Well, we're right grateful for that, but he ain't one of us. Take him back wherever he came from."

"What about them?" Jack said, pointing to Tony and Sammy.

"You forget about them. We're all gonna have us a nice chat, then we'll send 'em home."

"But–"

Levi grabbed his arm and pulled him away. "No questions. Let's go."

Elvin and Saree were already in the buggy. As soon as Jack and Levi settled on the rear couch, Elvin put it in gear and they roared off.

"What happened back there?" Jack said.

He was feeling weak and shaky. That guy had almost drowned Saree, and he'd never been shot at before–never dreamed it would ever happen and never wanted it to happen again. Ever.

Levi shook his head. "Nothing. And don't go yakking about it."

"You kidding? Tell my folks I snuck out tonight to see some toxic dumpers we trapped and wound up getting shot at? Yeah, right. Soon as I get home I'm gonna run into their bedroom and blab all about it."

Levi laughed. "Okay."

Of course he'd tell Weezy. She'd eat it up.

But Jack hadn't been talking about the dumpers.

"I meant you. What did you do to those guys?"

The smiled vanished. "Nothing."

"But I saw–"

He stared straight ahead. "You saw a couple of guys slipping around on a mucky cripple bottom and getting stuck. That's all."

He was sure it had been more than that. But what exactly?

Saree turned to face him. "Yeah, that's all it was, Jack. But what about you? What's your talent? Is it being able to hide? Is that why I can't see you?"

What was she talking about?

"I don't have any talent."

"Maybe you just don't know about it yet. You're hiding something, but that's okay. You came back for me. I never expected that. I still can't see you, but I like you."

Jack had no idea how to respond to that, so he didn't.

They dropped him off about a block from his house. As they raced off he saw their bumper sticker flash in the moonlight.

Piney Power.

He had an idea why those kids liked the sound of it.

4

"I can't believe all that happened without me," Weezy said as they entered Jack's house though the kitchen.

He'd waited till after school to tell her about it.

"Believe me, you were better off at home." He shuddered at a vision of that Tony guy holding Weezy's head underwater instead of Saree's. "While it was happening, I wanted to be *anywhere* but there."

As they stepped into the front room where his folks were watching the 6:30 news, a TV reporter said, *"The two bodies found inside those barrels of toxic waste have been identified."*

Jack stiffened as he recognized the mug shots on the screen.

"Anthony Lapomarda and Santo 'Sammy' Carlopoli have long rap sheets. Their bodies were found outside a South Philly body shop this morning along with two dozen barrels of toxic waste. More waste was found inside the body shop, along with a number of stolen cars. The suspected chop shop—"

He nudged Weezy and whispered, "That's them!"

The old Piney's parting words came back: *We're all gonna have us a nice chat, then we'll send 'em home.*

He hadn't mentioned *how* they'd be sent home. He glanced at Weezy and found her staring back with wide, dark eyes.

"Piney justice," he said, feeling a chill.

His father looked up. "What?"

"Nothing."

Dad pointed to the TV. "That's why we live out here. To get away from scum like that. You don't have to worry about running into any of their sort in these parts."

"I guess not, Dad."

At least not anymore.

In the not-too-distant past, a teenage secret agent in training learns the one thing spies should never do!

SIDETRACKED

Jeffrey Westhoff

January 1985

The train lurched and so did Sophia's stomach. She was in the central corridor of the sleeper car with no window in sight, only doorways, so she doubled back toward the connecting door she had just passed through, running against the train's undeniable forward motion. "No, no, no, no, no!" she said as the train incrementally built up speed.

Passing through the accordion passageway between the cars, Sophia felt the corrugated iron floorboards shift with the train's motion. This couldn't be happening. Why had the train left early? The connecting door slid aside with a pneumatic sigh, and Sophia stepped into the lounge car. She stooped to look through the nearest window and saw Grand Central Station's cavernous train yard rolling past. Sophia caught her face reflected in the window. Panic filled her eyes. She could hear the increased heartbeat racing in her chest. Sophia looked down at the slim Swatch watch with the plastic lavender band. It said she still had nearly ten minutes before the train's departure. Then she noticed the second hand wasn't moving. Her watch had stopped, probably right when she climbed aboard the train. "So much for Swiss goddamned timing," Sophia muttered.

This was bad, Sophia told herself, but not disastrous. She simply had to get off the train at the first stop. It would be a suburb in Westchester County, maybe Yonkers. She wouldn't be on the train more than an hour. She just had to avoid the conductor asking for her nonexistent ticket. She just had to avoid being noticed by Janov.

She could hear Ms. Chambers' mantra: "Observe and report. Don't engage. Never engage!" All right, but Sophia hadn't engaged Janov. This still counted as observation, though perhaps observation more aggressive than Ms. Chambers would approve.

Another iron stanchion went by the window. Sophia looked at her face again, pleased to see it had relaxed now that she had an escape plan. A lock of her auburn hair had fallen across her eyes. Sophia pushed it away and used the moment to appraise her features. She wished that her cheekbones were a bit higher, that her lips were a bit fuller, that her nose was a bit smaller, that her gray eyes were a bit bluer, but she was pretty enough that the boys sometimes turned their heads. She wasn't a striking beauty, but Ms. Chambers didn't want striking beauties in the program. They attracted attention.

For the last four months, shortly after beginning her junior year at the Elleston Academy for Girls, Sophia Layton had spent after-school and weekend hours as part of a secret FBI program of teenage girls shadowing foreign diplomats throughout Manhattan. The diplomats were all possible spies, so the program focused mostly on the Soviet delegation to the United Nations, though Sophia heard a rumor one of the other girls spent two weeks tailing a woman from the Israeli consulate.

The girls' administrator, Ms. Chambers–Special Agent Chambers, to be technical–informally referred to the program as her Harriet Brigade, named for the title character from *Harriet the Spy*. Sophia subsequently read the book and was disappointed it didn't feature genuine espionage.

"You won't be paid much," Ms. Chambers told Sophia during the interview, "but each member of the Harriet Brigade will receive a letter of recommendation to the university of her choice. The ranks of the FBI are well-stocked with Ivy League alumni." Sophia smiled hungrily at the offer. Straight As from the Elleston Academy might be adequate enough for Princeton, but straight As plus a letter of recommendation on Department of Justice letterhead should put her over the top.

Sidetracked

Sophia's parents and friends believed she had an internship in the FBI's file room at 26 Federal Plaza. That was the position she thought she was applying for when she saw the posting on the jobs board in the guidance counselor's office at Elleston Academy. Sophia later learned Ms. Chambers recruited exclusively from private girls' schools because she didn't want teenage boys in the program. The biggest reason was the maturity factor. "If a boy took this position," Ms. Chambers told Sophia at the start of training, "he would leave this room pointing his finger like a gun humming 'The James Bond Theme.' Then a week into his first assignment he would get bored and quit." Another reason, also important, was that Ms. Chambers believed girls were more observant. "If your subject changed his haircut or wore a new pair of shoes, you'd notice. A boy wouldn't," she said. "More pertinent, you'd notice if your subject was wearing a carnation in his lapel when he usually doesn't, or was sitting in a coffee shop reading the Times when he usually reads the Daily News. Both could mean he's signaling a contact."

Sophia recognized Ms. Chambers' reasoning as sexual discrimination. It made Sophia mildly uncomfortable, but as long as it worked in her favor she didn't see a need to complain. And whom would she complain to? The federal government?

The weeklong training period began with a lecture from Ms. Chambers on basic surveillance and shadowing techniques. "Your job is to be invisible. Do not go on assignment dressed like Cyndi Lauper or Madonna." That got a laugh from the girls. Both singers had become MTV sensations the previous summer. Sophia was certain that even though Cyndi Lauper dressed like a thrift shop explosion and talked like Betty Boop when she appeared on David Letterman, hers was a true talent and she would be a star for years while sex kitten Madonna would fade quickly.

The day following Ms. Chambers' lecture began what Sophia considered the most organized tournament of hide and seek ever played on the streets of Manhattan. The girls were paired off each afternoon. One girl was instructed to tail the other without losing her, and the other girl was instructed to shake her follower. The sessions lasted two hours. Ms. Chambers insisted it wasn't a competition. Yet Sophia was the only girl who "won" every session, whether she was the tag or the tail. At the end of the week, Ms. Chambers' eyes lingered on Sophia and the instructor gave her a slight nod. Sophia felt a rush of satisfaction.

As the assignments started, Ms. Chambers reiterated that the girls of the Harriet Brigade were "extra sets of eyes," a backstop to regular FBI surveillance that might result in added, beneficial intelligence. If the subject lingered on a park bench or walked up to a tree, the Harriet was supposed to pass along the location of the bench or tree, but not approach it. The Harriet Brigade would be called off if involved if a subject was suspected of active involvement in an espionage operation.

Even so, those early assignments carried a sense of danger. Late last summer, only a few weeks before Sophia joined the Harriet Brigade, President Reagan made a joke when he thought the microphones were off. "My fellow Americans," he began, "I'm pleased to tell you that today I've signed legislation that will outlaw Russia forever. We begin bombing in five minutes." The already frosty relationship between the super powers went into a deep freeze overnight. "This is the worst it's been since the Cuban Missile Crisis," Sophia's father said a few days later. Her mother grimaced and changed the subject to the new Clint Eastwood movie, something about a detective on the edge.

It was into this charged atmosphere that Sophia joined the Harriet Brigade. During her early days she felt a thrill watching suspected spies from the "Evil Empire," as President Reagan once called the Soviet Union. But the thrill faded as routine set in, and Sophia understood why Ms. Chambers believed boys would quit the program once they realized their James Bond fantasies would go unfulfilled. Sophia had never seen a subject go anywhere near a park bench. Most of her assignments came down to watching her man leave the United Nations and get into a cab or limousine. Sophia would call in to the FBI, report the vehicle's license plate number, then go home.

Such had been the nature of her job for months until this evening, a Friday, when Janov broke his pattern.

Sidetracked

Sophia knew slightly more about Vasily Janov than her prior subjects, which was their name and nothing more. When Ms. Chambers gave her the new assignment, Sophia joked, "Oh, another KGB guy?" and Ms. Chambers made an uncharacteristic slip when she murmured, "More likely a GRU guy." Ms. Chambers caught her indiscretion immediately, refusing to add anything else, except that Sophia was to identify Janov by the code name TENSPEED. A trip to the library informed Sophia that the GRU was the Soviet Union's military intelligence agency and that it had a rivalry with the KGB just as the FBI had a rivalry with the CIA. If Janov were a GRU agent operating in the United States, he might be stepping on the KGB's toes.

Early on, Sophia had witnessed nothing to indicate Janov was any sort of spy. To her eyes he was a U.N. diplomat who slipped into a limousine every afternoon and drove off into the care of the FBI surveillance team watching his residence. That had been his daily pattern until this evening. This evening he had ignored the taxis and limos in the circular drive and crossed First Avenue at the busy Forty-second Street intersection. He continued West. Sophia fell in a cautious half block behind him. This was an unusually cold January, and Sophia was underdressed for it, with only a light blue ski jacket (a recent Christmas present), stocking cap, earmuffs, and a pair of mittens to protect her from the frigid air. She envied Janov, who wore a heavy pea coat and a fur hat. At least it wasn't snowing.

After two blocks Janov stopped in front of a shoe store to look at the display window. Anyone else would think he was considering a new pair of shoes, but Sophia knew Janov was using the window's reflective surface to check for tails. She slowed her pace but didn't stop. Janov would be looking for anyone who stopped at the same time he did or who ducked into another shop. The thing about Manhattan, Sophia knew, was that the sidewalks were always crowded, especially this close to Midtown, so spotting suspicious behavior in fellow pedestrians was nearly impossible. Besides, Janov would be looking for a suspicious man, probably with a short haircut. He wouldn't pay any attention to a sixteen-year-old girl. Janov started walking again after about twenty seconds, and Sophia paused at a bookshop window to let him gain a half a block on her.

As they passed the Chrysler Building Sophia had a suspicion where Janov was heading. She closed the distance between them, and her instincts proved correct when he turned toward Grand Central Station.

Sophia risked closing the gap between herself and the Russian as she followed him into the station. Rush hour had passed, but the nation's largest train terminal was still bustling with borough dwellers arriving for a Friday night on Broadway, Amtrak travelers squinting at the departures board, and sightseers eager to imbibe expensive cocktails at The Campbell Apartment. If Janov was meeting a contact here, Sophia needed to witness it. She must not lose him in the crowd. Luckily, Janov was a tall man and he had left on his fur hat. The hat was an ermine beacon that Sophia followed through the shifting masses.

Sophia watched the hat separate itself from the pack and disappear into a men's room. If Janov was meeting a contact in there, Sophia could do nothing about it. She slipped into a nearby newsstand and picked up a fan magazine with Duran Duran on the cover. Not her favorite band, but the Talking Heads weren't available. She flipped open the magazine and pretended to read as she angled her body so that she could see the men's room door from the corner of her eye. After maybe two minutes Janov emerged and Sophia was about to replace the magazine when she saw it wasn't Janov, but a man of similar build wearing an identical pea coat and fur hat. Sophia kept to her post.

Thirty seconds later Janov appeared, bareheaded and wearing a camel-hair coat. He and the other man must have switched coats. A thrill jolted through Sophia. Janov was trying to shake a tail! He was trying to shake a tail, but he failed because he didn't shake her. She set down the magazine and fell in behind Janov again. It occurred to her that perhaps Janov had just made contact, that signals were exchanged along with the coats, but her intuition told her something else was up.

Janov entered the large alcove filled with coin-operated lockers. Following him and pretending to find a locker would be too conspicuous. Sophia slowed her gait and walked past the area, watching him obliquely. Janov headed straight for a locker, pulling one of those keys with the thick orange fob from the pocket of his newly acquired coat. He opened the locker and extracted a suitcase and overnight bag, which he slung over his shoulder.

Sophia remained outwardly calm as another wave of excitement raced from her scalp to her fingertips. Janov was leaving town! After weeks of boring surveillance work, one of her subjects was behaving like a spy. The moment was almost surreal. Now she had to learn what train he was taking and report in to the FBI. She could practically feel that acceptance letter in her hands and see the Princeton seal atop the page.

Sophia stopped in front of a rack of Amtrak brochures and schedules and waited for Janov to return to the concourse. Within moments–before she had time to pick up a brochure– Janov exited the locker area.

That's when he looked at her.

Sophia immediately unfocused her eyes and pretended to watch at someone in the distance. Janov looked away quickly, no more than two seconds. Sophia's skin tightened. She reminded herself that hers was one face among hundreds and that Janov in no way would consider a teenage girl a threat. Yet in those two seconds he glanced at her, Sophia had the feeling her face had been photographed and filed away.

Then Janov was moving again and, though spooked, Sophia knew she had to follow. This was the most important part of her assignment. She had to learn what train he was taking. Janov quickened his pace and so did Sophia, hoping she would be seen as merely another passenger rushing for the same train. She glanced up at a clock to see it was 7:11 p.m. The track entrances were ahead. Janov was walking toward a door marked THE LAKE SHORE LIMITED. Below the name was a list of cities– Boston-Albany, Cleveland-Toledo, Chicago–and the departure time, 7:30. Sophia dodged through a family in front of her. Getting close to Janov was chancy, but she needed to know his destination. The noise increased and the temperature dropped as she stepped onto the platform with only four people between her and Janov. He approached a redcap and Sophia pressed close enough to hear.

"Where to, sir?" the redcap asked.

"Chicago," Janov replied. "I have a bedroom, a roomette."

"Slumbercoach? Yessir. Allow me to take your bag, sir. All right then, follow me."

Janov and the redcap retreated down the platform. Sophia was about to find the nearest pay phone when another redcap approached her and asked, "Where are you traveling to tonight, miss?"

At that moment it occurred to Sophia there was one more key piece of intelligence she could obtain. The FBI would want to put a man on the train somewhere down the line. It would save them time if they knew Janov's room number. The train wouldn't depart for fifteen minutes. Enough time to locate Janov's room and get off. Sophia would show initiative and maybe earn another approving look from Ms. Chambers.

"Where to, miss?" the redcap repeated.

She thought quickly, recalling her train trip to Florida the previous summer to visit her grandparents. Coach passengers did not have to produce their tickets until the conductor came through once the train was underway. She would have to board at a coach car and make her way back to the sleeper cars. She didn't have a suitcase, which meant the redcap would assume her baggage had been checked. But only the larger stations were equipped to handle checked baggage.

"Cleveland," she said.

"All right, miss, you go on up to the sixth car ahead and get on board there. Have a good trip."

Sophia thanked him and jogged along the length of the silver train, ducking around other last-minute passengers. She wished she had a walkie-talkie to contact the FBI, or a wrist-radio device like Dick Tracy wore. She once asked Ms. Chambers if the FBI issued equipment like that. Ms. Chambers replied, "Are you kidding? I have enough trouble requisitioning a computer."

When Sophia reached the sixth car, she bounded up the metal steps into the tiny foyer and slowed down. Running through the cars would draw attention, especially from the conductors. She

Sidetracked

would prefer they ignored her. As she walked into the car she saw few empty seats. Most of the passengers were already settled. The adults read books, magazines, or newspapers, and the teenagers listened to Walkmans. Only the children squirmed. Above the rows, thin slips of paper sprouted from the luggage racks. The slips bore three-letter codes for each passenger's destination. Most of the strips in this car said CLE for Cleveland with several that said ERI, which Sophia figured meant Erie, Pennsylvania. A few said ELY, but Sophia didn't know what city those initials signified.

Moving through the coach cars, Sophia noted the alcoves containing suitcases at the front and rear of the seating areas. Briefcases, duffle bags, and backpacks filled the luggage racks that ran the length of the cars above the seats on either side of the aisle. Sophia knew she had reached the last coach car when almost every destination tag read CHI for Chicago. She checked her watch as she passed through the lounge car, and it told the lie that she still had ten minutes to find Janov's compartment. When she entered the sleeper car, Sophia realized the flaw to her plan. The corridor was empty. The passengers were already in their rooms. She had no way to know which one was Janov's unless she started knocking on doors. That might not be a terrible idea, she had reasoned with herself when the train started to move.

And now she was in the lounge car, a stowaway watching through a darkened window as the Lake Shore Limited made its passage beneath the streets of Manhattan en route to the Midwest. The train had reached cruising speed, and the wheels clicking on the tracks seemed to say, "Connecticut, Connecticut," over and over, emphasizing every syllable and hitting the *C* sounds hard. Sophia surveyed the lounge car. With the voyage just begun, the car was empty except for her and the steward, who stood behind the stainless steel counter in the middle of the car. Like most of the train crew, he was African-American. He was setting snack size bags of potato chips on the counter when he looked up at Sophia.

"Food service doesn't start for another thirty minutes, miss, but I could get you a cup of coffee if you want," he said.

"No, thanks," Sophia replied. "But do you have a schedule?"

Young Adventurers

"A timetable?" he said. "I happen to have a few. Here you go."

Sophia stepped up to the counter as the steward handed her a timetable, which was printed as a trifold brochure. The steward's name badge identified him as Aaron. Sophia thanked him as she opened the schedule. Reading down the timetable's left-hand column, she learned the train made its first stop at 8:18 p.m. in Croton-Harmon. That would be Croton-on-Hudson. A bit farther north than Sophia expected the first stop to be, but it should give her enough time to take a Hudson Line train back into the city and be home by eleven. She would tell her parents she got roped into seeing a movie with friends. She'd pick one she had already seen, probably *Beverly Hills Cop*, in case her parents asked about it.

Sophia wondered again if lying to her parents had become too easy since she joined the Harriet Brigade. Perhaps, but did this make her any different from the average American teenager? Anyway her parents were easy to deal with. Sophia was sure to catch hell from Ms. Chambers for getting herself trapped aboard a train.

She thanked Aaron again, stuffed the schedule into a coat pocket, and left the lounge car. Sophia spent the next thirty minutes moving from one restroom to another to dodge the conductor. She was in a lounge car restroom when she heard the announcement for Croton-Harmon. She stepped out of the restroom and took one last glance down the length of the car before heading for the exit. She gasped at what she saw.

Janov was in the lounge car. He was seated alone at one of the pale yellow Formica-top tables, drinking coffee from a paper cup and reading the Times. Janov was on the side of the car facing the station and was positioned next to the window. Anyone on the platform would see him clearly. He was turned toward Sophia but didn't notice her. As the train slowed, Janov set the paper down and looked out at the platform. He rested his cheek nearest the window on his hand and gripped an earlobe between his thumb and folded forefinger. With a bored expression on his face, Janov tugged at his ear. Twice.

Sidetracked

It was a signal. Sophia was sure of that. Janov was signaling someone on the platform. He was meeting a contact aboard the train. If Sophia got off at Croton-on-Hudson, she would not know which new passenger was Janov's contact. She let out a frustrated, nearly silent growl. She needed to stay aboard to get a good look at the contact and pass along a description to the FBI. Sophia did some mental calculations. The next stop was Poughkeepsie. She had to get off there whether she saw Janov's contact or not because Poughkeepsie was the last stop the Hudson Line. Beyond Poughkeepsie there was no commuter train to return her to Manhattan.

The restroom was adjacent to the passage leading to the sleeper car. Sophia went toward the sleeper car without attracting Janov's attention. She went to the rear of the car and waited inside the far doorway, listening. She was counting on Janov wanting to confer with his contact in his compartment. As soon as she heard someone in the corridor she would make her way forward and hopefully get a good look at Janov's contact before they vanished into his compartment. It was also possible, Sophia knew, that Janov would meet his contact in the dining car, which was at the other end of the train, but that would afford them less privacy. Spies wanted privacy, right?

Apparently they did, because Sophia heard masculine voices down the corridor. She started walking, and Janov came around the corner with another man. They didn't acknowledge her.

"How was your drive?" Janov asked the man.

"Not too bad once I hit the New York line," the man replied. "I tell you, it's snowing a shitstorm in Groton."

Janov frowned when the man mentioned Groton, as if he had been indiscreet. Sophia could guess why. Like any New Yorker who read the newspapers, she knew the Connecticut port was home to most of the U.S. Navy's Atlantic submarine fleet. It was also home to the shipyards that built those submarines and an array of defense contractors that designed the systems that powered the subs. Most of what happens in Groton would be of interest to Soviet military intelligence.

Still moving toward them, Sophia studied the man from Groton. He was in his mid-thirties and handsome, with clear blue eyes and a firm jawline. The only thing Sophia disapproved about his appearance was that he wore his light brown hair puffed up above his forehead, that ridiculous Jack Kemp look. He wore a belted trench coat and carried a briefcase. Sophia looked down at his shoes to see what they would reveal about him, but they were encased in a pair of galoshes. He had spoken with a Boston accent. The FBI would want to know that.

Sophia wondered if the man was Navy or a defense contractor. He wasn't in uniform, but she doubted a Navy man would wear his blues to rendezvous with a Soviet spy. His poofy hair may have looked ridiculous on a grown man, but the part was immaculate. Sophia knew an expensive salon cut when she saw one. She looked at the man's fingernails. They were trimmed so that no white showed at the tips and were buffed to a dull glow. A recent job. Maybe a Navy officer might get a pricey haircut, but Sophia doubted he would schedule a manicure on a Friday afternoon. Most likely, the man was civilian.

Sophia was now confident she could file a detailed description. Janov was reaching to open his door as she passed them.

"Excuse me," she said, giving the men an innocent smile.

"Not at all," Janov replied as he grasped Sophia's upper arm and pushed her into his compartment. His other hand came up to cover her mouth as he maneuvered her into a seat next to the window. Its shade was drawn. As the other man closed the door behind them, sealing the three of them into an Amtrak "roomette" designed for two, Ms. Chambers' admonition echoed in Sophia's thoughts: "Don't engage. Never engage!" This situation was beyond engagement.

"Please don't scream, young lady," Janov said. "I only wish to have a conversation."

The other man's face registered shock. "What the hell are you doing, Vasily?" He pulled his briefcase against his chest.

Without looking at the man, Janov responded, "You should return to your seat, Mr. Jones. I will collect you when this girl and I are finished."

Mr. Jones, who couldn't possibly be named Mr. Jones, said, "I think I had better stay and see what this is about."

Sidetracked

Yes, please stay! Sophia thought. Don't leave me alone with this Russian!

"Very well," Janov said, though his eyes told Sophia this wasn't very well. "Let me do the talking." He settled into the seat opposite Sophia. "Now, my dear, do you promise not to scream if I remove my hand?" Janov's Russian accent was distinct but pleasant. Sophia found this confusing. "I have only a few questions for you," he continued. "All I am is curious."

Sophia nodded her head. She realized all her muscles were clenched. She forced herself to relax them. Mr. Jones, who remained standing in front of the door, watched her nervously. His trench coat had come open, revealing a Burberry lining.

Sophia decided to handle this situation the way she imagined Ms. Chambers' would–coolly. Janov's eyes were sympathetic rather than menacing. That threw Sophia. She decided she would remain cool, or fake it, until the moment she sensed imminent danger. Then she would scream.

Janov took his hand away. Sophia channeled defiance into her voice and said, "Who the hell do you think you are grabbing me like this? It's illegal. It's kidnapping."

Mr. Jones let out an anxious little laugh. "I mean, if you wanted a girl, Vasily–"

"Be quiet!" Janov said, a sneer revealing his distaste for Mr. Jones' words. "I assure you that is not why you are here, young lady."

"Then why am I here?"

"Perhaps I am simply laboring under a misunderstanding, but I have the impression you were following me this evening."

"Following you? Why would I be following you? I don't know who you are."

"Perhaps not, but I saw you several times tonight. Behind me on Forty-second Street. In Grand Central. In the lounge car. And just now right outside my compartment. That seems more than a coincidence to me."

Sophia couldn't believe he had spotted her on Forty-second Street. She wasn't as good at tailing as she thought. "Well, that's all it is," she said, "a coincidence. I think maybe I saw you in Grand Central, but I must have seen dozens of other people who are on the train now. People in train stations tend to ride trains." OK, that's enough, she told herself. Don't protest too much.

"Perhaps, but I am wondering if you are playing a game with your friends. You select a person at random and follow them. Young people play such a game in my country. Although you must have been very determined to win if you followed me aboard a train."

"I'm not playing any game," Sophia said. "I'm just going to Albany."

"Oh, what is in Albany?"

"SUNY. I'm visiting the campus this weekend. I'm thinking of going there."

"A fine school, I am told. But we will be arriving there late tonight. How will you get from the train station to campus? You were alone in Grand Central, so I assume you are traveling alone."

"A student there is picking me up. I'm staying in her dorm room this weekend."

"What is her name?"

"I don't see how that's any of your business."

"I'm merely curious," Janov said casually.

"Allison Stephens, I think. Or maybe Stephenson. I have it in my backpack."

"Oh, when I saw you earlier I don't remember you carrying any luggage. I must have been mistaken." His tone became more convivial and he leaned forward. "What is the name of the dormitory? Is it Adam Hall?"

A warning sounded in Sophia's head. Why would a Russian know the campus of a state school in Albany? She suspected Janov was feeding her the name of a phony dorm to trap her in a lie. "I'm not really sure of the dorm's name," Sophia replied, "and I'm not really comfortable telling you where I'll be spending the night."

"I can respect that," Janov said. His expression indeed conveyed respect, like that of a swordsman acknowledging his thrust had been parried.

Mr. Jones grunted to remind them he was still there. As if he needed to, Sophia thought. The compartment was scarcely larger

Sidetracked

than two phone booths stuck together. Standing at the door, Mr. Jones loomed over her and Janov. Sophia wondered why he didn't take the third seat, the hard plastic one right next to him. A second later, Sophia realized it was a toilet.

Janov resumed his questions. "Now, if you are only going as far as Albany, you must be riding coach. What were you doing in the sleeper car? I could report you to the attendant."

Sophia shrugged. "So report me. I was just exploring. I wanted to know what one of these rooms looked like. I suppose I was curious, too. Like you."

"Well, now that you see what one of these rooms looks like, I hope your curiosity is satisfied."

"It is, and I'd like to go now."

"Soon," Janov said. He gave her a reassuring smile. "I don't suppose you would mind sharing your name?"

"Harriet Welsch," Sophia said. She left out the "M." That would have been pushing it.

Janov's reaction was unexpected. He chuckled delightedly and slapped his knee. "Do you get teased?" he asked.

"For what?" Sophia replied.

"You share your name with a character from a famous American children's book."

Before she could reply, Sophia's voice faltered. She had told the wrong lie. She cleared her throat and said, "Only by people familiar with the book. Not that many people know it, really. I'm surprised you do."

Janov waved his hand in a "la-di-da" circle. "I bought a copy several years ago to send back home to my daughter as a birthday gift. The title amused me."

Sophia didn't respond. Mr. Jones, clearly perplexed, looked from Janov to Sophia and back. "Well," he said, "what's the name of the book?"

"*Harriet the Spy*," Janov said, still smiling at Sophia.

Mr. Jones reacted as if Janov had slapped him. "What?" he asked, filling the single syllable with a soliloquy's worth of apprehension.

"She's not really a spy," Sophia said, feeling compelled to offer Mr. Jones an explanation and allay his fears. "She's just a little girl who snoops on her neighbors and classmates. She would have made a terrible spy. She gets caught."

Sophia turned back to Janov. His smile was gone. He sat watching her, nodding sagely with his folded hands resting between his knees. "Yes," he said. "Spies should not get caught."

Sophia and Janov looked at each other in silence. His gray eyes appeared old. Observing him from a distance over the last few weeks, Sophia had figured he was in his early forties. Now, with Janov less than two feet way, she reckoned he was nearer to fifty. He looked at her as if he wanted to ask another question but didn't know how to form it.

She considered his words: "Spies should not get caught." Was it an admission or an accusation? Perhaps both. Maybe he was acknowledging they had caught each other and had hit an impasse. His manner was not malevolent, but conflicted. Sophia sensed he wanted to work out a solution, and maybe they could if they were alone.

But they were not alone.

"All right," Mr. Jones interjected. "All this talk of spies is making me nervous. This isn't a joke anymore. I don't know why this girl is here, but she's dangerous. She knows who I am."

"No I don't!" Sophia said.

Janov added, "I am sure she has guessed your name isn't really Jones."

"Well, she knows what I look like, and that's bad enough. I don't like it, and I want to know what you plan to do with her, besides discussing children's books."

For the first time Sophia sensed the greater threat was not the Russian spy but the man from Groton, the man probably betraying his country.

"Do you realize that your words are only feeding this girl's imagination?" Janov said. "I asked you earlier to leave. I still believe that is a good idea. Let me handle this."

The train started to slow. It was approaching a station. Poughkeepsie. Sophia despaired. She couldn't make a break for it, not with Mr. Jones blocking the door. Now when she got off the train–if she got off the train–she had no idea how she'd get back to New York.

"Not on your life," Mr. Jones snapped back at Janov. "This involves me. I'm the one who will be ruined if the girl talks. So what are you going to do about it?"

Janov fixed a baleful stare at Mr. Jones. Sophia's attention was divided between their showdown and the train's arrival at the Poughkeepsie station. The train stopped and she heard voices from outside the window. A quick shout of "All aboard!" and the Lake Shore Limited was moving again, leaving hope behind for Sophia.

Janov seemed to have been waiting for the train to resume its journey. He said, "It so happens that I have an ample amount of cash with me. Perhaps we can buy Miss Welsch's silence."

A bribe? Sophia wasn't expecting that. How much would Janov offer her? Enough to buy that diamond necklace she had been eyeing at Macy's? Not that she'd be able to wear it. Her parents would demand to know where she got the money. She would be in enough trouble with them anyway when she got home. It was now after nine o'clock, assuming the train was running to schedule. If her parents weren't worried about her yet, they would be in another hour. Anyway, why was she kidding herself? Her conscience wouldn't allow her to take money from Janov. Still, if it meant getting out of this compartment alive, maybe she should take it.

The rage on Mr. Jones' face told her that wasn't likely to happen. "Are you shitting me?" he shouted. "That money is mine! You're not giving it to her!"

"Please keep your voice down, Mr. Jones," Janov said. "And relax. I can get you more money."

"You bet you can. A lot more money. We're renegotiating this deal." Mr. Jones hugged the briefcase closer to his chest. "You assured me this train would be the safest place to meet. But you've left me exposed. To a kid! What kind of amateur are you?"

Janov stood and faced Mr. Jones. His voice hardened. "We will not have this conversation here."

Sophia pushed herself back into her seat as if she could escape through the wall behind her. She realized, finally, that she had intruded into a world where she did not belong. She thought that by following Janov aboard the train to learn his compartment number she would score points with Ms. Chambers. She had treated the whole thing as a game, but now she knew this wasn't a game to men like Janov and Mr. Jones, whoever he really was. This was a fierce reality.

Janov continued, "If you would calm down, you might see that you are the one making this situation dangerous to yourself."

"Bullshit! You made it dangerous the minute you grabbed the girl. Now stop pussyfooting around and get rid of her."

Sophia's skin went cold. She pulled her ski jacket tighter.

"And how do you suggest I do that?" Janov's back was to Sophia now. Sophia wondered if she could break the window and jump through it.

Mr. Jones shrugged. "Shoot her."

Janov laughed. "I don't know what books you've read, Mr. Jones, but your government doesn't approve of foreign diplomats carrying concealed firearms, especially not diplomats from my country."

Mr. Jones pulled a gun from beneath his trench coat and pointed it at Janov. He continued to grip his briefcase with his left hand. "Lucky me," he said. "I'm covered under the Second Amendment. And stop calling me Mr. Jones. I'm sick of it."

Sophia didn't know much about guns, but she could tell Mr. Jones was holding an automatic and not a revolver. She also recognized the six-inch cylinder protruding from its muzzle as a silencer. That was the extent of her gun lore. She wondered if this finally was the time to scream, but that might get her shot. Sophia remained quiet and waited for Janov's reaction.

She could not see Janov's face. When he spoke his voice was icy. "Did you bring that to use against me?"

"Just being careful," Mr. Jones replied. "I've never done this sort of thing before. I didn't know how it would turn out."

"It would have turned out with your debt being erased," Janov said. Mr. Jones flinched at the mention of debt. As the two men stared each other down, Sophia turned in her seat so that her knees faced the door.

Janov shook his head. "I warned my superiors about your volatility."

Sidetracked

"I'm not the one at fault here, asshole. I followed all of your instructions to get here without being tailed. You're the one who dragged the girl along." Mr. Jones gestured toward Sophia with the gun.

In a flash Janov's right hand shot up and grabbed Mr. Jones' gun hand by the wrist. He forced the pistol upward. A silenced *phut* sounded and a small black hole appeared in the bulkhead that hid the upper berth. Sophia yelped.

Janov grabbed Mr. Jones' other shoulder with his left hand and twisted him into the wall behind his seat. Mr. Jones' briefcase hit the floor. Janov continued to press his opponent against the wall, clearing a path to the door. Sophia crouched and pushed past the struggling men. Mr. Jones lashed at her with his left hand and caught her arm.

One benefit of attending an all-girls' private school in Manhattan is the frequent self-defense demonstrations during physical education class. Sophia thrust her elbow into Mr. Jones' stomach. He grunted and released her arm. She grabbed his briefcase before unlocking the door and sliding it open. Janov and Mr. Jones looked at her with intense eyes. Each had an arm across the other's throat. Neither could come after her without losing the advantage–and perhaps his life–to the other man. Sophia squeezed through the door and into the empty passage. She slid the door shut behind her.

Sophia had to move fast. She didn't know who would win the fight, but her money was on Janov. The best outcome for her would be if they killed each other. Merely thinking that made her a little sick. Sophia sprinted to the end of the sleeper car, then slowed to a fast walk as she entered the lounge car.

The lounge car had changed since her last visit. It was now crowded and noisy. Every table was filled to capacity, and nearly every person was waving a cigarette. The solid ceiling had become a moving miasma of smoke, and the overhead lighting was dulled by the haze. The sudden stench of the tobacco made her gag. Aaron looked up at her from behind the counter as he pulled a saucer-sized pizza from the microwave. Sophia considered asking him for help, but decided that could lead to a violent, public situation the FBI would want to avoid.

Young Adventurers

Her wristwatch was useless and she didn't have time to consult the train schedule, so she didn't know the next station or when the train would arrive. She wanted to hide in the nearest restroom until the train reached the next stop, but she had to get the briefcase to the FBI. Janov or Mr. Jones still might ambush her as she tried to leave the train. She needed to do one last thing before she could hide. If Sophia remembered correctly, there was something she could use two passenger cars ahead.

Sophia glanced over her shoulder as she left the lounge car. Neither Janov nor Mr. Jones was following. She entered the first coach car to find it dark. The overhead lights had been switched off. Dim illumination came from small lamps where the seats met the floor. Many of the passengers already were asleep. Sophia hoped that held true in the next car.

In the next car her eyes went to the overhead luggage rack and despite the low light, she felt a surge of hope when she spotted what she needed. Now if she could just move casually. No one noticed her pause by the luggage alcove at the rear of the car. As she counted down the rows Sophia prayed her luck would hold. Thank God, she thought as she looked at the man in the target seat and found him sprawled out and snoring. She reached up nonchalantly and moved away, hesitating to see if anyone had observed.

Sophia had one witness. A young Hispanic girl, probably six, gaped at her from the opposite seat. The girl turned to her mother for advice. She found none because her mother was asleep. Sophia put her finger to her lips and grinned at the girl. She grinned back, and Sophia continued her journey to the front of the car. She was ready to hide in the next restroom.

Sophia didn't realize how much time the encounter with the little girl had cost her until Janov appeared behind her like a vampire formed from the darkness. She gasped as he pushed her into the narrow, accordion-covered vestibule between the cars.

The clacking of the train wheels rose loudly through the iron floorboards, giving Sophia the impression they were suspended in midair. Snow fell through a tear in the rubberized accordion fabric, and Sophia's breath crystallized into white puffs. She and Janov were pressed together between the two doors. She had to crane her neck to look into his face and even in the dark could see a bruise forming above his left eye. She shifted her hand to open the door behind her, but Janov restrained her. Sophia leaned to the side in an attempt to look through the window behind Janov, but his torso was too wide.

Janov noted the attempt. "Mr. Jones won't be joining us," he said, "but I do need you to give me his briefcase."

"I can't do that," Sophia said.

"You are a courageous and admirable young woman, Miss Welsch, but I wonder if you also realize how lucky you are."

That almost made Sophia laugh. "This doesn't feel lucky."

"You are lucky because you remind me of my daughter, who is also brave yet foolhardy, and because I don't value my career so highly that I am willing to murder a teenage girl. Many of my"–he paused a beat to give the next word emphasis– "*comrades* would have no such compunction."

Sophia said nothing. She shivered, but not from the cold.

"I am giving you your life, Miss Welsch. All I ask in return is that you give me a briefcase."

Slowly, Sophia raised the briefcase and let Janov take it.

"Thank you," he said. He moved back a step, opening an inch between them. "I expect you will depart at the next stop. You will contact your authorities. Yet even though I still have to deal with Mr. Jones, I will be out of the country before anyone can find me."

"Good luck," Sophia said. It was lame, but she didn't know what else to say.

"Goodbye, Miss Welsch," Janov said as the door behind him slid open. "I hope this episode has taught you not to follow strange men."

Sophia stepped into the warmth of the coach car as she watched Janov retreat to his compartment, holding her breath until he passed the rear luggage alcove. When he left the car, Sophia relaxed. She remained where she was at the opposite end of the car and counted to three hundred, approximately five minutes, before walking to the luggage area and reaching behind a suitcase to retrieve Mr. Jones' briefcase. She looked down the length of the car and mentally begged forgiveness from the sleeping man whose briefcase she just handed to Janov. She hoped Janov would be too busy "dealing with" Mr. Jones to examine the briefcase, at least until she was off the train.

Once again she considered informing the train crew about Janov, but now that he had a gun she would probably be endangering them. Instead she ducked into the nearby restroom and sat on the toilet until the train slowed for the next stop. She didn't wait long at all. When the porter opened the carriage door, she saw that the station was Rhinecliff. The porter placed a large blue stepping stool on the station platform to make it easier to get down from the train, but Sophia leaped right over it and ran into the cold toward the nearest pay phone.

The following Thursday afternoon Sophia met with Ms. Chambers at a Sbarro off Times Square. This was to be an informal session, Ms. Chambers said. She had formally debriefed Sophia on Monday and told her she would not receive any further Harriet Brigade assignments "pending review." Sophia wasn't surprised, and her parents had grounded her anyway for not getting home until two o'clock that morning without calling to let them know she was all right. The FBI had sent a car from Albany to fetch her in Rhinecliff, and the journey home was slow because she had to answer plenty of questions along the way.

She told her parents that after seeing *Beverly Hills Cop*, she went over to her friend Kayla's apartment and they fell asleep watching *Friday Night Videos*. This had necessitated a late-night call from an FBI car phone to ask Kayla to back up Sophia's alibi. Sophia told Kayla she didn't want her parents to know she had spent the evening with two older guys from out of town. That was true, but not in the way Kayla imagined. Sophia knew her reputation at school might be tarnished, but Kayla was generally good at keeping secrets.

Ms. Chambers settled into the booth across from Sophia. She had bought a salad instead of pizza. "Most of this will be off-the-record," Ms. Chambers said. "I just wanted to catch you up on several developments since your experience Friday evening."

Sidetracked

Sophia folded her sausage slice down the center as New Yorkers do and bit into the juicy tip as Ms. Chambers caught her up.

The body of one Alton Boehm was discovered late Saturday morning along the Conrail tracks between Hudson and Albany. He had been a vice president of development at JennDyne, a defense contractor based in Virginia Beach with a plant in Groton. He had died of a broken neck. A brief investigation found that Boehm had bet badly during the New Year's bowl games and owed a total of $44,000 to several Atlantic City bookmakers. Given that knowledge the local coroner ruled that Boehm had committed suicide by leaping from Friday night's Lake Shore Limited.

On Friday evening, Vasily Janov–Ms. Chambers continued to call him TENSPEED–had sent out a decoy limousine from the United Nations. His usual FBI weekend surveillance detail followed the limousine, but fortunately Sophia had missed it and trailed him to Grand Central. Ms. Chambers viewed that as a triumph for the Harriet Brigade. Sophia felt a flush of pride.

As he had predicted, Janov did get out of the country before the FBI could find him. However, the Royal Canadian Mounted Police did find him, Sunday, in Toronto and arrested him. A satisfactory outcome, Ms. Chambers said, even though the FBI hated owing the Canadians a favor.

Ms. Chambers took the last bite of her salad. "Now this is the part I have been forbidden to tell you, but I feel you deserve to know. So keep it confidential."

"I will," Sophia said.

"The briefcase you recovered contained plans for the sonar array that will be introduced in the next block of Los Angeles-class fast attack submarines. Obviously, it would have been a catastrophe if the Soviets had gotten their hands on those plans."

Sophia opened her mouth to speak, but could say nothing. She took a sip of Coke because her mouth had gone dry.

"If you were a field agent, you would get a medal for what you've done," Ms. Chambers said. "But, because of your age and the secrecy of the Harriet Brigade, I'm afraid all I can offer you is a slice and a Coke."

Young Adventurers

Sophia shrugged, "That's OK."

"You displayed courage and quick-thinking under pressure, qualities desirable for a career in counterintelligence. However…"

Sophia knew a "however" was coming.

"However," Ms. Chambers continued. "You grossly exceeded your instructions and made a reckless decision when you boarded that train, a decision that may have cost you your life."

Ms. Chambers let that sink in.

"You also might have exposed the Harriet Brigade. We don't know if TENSPEED was able to contact his people before the Mounties got him. We've decided to continue with the program and observe if our subjects suddenly seem aware of teenage girls in their area."

She placed her hand over Sophia's.

"But I'm afraid you will no longer be a part of the program. I promised you at the beginning you would receive a letter of recommendation to the college of your choice, and I guarantee you will still get that. Your country owes you at least that much for preventing the Soviets from obtaining military secrets. But I'm afraid I have to let you go." Ms. Chambers shook her head sadly. "You were brave, but you got caught."

Sophia looked down at her paper plate. All that remained of her pizza was the crust. She never ate the crust. She looked back up at Ms. Chambers and reluctantly nodded.

"Spies should not get caught," Sophia agreed.

In today's Washington DC, even a visit to a museum can hold mystery and adventure for curious and observant students.

AIR AND SPACE AFTER DARK

Jeff Ayers and Kevin Lauderdale

"Do you think they could hang a whole space shuttle up there?" asked Jake.

Hannah looked up at the ceiling of the National Air and Space Museum. From the huge grid of white support beams overhead, several planes were suspended from cables. There was the gray *Spirit of St. Louis*, with its wooden propeller, that Charles Lindbergh had piloted to become the first man to fly non-stop across the Atlantic Ocean. Nearby hung the *Glamorous Glennis*, the orange dart of a jet in which Chuck Yeager had broken the sound barrier. To Hannah's left was the X-15, stubby-winged and bat-black with a bold "NASA" painted on its tail. More rocket than plane, it had once gone over 4,500 miles per hour–more than five times the speed of the *Glennis*.

Hannah shook her head. "The beams can hold up a lot, but not *that* much. And, even if they could, would you trust them enough to stand under it?"

Jake laughed. The two of them were in the vast, open space of the museum's main entrance hall. Most of the planes floating a couple of stories above them were fairly small. If one actually did fall, they could duck out of the way. The X-15, though, was so long that it nearly reached the second floor's chest-high balcony railing. Hannah thought that, if she were up there, she could probably just touch its left–*port*, she reminded herself–wing.

Not that anyone could touch anything on the darkened second floor now. For tonight's party, the elevators had been shut down and everything upstairs was blocked off. Large metal signs reading "RESTRICTED" hung from red velvet ropes on all the staircases.

Usually crowded with tourists in t-shirts and jeans, tonight the museum was filled with suits and nice dresses. Waiters walked around carrying trays of tiny munchies. There was supposed to be music later.

Hannah said, "They've got a shuttle at the Udvar-Hazy branch of the Air and Space out by Dulles airport. It's on the ground. People like being able to walk around it and get a view of its top–oops, its *dorsal* side."

"Hey, you're really picking up the lingo." Jake sounded impressed, and Hannah felt herself blush. She'd been doing a weekend internship program at the A and S for a solid month now. It was only open to high school seniors. She saw the dark-haired, dark-eyed Jake and his twin sister Kayla at school all the time, but they never just hung out anymore. Specifically, she and Jake never just hung out anymore.

Jake asked, "So what happens next? Are they going to turn on black lights? I'm wearing white socks. They'll glow."

Tonight's "After Dark Exhibit" at the A and S was a thank-you to the D.C. area's scientific community. The second floor was closed, but the museum was premiering the new IMAX film shot aboard the International Space Station. As an intern, Hannah had been allowed to attend. Jake and Kayla were there because they were on one of the handful of Academic Decathlon teams from the area that had been invited. Hannah hoped that Jake would see her differently–as something other than his sister's best friend–in this different setting. She was wearing a new green dress to bring out the red in her hair.

"Who's Kayla talking to by the Hubble Space Telescope?" Jake leaned forward. "Either someone's modeling a space suit or that's Lady Gaga. I read a couple celebrities were coming."

Kayla had left fifteen minutes ago to go get them all some punch. "Take your time," Hannah had suggested, and Kayla had disappeared with a wink.

Carefully, Hannah put her hand on Jake's arm, and turned him. "There's no one over by the unmanned spy planes. Let's go look at those."

Air and Space After Dark

"I'm dying of thirst," said Jake, as if he hadn't heard. "I'm gonna go get the drinks myself." He started walking away. "You still want one?"

"Sure," Hannah said. "Why not?" She turned around and leaned against the blue cone of the Friendship 7 capsule, crossing her arms over her chest. John Glenn had become the first American in space when he'd circled the earth three times in that. *All by himself*, Hannah thought. She could relate. Seventeen-year old boys! You could put on a green dress, do up your hair, and you were still second place to something cold and fizzy.

She heard a booming voice thank everyone for coming. It was the museum's director, Dr. Palmieri, beginning his speech. Everyone began to move towards him at the east end of the museum, where all the moon-landing artifacts were. She could just see him standing next to the Apollo 11 lunar module, which was all gold foil and flags and had two mannequins dressed in space suits.

Hannah checked her reflection in the clear plastic that surrounded the *Friendship 7*. Her hair was starting to lose its curl and–What was that person doing on the stairs?

She stared harder into the plastic. Someone tall–a man, she assumed–crept under the rope at the top of the stairs and disappeared on to the second floor.

She spun around. The sign was still up at the bottom of the stairs, and she was willing to bet that guy could read. She looked around, but didn't see any security guards. They were probably all at the other end of the building. *Everyone* was at the other end of the building, half a football field away. No one else had seen him go up.

Hannah took a deep breath. As an employee of the National Air and Space Museum, it was up to her. She ducked under the rope and went upstairs after him.

The second floor was usually flooded with light from the ceiling skylight and glass walls of the museum. But at night it was dark.

A long beam of yellow sliced into the darkness. A flashlight! The beam grew and shrank. Hannah knew what that meant: he had opened and closed a door down at the other end of the building. Wow, he was fast.

The door was still open a crack when she arrived and peered inside.

He was crouching in the area where exhibits that were still being built were stored. He had on a black knit ski mask and gloves. Obviously a thief.

He was hunched over...the Mars Rock exhibit! *Her* Mars Rock exhibit.

The glass case held a fist-sized, rust-red colored stone that one of the landers had sent back from Mars. To its left was the cutaway model Hannah had made showing Mars' crust, mantle, and the liquid iron core that took up about half the planet's interior. On the rock's right were maps of Mars: modern satellite images, and some from a hundred years ago when people thought the planet had oceans and canals. She'd read a dozen books on Mars and surfed all over the web learning about geology. And now this guy was trying to steal her rock!

Oh, no, she would not let him ruin her exhibit. Her hands had been orange for a week from the dye she'd made just so that the exhibit's background was exactly the same color as the Martian sand you saw in NASA pictures. Hannah stood up as straight and tall as she could. She needed stuff like this for her college application. She desperately wanted to go to Yale, but the university only accepted one student from her school each year. She needed every possible advantage if she was going to beat out Louisa Wu, who had been playing the cello at Kennedy Center concerts since sixth grade.

The thief carefully turned on a small lantern and laid out a black cloth with a bunch of tiny tools on it. He knew his stuff. Even now the case was wired to an alarm system, so he wasn't going to smash and grab. But he might be able to pick the lock.

There wasn't time to go all the way back down and get some help. She would call Kayla on her cell phone.

No, she didn't dare make any noise.

She'd send a picture!

Hannah flipped open her palm-sized phone and aimed it at the crouching man. She clicked and selected Kayla's name from

Air and Space After Dark

the menu. Her thumb slid to the red dot in the center of her phone to send–and a hand grabbed her mouth!

She let out a muffled yell and struggled, but a second hand twisted her right arm behind her back and pushed her onto the floor. Her phone fell and skidded away. Before Hannah knew it, something had bound her wrists behind her. She tried to bite the hand at her mouth, but her attacker wore thick gloves. She heard a tearing sound and then tasted the rubbery flavor of glue as a length of duct tape was stretched over her mouth. She was flipped over and her legs quickly bound with a plastic cord. A tall figure stepped over her and crushed her phone with a stomp.

The glow of the screen faded to black.

Where the heck was Hannah?

Jake stood there with two sodas in his hands. He craned his neck. No, she hadn't gone over by the spy planes. He put the drinks down at the base of *Friendship 7*. He hadn't been gone that long, had he?

Man, she'd sure looked great in that dress. Now, if he could just keep it together and not mess up long enough to ask her to dance, everything would be okay. The DJ was all set up. There would be music, and later the movie, and everything would be fine.

No problem.

But also no Hannah.

He turned around and saw Kayla running towards him. Like she always did when she was excited, she was talking so fast that he couldn't make out a single word.

"Sis, slow down. What's up?"

"Hannah's in trouble. She sent…"

"Wait a minute, how can she be in trouble? She's just here– Oh. Yeah. Where?"

Kayla raised her eyebrows and gave him a look he knew all too well: the look that said he was an idiot. She held up her phone and showed him.

The image was dark and blurry, but could only be someone messing with a museum display case.

"I bet it's her rock, right?" he asked.

"Gotta be," said Kayla. "It's not ready yet, so it's in a prep area. She showed me where it is last week when I met her for lunch. There's a closed room in the far corner on the second floor, directly above the moon stuff where everybody is right now."

Jake said, "She probably sent a picture because she can't talk. Something's wrong." He started walking towards the nearest staircase.

"We can't go up there," said Kayla.

Jake looked around. "No one'll see. All the security folks are way over at the other end."

"Then we should get them for help," said Kayla. "We know there's a problem."

"She called *you*. We'll go up and check out the situation. If it's something we can't handle, *then* we call for help."

They hopped the red rope and quietly climbed the stairs. They could get tossed out of the museum for this, but Jake found it exciting. Besides, if it was something serious, here was his chance to be a hero in Hannah's eyes. How cool was that!

When they were about three steps from the top Jake got down on his knees. He motioned for Kayla to do the same. *Just like Christmas*, Jake thought. *Sneaking upstairs to try to see what Mom and Dad were wrapping*. Jake peeked over the top step. It was dark, but there was enough light that he was confident there wasn't anyone else around.

Kayla held a finger to her lips, and Jake nodded. That made sense. If Hannah couldn't talk, then obviously they shouldn't make a racket by yelling for her.

Jake and Kayla stood up and moved across the main corridor to the shuttered gift shop. Light from the full moon came through the skylight, casting shadows and giving the flying machines the illusion of being alive and watching the two of them. *Just like those Ben Stiller movies*, thought Jake.

"Down there, right?" Jake whispered, pointing to the end of the corridor. Kayla nodded. They slid around the corner from the shop and into a side passageway. "Okay. I'll go see what's up. If I'm not back in three minutes, get help."

Air and Space After Dark

Kayla shook her head and whispered, "We should go *together*."

"If something...happens to me, someone else has to go get help."

"Fine!" she hissed.

With his back to the wall, Jake started down the main corridor, keeping his eyes forward. It was slow going, but he eventually made it past the giant F-1 engine as big as his bedroom. The next room was the prep area. Jake tried the door's metal handle and found it unlocked. He eased it open just a crack and put his ear to the gap.

"She's tied up and'll be quiet, guaranteed," said a man. He sounded like he had enjoyed way too many cigarettes and his throat was starting to pay the price.

"What do we do with her?" a second voice asked. This one was squeaky, with a touch of desperation.

The rough voice spoke up again. "Forget her. Just let me finish with the rock and we'll go."

Jake was tempted to leave, but he had to see. He had to be sure that Hannah was okay.

He risked looking through the gap with one eye. Both men were dressed all in black. Something was making a small amount of light on the floor. Jake could see they were working on a display case, and about ten feet away was a second case. Beneath that, he could just make out the edge of a dress with two legs sticking out. Hannah was moving slowly, as if she were trying to wriggle out of whatever held her.

He turned around and started walking, full of determination. He was getting her out of there no matter what! He didn't like the idea of leaving her even for a minute, but this required some backup.

He ran back down the corridor and turned at the side passageway to join Kayla.

He quickly told her what he'd seen.

"Get security up here." He looked back around the corner. No one was coming. "I'm gonna stay here. You go down and get help." When help arrived, he was going to lead the charge and rescue Hannah.

Young Adventurers

"I'm not going downstairs," said Kayla. "Do you know what kind of trouble we'd be in?" She smiled. "Besides, I've got a better idea."

"What? You think we can help Hannah and no one will ever know we were up here?"

"If we're careful."

Jake smiled. "Okay." That would be the best of both worlds.

"While you were gone, I had a quick look around." She held up a flashlight and turned it on.

"Where did you–?"

"Follow me," said Kayla.

Just a few steps down the passageway was a janitor's closet.

"You know what Dad always says," Kayla whispered, "It's always time for chemistry." Their father was a chemistry teacher at their high school, which made for some awkward moments.

Kayla opened the closet door and shined the light. The tiny space held the standard mop and buckets as well as a shelf with some rags and bottles.

Jake heard the music start down on the first floor. It was muffled but loud.

"Hold this." Kayla gave Jake the flashlight, grabbed a bottle of chlorine bleach off the shelf, and began to pour the contents in a bucket. Jake knew that mixing bleach with other chemicals was a bad idea, but the circumstances were dire, and they had mixed much worse things with Dad in their basement.

Kayla grabbed another bottle and started pouring it in as well. While she was doing this, she said, "Jake, get a couple of rags off the shelf and get ready to hold your breath."

There were only two cloths. "What's your plan, Sis?"

She reached into her purse and pulled out a bottle of fingernail polish remover.

"Be prepared," said Kayla. "That goes for Girl Scouts as well as Boy Scouts."

He couldn't argue with that. Jake tied one the cloths over his mouth and nose, and Kayla did the same. Then she up-ended the entire bottle of the stinky fluid into the bucket.

"Oh, man!" she said. "We need another cloth quick. Something to cover the bucket while we carry it down to the

Air and Space After Dark

prep area." Kayla had just made chloroform: perfect for knocking out anyone getting a deep breath or two of the smelly concoction. But the vapors it was giving off wouldn't last forever. "You should have worn a suit jacket with those pants. That would've worked."

"I got ink from a printer cartridge on it." Jake moved the flashlight beam around the closet. "A dust pan would cover it, but they don't have one. They must vacuum everything."

Kayla said, "I'll go see if there's anything we can use in the bathroom. Be right back."

Jake stepped out into the passageway and watched her leave. He tightened the mask on his face. That would help a lot, but it was best not to get too close to the bucket of chloroform. He turned his back on it. He could hear another song playing down below. *I'd give the shirt off my back to be dancing with Hannah right now*, he thought. And then: *Shirt!* For smart kids, sometimes they missed the obvious. He could just take off his shirt for the bucket. That would–

"Are you trying to be a hero, you stupid kid?" Jake immediately recognized the squeaky voice. He turned around and faced one of the thieves, who said, "I thought I heard something going on down here."

The thief shot out a hand to grab Jake, who ducked but slipped and ended up face down on the carpeted floor.

"And what's with the mask?" laughed the thief.

Jake started to crawl towards the bucket. That was the only way. Make him think the bucket was important. Jake made it and looked inside as if he was searching for a cell phone or some weapon.

The man in black bent down to the bucket. "What have we here?" He looked inside and then, taking a deep sniff, said, "What's this junk?" He then took a second, even deeper sniff. "Oh yeah, that's horrible." He left the bucket next to Jake's head.

The thief straightened up, took one step, and toppled over.

"Jake, are you okay?" he heard his sister say right before he lost consciousness.

Young Adventurers

Kayla looked at both her brother and the thief on the floor and realized that she needed to hurry. The two of them were out cold. The contents of the bucket worked, but the gas would soon spread and loose strength. *Dissipate*: that was the SAT word for it.

Kayla hadn't found anything she could use in the bathroom, but now she didn't need to. "Sorry about this," she said, as she quickly undid Jake's face cloth. She stretched it over the bucket and gripped the rim hard to keep as much of the chloroform fumes inside as possible. She made her way up the passageway to the main corridor.

As she crept, she thought, *Okay, be quiet, slide the bucket into the prep room, and then quietly walk away. That'll knock them out, and I'll run downstairs and tell everyone.* The time for trying to keep this secret was over.

She was almost to the door when a man in black stepped out and said, "Ray, what the–"

In the time it took him to realize that Kayla was not Ray, she'd dropped Jake's face cloth and splashed the man in the face with the contents of the bucket. He was wearing glasses, but his knit facemask was soaked with the liquid. What wasn't absorbed splashed back at Kayla. She closed her eyes, but the stuff soaked her face cloth as well, delivering a constant supply of chloroform vapor.

Kayla turned and tried to run, but his hand was on her shoulder. Both of them were breathing hard, taking in more and more of the fumes as they struggled. With a loud yell, she burst free from him and began to run. She could hear the roar of the music downstairs.

After two long steps, Kayla felt tired. Her feet were heavy. Forget running. Just walking was like swimming through a pool of sand.

It was so unfair. It was cruel fate. It was worse than cruel. It was...what was that SAT word? Ex-something. Ex-cr...she shook her head. *Stay focused!* She thought to herself.

She looked back. The man was slowly following her. She couldn't go very fast, but he was moving through sand as well. The fumes affected them both, but if she could just make it far enough away from him...if she could just get someone's attention down on the first floor. But no one down below would hear her. She was too high up, and the music was too loud.

If she could...he was closer. Where could she go? She was tired. She felt her back bump against the balcony railing. Behind her–below her–was a two-story fall into the entrance hall. Facing her was the Pioneers of Flight gallery. She'd always loved Amelia Earhart's snub-nosed 5B Vega. Amelia had flown the Atlantic solo in that. *It's so red and shiny...*Kayla bit her lips. *Focus!*

The man came closer. Then closer.

I can be Amelia Earhart, Kayla thought, turning around. *I can fly.*

He lunged towards her, and Kayla threw herself over the railing...onto a cold, black wing of the X-15 rocket plane. The plane jerked forward with a horrible creaking sound from the cables, but Kayla held on with a fierce grip. She looked back. The man was unconscious on the floor. She pulled herself onto the body of the plane and tugged the cloth from her face. She took a deep breath of clean air.

Kayla looked down. Dozens of people were dancing. She slipped out her cell phone and let it fall. It shattered as it hit the plastic surrounding one of the space capsules below.

A girl near the capsule screamed. People around her looked up and saw Kayla.

The music stopped.

LouisaWu: OMG! Kayla! I saw you in the Washington Post!
KaylaStrand: Yes, it really happened.
LouisaWu: How did you get down? Did you have to JUMP?
KaylaStrand: No. They didn't want me to even TRY to move, on account of being so groggy. They brought in one of those super-long cherry-picker cranes and put me in that. It was TOTALLY embarrassing. It was slow, and everyone was standing around taking pictures with their cell phones. Some video of me on YouTube already has about a million views.
LouisaWu: So, are you, like, a hero now? Is Selena Gomez going to play you on TV?

KaylaStrand: No. Even though we saved Hannah and the rock, Jake and I got grounded for two weeks for going into restricted space.

LouisaWu: Ouch. Cruel.

KaylaStrand: Double Ouch. Excruciating.

Sometimes people just disappear. But as every aspiring young reporter knows, sometimes there's a bit more to it than that…

THE MYSTERY OF RAVEN'S HOLLOW

Victoria Pitts Caine

"Listen, Debbie, you can hear the thundering hooves."

Grams always said that when it rained. She told me the noises were the sounds of horses as they raced along the gravel strewn pathway down by Willowby's Creek. To me it sounded like the branches of the old oak tree as they scratched on the roof when the wind blew. Scratch, scratch, scratch. Night had fallen and the January cold front dropped in on us making the wind whip rhythmically. The noise turned into a thump. The sound grew louder. Thump, scratch, thump, scratch.

As I walked to the window, I looked out onto the dark, barren yard of the old farm where we lived. The rain ran in little rivers down the panes of the wavy glass windows. Most of them had been replaced in the hundred year old house, but Grams was proud of those that hadn't. They were the original glass from when her grandpa built his home in these Missouri backwoods. The wavy panes were the only ones that made rivers.

I couldn't remember a time Grams wasn't around. My parents died in a car accident when I was two. My mom, Opal, was one of three girls who belonged to Grandma Em and Grandpa James. When I was older and found out, I was disappointed that neither Aunt Ruby nor Aunt Pansy took me. They both lived in Kansas City and that would have been far more exciting than living out here in Raven's Hollow, but then I'd never known the story of old man Parker and his daughter who drowned in Willowby's Creek almost eighty years ago. I'd heard it all my life, the mystery that haunted this area. Their deaths brought shame to the little town up at the Four Corners and I planned to solve the mystery now I'd turned thirteen.

My name is Deborah Jean Woods. Back then, much to Grams' dismay, I liked to be called D.J. My best friends were Kevin Finnegan and Tommy Miller. Kevin had a prissy sister, Katie, about my age. I used her for an excuse when I wanted to play with the boys. I'd rather climb trees or fish down by the creek than play with dolls or stupid dress up games, but if I told Grams I was going to Finnegan's, she figured I'd be with Katie. Not wanting to disappoint Grams who wanted me to be prim and proper, Katie became an excellent excuse.

"Grams, tell me the story again." I pulled the footstool next to her old rocker. When I looked into her wrinkled face, I thought about how old she was. Grams must have been in her thirties when Mom was born. She died at twenty-seven. Adding my age minus two, I did the math, my most hated subject, and figured Grams at around sixty-seven.

"Deborah Jean, don't you ever tire of that old story? I'd think you'd have it memorized yourself by now." Her wrinkles turned into little smiles all over her face while she talked to me. Soft wrinkled smiles. "Let's move our chairs toward the fire. I always get a shiver up my back when I tell it."

"Can I write it down this time, Grams? Act like I'm a reporter? You know I want to work in Kansas City for the newspaper when I grow up." Yearning to learn everything, I needed details of what had happened. The boys and I planned a camping trip out to the creek once it got warm enough. There was an old house near the clearing, the Parker house. Our strategy was to explore it and look for clues. If I wrote down the story, I'd be ready once spring came.

"Go get that journal of yours. I'll let you read it next time. Run along now. I'll make some hot chocolate while you're gone." Grams got up and limped into the kitchen.

My small room suited me. It had been my mom's. I slept in her same bed and read her same books. Grams had been slow to redo her girls' rooms once they married and moved into town.

She hadn't even touched my mom's room when I came back to claim it. Finding my journal, I returned to the living room.

Grams placed the steaming cups of chocolate on the small table between us then pulled her lap robe from the back of her chair and tucked it in behind her knees. She flinched some when she folded it beneath her bad leg. Moving my hand over hers, she smiled. "Ready, girl?"

"Ready, Grams." I pressed the pages of my journal flat on my lap.

She began… "Back a long time ago when my grandpa lived here, there was a man named Parker. No one in town liked him. He wanted to be alone and lived down there by the creek in that old house, came to town when he needed something which wasn't often, and raised his own food. He ran everyone off with a shotgun if they came close to his place.

"He came to Four Corners like clockwork. Every three months on the first. Dirty and dressed in near rags, he spoke in single words like he had no education. He'd point and grunt for things at the mercantile. At the post office, he always picked up a single letter from the city.

"The odd thing about it was that some people knew him as a young man. They said he'd been a scholar. Sent back East by his family to college, but something happened. He wanted to marry a young woman whose parents despised him because he was from these hills. Her parents told him he wasn't good enough for their daughter, even though he had a college degree and held down a promising job.

"Parker came back here to live after that. Never ventured out, never left Raven's Hollow except for once. One day after the delivery of one of them letters he went back to the city and came home with a baby girl. His baby girl.

"When he got off the train at Four Corners, all dirty and ragged, someone saw him with the baby. They jumped to conclusions he'd kidnapped her and got up a vigilante group to go after him. By the time he'd recovered his horse and wagon at the livery stable, they were hot on his trail.

"He raced down the narrow road by the creek, branches cutting his face, the baby drawn close to his chest. Thunder bellowed overhead and lightening ignited the sky. The cold wind tore through his thin coat and pounding wind-blown raindrops turned into sleet and cut like razors into his exposed skin. When they were in sight of his place, there was a tight turn in the road. Pressing harder and harder the urgency to escape drove him to whip the horses, their backs marked by braided leather. The tail end of the wagon swung around sideways as they neared the sharp turn. His horses panicked and reared. The wagon overturned and he and the baby drowned in Willowby's Creek.

"Later when the towns' people found out the true story, there was so much shame brought to Four Corners. It's on nights like this that you can hear the horses gallop. The stallion and the bay he switched to get home and the thundering hooves of the vigilante group. It was a sad day for Raven's Hollow. Some people say you can see a light like a candle or an oil lamp in the old house going from room to room. Story is his ghost is still out there as he searches and calls for his little girl. 'Elizabeth Ann. Elizabeth Ann.'"

Grams pulled another blanket around her shoulders. "That poor baby drowned in that icy creek in the middle of winter."

"Did your grandpa know Mr. Parker?"

"In fact, he did. Always told me he was a nice enough man. Grandpa traded him eggs for fish he'd catch out of the creek. Grandpa said he was a little odd. His mind just snapped when he couldn't marry that city girl."

The story was always the same, sad, scary, and heartless. "Why did people hate him so much, Grams?"

"He was different. Back in those days people didn't like others who were different. The people at Four Corners made it hard on him and he reacted the only way he knew. I guess he figured they'd just leave him alone, and they did, all except for that awful night down by the creek." Grams sipped her chocolate. We'd never talked much beyond the telling of the tale, but I guess she figured that now I was thirteen, almost a grownup, I'd understand more about people's injustices to others.

While I'd jotted down the information, I reached for my drink, but it had turned cold. The top of the liquid had a thin coating like Willowby's Creek, I thought, when it is freezing over. "How about the house? Did anyone ever check where the light came from?"

"I doubt anyone has gone into that house since it happened. I don't even know who it belongs to. It was his folks, then his. It's good river bottom land. His parents made a lot of money farming. That's how they could afford to send him East to school." A rumble of thunder and a flash of lightning made us both jump, and the mood changed. "Better get ready for bed, Debbie. You have school tomorrow."

Kevin and Tommy pressed their faces against the glass of the old yellow school bus as it lumbered down the drive towards my pick-up shelter. I walked a mile from the farm to the enclosure and shivered in the damp, cool morning. All around slush encrusted the ground. The puddles lay concealed underneath thin, brown ice. I stuck a stick in one of them. The crust cracked and exposed the water beneath. I thought about old man Parker.

"Mornin', D.J., been waitin' long?" The bus driver smiled. I smiled back and looked for a seat. Kevin and Tommy waved me to the back of the bus. There was a place next to Katie.

I slid in next to her and she made one of her long hissy sighs. "Good morning, Deborah Jean. If you're going to sit next to me, don't wrinkle my new skirt. Mother just bought it for me in Kansas City."

I would remember that when we were on the playground. Maybe the boys and I could give her a few wrinkles. "Hey, guys. Some storm last night, wasn't it?"

"Well, did ya ask her? Did she tell you the story?" Kevin drew close across the aisle.

"Shhh. Do you want the whole school to know what we're up to? I'll tell you at recess. I have it all down here in my journal. We'll meet in the library at 10:00.

When the bell rang, Tommy turned around, winked, and headed for the hall. I caught up with him and Kevin. "I got all the information. We need to plan our camping trip."

Young Adventurers

"We probably won't be able to go until April, maybe even May as cold as it is this year. That's a long time." Kevin always saw the gloomy side of things.

"No, that's perfect. You guys have Boy Scout stuff don't you?"

"Yeah. My dad has some lanterns we can use, too. This will be so much fun." Tommy, who was more of an adventurer, would be my ally.

I studied their faces. Tommy still looked like he did when he was six, but Kevin was changing. His voice cracked sometimes when he spoke. I wasn't sure if I liked that or not. They'd put up with me until now, but once we finished our eighth grade year and went to the Willowby Creek High School, I wasn't sure they would. "Have either one of your folks ever let you camp in the woods before?"

"I did once, with my cousin Jake. I'm not sure I can go out there on my own, but I can figure something out." Tommy forever the optimist.

"You, Kevin?"

"I don't know. They might." He thought for a moment. "If I tell my mom Dad said it was okay and vice versa, we'll be gone before they figured out I'd buffaloed them."

"You use that all the time. They aren't stupid. I'm the one that has the problem. Where am I going to tell Grams I'll be over night?"

"Katie has a birthday in May. She's having a sleepover."

"Perfect. We'll go in May."

Kevin was right. Spring took forever to arrive, but everything fell into place. Our camping gear lay stowed in the barn at Grams' and I'd received an invitation to the sleepover, but it was because there were so few girls in our class. Since school closed for end of the year state exams, we had an extra day. I hoped I'd passed to seventh grade. I was a good student. It might depend on what happened that weekend. It might not matter.

Alone in the barn, nervous and scared, afraid we either might get caught by the grownups or old man Parker's ghost, my stomach clenched. A noise jolted me from my thoughts. I

The Mystery of Raven's Hollow

crouched down and raised my head enough to peek through the window. Kevin stood in the yard. I opened the latch and motioned him in. "You look upset."

"Just a little scared, I guess." His voice went up an octave. "Tommy here yet?"

"No. Soon. You two will take our stuff and go down by the pond. I'll go tell Grams I'm leaving for your house. Then I'll double back and meet you. I can't believe our trip is finally going to happen." I looked at Kevin, who had turned an odd shade of green.

"Ya guys in here?" Tommy pounded on the wooden exterior.

I yanked him through the opening by his sleeve. "Grams isn't deaf. Get in and be quiet."

"You know the plan, Tommy. You and Kevin go on. I'll be there in fifteen minutes." I went in and told Grams I was leaving for Katie's party. She reminded me to be polite and not to forget to thank Mrs. Finnegan. She expected me home by 10:00 in the morning. A pang of guilt stabbed my chest. I'd lied to her.

While I walked to the water to meet the boys, I couldn't believe how lucky we were to have such a great day. It was warm, but not hot. The fields were full of wild flowers. My favorite, Goldenrod, bloomed into a bumper crop that year. My belly tied in a knot. "I'm here. Let's go."

Tommy hoisted his backpack onto his shoulder. Kevin looked like he would throw up any minute. I fell in line behind Tommy while Kevin brought up the rear. As we trudged down the dirt path, we sang a few rounds of "Row, Row, Row Your Boat" when I noticed Kevin's voice had grown fainter. I turned around, and he had disappeared. "Wait, Kevin's gone," I yelled at Tommy as he advanced forward and almost out of sight in the opposite direction.

"Kevin, Kevin," I screamed. "Where are you?" I took a deep breath and strained my ears waiting for an answer. Nothing. The wind whistled through the pines and prickles raised on my neck. *Where could he have gone?*

I ran down the path. *Had the ghost taken Kevin? Come on D.J. There's logical explanation.* I couldn't run anymore. I knew the distance between Tommy and I had grown, but I wouldn't leave Kevin out here alone. Not in the middle of nowhere as scared as he was. *I'm going to have to admit how scared I am if I don't find him.* I took in a deep breath. "Kevin?" I yelled.

"D.J." I jumped at the sound of my own name. "D.J., here," Kevin called. What little color he had in his cheeks had vanished. "I'm scared D.J. I lied to my parents. I'm afraid of that ghost and…"

Running toward the big granite rock where he cowered my foot snagged on an exposed root. Tumbling, sprawling toward the boulder, hands scraping against the dirt and jagged rocks on the path, I slid head first. "Ouch!" I yelled.

Kevin laughed. "That was pretty funny, D.J."

"Well, I'm glad I amused you. At least you aren't terrified anymore."

"You're bleeding."

When I checked my hands, my right palm had a nasty gash, blood gathered at the ragged opening. *How was I going to explain to Grams I got hurt at a sleep over?* Walking over to the pond, I rinsed it off.

"D.J., you're hurt." Tommy had found us and dropping his backpack he retrieved a first aid kit. "Let me bandage your hand."

I gritted my teeth. The boys wouldn't see me cry, but it shouldn't have worried me because now Kevin was sniveling. "I want to go home," he moaned.

"Oh for Pete's sake, Finnegan, pull it together." Tommy shot a glance at Kevin that would have frozen the pond over had it not been spring.

Tommy applied ointment and wrapped the bandage like a regular paramedic. When he finished, he gently patted my hand. "I think it will be okay, but let your Grams look at it when we get home."

He smiled and my stomach did a little flip. *What was that about?* "Let's go boys. We've wasted enough time on this little detour."

The Mystery of Raven's Hollow

"This place looks good as any." Tommy dumped his gear on the ground near the corner of a clearing. We had a good view of the house, but were back far enough in the trees not to be seen.

"Let's set up. I made jelly sandwiches for dinner and Grams baked fresh cookies this morning. I got us each a couple."

We waited for nightfall taking turns watching the house, but nothing moved. Even though it was spring the setting sun disappeared quickly. The shadows grew longer and the sound of coyotes echoed in the distance. Something scampered in the bushes and big yellow eyes peered out at us. I shivered and nudged Tommy on the shoulder. I stiffened my back determined to meet the beast. "What is that?" I asked.

Tommy picked up a rock and threw it into the undergrowth. A big black barn cat made a zig zag path between us. We laughed. "Just a big old tom," Kevin said, his voice shaking and my heart hammering in agreement. *It could have been a panther. We don't have panthers. Mountain lions, no, not this far down. Right. Just a cat.* I shifted a little closer to Tommy.

By 7:30 total darkness engulfed us. It was my turn to stand watch. I had just taken my post at the mouth of the clearing. Propping my back against a pine tree, I nested down into the mound of needles Tommy had pushed into a cushion.

The cold seeped in and I jammed my hands into my pockets. A brief flicker in the window prompted me to rivet toward the house. It caught me off guard, but I saw it just for an instant scrunching up my eyes to make sure. "I see the light." I whispered. "Come over here." Tommy and Kevin knelt next to me. We watched the glow move from room to room, just like the story. We crept from edge of the clearing, out of the cover of the trees and had gone too far to turn back. Inching out on our stomachs we used our elbows to drag ourselves along.

Kevin whimpered.

"Shut up, Finnegan," Tommy hissed.

"My allergies. All these weeds and flowers are making me sick." Kevin snuffled.

"You're making *me* sick." Tommy huffed as he slid along on his stomach. "Be quiet."

Kevin sneezed. A loud dinner bell clanged from the porch.

Young Adventurers

We froze. Kevin buried his head into the crook of his arm to ward off another sneezing fit. Tommy reached over and took my hand, but didn't say a word. My heart ricocheted against my ribs. I agreed to acknowledge the knot in my stomach that had grown since this morning.

"Who's out there? I'll shoot if you don't answer." The tall, thin, elderly woman stood in the doorway, a 12-gauge shot gun resting on her forearm.

"You go D.J. She won't shoot a girl." Kevin, once more about to cry, sounded all too ready to give me up for slaughter. I stood and slowly walked toward the house.

"What do you want, girl?" She moved the gun to stand beside her, the wooden stock against her leg.

"We came to solve the mystery." My voice quivered more than I'd intended.

"What mystery?" Her voice softened from harshness to inquisitive.

"The lights floating around in this house—story is it was a ghost. We didn't know you lived here."

"Few people do. Who's the 'we' you're referring to?"

I motioned the boys onto the porch. They stood and walked up beside me.

"You three into the entryway," she barked. "Tell me this ghost story."

I told her everything I knew. The corner of her mouth trembled now and then and wondered if she'd heard it before. The astonishment that tore through me must have registered on my face when the woman finally spoke.

"I'm Elizabeth Ann. I'm not a ghost, don't look so scared." She reminded me of Grams, just older.

"You're supposed to be dead," Tommy interjected. Kevin's skin took on the color of split pea soup and he stayed bolted in place.

"I would have been, too, if it wasn't for Jack Swan."

"Jack Swan? My Grams' grandfather? What did he do?"

Miss Elizabeth turned facing me. "First, what happened to your hand?"

The Mystery of Raven's Hollow

I looked down at the bloody once white bandage. "I fell on the trail near the pond this afternoon."

She held out her hand. "Let me see it. Your bandage is dirty. You could get an infection." Reaching for the handle she opened the door. "Go on in now, through the living room and into the kitchen."

The huge house reminded me of the Kansas City Museum, a seventy room house owned by some guy back in the 1800's. The old furniture, antiques as Gram would call them, sparkled with a fresh coating of orange oil. A large couch and two side chairs in leather then another arrangement of furniture upholstered in a velvet looking material sat near a bay window. The room, warm and inviting, resembled a page torn from the museum pamphlet.

I hesitated taking it all in when Elizabeth pointed to a chair at the kitchen table. "I won't hurt you. Now let me look at that hand."

Peeling back the bandage, the cut oozed again. I bit into my bottom lip as the last bit of gauze stuck to my flesh. I held my upright palm in her direction. "You didn't answer my questions about Jack Swan."

"Tell you what." She turned to the boys. Her mouth tilted up at the corners when she looked at Kevin then her gaze came to rest on Tommy. "You two go right through there and wash up and come back. I have a job for you."

Kevin and Tommy obliged returning in a flash. "Did you even get those hands wet?" she asked.

They held their hands up for her approval. "Ok, then. Go over there to the stove and turn on the kettle. What's your name?" She nodded to Tommy.

"Thomas, ma'am."

Thomas! I almost laughed and if I hadn't been afraid I'd be grounded all of my high school years when this woman talked to Grams and the boy's parents I might have. Tommy was never that formal.

"I'll bet it's Tommy, isn't it?"

He shook his head in agreement and turned the burner on under the kettle. "Thanks, Tommy, now get some plates from that cupboard over there and you and…"

"Kevin, Miss Elizabeth." Tommy answered for him.

"Cat got your tongue?" she asked.

"Nnnnno, Kevin Finnegan," he stuttered.

"Okay, Mr. Finnegan. There's a chocolate cake yonder in the pantry. Go get it and slice us each a piece while I fix her up." The boys went to work and Elizabeth continued to examine my hand.

"Well, if your Jack Swan's great great granddaughter you must be Deborah Jean. Do they call you that or Debbie?"

"D.J., Miss Elizabeth."

"Ahh that suits you. You're a brave girl. This hand must have hurt like the dickens."

With the temporary bandage Tommy had wrapped on my hand removed, the cut throbbed red and angry. Grams would be upset with me, not only for getting hurt but lying and dragging the boys into my adventure. I cringed from the pain–the reminder I'd have to face Grams and whatever punishment she dispensed.

Miss Elizabeth went to the sink and came back with a bowl of warm water, a cloth, and a bar of white creamy soap. She gently washed away the dirt and the blood then applied a salve from a fruit jar.

"Be still, now and I'll tell you what you want. Then we'll have cake with the boys."

I bobbed my head in agreement but a tear threatened to fall. She handed me a towel and smiled.

"The night of the accident, when my papa drowned, my little body came to rest on the bank under the scrub brush. The men assumed I'd drowned, too. After all the commotion, Mr. Swan walked down to the creek to see what had happened and found me. I'd been out in the cold for close to an hour. I almost died. When his wife nursed me back to health, they found my mother. I went to stay with her. I spent most of my childhood in boarding schools. When I finished, I realized I didn't fit into my mother's life and returned here to Papa's land."

"Why didn't you let anyone know who you were?"

"I didn't want to be treated like my papa just for being different. When I go into town, I use my mother's name,

McCrackin. No one knows who I am and few are aware I'm out here. I have a hired man to help and I stay to myself. I have no friends in Four Corners. Jack Swain, bless him, never told a soul."

"Miss Elizabeth. My Grams would be your friend." With halting steps I moved closer to the old woman and watched a tear run down her weathered face.

"Do you kids want me to take you home to your parents?"

Our biggest fear. "No!" The three of us echoed.

"We need to go," Tommy said edging toward the door.

Kevin who'd found his tongue chimed in, "Our camping gear is out in your clearing."

"It's cold out there. Come up and stay in the barn. This will be our secret. I won't tell if you don't. I'll remain the ghost of Parker house."

We couldn't get out of there fast enough, but I looked back at the porch and she waived a frail hand.

We slept until eight the next morning tired from our adventure with a chocolate induced daze from the wonderful cake we ate in Miss Elizabeth's warm kitchen. When we got home, I for one couldn't keep my secret from Grams since the first thing she noticed was the bandage on my hand.

"Well, D.J., what do you think your punishment should be?" Grams eyed me from across the table.

"I'm sorry." *Of course I was sorry. I owed Grams something better, but I wanted to solve the mystery and write a story about it.* I wound up getting the boys in trouble, too."

"Yes, you did. I talked to Tommy and Kevin's parents." Grams shook her head. "I just never expected this from you." She laid her wrinkled hands in her lap waiting for me to speak. "You could come up with your own penance."

I traced the squares on the oil cloth table covering with my fingertips. I enjoyed being outside so working in the yard wouldn't be a burden nor would sitting in my room and reading all day. One thing crossed my mind. "I could spend more time with Katie," I offered.

Grams laughed. "I think that might be punishment for her, too." She rose from her seat. "How about you spend your summer working for Miss Elizabeth?"

"She won't even come into town and she wants no one to know she's out there and she's kind of scary," I said all in one breath.

"Maybe we all should get to find out who she really is," Grams said then shuffled over to the stove. "We'll see."

Grams mentioned nothing more about it, but three weeks later Miss Elizabeth stood at Grams' front door. She was tall and proud as she extended her hand, "I'm Miss Elizabeth Ann Parker."

The summer of my thirteenth year whizzed by working for Miss Elizabeth and while at first there seemed to be so much to do and so many instructions to be carefully followed by September we were fast friends. I cleaned that marvelous living room of hers and she taught me how to oil the furniture just right and turn the cushions. Opening the curtains in the morning and closing them early afternoon to keep the sun away from her fine furniture and paintings.

We went into town every Monday to buy her groceries and she let me drive her old car when we were on the farm roads. I never told Grams that one. We even attended a few of the summer parties and the Fourth of July picnic in the park. The town people accepted her, too. It brought them some redemption.

That was how it happened fifteen years ago. Miss Parker died while I was away at college. She left me the house and that good river bottom land. We live there now; me, Tommy, and our little girl, Elizabeth Ann.

The Girl Who Slipped Through The Mirror

How could a 14-year-old girl end up facing herself and being pursued by a monster? Well, if she happens to cross through a portal into a parallel universe…

THE GIRL WHO SLIPPED THROUGH THE MIRROR

Kevin Singer

Mina was afraid her father was lost. They'd driven along a darkened wooded road with no sign of life for what seemed like forever. The cabin should have been close, but there was nothing but hulking trees and swallowing blackness.

Her father fumbled for the yellow paper wedged between the seat and console. He passed it to Mina beside him. "What do the directions say?"

"Are we lost?" Reed clambered up from the back seat.

"No," Mina said. "We're fine. Don't worry."

She followed the scrawl of her father's writing, retracing their path. "Did you make the left on County Road 772?"

"About 20 minutes ago."

"Then a right on McGee Road?"

"Yep. I think that's what we're on now."

"It says to stay on this road for five miles, then a left just past a boarded up white church. That's his road."

"I hope this is right," her father said. "Your mother gave me directions from her memory. It's been years since we've been up here. I tried calling Tao for the last few days but no one answered."

Mina struggled for something to say. If her mother were here she would calm him no problem. But she wasn't. She looked at the bracelet on her wrist–thin spun silver with rectangular blue stones the size of grains of rice. It was one her mother had worn when she was Mina's age. The clasp had come loose; it always did. She secured it tight again.

The cabin they were headed for belonged to Mina's great uncle Tao. He lived alone in Manhattan but owned this weekend house tucked in the woods. Mina had only met him a few times. She remembered him as hunched and wrinkled with tired black eyes and skin that smelled vaguely of motor oil. The plan was that Mina, her little brother Reed and their father would spend the weekend. "You all spend too much time in the hospital," her mother had said. "It'll be good for you to get away." Mina was secretly glad to leave, and that thought filled her with shame.

They'd already been driving for three hours. After they left the highway the streetlights became fewer and fewer. The bait shops and diners and gas stations disappeared, as did the rambling farmhouses and their glinting silos. Darkness seeped in around them. The Honda's high beams exposed a crush of forest on either side. Mina checked her phone. Only one bar, then none.

"You're doing great dad," Mina said, hoping her father was not lost after all.

"You're doing great dad," Reed mimicked in a sing-song voice.

"Shut up."

"You shut up."

Reed glared at Mina. He was 11, three years younger than her, and at the age when everything he did seemed to be aimed at getting her mad. She fought the urge to reach back and pinch him hard.

"Stop it, both of you."

"Sorry," Mina said.

Ahead Mina spied the church. Its windows were gaping holes. The front door swung partway open like a gasping mouth. On one side were black scorch marks. The steeple lay broken on the ground. Mina wondered who would ever want to live around here.

"This is the road," her father said.

He turned onto a rutted dirt road and they bounced along on the Honda's weary shocks. Darkness surrounded them. Mina

The Girl Who Slipped Through The Mirror

gazed out the window at the black woods. She imagined a pack of gray wolves, saliva dripping from fangs, encircling them in the car. She had to close her eyes and let the imaginary monsters run away. Instead she thought of her mother. What was she doing now? Sleeping? Reading a book? "Don't you worry about me, I'll be fine," her mother had told her before they left. "There are so many nurses, I'll be lucky to get a moment to myself." Mina still hadn't gotten used to the sight of her mother without hair. The black pageboy wig only made it worse. She hoped it would grow back again.

"Do you think there'll be a swimming pool?" Reed asked.

"You're too much of a city kid," their father said. His cheekbones rose as he cracked a smile, and it made Mina forget about the wolves and the hospital. "No pool, but there's a lake."

"A lake? Yuck. It's probably full of fish and monsters."

Mina kept silent but she agreed. Just the thought of something disgusting lurking beneath the surface, waiting to grab her with its tentacles and claws and pull her under, terrified her.

The road curved, and a quarter mile ahead a house came into view. Light from the car drenched the house. Three stories tall, it sat huddled in a clearing of pine trees. Thick ruddy beams framed by wood-slat trim of a peeling, melted yellow ran across the house. Its cement base seemed to be sinking into the ground, while the third floor, with its tall-slanting gables, edged high as if trying to escape. Behind the house the lake glinted, flat and boundless.

A single light shone from a gabled window on the top floor.

"Is this where monsters live?" Reed asked as he climbed out of the car.

"Only the nice ones," their father said.

"There are no nice monsters."

Mina stared at the lit window as she climbed out of the car. The autumn air gave her a chill, and she hugged her arms.

"Come on and help me with the groceries," their father said.

The trio grabbed their backpacks and the sacks of groceries picked up along the way. Their father pulled the key from underneath the mat and unlocked the door. It creaked open.

Young Adventurers

Mina expected it to reek of dust and dead mice but it was pine fresh with a hint of stale water. The foyer was about ten feet square with red walls and dark stained floors. A clock ticked on the wall. On either side of it hung two portraits–a man and a woman with milk-white skin–dressed in Revolutionary War-era clothes.

"Looks like the old boy is keeping up the place," her father muttered.

They set down their backpacks and wandered with the groceries until they found the kitchen, bleached white with scratched butcher-block counters. A lone cup of tea steeped a dark brown sat on the counter. Mina touched the cup. It was cold.

She inspected the counter for dirt but there was none. Her mother would probably scrub it down with bleach anyway. What was she doing right now? More sleep, she hoped. She remembered the time at the hospital when she eyed her mother's chart while the doctor was lost in conversation. Norah Li. 42. Stage IV. Recurrent. Acute Myeloid Lymphoma. The words were alien to her. When she looked those words up on the Internet, she wished she had never peeked at the chart.

The blue and silver glint of Mina's bracelet caught her eye. She checked the clasp and felt calm again. She was about to unpack the groceries when she heard a distant clang.

"What was that?" she asked.

"Just your overactive imagination again, honey," her father said. "Why don't you kids go explore while I fix us some grub."

"Let me help," Mina said.

"No way, missy. Go have fun. That's an order. You too, Reed. Be back down here in a half hour."

Mina wandered through the first floor. The dining room had a long dark table, twelve chairs and windows covered with green velvet drapes. In the living room was a floral couch, end tables and lamps with crystals hanging from the shades. The library had too many books to begin counting and a fireplace with an opening nearly large enough for her to fit inside. And there was a

The Girl Who Slipped Through The Mirror

bedroom, spare with a metal-rail twin bed and a single scratched dresser, and no curtains. Mina peered out. Wisps of branches swayed in the wind. Despite the darkness, she was glad to be far away from the hospital.

"This should be your room," Reed said. "Because it's ugly."

"Why are you here? Quit following me."

"You quit following me."

"How can I be following you if I'm always in front of you?"

"Because you're a freak and you're reading my mind, so you know where I'm going."

"Don't be silly. No one can read minds."

"That's your problem. You don't even try. You just do whatever people tell you. Come on, try and read my mind."

"No."

"Try."

"Okay." She pretended to think hard. "You're thinking about how you're going to sneak outside and dig up some earthworms and leave them on my pillow."

"No but that's a good idea. I was calling you a bad name."

"Stop it."

"I just did it again."

"Stop."

"And again. And again. And again." Reed laughed, then he spun around and headed away in the opposite direction. "I'm going to find the basement. That's where the monsters live I bet. I'll make friends with them and send them to get you."

"Finally," Mina whispered. "Thank God."

She climbed to the second floor. The stairs were covered with a fraying blue runner. The varnished railing was as cool as glass. At the top of the landing she put the lights on. There were pictures on the walls, much like the old-style portraits in the foyer. Animals forlorn in a pen. A man on his knees during a thunderstorm, hands raised to the heavens.

She walked through the L-shaped hall and counted eight doors. She was about to open one when she spied the staircase to the top floor. It was narrow, with bare worn treads. She climbed.

Young Adventurers

The stairs groaned with each step. The air grew colder as she rose. At the top was a door. She turned the handle. It opened, revealing a single, large room, larger than even her classroom at school. Tables stacked with jumbles of computer parts and machinery lined the edges of the room. On one end was a whiteboard with numbers and letters squiggled–nonsense, almost like a five year old would write. She inspected it, trying to decipher the random writing. Only one line stood out:

Crossover portals theoretically infinite??

At least it was English, but still, it made no sense to Mina.

From the looks of the haphazard junk and abandoned contraptions, she guessed Great Uncle Tao had too much time on his hands. Was he a scientist? She wasn't sure. All she knew was that he was old. She picked up a metal spider web-like mesh panel. It glowed in the light of the dim bulb. She shook it, and it left rainbow fluorescent swirls in its wake. She shivered in the cold air and spun around to leave. She was about to step down the stairs when she heard three distinct knocks.

Her heart pounded. Was Reed playing one of his usual pranks on her? But how could he have gotten up here without her seeing?

Slowly she turned around and looked to where the knocking came from. At the far end of the room, half hidden behind a steel-ringed contraption, was a mirror. It wasn't an ordinary mirror. It was as tall as her father, and wide too. It had a swirling metal frame and the dingy glass was pocked at the edges. It was suspended from the ceiling with a thick silver chain. Mina was certain that the knocking came from the mirror. She tiptoed closer, waiting for Reed to jump out from behind it and scream.

"Reed, I know you're here, so just come out."

She tiptoed closer.

"Reed, I'm serious. Quit being a jerk."

She was at the mirror now. It was suspended six inches off the ground. Her heart thudded as she bent down to look underneath. No feet. She climbed back up. She was sure she'd heard the knocks. Her heart kept on pounding. She poked her head around the backside of the mirror. Nothing except wood beams.

She tried to convince herself it was all in her head. Just as she turned away she heard the knock again. She froze. Slowly she pivoted back. What she saw in the mirror made her gasp.

The girl in the mirror was her, but it wasn't her. The girl in the mirror wore a white shirt and black skirt, while she wore jeans and a t-shirt. The girl in the mirror had hair cut in a bob just below her chin, while her own hair hung free past her shoulders. And the girl in the mirror wore burgundy lipstick.

Mina struggled to make sense of it. Was she dreaming? Hallucinating? Then the other Mina waved. Mina stumbled back. She had to remind herself to breathe. Slowly she raised a hand and shook a tiny wave. The other Mina smiled. Then she beckoned her forward.

Mina touched the glass. It was cool and hard, and then it turned pillow soft. She gasped and pulled her hand back. The other Mina laughed and beckoned again.

The second time Mina touched the mirror the glass rippled. She pushed her fingertips into the mirror. It was some sort of pliable membrane, cold and squishy. She pulled back.

The other Mina mouthed words and smiled warmly, a smile so like her own, then beckoned again. Mina thought of her father and brother downstairs. She looked toward the staircase. Then she turned back and she slipped through the mirror.

Crossing over felt like plunging into ice water. It felt like her body was taken apart and put back together again in an instant. Once on the other side she took a breath and blinked.

The room was not the same. Instead of mangled computers and metal-heavy contraptions there were boxes, crates, dusty suitcases, the smell of old paper and closed up windows. Nothing looked familiar. The other Mina took her hand, and the solidness brought Mina fully into her reality.

"You're me, aren't you?" Mina asked.

She shook her head and laughed, the edges of her cropped hair hitting the corners of her eyes. "No, I'm me."

"Mina."

"Yeah, well everyone calls me M1."

"That's strange. Why?"

"M for Mina, and because I'm number 1." M1 smirked. Mina wondered if she looked like that–as if she ruled the entire universe–when she smirked. She couldn't help but stare at this girl, M1, or whatever she called herself. It was like looking at another world of possibilities.

M1 snapped her fingers. "Hate to be a buzzkill, sweetie, but we can't stay here staring at each other forever."

Mina blushed and gazed at her feet. "I was only..."

"Don't worry." M1 put her hand on her hip. "Jeez, don't you have any questions? You act like this is no big deal."

"Of course. I mean, where are we?"

"Uncle Tao's house, silly."

"I know. I was there already." She pointed to the mirror. She peered in it. She saw the room where she came from. Then the image faded, and all she saw were two girls who could be twins.

"And now you're here."

"No, I was there already. This can't be Tao's house."

"It is."

"How can there be two of them?"

"Do I look like a scientist?"

"No, you look like a stuck-up cheerleader."

M1 rolled her eyes. "Okay, here's the story. I was at Tao's house with my parents and Reed."

"Your parents? Both of them?"

"Yes."

"Your mom–she's fine?"

"If by fine you mean annoying and always getting on me about my clothes, then yes."

Mina had to shut her eyes for a moment. There was another place where her mother wasn't sick. "You're lucky."

M1 fluttered her hand. "Whatever. Anyway, I was there. I wanted to be alone. Me and Tyler had a fight before I left."

"Who is Tyler?"

"My boyfriend."

The Girl Who Slipped Through The Mirror

"You're allowed to have a boyfriend?"

M1 rolled her eyes. "Anyway, I was up there and I was mad, and I walked up to the mirror and punched it. My fist went through. So now here I am."

"So this isn't your real house?" A bellowing groan echoed from somewhere in the house. Mina jumped. "What was that noise?"

"The reason why I brought you here." M1 grabbed Mina's hand and pulled her close. "Come on. We've got to go. Now."

They ran down the narrow staircase onto the second floor landing. It seemed the same as the house she left, until they turned a corner. The hallway twisted and they passed the staircase leading back up to the attic. "Wait, didn't we..."

M1 pulled her. "We can't stop."

They rounded another corner and passed another identical staircase. A left turn took them past more doors and another staircase up. A right turn, the same. Mina shook her hand free and stomped her feet on the floor. "Stop. This house–it's not possible. Tell me what it is."

M1 sighed. "I don't know."

"We're going in circles."

"No. It's the house. It keeps adding, growing. I don't know. I can't explain. I didn't make it like this. I hate it here."

"Then why don't you go back?"

"Because I can't."

"What do you mean you can't?"

"I can't find my world."

The words tumbled down on Mina like a collapsing house. If M1 couldn't find her way back, how would Mina? She looked at the staircase nearest to her. Was it the one back to her world? Were they all the same? All different? She reached down for her bracelet. It wasn't there. The clasp must have loosened, and now it was lying somewhere in this endless house. She fought her tears. "How could this be happening?" She looked up at the other girl, so like her, but so different. "How could you do this to me?"

M1 stroked Mina's arm. "I'm sorry. I didn't mean to hurt you. But I promise you. Once we defeat it, we can find our way back to where we belong."

"It?"

"The monster."

It was all too much for Mina–this other world, this other girl, and now a monster. "I need to sit."

M1 bit her lip. "Okay. Just a couple of minutes."

The tread beneath her was stripped to its bare, rough state. Just a couple of minutes, she told herself, just to accept it all. So here she was, trapped in a world that wasn't her own, with another version of herself and a monster. What choice did she have but to listen to M1? She could trust her, right? After all, she was her. It hurt her brain to think about it too much. "Okay, tell me about this monster."

M1 hugged Mina. "Thank God. I was terrified you'd leave me alone."

Mina didn't tell her how she wished she never stepped through the mirror. Too late for regrets. "No, I'm not that type of person."

M1 smiled. "All I know is I've been here maybe a week."

"A week?"

"I told you I couldn't get back."

"Did you try?"

"Of course I tried. Some mirrors I couldn't step through."

"And the others?"

M1 looked down at her shoes. "There were four that I could step through. None of them were my world. All of them were even worse than this place."

"What about leaving this house? I mean, if there's a monster in here, then why didn't you just run away and get the police?"

"I'll show you why."

M1 led Mina to the nearest door and opened it. Inside was a queen-size bed covered with an ivory comforter. A double bureau was on one wall, and a writing desk sat near the window.

"Look outside."

The Girl Who Slipped Through The Mirror

Mina gazed through the glass. The sky was a twilight gray. It could have been morning, or evening, or simply overcast. There was no way to tell. A mist coated the ground. In the distance the lake glowed with a greenish phosphorescent tint.

Then she saw it, clambering on the edge of the lake. About the size of a pit bull, it looked part lobster, part tarantula, with yellow fangs and bulbous eyes, and great big claws that clacked and snapped at the air. Then she saw another one. Then another. There were hordes.

"That can't be."

"Like this house can't be? Like me and you–two of us–that can't be?"

"Those are monsters."

"Some kind of chemical mutations, I suppose. They're the reason I can't leave. I tried. They're faster than they look. One nearly got my ankle."

Mina wished her father was here. He would surely know what to do. He always had an answer. He could always solve any problem. Well, almost any problem. "What are we going to do?"

"Don't worry." M1 draped an arm around Mina and pulled her close. "I've been plotting a way to get out of here."

Mina shuddered but she took comfort in M1. She seemed so strong, so resolute. Surely if anyone could save them, stuck here, it would be her. "Okay. So what's the plan?"

M1 grinned. "We find this bastard and kill him."

Just then Mina heard a groan. It stretched into a screeching, like crows cawing in the wind. Then it sunk back down into a low rumble that carried through the air, moving closer and closer.

"It must have heard us," M1 hissed. "Come!" She pulled Mina toward the closet, shoved her inside and then followed, easing the door closed behind her. The closet was full of women's clothes, and just before the latch clicked shut Mina could have sworn she noticed one of her mother's dresses–light yellow with a white collar–hanging inside.

Mina could hear her own heart pound. She begged it would stop. M1's hand rested gently on her forearm and Mina took a scrap of solace from her touch. The door to the bedroom creaked open, a painfully long cracking. Mina gasped despite herself. M1 pressed a lone finger to her lips.

Outside the closet door the thing scraped along the wood floor. It scrape-shuffle-scraped, stopped, then scrape-shuffle-scraped again. Mina imagined a misshapen thing sniffing the air, drunk on the tantalizing scent of two human girls. It scraped-shuffled-scraped closer, closer to where they hid. Mina wanted to grab in the darkness for anything that she could use as a weapon but she dared not move. Beads of sweat itched their way down her forehead. She fought to keep herself upright.

Then she heard a clatter from somewhere deeper in the house. The creature outside the door released a sound like gurgling, choking phlegm. Then it scrape-shuffle-scraped away from the closet.

The girls stood like statues long after the noises faded away.

"We are so lucky," M1 whispered.

"What would it have done to us?"

"What do you think?"

Mina regretted ever asking the question. "I didn't want to believe you. I hoped you were crazy, or a liar."

"Well I'm not." M1 carefully opened the door. She poked her head out and looked around. "All clear."

"What was that noise?"

"I don't know."

"Is someone else here with us?"

M1 shot her a cold stare. "I hope not, for their sake."

The air smelled like a mixture of burned meat and vomit. Mina scrunched her nose. "What do we do now?"

"Simple." M1 flashed a devious grin. "We go to where it lives, we trap it, and then we kill it."

Mina would rather spend an eternity trying the endless mirrors until she found the right one to lead her home. But she nodded. "Okay, let's do this."

"Just to warn you, it won't be easy."

"I'm braver than you think I am."

"I sure hope so, for both our sakes."

The Girl Who Slipped Through The Mirror

The hallway was dead. Mina followed M1 through the maze-like second floor corridor. She passed a painting on the wall. She recognized it from the original house. It was the one with the man on his knees, head twisted toward the sky as if begging God for mercy. But this one was different. The man was the same, but now he was surrounded by monstrous boars with giant tusks, sheep with fangs, sharp clawed birds, all tearing the flesh off his bones.

"We're close, I can feel it," M1 whispered.

"To what?"

"To the staircase down to the first floor. There's only one. Sometimes it moves."

"What if we never find it?"

"We will. Getting downstairs is never the problem. It's getting up to the third floor and out that's almost impossible."

"Impossible?"

"I said almost. God, you don't have much faith, do you?"

Mina thought of the moment when she discovered that her mother wasn't just a little sick, that she would never live to see Mina graduate high school, or get married, or have children. She lost her faith that day, in her room, all alone on the Internet, when she learned what stage 4 recurrent really meant. She reflexively reached for her vanished bracelet. "Never mind about my faith. Let's just go kill this thing and get it over with."

M1 glanced back and grinned. "That's my girl."

They rounded another corner, past a staircase up and several doors identical to the ones they'd just seen. Ahead of them was the staircase down. It looked exactly like the one Mina remembered from Uncle Tao's house. Hand in hand they tiptoed down. A dull light filtered in through the windowed door, and outside the clack clack clack of the creatures' pincers called out their threat.

"Do you think the monster is somewhere on this floor?" Mina whispered.

"No, I don't think so," M1 said loudly. "It doesn't come here for some reason. Only the basement and sometimes the second floor."

Young Adventurers

"Why?"

M1 stopped in the foyer and stood face to face with Mina. "How the hell would I know? You think I made this place? You think I want to be here? You think I'm just hanging around to try and figure out the rules here?" M1's hands trembled. "Well, no, I'm not. I'd do anything to leave. Anything. Get it?"

"Yes."

"Good. Now I'm hungry. Let's get something to eat before we give this bastard what it deserves."

The foyer looked identical to the one that Mina remembered in the original house. Except for a few differences. There was the clock. As it ticked the hands moved backward. And the numbers themselves, not only were they out of order, but there were three numbers she didn't even recognize. And then there were the portraits that hung on either side of the clock. In her world they were a colonial-era man and woman–normal and boring. Here the man's flesh fell off his cheeks in gray chunks, his lips chewed off. The woman's eyeballs dangled from her sockets, a spear skewering her skull.

Mina turned away. "I'm not that hungry."

"Your loss."

They treaded lightly into the kitchen. This kitchen was not the same as the one she'd remembered. This one wasn't tidy and old, it was sleek and new: black cabinets with white marble counters and a double-sized stainless steel refrigerator.

M1 opened a cabinet. It was stocked with food–cans and bags and boxes. "Whoever was here before me sure liked to eat well, thank God." She pulled out a bag of Doritos and hopped up on the counter.

Across from the counter was a dark wood table with four chairs and four plates laid out. Scraps of uneaten food lay gray and moldy on the plates–abandoned, as if someone had fled in a hurry.

"What about that?" Mina pointed to the plates.

M1 shrugged. "Not my problem."

"You couldn't even wash them?"

The Girl Who Slipped Through The Mirror

M1 narrowed her eyes. "Like I said, not my problem." She ripped open the Doritos bag and began stuffing chips into her mouth. "I could eat these forever."

Mina pulled one of the chairs away from the table, far enough so she wouldn't have to look at the abandoned dinner. "Okay, but please don't take forever."

M1 crunched a chip slowly. Crumbs fell on her skirt. She flicked them onto the floor. "I'll take as long as I want."

"Why are you being so mean?"

"Why are you being such a pain?"

"Because I don't want to be here."

M1 stuffed more chips in her mouth. "You know, it's not too bad here, besides there being a monster and all."

"How could you say that?"

"Simple. No one here to tell me what to do. No one to tell me what I can and can't eat. No one to yell at me for dressing how I want."

Mina glanced at the table set for four, then she remembered the closet with the dress that looked so much like her mother's. "But you only have the clothes you came in, right?" M1 glared at Mina and kept chewing. "Right?"

"I found some more, in a bedroom, and, well, they fit me."

That's when Mina realized there must have been another version of her own family here–Reed, her father, her mother, maybe even Uncle Tao, and herself as well. And they were all gone. Mina pointed to the table. "They're all probably dead, you know that."

M1 put the bag down. "I had nothing to do with it."

"But you can at least act like you care. You can pretend to be sad or respectful. You shouldn't act like it was just nothing."

M1 wiped her mouth with the back of her hand. "I know it's not nothing." She gazed at the floor. "I just want to live, that's all. Don't hate me."

Mina sighed. She walked over to M1 and held her hands. "I don't hate you. I couldn't. That would be like hating myself, kind of."

"You promise?"

"Yes."

M1 smiled. "Thank you. And I promise you that together we'll take care of this monster."

The thought of actually seeing–and fighting–this creature made Mina want to disappear. But M1 was right: they had to fight.

Through the kitchen they walked into the parlor. The light that filtered through the window cast the room in a dusty haze. Mina followed M1 to the fireplace. Above the mantle was a deer head. As Mina came closer she realized it was not a deer. The thing had four eyes and fangs that curled outside an elongated jaw. The antlers were a greenish blossom of razor tips.

"Here." M1 hoisted a metal poker. "Give it a feel."

It was heavy in Mina's hands. She gave it a swing and imagined breaking the monster's spine. She wondered if she would have the strength, even with such a weapon. She passed it back. "Is there one for me?"

"You can have the shovel, I suppose. Don't worry, I'll be the one taking care of it. I've been practicing."

The shovel with its smudged brass base wasn't half as solid as the poker. Mina was surprised to find herself disappointed. "Okay."

Mina followed M1 back out through the kitchen and into a small pantry. Inside the pantry was a scuffed door that led to the basement. M1 rested her free hand on the knob. "This is it. Are you sure you're ready?"

"Yes."

"Absolutely sure?"

"I said 'yes,' didn't I?"

"You better be."

"Come on. Stop treating me like a baby."

"Listen," M1 leaned in close. "I have a plan, and you've got to trust me 100 percent, no matter what. If you don't, we'll both end up dead. Do you understand?"

Mina nodded.

"Say it."

The Girl Who Slipped Through The Mirror

"I trust you, no matter what." Mina didn't quite believe her own words, but there was nothing else for her to say.

"Good." M1 grinned. "Let's do this." She opened the door and both girls descended into the mildewy darkness.

Each step was an eternity. Each creak was a scream. A thin-wired bulb shed a wisp of light at the bottom of the stairs. Mina almost wished it could remain pitch black.

"Were you..."

"Quiet," M1 whispered.

"Sorry. Were you ever down here before?" M1 nodded. "And you weren't scared?"

"Of course I was. But you fight through it, 'cause you have to."

The girls touched down on the concrete floor. Mina peered through the meager light. The basement didn't seem nearly as large as the endless second floor. A long narrow space was framed by shelves and topped with tiny rectangle gray-lit windows. On the other side was a long cinderblock wall. Mina couldn't make out what lay at the end.

M1 walked through the corridor with Mina close behind. The shelves were lined with board games, stuffed animals, balls and blocks, all cobwebbed and dusty. She grazed a finger against the arm of a headless doll. It was slimy. She wiped it on her jeans. "This place is gross."

M1 shook her head and didn't even turn around. "You have no idea."

At the end of the corridor was a door. It was hard, maybe steel, Mina guessed. And there was a bolt on the outside. M1 gripped the fireplace poker tight. She spun around and whispered in Mina's ear. "We've got to be quick. If I say 'run' that means the creature's in there. You run back up to the kitchen. If it's not in here, then we can move on with our plan."

"But I don't even know what the plan is."

"Ssh." M1 unlatched the bolt. She turned the knob and opened the door. Then she slipped inside.

Mina pressed her back against the wall. The cinderblocks were rough against her head. Every creak of the sagging house was the monster on its way. She hoisted the thin shovel but it felt silly in her hands. Maybe it would buy her a minute, if that. She stared at the stacks of toys and thought of the children who played with them. Where were they now?

M1 poked her head out. "It's clear." She beckoned Mina inside. "Hurry up. It'll smell us soon enough."

Mina dashed into the room. It was larger than she'd imagined. There was a brown-splattered sink and a cage of mechanical equipment–large rusted tools, crushed and twisted metal–at one end. The floor was littered with newspapers and tufts of cloth–sheets and towels, matted and stained. The smell was feral.

"This is where it lives?" Mina asked.

"Where else?"

"It's worse than I imagined."

M1 shrugged. "Well, don't start crying now."

Mina hated that this other her might think she was nothing more than a scared baby. "I'm fine."

"Good, because it's only going to get harder from here."

"What do you mean?"

M1 led her to the far wall. There were piles of clothes and blankets stacked like firewood. Beside the stack was a metal loop embedded in the wall. Attached to the loop was a handcuff. One end dangled open.

"What's that for?" Mina asked.

"You ever see in movies how there are two soldiers and one of them runs across a field to draw fire from the bad guys while the other one shoots the bad guys?"

Mina didn't like war movies. "I guess."

M1 cradled the fireplace poker. "Guess which one you're going to be?"

"I...have no idea."

M1 rolled her eyes. "God, what is it with you? Okay, here's the plan. You're going to be bait, and I'm going to hide. When the monster comes for you, I sneak up behind him and bash his head in."

The Girl Who Slipped Through The Mirror

Mina looked between the cuffs and M1. "Are you serious?"

"Yes."

"No way!"

"Don't you want to get out of here? Don't you want to see your parents again?"

Mina glanced at her arm where her bracelet had been. She couldn't bear the idea of her mother dying knowing that Mina was gone from her. "Yes, more than anything."

"Well, then you're going to have to trust me."

"Why don't you be the bait?"

M1 looked down at the poker, then back up at Mina. "You seriously think you can nail him with this?"

Mina shrugged. "But why the handcuffs?"

"This monster isn't dumb. That way his guard will be down. He'll know you can't fight back." Just then a groan rumbled from somewhere in the house. "We don't have time," M1 said. "He's smelled us. He's coming."

Before Mina could even think M1 thrust her wrist into the handcuff. She clicked it so tight that it dug into Mina's skin. Then M1 scurried back and ducked between stacks of crates midway across the room.

The monster groaned again, this time closer, then the air turned quiet. Mina could see M1's head poking out from between the crates, just barely. Her hand throbbed, and she began to sweat. She gave a jerk to the handcuffs but all it did was give her pain. Her eyes darted around the stacks of clothes by her feet. In the gray light she caught the glint of a gold thread. She leaned in as close as her cuff would allow and saw it was a necklace threaded between a yellowed husk of something and a sweater. Mina nudged it with her foot. The bundle tumbled down and she saw a dried out, shriveled face framed with black hair.

"Oh my God, what is this?"

But she knew instantly what it was, who it was. The face, twisted, shriveled mouth, hollowed eyes, was hers. She looked back at the pile of bundled clothes. They were all her, different versions of her, all drained and dead.

Young Adventurers

"What is this? What are you doing?" Mina tugged hard at her cuffed hand.

The other girl poked her head out. "It's not painful, not at first, I think, anyway. It's kind of like a vampire biting you. All the other ones screamed at first but in a couple of seconds they looked like they were drunk or on drugs."

"But why? Why would you do this?"

"Because I don't want to die."

"I thought you said you were going to kill it."

M1 shrugged and tossed the poker behind her. It clanged against the concrete floor. "You'd be surprised how hard it is to kill a monster. So I figured out that as long as I keep feeding it, it leaves me alone. Lucky for me there are a lot of other Minas out there. Hundreds. Maybe even thousands. And lucky for me they're all as nice and trusting–and desperate to get back–as you."

"But I thought you wanted to get back to your world."

M1 laughed. "My world? Why would I want to go back there? My mom's an alkie and my father's in jail. Even if I could find the right world, I'd rather live here among all these monsters than go back there."

A rolling moan floated through the air. It was a sound barely human, the sound of something coming to devour every shred of life. Mina screamed and pulled uselessly at her cuffed hand. She glared at M1. "You can't do this!"

M1 turned away. "Funny how it gets a just little easier each time."

With every tug of the handcuff pain seared down Mina's arm. There was a door to her left, past the stacked bodies of the other Minas. The sound of the creature came from that direction.

"Please!"

Behind where M1 was hiding Mina spied movement. It was a form, small and shrouded. Was it another creature? One of the lobster monstrosities from outside? It was too much, all too much. Mina prayed, though she knew she had little chance against one monster, let alone two.

The Girl Who Slipped Through The Mirror

The form crept closer to where M1 crouched. Then a flash of metal in the gray light–the fireplace poker that was discarded by M1–swung down upon M1's head.

"Aah!" M1 stumbled into the open basement. She sunk on her knees, holding her head. The shrouded form swung the poker again. It glanced off the top of M1's skull. M1 fell limp onto the cold concrete floor.

The figure pulled its cloak off. Mina gasped. "Reed! What are you doing here?"

The cloak was just a brown bathrobe. The boy was dressed in a stained white T-shirt and shorts. He wouldn't take his eyes off M1.

"Reed! Look at me. It's me, your sister. It's me, Mina.

"You're not my sister. My sister is dead."

Mina was confused, then she realized that if there were infinite Minas, then there were infinite Reeds. He kept staring at the slumped body of M1. Mina was afraid she was dead until she noticed the slight rise and fall of her back, air inhaling and exhaling. The monster's groans came closer. She looked at her cuffed hand.

"Listen to me," Mina said. "She has to have a key."

"A key?" Reed glanced up at her. He seemed as if he'd just woken up.

"Yes, for this." Mina pointed to her cuffed hand. The monster cried out. It was nearly at the doorway.

Reed thrust his hands in the pockets of M1's skirt and pulled out a silver key. He carefully stepped over the husk of a body and gave Mina the key. She freed herself just as the monster groaned from the other side of the door.

Mina grabbed Reed's hand. "Hurry." She pulled him toward the other exit. Then she stopped.

"What is it?"

M1 was so much like Mina, yet so different. "I can't just leave her."

"But she let all those others die."

"I can't do the same to her." Mina tried to hoist M1's body up but she was too heavy. It was all she could do to raise her off the floor; she'd never be able to carry her up the stairs, not even with Reed's help. She lugged M1's unconscious body to the far side of the basement and rested her against the cinderblock wall. She piled blankets on top of her, hoping that maybe the monster wouldn't find her.

Just then the door opened. Mina caught a glimpse of the monster. It looked like it had been human, once. Now it was a lumbering thing, hunched and covered in tumors that glowed in the gloom. She fought the urge to coil up from fear. She pulled Reed out of the room, through the corridor and its ruined toys, and up the stairs to the safety of the first floor, slamming the door behind her.

"It won't come up here." Reed sounded almost robotic. "It never does."

Mina cradled her wrist. It was bruised but she was thankful she was alive. "That's what she told me. Why? What is it?"

"Uncle Tao slept in the bedroom out front. He had trouble walking, so he moved down here." Reed wandered out into the kitchen. He stared at the dirty plates. "I should clean these."

"Reed, do you know what that thing is?"

The boy kept his back to her. "Uncle Tao was getting sick. Mom said he had cancer. Then there were these weird flashes, like bursts of light. They were all around the house and then by the lake."

"Where did they come from?"

"I dunno. Uncle Tao was yelling one night. Mom tried to calm him down but I knew something was really wrong with him. She wouldn't even let us look at him. Then he was gone."

Then it dawned on Mina. "You didn't come through the mirror, did you?"

"No." Reed picked up a plate and scraped the moldy food into a trash bag.

This Reed had always been here, in this world that had suddenly, somehow, turned horrific. "So this is your home."

He dropped the plate into the sink. "There was screaming noise from the basement. Dad went to check. He didn't come back up. Mom called after him but he didn't answer. Then she

The Girl Who Slipped Through The Mirror

went down. We heard her scream. She never came back up." He cleaned off another plate and rested it in the sink.

"What about Mina?"

He turned and glared at her. "The real one, you mean?" Mina nodded. "She tried to call the police but the phone wasn't working. The sky was gray by then, always gray, even at night. She told me not to go into the basement. She told me to hide. She told me to keep safe. Then she left for help. I haven't seen her since."

Mina thought of those mutants crawling all over the property. "Oh, no," she whispered. "So you've been alone here."

Reed cleaned the last plate. "Until the one down there came. I knew she wasn't my sister. I knew she was an impostor. I thought she was going to get eaten by the monster but she never did. Then there was another, then that one was gone, and then there was another one. I kept count. You were the fourteenth."

Thirteen dead Minas. Or was it fifteen, counting the one who lived here in this world? She tried to imagine all these other Minas and what their lives were like. Maybe they were as different as she and M1. Maybe some of them were even happy. "We have to get out of here."

He sprayed water on the dishes. "But this is my home."

"I know, but we can't stay here. It's not safe anymore."

He shut the water off. "What if my sister comes back?"

"We'll leave a note letting her know where to find us."

Reed knelt beside Mina. "She's not coming back. I know that."

She stroked his black hair. It was longer than her own brother's. "I promise you, I'll take you to somewhere safe."

"Okay."

She touched her bare and damaged wrist, more determined than ever to find her way home.

The second floor was where the monster roamed. Mina couldn't guess why, and she didn't have time to solve that puzzle. If the monster found M1 and fed on her–just the thought made her sick–they might have some time to spare. If it hadn't found her, the monster might be ravenous. They had to be quick.

There was no sound in the corridor aside from their own footsteps and the clacking claws of the creatures outside. She hurried through the hallway, Reed in tow.

"Where are we going?"

"I don't know."

They came upon a set of stairs leading to the attic. Mina bounded up two at a time, nearly tripping. This attic was like the one she came through–a standard attic used to stow the extras of life, not the mad scientist workshop of her world. She spied the mirror on the far wall and ran toward it. She reached out a hand and touched the glass. It was solid. She pressed both hands hard on it, staring at her own angry face. Nothing happened.

"It's dead," she said. "Come on."

They ran back into the hallway and found the next set of stairs. The attic looked exactly the same. She touched the mirror but it was solid too. They tried attic after attic, but nothing.

"We'll never find it," Reed said.

"Of course we will," Mina told him, trying to sound certain.

The mirror in the eighth room vibrated with a slight hum. Mina touched the glass. It shimmied and vibrated as if it was no more than a viscous film. She pushed her hand all the way in and then pulled it out. She turned to Reed. "Let me check first." She pushed her head through the mirror. A few seconds later she pulled it out.

"What's wrong?"

Mina touched her bare wrist. "I think there was a fire in that house. It's all black, charred wood, nothing else."

"What if they're all like that?"

"They're not. Don't say that. Let's go."

The mirror in the next attic was dead. The one after that, though, vibrated and hummed. Mina peeked into that world and drew her head back out. "It's okay there, but it's not my world."

"Maybe we should just go there. At least we'll be safe."

Mina thought of her mother, daughterless in the last days of her life. "No. I want to go back to my home."

The Girl Who Slipped Through The Mirror

Three more attics with three more dead mirrors. Mina worried they were doubling back on their path, repeating attics. She wished she had a pen to x off the doors. As they ran to the next attic they heard a low groan.

"It's going to eat us unless we hurry and find it," Reed said, "or someplace good enough."

They dashed up the next set of stairs. The mirror was alive. Mina pushed her head through and pulled it back grinning.

"What did you see?"

"Uncle Tao's workshop. I think this is it."

Reed took a look around the attic. Mina understood that this was his world, and he'd be leaving it forever. "Okay," he told her. "Let's go."

She watched Reed approached the mirror. He was so like her brother; it hurt to see him so sad. If they made it back to her world, how would she explain this new sullen Reed to her family? How would he fit in their lives? Then another thought hit her. What if he couldn't pass through the mirror? What if she alone had that power? "You go first, she said. "Just step through and I'll be right behind you."

He looked back at her, then he slipped through the mirror. Mina breathed in relief, then she followed.

The shift felt like walking through a cool shower, though she remained dry. She raised her arms and wiggled her fingers, noticing with a pang of regret the bare wrist where her mother's bracelet used to rest. She smiled at the hodgepodge of steel contraptions in the attic of this safe world. She brushed her hair from her face and breathed a long sigh of relief.

"Are we okay?"

Reed wore a frown, and Mina wondered if it would ever leave his face. She crouched down and hugged him. "Nothing can hurt us here."

Then came a voice from the floor below. "Mina? Where are you hiding?"

Mina's heart jumped, though she knew in that instant that she shouldn't have let it. The voice belonged to the one person who should not have been in this house. She stood and backed away.

Young Adventurers

"What is it?" Reed asked.

"Something's wrong."

Reed scurried away and hid behind one of Tao's overloaded workbenches. "Another monster?"

Mina waited as the feet climbed the stairs. She stared at the door, caught between ecstasy and fear, while it opened. There, before her was her mother, Norah, looking like she did before cancer ravaged her body

"Where have you been? Didn't you hear me calling for you?" Norah gave Mina an exasperated look. "Dinner's been ready for ten minutes."

"I'm sorry."

"Have you been up here the whole time?"

Mina couldn't help but stare. She nodded.

Norah cocked her head. "You look different. Did you do something to your hair? It looks longer for some reason."

Mina couldn't take it anymore. She ran over to the woman and hugged her tight. Her body was warm and alive and vital, not weak and dry. Her skin smelled perfume fresh, not like tangy sweat. "Tell me you were in the hospital, and you got better and you drove up to meet us. Tell me, please."

Norah pulled back. "What on earth are you talking about? I haven't been in the hospital since I gave birth to your brother."

Then Mina noticed her mother's wrist. On it was the blue and silver bracelet. This was not her world. This was not her mother. Her heart felt shredded into a thousand pieces. She glanced back to the mirror. "How long have I been up here?"

"I don't know, maybe a half hour or so. Are you feeling okay?"

She looked between the mirror and this woman, and then a horrible realization came upon her: this woman's daughter was most likely one of the dead Minas. This woman would never see her daughter again.

"Mina, is something wrong?"

Her mind spun. She could stay in this world: she was soon to be a motherless daughter, and this woman was now daughterless. They could both be happy. They could both have what they

The Girl Who Slipped Through The Mirror

needed. All it would take was for her to say yes, to break that mirror and sever the link with all the other worlds.

"Nothing's wrong," Mina said. "I'm just so glad I'm here." She gripped Norah's hands. They felt so warm, so healthy. Her heart pumped with joy at the idea of this new, safe life.

"I swear I will never understand teenagers," Norah laughed.

The laugh was so clear and bright that it brought Mina back to the last time she heard her own mother laugh so freely, before she fell sick. Mina couldn't help imagine her own mother in her hospital bed, dying. And in that moment, because of that laugh, she knew she couldn't let her mother die with a vanished daughter and a broken heart. This was not her world. She didn't belong here.

The mirror lay against the wall, beckoning her. It almost seemed to be laughing at her pain. She turned back to Norah. They looked so much alike. It wasn't fair. "Don't worry about me, mom. I'm fine."

The instant Norah let go of her hands Mina wished she could grab them again and hold them forever. "Well, come on down for dinner before it gets cold. We're all waiting for you." Norah cocked her head, and Mina wondered if she knew she wasn't her daughter.

The sadness of the coming loss caught hold of Mina. She thought of what this woman would go through when her daughter never returned. "Mom, I love you. Remember that, always, okay?"

Norah shook her head and chuckled. "I swear, sometimes it's like you're someone else's child." Then she was gone.

Reed came out of the shadows. His frown was firmer than ever. "I know," he sighed. "Back again."

"I'm sorry. I've got to try."

The attic was the same jumbled mess as before. The air smelled sour and the light from the window carried that familiar gray glow. Mina snapped into warrior mode and ran back down to the maze of the second floor, Reed in tow. They turned a corner and came across a puddle of greenish ooze.

"What is that?" Mina bent down. It smelled like horrible cheese. She didn't dare touch it.

"It comes from the monster." Reed's eyes were wide with terror. "It's here."

They ran for the nearest stairway up to the third floor. The mirror there was dead. They dashed back down and ran the maze again. Just before they reached another staircase they heard the monster's groan. It was the sound of emptiness, of death.

"We should go back to that other place," Reed said.

"Just one more."

The mirror in that attic was dead too. Mina wanted to scream but she had to keep strong for the boy.

Back down they went. Mina was nearly breathless. Reed's sweaty hair was stuck to his forehead. They jumped over another puddle of ooze. Mina rounded the corner ahead of Reed and slammed into someone standing there. She stumbled to her feet, afraid to look up at the hideous face of the monster. But she did, and it wasn't the monster. It was M1. Crusted blood covered half her hair and ran down her forehead and cheek. Her eyes were dazed and she had to steady herself against the wall.

"I've been looking everywhere for you."

Mina pushed herself up. "Oh my God, I can't believe you're alive."

M1 swayed on her feet. She let loose a gleeful laugh. "You tried to kill me."

"I tried to hide you."

Just then the monster groaned so loud that Mina had to cover her ears. Reed tugged at her shirt. "It's coming."

Behind M1 stood a staircase. M1 saw where Mina glanced. She barricaded Mina's way. "You're not going anywhere."

Mina grabbed M1's shoulders but she wouldn't budge. Mina thrust her body against M1's blocking arm, again and again until M1 gave way.

"Hurry, Reed."

He dashed up the staircase. Mina was about to follow but M1 reached out and clawed a hand on her throat. Mina flailed her arms and caught M1 on the side of the head, smacking her

The Girl Who Slipped Through The Mirror

bloody wound. M1 gasped, her hold slacked. Mina wiggled past and climbed the stairs on her knees. M1 recovered. She followed Mina up the stairs and grabbed her ankle. Mina wiggled and kicked. With her free leg she nailed M1 square in the head. M1 tumbled down the stairs and lay sprawled in the hallway.

Dazed, M1 stared up at Mina. "Should have been you."

The monster came upon M1's body lightning quick. It hovered above her and descended, covering the screaming girl.

Mina couldn't watch. She wheeled around and prayed this mirror was alive. If not, then she and Reed were as good as dead. Reed stood by the mirror, his frown deeper than ever. Mina ran over, desperate to the point of tears. She thought of the monster at the bottom of the stairs, devouring, waiting. She was halfway across the room when she heard the clatter of the monster on the steps behind her. She wouldn't turn back.

"Hurry," Reed said.

When she reached the mirror Mina held up her hand. She prayed harder than she ever did in her life. The monster growled a scream of twisted pain. She poked the glass and felt an electric surge. It was alive!

"Go, Reed." She grabbed him by the shoulders and shoved him forward.

"What if it's worse?"

"It can't be."

He slipped through the shining film. Mina stepped in after him. She was halfway through when she felt the monster's hand grab her foot. Caught between two worlds, Mina kicked her foot hard.

Reed stood in the other attic–a laboratory mess. "Pull me!" Mina said.

He took her hands and tugged hard, but the monster was too strong. She felt herself slipping back to the dead mutated world, back to a thing that wanted nothing more than to devour her. I am going to die, she thought, and she almost succumbed. But then she remembered her mother. Mina wiggled and kicked her trapped foot as hard as she could. She grabbed onto the edges of the mirror and thrust herself forward. Then she broke free and tumbled into the new attic.

She lay on the floor for just a moment and caught her breath. Then she saw the hand poking through the mirror. It was a gnarled claw with a mess of tumors and sores that oozed a glowing green puss. The hand moved slowly, as if it had to fight its way between worlds.

"Quick, give me something hard," she called out.

Reed grabbed a hammer from the workbench. He tossed it to her and she caught it in midair. She smashed the hammer against the mirror. It shattered into a thousand crystal shards as the hand vanished back into that other world.

"Are we safe now?"

"Yes," Mina said, though she had no idea what this final world would hold for them. What if this world was wrong, and even worse than the monster's world?

Among the jagged glass Mina spied a sprinkle of blue. She brushed the broken glass aside. It was the silver and blue bracelet, the one from her mother, the one she'd been missing her whole time in that other world. She slipped it back on her wrist.

"What's that?" Reed asked.

"It's home."

Puppy Love And Zombies

Becca's life changed dramatically when she became infected with the Z virus and turned part-zombie. Now she must put her fear of dogs aside to rescue one little puppy and find the other dogs that went missing. She'd do almost anything, she realizes, to do that…even break a few laws if necessary.

PUPPY LOVE AND ZOMBIES

C.A. Verstraete

Most of us had been too busy surviving, and trying to avoid the roaming hordes of ravenous undead, to notice something else was going on.

Yeah, like the rest wasn't bad enough? It was, but this new thing nearly did what the mutated Z virus didn't already do–kill me.

The morning started great when my Uncle Franco brought this beautiful, year-old white German Shepherd puppy over for us to meet. Unlike my first dog experience (more on that later), the puppy bounced around, played, barked, and most important, didn't make me afraid.

Call it love at first lick.

For once, I forgot all the zombie stuff that had plagued me for the past year. I threw a ball and laughed at how she ran and brought it right back. "Ooh, she's so cute and smart! I'm going to call her Fluffy! Is she mine? Can I keep her, can I?"

I begged and begged, though I knew my *Tia* (Spanish for Auntie) Imelda already loved her as much as I did. Then we heard the yells outside. My uncle's cries of "look out!" came too late. My cousin Carm opened the door and jumped back at sight of the chaos in front of our house. Our neighbor Mr. Thompson screamed, "go back in, shut the door!" as two of the zombies came at him.

In the last few months, most of the full Zs had been rounded up and exterminated, but a few wanderers like these kept us on our toes–at least they should've. My uncle grabbed his gun and fired at the monsters. The excitement was too much–the puppy panicked and pulled out of her collar. I screamed as she darted out the door and ran off in the opposite direction.

"NO-NO!" I yelled and tried to catch her, but she was gone. I would've followed if not for the strong arms of my cousin and aunt holding me back.

"No, Becca honey, let her go," *Tia* implored. "She'll come back or someone will find her."

"No, she won't," I cried. "She won't!"

And she didn't.

My aunt's friend Amelia from down the street stopped by later and let us know my suspicions had some truth to them. As a nurse, she had a way of hearing what was going on in the community.

"Sure glad they got those creatures." She gave a mock shiver. "The National Guard's been doin' a fine job of watching out for stragglers, so I can't imagine how those two made it into town."

I shrugged and tried to be polite, but my heart wasn't in it.

Amelia reached out and patted my chin. "Oh sweetie, I wanted to see how you're doing. I saw that cute little dog of yours run by my house. I tried to stop her, but couldn't catch her."

She paused for a minute. The concerned look on her face did make me pay attention. Amelia was a sweet, caring lady, who also told us when she heard something we should know about. What made her even more special to me was that of all the people in our neighborhood, she'd been the only one who welcomed me back home after I'd been infected. She treated me the same as always, like she was my aunt.

"Amelia? Is something wrong?"

The older woman paused a second, then leaned in, and looked me straight in the eye. "At first I didn't think much of it, but now, well, I'm not so sure. Two of my other neighbors' dogs are missing, too. One ran off and never came back. He told me his dog never went further than the house next door before this zombie thing hit. My other neighbor said her dog was in the yard and when she went to call her in, the dog was gone, and the gates were still locked."

Puppy Love And Zombies

The uneasy feeling I'd had earlier came back with a vengeance. I tried to ignore it. No way did I want to think that those *monsters* had found the dogs and attacked them, too. I couldn't bear the thought.

"Maybe the dogs snuck out and got lost?"

Amelia shrugged, her face questioning. "Maybe, maybe, but a couple people I work with at the hospital said their dogs also disappeared. I think something's going on and the police aren't bothering with it, not with all the other things going on. My co-workers called and both were told, real sarcastic-like, to file a report and it would be looked into when things let up. No one at city hall took their complaints seriously, either."

She continued, her voice lower. "It's simply been too chaotic to worry about the smaller things happening, not that it's small to any of us, of course. Now, you didn't hear it from me, but the rumor is somebody's taking those dogs. And no, it's not those *things*."

My gasp prompted her to squeeze my hand and tell me not to worry before she left. It didn't help. Now I was more worried than ever about where Fluffy had gone and what was happening to her.

The rest of the day I ignored everyone. I didn't want to talk, or hear their well-meaning attempts to console me. Instead I sat by the window, my eyes on the street (*well, one of them when my other eye crossed*), my senses ever alert for a streak of white fur and the sound of a playful yip or bark.

Nothing anyone said could stop me from making those weird hiccupping sounds that passed for crying since I'd been infected with the Z virus. It was one of the odd side effects of my new life as a part-Z, which luckily, didn't include the disgusting things done by the full-zombies, nor their horrible diet. Ick. I let out a big sigh. Chalk it up to the latest bad event in what had been a bad year. I felt a big pity party coming on.

After a couple hours, I rubbed my still-too-dry eyes and wished real tears would appear again. Like hitting replay on my iPod, I heard *Tia's* voice in my head saying her favorite, often repeated phrase: "*Wishing don't make it so, honey.*"

Young Adventurers

I knew that. All of it was pointless, so, so, pointless.

My mood dark and growing worse by the minute, I stumbled to my feet and headed for the stairs, my limp more pronounced from my self-confinement. I motioned Carm to come upstairs with me. Once in my still-too-messy room, I shoved over the pile of clothes my cousin, ever the *fashionista,* had brought over for me from her always overstuffed closet.

I plopped myself on the bed and told her we needed to do something. "We need a plan. We need to find Fluffy and find out why all these dogs are disappearing."

Carm stopped folding clothes and stared at me. "We? As in me and the person who freezes like a statue when a dog comes near her?"

No way did I want to go over our *stupida* argument again about my fear of dogs and my, um, "scent" problem since my other cousin, Carm's brother, Spence, infected me with the Z virus via a scratch. Given the circumstances, I didn't think it irrational at all.

"No, this is different."

She raised an eyebrow at me and kept on sorting. "Really?"

I snorted and kneaded one of the shirts she'd handed me into a ball before tossing it back on the bed. "Yeah, Fluffy's different. She doesn't scare me. I can deal with the other dogs if it means we find her. Really."

My cousin flashed a "who-are-you-kidding" look and went back to straightening out the pile of clothes on my bed. Okay, so she had good reason not to believe me after my last experience. Our uncle brought a big black German Shepherd dog named Chico over, *Tia* thinking it a good idea for protection before me and Carm left to go find our mothers.

Yeah, the dog had scared me–a lot–especially after Carm's declaration that I had a certain "smell" since becoming a part Z. "Something like going by a landfill and then it's gone real quick" kind of scent, she'd said. Great.

The whole situation scared me even more since I figured the D-O-G with its big head and even bigger teeth would notice. He didn't–that time. So, after that incident, I understandably never, ever, hoped to see another canine up so close and personal again.

Then my uncle came over this time with Fluffy, the cutest, fluffiest, and friendliest little German Shepherd pup I'd ever seen.

Now she was gone, and even if I couldn't feel my heartbeat anymore, I knew my heart was broken.

Unable to sit still, I paced across the room, trying to think of what to do when Carm interrupted. "Hey, look at this." She unfolded a newspaper and pointed at the back page.

"What?" I asked, getting more aggravated. "C'mon, Carm, help me think of something. I have to find Fluffy!"

She gripped my arm and thrust the paper in front of my face. "You better read this."

I stared at the page, focusing on the small square of black and red print she tapped her finger on. "Great Job! Great Pay. No Experience...So? What's that have to do with anything? We need to find–"

She cut me off. "Keep reading."

The last line got me–*Must be able to follow step-by-step instructions and work with animals*. "That doesn't sound good. Do you think they're doing something there with the dogs?"

A shudder hit me at the idea of what that could be. Our eyes met. I didn't have to say anything else. "Call the number. I can't go there, you know, because of how I look...but you can."

When Carm got nervous, she sounded like a mouse. Like now. "You-you want me to call them?" She took a breath and squeaked out another answer. "I don't think it'll work. We shouldn't get involved in something like this. Maybe we better tell someone else like *Tia* or Uncle Franco."

I rolled my eyes. Well, one of them, since the other one had a way of not cooperating. "Carm, you know what'll happen. They'll call the police. The police will tell her they'll look into it, and they won't. That's what Amelia said. They're too busy with all the zombie mess and chasing down vigilantes."

The moment the V word left my mouth, I knew I'd made a mistake. A big one. I cursed under my breath as Carm's eyes went wide.

"Vi-vigilantes," she murmured. "Did you forget how they attacked our car? How they broke into the house? It's still not totally safe for you out there yet. I saw it on TV. It isn't. People still don't trust people like you."

The best way to deal with my cousin's paranoia was to divert her attention. My thoughts whirled as I figured out the best way to do it. I had to get back to the dogs–in a hurry.

"Most people are used to part-Zs like me now. Never mind the few troublemakers. We have to see what's going on with those dogs. Who else is going to do it? You can get Jesse to help if it makes you feel better."

I intentionally left out Jesse's brother Gabe and hoped she didn't bring him up. I couldn't think about him. Not right now. Her face grew thoughtful. I could see the wheels turning, a good sign. My determination grew.

"C'mon, cuz, I know you can do it. Just call and say you're interested in the job, ask what it's about. Arrange an interview in a couple days. Once you get the address, we go check it out and see what's going on. "

Carm's eyes went wide. "I don't know..."

Time to pour on the guilt, I decided. "All right, what if Fluffy's there–and they have other dogs, too? I know you don't want to leave all those dogs there, alone, scared, waiting for who knows what to happen, who knows what someone is doing to them..."

I gave her my best puppy dog look.

"Okay, okay, I give."

"Now, don't talk a lot. Only ask what the job's about and what you'd be doing. Most important, get the address. Keep your voice low so you sound older."

She nodded, grabbed her phone, then stopped, her face worried. "Wait, what if they have Caller ID? They'll know who I am."

I almost hit my forehead with my palm, but stopped myself. With my easy-to-erode skin condition, it wasn't a good idea doing anything that could make my skin crack again, especially when it had been clearing up so nice lately.

"Ugh, you're right, *stupida* me. I didn't think of that. I think there's a Caller ID blocking thing on our phones. You can use mine."

Puppy Love And Zombies

Grabbing my cell phone, I checked the settings, and after several minutes of fumbling and going to the website, set up the temporary Caller ID blocking system. "*Hmm*, looks like it'll work. Let me call your phone first to make sure."

I pulled up her name, hit send, and waited for her distinctive ring. The Beatles' *Lucy in the Sky with Diamonds* rang out. We both were big Beatles fans thanks to our mothers constantly playing the CDs and albums since we were little.

"Good song," I remarked. Last week it had been Lady Gaga and Taylor Swift. By Christmas, she'd be through the top hundred hits at the rate she changed ringtones.

Carm looked at her phone and nodded. "Okay, it works. It says number unavailable."

"Good, now remember what I said."

Perched on the end of the bed, she quickly punched in the numbers. "It's ringing," she whispered. "Oh, hello, um, yes, I'm calling about the ad, about working with animals. My experience? I've worked at a dog groomer's. I'm taking classes now to be a vet technician."

I gave her a thumbs-up. Both of us had hoped to begin checking out colleges soon, especially since my condition finally seemed stable. She'd talked about going to veterinary school since we were kids so her little white lie wasn't totally false.

"Uh-huh, so you're hiring people to care for animals? Medications?" Her face grew worried. "Sure, I can give them medicine. I've done that. My name? Alicia, Alicia Simmons."

I gave her the okay sign.

She continued, her voice more confident. "You're at the Tallman Business Park, Sheridan Road. Number one, two, one. Day after tomorrow? Yes, I can be there. Four p.m. is perfect. Thank you."

She ended the call and let out a huge sigh of relief. "Whew, glad that's over. Why are they in the business park? Wouldn't somebody know what they're doing there? How come the police aren't looking into it? You know, maybe we should call them first."

"Hey, one question at a time. C'mon, they don't believe the adults, you think they'll believe us? Besides, they're too busy trying to round up the rest of the Zs. We talked about this. It'll be fine."

Carm's face grew thoughtful. "I suppose, but the police still have to take care of other crimes, too, right? I still think we should call them."

I sighed and looked at the ceiling. "All right, you call then. Tell them your dog is missing and see what they say."

"No, I'll tell them someone *stole* my dog." She ended with a pout.

I couldn't help turning on the sarcasm. "And they'll get right on it, huh? Gee, Miss, we're kind of busy right now getting all these zombies and hoodlums off the streets, but we'll drop that and help you look for your dog. Think they'll do that?"

"Fine." She crossed her arms. "You don't have to be so snotty. You win. We'll go look. I think we should have Gabe and Jesse go with us, though. You know, in case."

This time I raised my eyebrows at her. Gabe? She knew we weren't talking. Not since he'd gone all quiet on me two weeks ago. We'd been together like almost every day for the past year. He'd been with me fighting Zs, and helped me in the hospital, and stayed with me when I got really sick. Then all of a sudden, he just goes off and disappears. No texts, no calls, nothing. I'd been really mad, but now I was just plain hurt.

"Carm, that's mean, even for you. You know what Gabe did."

"Bec, no, I'm not being mean," she insisted. "Jesse texted me. He said they got caught up in a Z sweep. Their attorney had to bail them out of jail. They're on their way here."

I looked at her in surprise. "Here? How come Gabe didn't tell me himself?"

Carm shook her head. "You better ask him that, and maybe talk about some other things, too. You guys always seem to be fighting."

My cousin was right. He and I had been arguing–a lot. I wasn't sure why except I'd been feeling, I don't know, kind of different lately. Cranky. Really crabby and icky.

"Never mind," I snapped, my annoyance growing at Little Miss Right Again. "I'll text him. I want him to bring his Nikon and his video camera. We might need them." I did that and

Puppy Love And Zombies

headed for the door. "Let's take a ride. I want to see what this place looks like. We'll just take a quick peek."

Carm gave me a look like I'd grown a third eyeball in the center of my forehead. The idea had me frantically touch my skin in case something had shifted or moved. It hadn't. As weird as it sounded, I knew with my condition anything could happen. But that wasn't the worst thing I had to deal with at the moment, of course.

"You forget something?" she asked. "You think *Tia* is going to let us go wander around like nothing happened after our visitors this morning?"

Big sigh. No, I hadn't forgotten. The idea of how to get our aunt to ease up on her restrictions had me feeling like I was trapped in a cage and had no choices, which I didn't. I was tired of being inside.

I needed to do something. I needed to find that puppy.

We went downstairs to the kitchen where I poured myself a fresh glass of cranberry protein juice and Carm grabbed some potato chips. I eyed the newspaper, noting the stories urging people to not be afraid to resume their lives. Spending money, reopening the stores, and getting people back to normalcy, was the only way to get the local economy recovering, one story said.

Should I push for my aunt to go out and take us shopping? I'd decided to make the suggestion when the phone rang. Carm and I exchanged glances as we listened to my aunt's side of the conversation.

"Hilda, that's wonderful," *Tia* said. "I'm so happy you and Enrique got the new office set up. I wondered if you would be able to make the move with all the terrible things going on outside. You say it seems safer? *Hmm*, funny, we caught two of those monsters outside our house this morning. Well, you're right. We hadn't seen any before that for a few weeks. It has quieted down a lot. The boxes? Yes, I still have them. Oh, it can't wait? I know, I'd love to see the office and...well, you know, maybe you're right. I've been cooped up in the house too long. Wait, *uno momento,* let me get a pen."

Young Adventurers

I passed a pen and paper to my aunt. As she wrote down the address, I felt more hopeful about getting out of the house. I tried to act nonchalant when she finished talking and hung up the phone.

"Well, *niñas,* it looks like my friends moved their business and need my help. I have some boxes of records I was holding for them. Why they need it now, I don't know..." She paused and glanced at the newspaper I'd moved closer. "*Hmm*, I see the mayor said things are clearing up. He claims it's safer." She gave a snort of contempt. "Huh, even with those two monsters at our door this morning?"

I shrugged and tried to sound encouraging. "I've seen more people outside. Even Amelia said she was going back to work."

My aunt raised an eyebrow, but seemed to come to terms with the changes. "She did? Well, I guess she knows better than anyone what's going on. You girls want to take a ride? Bring those boxes from downstairs out to the car. I have to admit I'm tired of being in the house. The ride will do us all good."

Once the two of us got settled in the back seat, *Tia* headed out on Route 83 and shot over to Highway 50. Carm pulled out her phone. "*Tia,* where are we going?"

Tia peered at Carm in the rearview mirror. "It's that new business park on Sheridan."

I gave Carm a discreet poke with my elbow and smirked at her little yelp. "I heard about that. It has a funny name. Tall–"

"Tallman Business Park," my aunt said.

"Yeah, that's it. What's the address?"

"One, four, one," my aunt said.

Carm leaned out of reach before I poked her again. Perfect! We wanted to see what was going on at one, two, one. With any luck, the two places were close, if not right next to each other.

We drove in silence the rest of the way. It was nice to drive normal again–no dodging Zs, no running over gory, yucky Z parts splattered all over the street now that the National Guard had rounded up most of them and cleared the city. Even *Tia* seemed to relax and enjoy the ride. She wasn't all hunched over as she drove. She held the steering wheel looser, not with her hands like talons, as she had been doing.

Even Carm seemed calmer. Good. Now all we had to do was look around without raising our aunt's suspicions. We rounded the curve and pulled to a stop at the stop sign.

"There it is." Carm pointed to the large painted wood sign across the street. *Tallman Business Park,* it said. *Business at Its Best.*

Tia turned right and swung onto a gravel drive. We followed the road, Carm pointing out the new buildings we passed. Giant cement warehouses lined the road interspersed with smaller, ranch-style office buildings featuring different but contrasting shades of vinyl siding. The park's past use as a trailer home park hadn't been totally erased, though. A small section of trailers remained barely visible behind a big wood fence in the back.

"I wonder how it is around here at night," I asked. "Mom said most of these old, run-down trailer parks are disappearing. They're getting closed down if they don't upgrade and make improvements."

Tia nodded and sighed softly. "It can get pretty rough down here at night. It has to be pretty bad if this is the only place you can live."

Me and Carm exchanged glances.

The first row had six large warehouses, three on each side. We pulled into one of the parking areas near the first building. My mind worked out the next step to take as *Tia* turned off the engine. I watched her scan the area before she opened the door.

"Girls, you want to stay here or come in with me? It seems safe enough."

My eyes met Carm's before I gave a nonchalant shrug. "We can wait here. It's nice to be outside."

"All right." *Tia's* face creased with concern and then relaxed. "I suppose it'll be fine. I may be a while as you know how Hilda likes to talk."

"You want us to bring the boxes in?" I asked.

"No, Enrique will get them. You girls keep an eye out. And if you do get out of the car, don't go far."

Young Adventurers

I smiled, pleased with how things were working out. "We'll be fine. Don't worry."

Both of us watched her walk away. Once she went inside, I reached for the car door handle.

"Now what?" Carm asked.

"We better not waste time," I answered. "Let's go see where our building is."

We got out and walked around the corner opposite of where our aunt had gone in. Lucky for us, the building had no windows on the side. I checked the numbers as we walked until we got to the second warehouse. A small sign in front indicated we'd found our destination. The sign also advertised spaces for lease and invited visitors to contact the management for information. I grabbed a brochure with a map and the names of the businesses to look at later.

We walked to the corner of the building, figuring there had to be an entrance for deliveries and unloading. Instead we found something better–a couple picnic tables which gave us a good view of both buildings.

"We can sit here and watch what's going on."

"I could go for a snack, I'm hungry," Carm said.

"You're always hungry."

Carm answered by sticking out her tongue. Luckily, any pending argument had to wait when a plain white van pulled up. A man wearing a dark blue jacket and pants got out and walked to the back of the van. He opened the door, took out two boxes, and set a clipboard on top before heading for the back entrance.

"Quick, Carm, get a picture."

She pulled the phone from her pocket too late. The man disappeared inside.

"Sorry, I missed it," she said. "Maybe he'll take some more boxes out?"

"Maybe, but if he doesn't, we better go. Something bothers me about those boxes he carried in."

"They didn't have any writing on them," Carm added.

"No, not that. I thought I saw holes on the sides.

"Holes?"

Puppy Love And Zombies

"Yeah. You wouldn't need those unless something inside needed air. The boxes might've been empty, but if they had animals in them, then they were knocked out or-or worse." I gulped. "It was quiet. Much too quiet."

The quiet didn't last long, though. A familiar sounding moan drew our attention. We turned and stared in shock at two ugly Zs staggering in our direction.

Almost on cue, Carm began to hyperventilate. "Bec-Bec, what're we going to do? What about *Tia?* What if she comes out?"

I grabbed Carm's wrist and tried to calm her, not easy to do since I knew how vulnerable we were. With things clearing up, I'd taken to not carrying around our BB guns or anything else to use in our defense. I now realized how dumb that had been.

I watched the two zombies shamble forward, still yards away, but close enough that I could see the ratty clothes hanging from their skeletal forms. My nose wrinkled. Even with my limited sense of smell, their distinctive rotten meat odor made me gag. More moans drifted our way.

"Carm, we don't have any weapons. All we can do is get the security guard. On the count of three. One, two–"

She bolted. I followed, the two of us running inside and raising the alarm. "Zombies! Security-security! Two zombies outside! Someone, help!"

Finally, in what felt like forever if only minutes, two security guards rushed out, guns drawn. Several office workers gathered by the door to watch. I saw our chance. Gunshots and screams signaled the two men weren't the best of shots. I signaled Carm to follow and ran down the hall to a large door. The sign said *Employees Only*. I peered through the window into some kind of workroom.

Urging Carm to get her phone ready, I pushed through the door into a room filled with two steel tables and several desks. To our surprise, rows of empty steel cages lined the back wall. At least I thought they were empty. Growls and barks sounded from two of the lower cages. One held a small black dog. A brown dog sat in the other. No sign of Fluffy. Heavy locks prevented me from grabbing the dogs and running.

Carm interrupted my observations. "Bec, we have to get out of here."

I nodded and told her to take a couple photos with her camera. "Make sure you get a photo of the wall. Hurry up. I'm going to yell about the zombies as a distraction, then follow me out."

A minute later, I ran out and around the corner, nearly knocking down two women dressed in white lab coats. "Hey, what are you doing in here?" one yelled. "Security!"

I cut off their calls of alarm with my own. "Run-run! Zombies are coming! Get security. Hurry, run!"

The women quickly forgot their questions about me and rushed down the opposite hall, yelling as they went. Their actions gave me and Carm enough time to get back to the entrance. The workers and the delivery man ignored us as they watched the security men directing the disposal of the two zombies now lying in the center of the road. The two of us ran and circled around the opposite end of the building to make our way back to the car.

The thought of what could be going on at that warehouse put both of us in a bad mood as we got home and went up to my bedroom.

"Bec, you think maybe it's some kind of animal hospital?" Carm asked.

I raised my eyebrows. "Over there? So out of the way?"

My suspicions could result from an over-active imagination and nothing more, but I doubted it. I plopped on the bed, then jumped back up and pulled the brochure from my back pocket. "I almost forgot about this. It's that map from the business park. Let's see what other businesses are there."

We studied the layout, the names of the businesses, and the details about the park. "There's a paper place, a trucking office, and a few places I can't tell what they do," I said, "plus the place we were at, Health Systems, Inc. and...oh, no."

"What?" Carm asked.

I pointed my finger at a name on the list and nodded as she gasped. "Yeah, and this."

It was a big surprise to see the name of my special makeup manufacturer, "Girls Like Us," listed under the business names. After I fell ill, finding a woman who not only had been infected with the Z virus like me, but had developed a whole line of fantastic, great-covering body makeup, foundation, and lip gloss had made my life tons better. I called the makeup "Ghouls Like Us" since she really understood our problems. This hit me. Hard.

"Carm, what do you think?"

My cousin hemmed and hawed. "Ugh, well, it could be a coincidence."

"Yeah, a big coincidence."

She remained quiet while I reasoned it out. "I saw her on some talk show a while ago. You can hardly tell she's infected unless you know or look real close." The disappointment threatened to drag me down. "She-she seemed so nice, so genuine. I can't believe she'd do anything terrible."

Carm screwed up her face in confusion. "Terrible? Like what?"

"Like steal dogs–and use them to test her makeup. I wonder...maybe it isn't a coincidence. Look the business up, Health Systems, Inc."

Carm scanned the list of sites that came up on her phone.

"There," I pointed. "Go to that one."

"Maybe you're right," Carm said. "It says Health Systems, a division of GLU." She went to several other sites. "There it is, GLU, Girls Like Us, LLC. I guess it makes sense that a business with the word health in it is tied to a cosmetics firm. Nothing wrong with that, though."

"Possibly not," I cautioned, "but the real question still is what this health place is doing with dogs and cages in their building? Not something they want anyone to know about, I bet."

At this point I knew talking to my aunt about the whole problem and my suspicions would be the best thing to do. Of course, I decided on a riskier plan of action.

"Call your mom," I told my cousin. "Ask her if you can spend the night. I need your help."

Carm's eyes widened. "Help? Help with what? Oh, you're not...we can't go back there. You saw the security guards.

Young Adventurers

Maybe the National Guard didn't get all the zombies roaming around at night yet. I-I don't want to run into any out there, not in the dark. We should let the police take care of it."

I sighed. Not again. We didn't have time for her to get all chicken on me. "We'll be fine, Carm. We can do it. Remember what my neighbor Amelia said? Do you think the police really care about some missing dogs?"

Carm began to search on her phone. I peered over her shoulder. "What're you looking for?"

"This." She pointed to the web page and began scrolling down the list. "The police have to care. Look. Wisconsin has laws against dog-napping–taking a dog that doesn't belong to you without permission–and animal cruelty, and other stuff. They have to do something if we show them what we found." She searched in her phone. "Oh, or didn't."

"What?"

She showed me something fuzzy and out of focus. "I need a new phone. None of the photos came out."

"Need a new operator is more like it," I grumbled. "You know what that means. No arguments. We have to go back. I'll text Jesse and Gabe to come pick us up."

Dinner over–mine the usual liquid protein kind since I'd really gotten sick of eating all that tasteless, boring, uncooked chicken–we helped *Tia* with the dishes and said goodnight since she was going to bed early. I wasted no time putting our plan in motion and pulled a bunch of black clothes from the back of my closet.

"Hurry up and change," I urged my cousin. "I have flashlights for both of us. I heard some trucks go by, so I think the Guardsmen are still patrolling. We'll probably have to avoid them more than the Zs. Okay?"

Carm looked like she'd jump and run at the slightest noise. I hoped she'd pull herself together once we got outside.

"If there's a security guard, one of us can distract him," I said. "I put some hair pins in your bag, in case you need to pick a lock. And I've got these. Found them in the garage." I held up a big pair of metal cutters. "Just in case. But hopefully we can find the keys. Once it's dark, we'll get out of here. You, ready?"

"What about the Zs?" she asked, her voice shaky.

I held up my souvenir bat, the surface stained red from past excursions. It would do. Besides, I didn't plan on us getting that close anyway. Not with more important stuff to do.

Easing out my bedroom window, we picked our way down the trellis and jumped to the sidewalk. The house remained dark and quiet, telling me *Tia* must've fallen asleep already. Good.

We jogged down the block and stopped when a car blinked its headlights. Carm climbed in the back seat next to Jesse and gave him a hug. "I'm glad you showed up!"

I didn't share her enthusiasm. I'd talked to Gabe earlier and told him how hurt and mad I was. We'd kind of worked it out, but I didn't want to let him off that easy for ignoring me. Still, I felt myself melt when he gazed at me, his eyes dark. No matter how much we fought, the two of us had a special connection, and it wasn't just chemistry. We had something I couldn't shake no matter how mad I got or how much I pushed him away.

"Now explain this idea to me again?" Gabe asked and pulled the car out onto the road.

I told him what we'd found and said we needed to get more proof. "We have to get those dogs out of there," I ended.

As expected, he gave me a look that told me my plan was as crazy as I thought it was.

"Breaking and entering? Theft? Burglary?" His face darkened. "You prepared to go to jail?"

I looked away. "Well, uh, no. I don't think it'll happen like that."

His eyebrows went even lower if that was possible. "You mean you didn't think."

My anger rising, I ignored my initial feelings of being happy to see him. Luckily, Carm headed off my outburst.

"I say we look around first," she said, ever the diplomat. "If we see any security we leave. Or one of us keep him occupied, though I don't think that's a good idea. Either way, it looks suspicious. Who else drives around there at night?"

The urge to stick my tongue out at her disappeared as we rounded the corner and turned into the park. It looked creepier at night though each row was well-lit. As it turned out, we weren't alone. Several cars sat next to the building. Gabe shut the car off as we parked in one of the open spaces at the end of the next row.

We watched and waited. After ten minutes of nothing going on, I'd had enough and grabbed the door handle. "We need to get out. We have to see who's inside. I'm going with or without you."

After what seemed like forever, Gabe agreed. "All right. You bring any weapons?"

I held up my bat and showed him the small pellet gun I'd also stuck in my bag.

"I guess we'll chance it," he said. "You two wait by the building next door while we try to find out how many people are inside. No matter what, if you see any Zs, don't yell. We don't want whoever's in there knowing we're out here."

We ran down the row between the buildings. I peered around the corner of the building next to our target location, bat in hand, and watched the guys sneak toward the back door. Of course, things never go according to plan. A telltale bad odor drifted our way. Carm turned and yelled, "Bec!" as two ugly Zs stumbled our way.

My cousin had gotten pretty good at defending herself when she didn't give in to her fears. This time, however, she gave me a panicked look and waved her empty hands. It was up to me.

"Get behind me," I whispered. "See if you can wave Gabe and Jesse over, but make sure no one else is out there. And don't yell!"

She ran to the end of the building and a minute later, began jumping and waving. I pulled out my bat and got into position. One of the ghouls moaned and grabbed at me, while the other seemed to shuffle faster. I backed up and hurriedly pulled out the pellet gun. The two came at me, low moans coming from what remained of their decayed lips. I readied to fire when Gabe rushed around the corner and warned me, his voice low.

"Bec, no guns, they'll make too much noise! Here, catch!"

He tossed me a metal garden spike. I picked it up from the ground, spun around, and stabbed out, catching the Z in the head and within inches of biting me. It fell, and with no time to reclaim the spike, I swung the bat at the second zombie. CRACK! The bat hit the ghoul's face and crushed in the side, yet it kept coming. I hit again and connected with the top of its diseased brain this time. It let out a final moan and fell in a disgusting heap.

A second later, Gabe and Jesse rushed around the corner and plastered themselves against the wall next to us. "Someone's coming out," Gabe whispered. "Shh!"

Voices drifted our way, but I couldn't be sure who was talking. I inched closer to the edge of the wall and peeked around the corner. Two people stood in front of the building. Watching a group of Zs approach would've been less shocking than seeing the lady I admired, the owner of the Girls Like Us Makeup Company, and Enrique, the husband of our aunt's friend, together.

No matter how you looked at it, something was going on. Something wrong.

Jesse peered around the corner and aimed his video camera. He finished and crouched down. I balanced the Nikon camera's long lens against his arm and clicked the shutter. Enrique stopped talking and looked up like he'd heard something, but then continued his conversation. I hurriedly took several more pictures and waved everyone to go. We ran past the dead zombies and back to our car.

"Whew." I plopped in the front seat and checked the camera images. "That was close. Okay, looks like I got some photos."

Jesse nodded to his brother. "I managed to get a video of the inside from the side window, too. We're set."

"Good," Gabe said. "Now we wait for them to leave. Everybody duck down and get comfortable. It could be a while."

I didn't protest when Gabe hugged me close. No matter what happened, or how mad I got at him, we had a special bond. Not only had he helped me adjust to life as a part Z, but he saved me quite a few times from my worst impulses. More times than I wanted to admit.

About twenty minutes or so later a light flashed as one car, and then another, pulled out. I almost hated for our adventure to end, but knew *Tia* would be frantic and call out the Guard if she didn't find us upstairs come morning.

Like before, Gabe parked down the block from the house and shut off the lights. The kiss he gave me made it harder to leave.

"Now, no more being mad," he urged. "Promise?"

"I promise."

"Good. I should be moved into the apartment next weekend. I want you to come over and help me set things up. We'll get pizza and spend some time together. You want to?"

"Yeah," I nodded. "I want to."

He kissed me again. "You better go. We're going to see my friend at the sheriff's department. I told him what you said about no one else wanting to help or look for those dogs. He was pretty interested. I'll let you know what happens."

I'd barely gulped down breakfast the next morning, this time a cranberry-orange-protein drink, when the phone rang. "Got it," I yelled. Gabe's voice greeted me on the other end. "Hey. Yeah, I'm up. How'd it go? Really?" I squealed and waved at Carm. "Yeah, we'll be here."

I ran to the steps and told Carm to hurry up. "Get dressed. They'll be over in fifteen minutes."

My aunt stopped us at the stairs. "What's the hurry? Who's coming over?"

"Buenos días, *Tia*. The guys are coming over with news about the dogs. Isn't that great?"

I let it go at that, figuring she'd hear about her friend's involvement and our roles in it all soon enough. Throwing on my clothes, I hurriedly dabbed makeup on my worst dark spots, brushed my teeth and smoothed my hair, finishing just as the doorbell rang.

I pounded down the stairs and waited as *Tia* greeted the sheriff's deputy, along with Gabe and Jesse.

"Good morning, ma'am. I'm Deputy Wilson. I wanted to share some information and get a statement from your nieces, if

Puppy Love And Zombies

that's all right? And I believe we have something that belongs to you."

With that, he took something from Gabe and held out a small dog carrier. I heard the excited barks and let out a squeal. "Fluffy! You found her! Is she all right?"

The deputy smiled. "She's fine, Miss. She was with several other dogs in the back of that warehouse. You'll be glad to know the business owners have been arrested and the other owners are getting their dogs back, thanks to you and your friends."

Tia arched her eyebrows at me, but thankfully the deputy had her ear while he explained what happened. I saw the shock on her face and felt bad when she heard about her friend's involvement. Of course, we'd have a serious talk later and she'd probably ground me. For now, it was worth it as I played with the energetic little puppy darting around my feet.

Once the deputy left, *Tia* made it clear she was unhappy with our actions. "I'm disappointed at your sneaking around, although I am grateful that everything ended well. I still cannot believe that Hilda and her husband were involved in such a terrible thing. Even worse, they kept records in those boxes they had me hold for them." She shook her head and sighed. "However, I think that you and Carm will probably be staying home this weekend helping me and her mother clean closets."

I saved my protests as *Tia* went to the kitchen, knowing she wouldn't relent and realizing I'd actually got off easy.

"I guess I won't be able to come over this weekend," I told Gabe as he sat next to me on the couch.

"Next weekend," he insisted. "I'll be there. No matter what, you and Carm did a good thing. You kept at it, and I'm glad you let me help. We make a good team, you know."

I smiled, realizing how lucky I really was. "Yeah, I guess we do make a good team, don't we?"

Becca is also the star of C.A. Verstraete's debut novel, GIRL Z: My Life as a Teenage Zombie.

SCIENCE FICTION

ADVENTURES

Young Adventurers

Our heroes and heroines have already handled spies, monsters, and even zombies. But what about aliens? The question is, how do two very human girls DEAL with their new friend from far, far away?

FANGIRL, RIP AND THE ALIEN

David Perlmutter

The two of them- one extremely tall and gangly for fourteen years old, the other short and underweight for that age- marched with determination towards their destination in the forest near their home. One might have thought they were mismatched, but this was not the case. They had known each other for nearly their whole lives, and were as devoted to each other as two girls of their generation could be. Chiefly because their personalities, physical appearances and attitudes tended to drive people away.

Although Morgan Robertson, the tall one of the pair, was extremely beautiful and athletically built, she was neither a beauty queen nor a jock. She was far too intelligent to limit herself like that. Her Achilles heel was that she was afflicted with Asperger's Syndrome, the still very much misunderstood stepchild of Autism. As a consequence, she was prone to vicious and unexpected mood swings at the least provocation, even though she regularly took pharmaceuticals designed to "control" them. False assumptions about her mental state among her peers had prevented them from befriending her.

Roberta Ripley–or, rather, "Rip", to Morgan–had been dealt far worse physical hands in life than her friend, but, unlike Morgan, she did not worry about or bemoan her fate. Born prematurely and asthmatic, and underweight because of it, she suffered from the further indignity of a club foot, which forced her to get around on a cane, not unlike Dickens' Tiny Tim. Her eyes were two different colors, her teeth so grotesquely "buck" that no braces could mend them, and her voice was a raucous, almost masculine rasp, in contrast to Morgan's more feminine (if occasionally hysterical) tones. Yet she would always be the first to tell jokes about herself when she entered a room–if only to prevent others from doing the same, or worse, to take advantage of her. If that didn't work, Morgan would come to her aid, for the taller girl possessed a noble virtue as a consequence of her Asperger's–firm, unbreakable loyalty–and was willing to fight to the death for her friend if she had to. Nobody else had dared do that for Rip, and it had sealed their permanent friendship many years ago.

The other aspect that sealed it was their joint interest in the literature concerning itself with impossibilities and improbabilities–namely science fiction, fantasy and horror. They were classic 'geeks' in that they were avid readers as well as adventurous and accepting seekers of film and TV narratives of the same kind. Morgan had received the derogatory nickname of "Fangirl" for daring to try to talk to more "popular" kids about her great love, while Rip generally kept her mouth shut about it outside of Morgan's company for that reason. But it went further than that. Unlike many readers and viewers of the speculative arts, who were content to view it as mere entertainment, Morgan and Rip maintained the belief that, while the narratives may have been fictitious, they were reflective of events that could have happened in the past and had every opportunity to occur again. And they intended to be there when they did, to witness them for themselves. No matter what it took.

This is how they got into the predicament which befell them.

As was often the case when they walked together, Morgan's longer legs and wider stride meant that she had soon established a wide gap between herself and Rip, and her distracted train of thought meant she did not notice this. On these occasions, Rip would either holler or whistle at Morgan so she would get it. She chose the latter option this time, startling Morgan in the process.

"What the...?" Morgan uttered as she spun around, only to see Rip taking a "hit" of air from the device required to keep her asthma at bay.

Fangirl, Rip And The Alien

"Oh," Morgan said when she realized what had happened. "Just you again, Rip."

"Who else would it be?" Rip asked, rhetorically.

"I don't know," Morgan said, missing the rhetoric. "It might have been something important."

"As in something other than me?" said Rip, sarcastically. "What, are you cheating on me? You know-seeing another "best friend" on the side?"

"Of COURSE NOT, Rip!" Morgan retorted angrily, missing the sarcasm this time. "I TOLD you that you were the only best friend I'm *ever* going to have, and I MEANT IT!"

"Whoa!" Rip quickly got close to her friend and put a reassuring hand on her torso. "I was just fooling with you, Morg'!"

"Well, don't! You know how I am with sarcasm."

"Sorry. Keep forgetting that. That's something you Aspies have trouble with."

"Don't CALL me that!" Morgan snapped. "For us, that's like me calling you a "cripple." Or a…a…"gimp"! Would you *like* that?"

"No," said Rip.

"Then I rest my case."

"Speaking of resting cases, do you think we could rest ours for a while?" She looked down at her sweat-stained yellow shirt with a Star Trek insignia on it (for she favored only the Shatner/Nimoy original.) "I'm getting sweat on the old velour."

"You're right." Morgan looked down at her own sweat-stained red shirt, with a vintage '60s–'80s Doctor Who logo on it (for she turned up her nose at the modern reboot). "I'm getting tired myself. I'm thinking today wasn't the right day to go hiking up here. It's too hot."

"Well," Rip said, after taking a "hit", "it *is* summer. We got the whole winter to curl up with the books and the videos and stuff. Outside of school, of course."

"Of course," agreed Morgan.

Young Adventurers

"Besides, it helps to be around you, Morg'. My parents say you're a "positive influence" on me, whatever *that* is. Thing is, I already know that just hanging around you."

"Awwwwww!" Morgan cooed. "Rip, you *always* say the *best* things about…"

She was interrupted by a blinding flash of light that seemed to come out of nowhere out of the sky, and vanished just as soon as it had arrived.

"What the hell was THAT?" Rip uttered, as soon they both recovered from the shock.

"I don't know," said Morgan. "But I'm game to find out. You in?"

"Of course," said Rip.

"Good," said Morgan, as she whipped out her smart phone from her brown corduroy pants, the same color as her now sweat-drenched hair (and Rip's, as well). "This could be important. We might, *finally,* be able to get some actual evidence of the spirit world or space, and show people we're not *nuts.*"

"Or *you're* not," Rip said, teasingly. Her mirth ended abruptly, however, when Morgan looked at her with her "game face", meaning that this wasn't a joke to her. Such instances of possible interaction with the worlds of their dreams always were, even if Rip viewed them in a bit more of a cockeyed fashion.

"Shut up and come on," Morgan said, meaning it. She walked forward, with Rip following obediently.

They wandered over to the glade where they had seen the lights originated from. They girded themselves for potential battle, prepared to face anything from a tentacle-laden Lovecraftian monster from outer space to an evil sorcerer banished from a Tolkienian fantasy realm.

What they saw was nothing of the kind.

It was a girl about their age, or slightly younger, about the same size as Rip, wearing patched-up old clothes and carrying a bindle on a stick over her shoulder, like an old fashioned hobo. Nothing supernatural whatsoever–or so it seemed.

"Ah, it's nothing big," Rip whispered to Morgan. "Just a kid like us, lost in the forest. We should help her get out."

"Are you *crazy*?" Morgan hissed, her confidence eroding as her Asperger's suddenly took control of her consciousness. "You know how *bad* I am at meeting new people."

"And yet," Rip retorted, "you say you're *always* ready to confront the things that woman was not meant to know—"

"That's different!"

"Be reasonable, Morg'. She doesn't look like she'd hurt a fly."

"All right. But if she does hurt a fly—i.e. us—let me be the first to say "I told you so.""

"She won't. She's probably from Gallifrey."

That insult directed at her favorite TV hero's homeland was something Morgan was only prepared to accept from Rip, just as only Morgan could get away with sassing the "Enterprise" crew in Rip's presence and not risk angering the latter.

"You," said Morgan, "are *terrible*. Let's go."

Their approaching footsteps made the girl turn around immediately, like she was fearful of being attacked. However, as soon as Morgan and Rip introduced themselves, all was well.

"I'm…Sibyl," the girl said, evasively. "Just got in from…away."

"Don't you have your family with you?" Morgan asked.

"I'm a…" Sibyl groped for the right word to say, as if English was not her first language. "I'm that…thing…where your parents die before you and you have to fend for yourself…"

"An orphan," supplied Rip.

"Right!" Sibyl slapped her forehead. "The word was right on the tip of my tongue."

"How old are you?" Morgan asked.

"How old are *you*?" Sibyl answered.

"Fourteen," said Morgan.

"Same for me," agreed Rip.

"What a coincidence," said Sibyl. "So am I. Listen, do you know a place where a girl can get a room?"

"Sure," Rip said, trying to be friendly. "There's a hotel in…"

"No." Morgan overruled her friend.

"What do you mean, Morg'?" Rip asked.

"I *mean* that she belongs in the orphanage."

"Orphanage?" Rip queried.

"No way!" Sibyl objected to the idea. "Orphanages are for BABIES!"

"No, they're not," Morgan said, touching a finger to her head. "Any minor who hasn't obtained their majority, and doesn't have parents or guardians, the way Rip and I have, has to be remanded to the care of the State until they obtain their majority…"

"Smart, isn't she?" Rip said. "She remembers a huge ton of whatever she reads. Wish I could do that."

Sibyl was less impressed.

"I'm not going," she pouted.

"Yes, you are!" Morgan's face and voice shifted to "game" mode.

"In my land," Sibyl said, "everyone is free to act according to their own free will and intelligence…"

"We're not in your "land", wherever it is." Morgan balled her fists aggressively as she raised her voice in anger. "In the United States of America, we obey the LAWS! And so will *you*!"

"You gonna *make* me, STILTS?" Sibyl challenged, balling her own fists.

"If I *have* to!" declared Morgan.

Before violence could break out, Rip stepped between them.

"Why don't you just go to the orphanage and leave it at that?" she said to Sibyl. "It's not that bad, really. You get looked after for a few years, and then you can be on your own again, like you want. And *you*…" here she addressed Morgan, "BEHAVE YOURSELF! She hasn't done anything to harm us, so *relax.*"

"All right." Morgan stood down and became friendly again. "Sorry, Sibyl. I know you're not from here, so I just wanted to…"

"I got it, Morgan!" Sibyl waved her hand dismissively. "I have stuff to learn about this place. Maybe you could help me learn about it."

"Maybe we could," agreed Morgan.

Fangirl, Rip And The Alien

Being that Morgan and Rip lived in a small town, where almost everybody knew everything about almost everybody else, it was a small and simple matter for them to introduce Sibyl to the local orphanage director, explain her situation, and get her taken on as a boarder. At the same time, Morgan and Rip, who had started to grow friendly with Sibyl, promised to help her assimilate into her new environment, and, they hoped, stay there, to remain friends with them for a long period of time, as Morgan and Rip themselves were.

This would prove not to be the case.

When Morgan and Rip arrived at the orphanage the next day to visit Sibyl, they found her in what, to them, was a rather unorthodox position on the floor. Still dressed in the same patched-rag outfit she'd been discovered in, for she seemed to own no other clothing, Sibyl was sitting beside her bed in a posture resembling a child in old-fashioned nighttime prayer to God, before sleep. However, what she was uttering was not prayer, but, rather, a one-way conversation.

"I got in fine," was what she was saying as Morgan and Rip entered the room. "No trouble. The thing runs like clockwork...no, no issues with the humans. Found a couple of kids my age in the woods to help me with the plan. Perfect patsies- they got no idea what...DAMN! Gotta go!"

She had, at this point, discovered the presence of her erstwhile "friends" in the room, and rapidly took pains to conceal whatever apparatus it was she had been speaking into. That, as was soon discovered, was something resembling an early 20th century model telephone-a black, clarinet-like stick with an earpiece of the same color attached by a hook. This she accidentally dropped, and it rolled on the floor towards Morgan, who picked it up.

"Hey!" said Sibyl, viciously, when she saw this. "Don't *touch* that!"

"How come?" Rip asked innocently. "It doesn't seem like much. Just an old telephone."

"Because..." Sibyl began, nervously.

Young Adventurers

Immediately, she regretted saying this, because Morgan, always alert to when things got "wrong" in her presence, pounced on the evasive excuse.

"Because *why*, Sibyl?" she demanded.

Sibyl realized immediately that her powers of deception were no match for Morgan's intelligence, and confessed.

"All right," she said, defeated. "You got me. I hid where I came from and how I got here. I shouldn't have."

"No," Morgan agreed, in an offended tone. "You shouldn't."

"But I can make it up to you," said Sibyl. "I'll tell you the truth. You deserve that much, for trying to befriend me and all."

"So tell, already," said Rip.

"You *better* have a good excuse," added Morgan. "I don't like being fooled."

"Not here!" Sibyl said.

"Why?" demanded Morgan.

"Because I don't want anyone else to hear it except you two," she said. "This is important stuff. And you're the only two people I know here who can handle it. You're the only two people I know here, period, but that's not the point. Can you handle it?"

Morgan and Rip nodded.

"And, after I tell you, you will not speak a word of this to anyone else. Agreed?"

They agreed, again by nodding.

"Fine," said Sibyl. "What say we reconvene in ten minutes, out where you found me?"

That was agreed to, as well. Ten minutes later, Sibyl spoke to them in the new venue.

"Okay," she said. "I told you I was fourteen and an orphan. That's true. But the rest of it is…I'm an alien."

"An immigrant?" Rip asked.

"No," said Sibyl, with a raised left eyebrow, in a *don't be more stupid than you already are* tone. "An *alien*. As in, a being not of this Earth, as your Hollywood would put it."

Morgan and Rip looked at each other, briefly and excitedly, as if they'd had met a favorite pop singer by chance and by accident. This was the moment they had been waiting their whole lives for! However, they were quick to retain their normal demeanors.

"How did you get here?" Morgan asked.

"The flash of lightning you saw before I came. Obviously, you've never heard of the Starlight Express. Fastest rapid transit system in the galaxy. You get in and out of places in seconds, no question asked. The trip from Ziltox to Earth is pretty fast even by those standards."

"Ziltox?" Rip asked.

"My home planet. And..." suddenly and fiercely, her voice took on an acidic, Satanic tone, "the one that will soon reduce yours to ASHES!"

"*WHAT*?" Morgan and Rip shouted, backing up from her in genuine horror.

"Ahhhh! DAMN IT!" Sibyl slapped herself on the forehead. "I gave it AWAY!"

"What?" Morgan asked, angrily, getting the picture. "Your plan for conquering the Earth?"

"Yeah," said Sibyl. "I got too much of a loose tongue. See, I'm the advance scout for the Army, and I'm supposed to see whether they can take you Earthlings in a fair fight. But, from what I can see, you can't do anything of the things we Ziltoxians can do, so it should be easy."

"What can you and your kind possibly do that people on Earth can't?" said Morgan. "I mean, you seem almost exactly like us..."

"Well, among other things..."

Sibyl expelled a beam of light from her right hand, which landed in a nearby tree and reduced it to a flaming ruin. This freaked Morgan out.

"YOU..." she shouted, in shock. "You...just..."

"Oh, that's nothing," said Sibyl.

Abruptly, she picked up Morgan and Rip and juggled them in the air, as if they were balls or clubs. Rip was simply reduced to awed silence by the act, but Morgan, who was reduced to

Young Adventurers

gibbering panic, started screaming almost as soon as she was lifted up in the air.

"AAH!" she shouted. "PUT US DOWN! *PUT US DOWN! PutusdownputusdownputusdownPUTUSDOWNNN!*"

Eventually, Sibyl agreed, and they were placed on the ground. Outraged by the alien's insensitive treatment of them, Morgan moved towards her.

"HOW *DARE* YOU!" she stormed. "Rip and I were trying to be friendly, and you…treated us…like…DIRT! I don't care if you *are* an alien, or what you can possibly do to us or to Earth! I will *not* have myself and my friend be treated like TOYS for your amusement…"

"PUT A *SOCK* IN IT, *EARTHLING!*"

Sibyl's voice and face darkened with these words, which drove Morgan back towards Rip.

"Now," Sibyl said, with firm seriousness, "here's how it's going to be. In one day–ONE–you two will come back here, and explain exactly why and how this pitiful excuse for a planet should be spared the wrath of the Ziltoxians. Because what I just showed you is a mere FRACTION of what we are capable of doing to this pestilent *rock*! And, if the INSOLENCE you just showed me is the best line of defense Earth has, then it'll be over faster than that your Six Day War was in the 1970s."

"How do you know about…?" Rip began.

"We just *know,* okay?" said Sibyl. "First rule of war is- know your enemy. You'll need to know that in the future–*if* you live."

"How can you just…decide…to…get…*rid* of us…?" Morgan began sobbing, weakly. "Don't you…*care*…about…?"

"Hah!" Sibyl growled. "If your "science fiction" stories are to be believed, Earth has never CARED about the civil rights of ANY alien race! So why should WE care about YOURS?"

She stormed off into the forest, turning back only briefly, to say one more thing.

"Remember. *One* day. OR ELSE!"

Having no other choice in the matter, Morgan and Rip resolved to meet the following morning to discuss what, if anything, they could do to save the Earth before Sibyl and the Ziltoxians chose to destroy it- if they were feeling so inclined. Rip, tired by the day's activity, slept well. Morgan did not.

When they met at the agreed time the next day, that much was clear. Morgan looked as if she had barely slept at all, by Rip's gathering, fueled by the coffee that still lingered on her breath. Worse still, the half-crazed expression she sported on her face meant that, in the rush to accomplish everything she wanted, she had forgotten to take the pills that typically kept her emotions in check. And, if Sibyl somehow set her off, or vice versa, something bad was going to happen.

This is going to be interesting, Rip thought, ruefully, to herself. But, to her friend, she simply said:

"You...slept okay, Morg'?"

"What does it LOOK like?" the taller girl shrieked. "Yes! I slept like a BABY!"

"No, you didn't," Rip replied, stating the obvious.

"Don't you know SARCASM when you hear it? You use it all the time on me, and I..."

"...can't "get" it 'cause you have Asperger's. Yeah, I know that. I also know that you've been pulling an all-nighter. That's not like you, Morg'. You're usually so prepared..."

"Not this time, Rip! I couldn't *find* it."

"Couldn't find what?"

"The INFORMATION!" She began pacing the street in front of them, almost ignoring Rip in the process.

"What information...?"

"About *Ziltox*! I went through the Internet and all my reference books, and I couldn't find it anywhere!"

"All of 'em?"

"Yeah. There's nothing about Ziltox anywhere. I'm starting to think we hallucinated when we saw those lights in the sky, and we somehow dreamed Sibyl into existence because we wanted to meet an actual alien..."

"Morg'..."

"I mean, people do have those kind of experiences, when they're on cocaine, or marijuana, or hashish or opium or something like that, and they read about far away or fictional places, but we were both totally sober when we saw those lights and we met Sibyl, weren't we?"

"Uh, Morgan…"

"And everything she said was so plausible! Aliens stronger than men and women, capable of killing us all! But there's no information related to the planet at all, ANYWHERE, let alone a *scientific* study of it. How can we understand the Ziltoxians if there's no information about them at all?"

"Morgan!"

"Oh, this is HOPELESS! We can't talk to anybody because of that gag order she put on us, and, even if we did, they would just laugh at us and say we made it up, or someone else made it up, like they USUALLY do, even though this time our butts are REALLY on the line…"

"MORGAN!"

This bellowing cry from Rip- about the only resource she had to stop Morgan from going on with her complicated and fear-laden speech- was enough to scare Morgan and stop her in her tracks. Which was its intended effect.

Rip took a needed "hit" and then continued.

"You're looking at this the wrong way," she said. "It's not important that we know anything about Ziltox if we want to deal with Sibyl."

"But that's where she comes from!" said Morgan.

"She's not there, right now. She's HERE!"

"You mean…?"

"I mean, we need to think about what things are here on *Earth* to stop her."

"Rip, there's no way we could get other human beings to help us stop her. She said so herself."

"That's not what I meant."

"Then what do you mean?"

"I believe we're both well-acquainted with H.G. Wells' *The War of The Worlds?*"

"We are. But how will that help us?"

Fangirl, Rip And The Alien

"Remember the end of the story. Why the Martians didn't win."

For the first time that day, Morgan's fear dissipated, and she became calm and rational again.

"I see what you mean," she said.

"Well," Sibyl said, when Morgan and Rip met her soon afterwards. "I see *someone's* been pulling an all-nighter. Won't do you any good, though."

The all-nighter reference was clearly aimed at Morgan, causing Rip to aim an "I told you so" glance at her friend. Morgan simply ignored the remark.

"It was worth it, though," Rip said, with a Cheshire Cat grin. "She found out the kind of stuff that'll make it *much easier* for you to take over Earth."

"Really?" said Sibyl, suddenly pleased. "Do tell."

"We can't," Morgan answered, with a Cheshire Cat grin of her own.

"How come?" Sibyl demanded. "What is it? You *blackmailing* me or something? 'Cause you know what I can do to…"

"No!" Morgan said, failing to hide the fear now emerging in her voice. "I mean…"

"We just want to convey our information to you in the same way you did to us- secretly," Rip finished on Morgan's behalf. "This stuff is so secret we got to whisper it in your ear."

"Fine."

Sibyl walked over to Morgan and Rip until they were only inches apart. Sibyl expected the two of them to begin telling her what she needed, but that was not what happened.

Morgan and Rip spat in her face, at exactly the same time, from two separate angles.

Repulsed and angered, Sibyl started to withdraw.

"How disgusting are YOU!" she proclaimed. "If you're going to act like *pigs*, then you might as well *die* like them. Nobody spits on a Ziltoxian and…URRRGGGGGHHHHHH!"

Abruptly, she clutched her throat and began rolling on the ground in agony, as she turned a ghastly pale. Morgan and Rip simply stood and watched.

"What the hell's going on?" Sibyl croaked.

"Nothing," said Morgan. "Except *you* getting your just desserts!"

"But how…?"

"You're an alien, right?" Rip explained. "Well, it stands to reason that you've never been exposed to the microorganisms of Earth. Therefore, if one of them gets inside of you, you get sick immediately, and, ultimately, you die."

"What do you mean, "ultimately?" said Sibyl. "I'm dying *now*!"

It was true. While they were talking, Sibyl's bones had begun to give way, reducing her body to a gelatinous mass. But she still had fight in her, and crawled threateningly towards Morgan and Rip.

"Serves me right for trusting you two!" Sibyl snarled.

"Well, you betrayed *our* trust first!" said Morgan. "We don't *like* that."

"Besides which," Rip added. "This is what happens to *any* alien that gets sick on Earth. Even you supposedly mighty Ziltoxians aren't a match for the germs of old Earth. That's why *nobody* can invade Earth successfully, 'cause they *forget* that!"

"You BITCHES!" Sibyl cried. "I'll…uuuuhhhhhhh…"

"RUN!" Morgan shouted. "She's gonna blow!"

Indeed, Sibyl's body had started to burn up and was threatening to explode. Carrying Rip in her arms, Morgan was able to escape the forest before the explosion happened, but only barely. Once they were safe, Morgan returned Rip to the ground.

"You were right about the microorganisms, Rip," said Morgan. "They certainly took care of her. Only I didn't expect her to go off and out like that."

"Well, I did," said Rip.

"You did?"

"Yeah. I knew she was a ball of fire the first time we met. I just didn't think she was LITERALLY!"

Fangirl, Rip And The Alien

All they could do after that line was laugh and go home.

In a future where science has gone horribly wrong, the greatest adventure of all may be a boy's rites of passage on the path to becoming a man.

COMING OF AGE

M. M. Rumberg

My Walking was tomorrow and I was scared, only knowing half of what to expect. The other half was what was causing my high anxiety–the unknown in the form of rumors and speculation. Everyone kept reminding me how dangerous it was. I guess being scared showed because Gran'father seemed concerned. Usually he ignored what I was doing or thinking, but now he seemed worried.

We stood in front of the heavy, gray metal door and looked through the thick glass at the missile in the space called a silo. Instruments with dials and knobs lined one wall of the room we were in. Gran'father checked the instruments and wrote a note on a clipboard. He clicked his tongue and shook his head. "I wonder if we'll ever have to launch it," he said, fingering the key that hung from his neck on a chain.

I knew the key was required to launch the missile–Gran'father had showed me how to use it. "Just in case," he said.

The song the little kids sang as they played war–throwing make-believe bombs at each other then running and hiding–came into my head. We all played it when we were little.

> *Missile, missile, in the room,*
> *Watch it go boom, boom, boom.*

"Tell me again why we would have to launch it, Gran'father."

"It's called retaliation. We're still at war and this is our reserve bomb. I'm sure there are others around the country in places just like this one." He shook his head. "After all these years, we've never learned. What a waste."

"What do you mean, 'We've never learned?' Never learned what?" I asked, but Gran'father began to get lost in his memories again. I hated when that happened, so I interrupted him. "Tell me about the Walking, Gran'father, one more time before I leave on mine."

"Ah, the Walking. You're ready for your Walking. You think you're ready to be a grownup, huh?" He looked at me sideways through his narrowed eyes.

I nodded, but he had turned back to the gray door and said, "Someday this key will be your responsibility. I just hope you're mature enough and understand enough to handle the responsibility." He glanced at me again and shook his head as if doubting his own words.

Every time we came by this room, I thought of the *boom tune*. I couldn't get it out of my head.

We turned from the gray door and walked into the common room of the bunker. "I used to think this day would never arrive," I said, "and here it is." I was excited.

"Calm down, boy. Don't get overconfident. When will you be eighteen?"

"In two days. I'm eager to get going." Actually I was very scared, but I wouldn't admit it.

"I can see that. I keep thinking we should wait until you're older–maybe twenty-one, or maybe two of you should go together."

I frowned and watched him as he seemed to get lost again in his memories, but he looked up and said, "Did you choose the Zone or the Mountain?"

"The Zone." I had told him this many times, but he always forgets.

"And you leave tomorrow?"

"Yes, in the morning."

Gran'father looked pensive, probably recalling his memories again. He did that often, going in and out of his memories. All the old-timers seemed to do that. Sometimes they talk to themselves. Now, he mumbled something like, "He's not ready

Young Adventurers

for the key. Will he ever be?" and shook his head. "So, you want to hear again what to look for on your Walking, what to prepare for?"

I nodded, waiting impatiently. Gran'father was one of the few "old ones" left. He has trouble seeing and keeps saying he wishes he hadn't misplaced his glasses. He's really getting forgetful. I brought him several pieces of glass just last week but he obviously forgot about them. He has a big, fluffy white beard like a cloud and it has little bits of dirt stuck in it. The top of his head is slick like a rock, except for the wild hair around his ears. His face is very wrinkled and he walks bent over with a cane.

"I'll tell you again, boy, the first thing is don't be so cocky. It'll be your downfall. You're supposed to kill a beetle, not be killed by one. It's very dangerous out there. Very dangerous. You've got the hot sun, the beetles, and the cold to contend with. Sometimes a Walker doesn't come back."

Soon as he said that, another tune popped into my head.

> *Beetle, beetle is outside,*
> *Waiting, waiting to cut your hide.*
> *Hurry, hurry, run away,*
> *Come on back another day.*

"I know, I know." Several of my friends hadn't come back from their Walking and we never knew what happened, although everyone thinks the beetles got them. I really didn't want to go, but it was required to be accepted as an adult. "It's your right of passage," the old ones said.

Like us, the girls had their own right of passage they had to go through, but theirs wasn't anything dangerous like a trip to the Zone or the Mountain. Something to do with babies and things like that.

Gran'father looked at me and frowned. "Now listen up, boy. When you walk into the Zone, pay attention to the size of the rubble heaps. The very big heaps like hills indicate that's where an apartment house was."

"Tell me again about a part ment houses, Gran'father."

Coming Of Age

"I keep forgetting you've never seen them before. An apartment house is where large groups of people used to live."

"Like we have now."

He shook his head. "No, grandson. Before the blast we used to have tall buildings with many people living side-by-side and on top of one another. Now people here only live side-by-side. No one is on top of anyone and we don't have so many people any more. Where we live now is called a 'bunker'."

I visualized many people standing on top of each other and smiled at his senile ways. Gran'father often doesn't make sense. Why would you want people to stand on top of each other? Side-by-side I could see, since that's what we do now. Everyone has their own place with their family, but no one has anyone on *top* of them. Suppose the person on top of you wanted to go to the pit but you didn't? And what happened if one of them fell? And how many people can you hold up?

"What about the things inside these tall a part ment buildings, Gran'father?"

"Well, each person's house was furnished differently. They could do whatever they wanted in their home. Furnish it however they wanted, come and go like they wanted. We called them apartments."

Even though I'd heard this before, I wrinkled my brow and smiled at his strange words. "What's a ment?" I asked.

"A ment?"

"You said 'everyone lived in a part ments.'"

Gran'father shook his head. "You've got a sense of humor, boy." But he didn't smile. I've never seen him smile.

There were so many times I didn't understand him, especially when he drifted into his memories. Now, he looked pensive again. He keeps going in and out of his memories. "What're you seeing, Gran'father?" I asked.

"Just thinking of the past, boy, way before your time. Before the blasts. Before the wars. Before all this damned rubble. When everyone had a father and a mother, good food, and new clothing."

I didn't want him to get lost in one of his memory lapses because he could go on and on, so I quickly asked, "What should I look for during my Walking, Gran'father?"

He looked at me for a second then said, "Look for white boxes with doors. We used to store food in them." He used his hands to show how big they were. "They used to keep food cold for us."

A box with a door that kept food cold? I smiled. "What else?"

"We had devices to heat our food. We called them toasters and microwaves and ovens."

"Why did you have so many things to heat food but only one to keep it cold?"

"We used these things to heat different foods. Some things we cooked quickly, others took a long time to cook."

I shook my head. "You made different fires for different foods? Isn't that wasteful?"

He sighed. "I keep forgetting you never saw any of these things. And now your food is…"

"Anything else, Gran'father?" I said, quickly, before he lapsed again into his memories.

"Bathrooms. We had bathrooms."

"I know. That's a place to take a bath. Like we do now."

"More than that," he said, shaking his shaggy head. "It was a room where you'd bathe or wash or use the toilet. The toilet was a place where you sat on a large white pot to poop."

That made me laugh. "Suppose you didn't have your white pot with you when you had to poop?"

"A toilet is like the pit you use now," he said. "It was always there."

"You also washed or bathed in the pit, I mean, the pot?" I asked, my eyes wide.

"No, no, boy. The pit…er…the pot was nearby. We washed and bathed in separate…uh, containers."

I always had trouble imagining what he was talking about and tried to visualize a pit with everyone peeing in it and some people carrying a small container to wash in. I shook my head at my doddering Gran'father. Sometimes he got lost in his memories and other times it seemed like he was losing them.

Coming Of Age

"Anything else, Gran'father?"

"You know that small piece of glass I gave you? The one that looks back at you? The mirror?"

"Yes." It was in my pack. I undid the strap, took it out, and looked at it. It easily fit in the palm of my hand. My eye stared back at me. If I held it farther from my face, I could almost see my whole face.

"Well, we used to have bigger ones," he said. He spread his arms out and up. "Very big ones. You could see your whole body in them. People would decorate their houses with them. It could make a small room look bigger."

I looked at the glass fragment, the mirror, I held in my hand. All I could see was my eye. I frowned and squinted at it, trying to make my eye bigger. I didn't know what he was talking about. "You'll have to show me how to make my eye bigger, Gran'father."

"Make your eye bigger?"

He's really losing it. He just said it could make a room bigger so why couldn't it make my eye bigger? "I've got to go and get ready, Gran'father. I'll see you in the morning before I go."

"One more thing, son."

"What's that, Gran'father?" I was getting anxious.

"Be very careful in the larger piles of rubble. That's where the beetles are."

I knew about the beetles. They were big like a cat, Gran'father said, only I've never seen a real live cat. I've seen pictures of them, but they seemed so small.

"The beetles move slowly but are very strong. They can only be stopped with brute force. They'll slice and cut you if they get close enough," he said.

I nodded. I've heard many stories about the beetles. They're the only animals that survived the blasts. They eat anything and are very dangerous. Once they see you they won't stop coming after you. They'll cut you to shreds and eat you. That's what probably happened to my friends who didn't return from their Walking.

"Remember, boy, if you see them, get away fast. Don't get cocky around them. They have big mouths and large pincers and slicers. It won't take much for one to cut you into little pieces and devour you in seconds. And they can fly at you. You got to be real careful or they'll kill you."

He raised his voice and his eyes locked on mine and seemed to burn into me. The beetle stories scared me, but I wanted to see one and kill it. That was the purpose of the Walking, to get a beetle and to show you could handle yourself out "there." To prove you were an adult. Most Walkers were afraid of them and many only brought back something they found in the Zone and then the old timers had to explain what they were. Only a few Walkers ever brought back a beetle or part of a beetle. And some of them never came back.

Beetle, beetle, is outside. Hurry away, you can't hide.

"Don't stay out too long. You shouldn't stay more than twelve hours. I mean twelve times. You need to be back when the sun goes down. It'll get very cold."

"I know, Gran'father. I know."

"But you have no way to tell the time."

There he goes again with that "time" thing. Like putting the sun on my wrist, he said. I shook my head. The old timers told great stories, but they were all crazy. Why would you ever want to put the sun on your wrist? And how could you do that? All I could think about was how hot it would get and burn your wrist. It didn't make sense. "I'll be back before it gets cold and see you soon, Gran'father." I stood to leave. "I'll bring you a piece of a beetle."

"Come hug your grandfather."

He pulled me tight to him. I could feel him run his hand over my back scales and heard him mumble something about green skin. Then I heard him sigh. I wonder why he did that?

"Remember, boy, mark your way and it's okay if you don't get a beetle. If you don't, bring me back something from the Zone. You can find some good things in the big piles of rubble."

"The a-part-ment things," I said.

He nodded.

"I will, Gran'father."

"Be careful of the beetles. If you're too cocky they'll get you."

Coming Of Age

I pulled away and watched him holding the key hanging from his neck. He always wore it. He looked at me and shook his head slightly. I turned and walked back to my sleeping place. The Walking would be my first initiation in entering the world of the men. All us kids went through it when we reached eighteen seasons.

"The underground bunker was where everyone stayed when war came," Gran'father had told me many seasons ago. "When the first war started, the Army selected who would live underground. Years later, when we came to the surface, the war started again, so we went back down. The wars happened several times, and each war was worse than the one before it. No one thought we'd have to stay underground so long and because of that we ran out of supplies and had to make our own food."

The old ones say it's yucky artificial food, but I think it's okay. Gran'father said the old food used to smell and get everyone's appetite going, but why would you want your food to smell? When I asked him, he only shook his head and got lost in his memories. He does that often.

Gran'father said we sleep on the ground because the beds rusted away years ago and the mattresses rotted and had to be burned. I remember what a mattress was, but they were big and heavy and would be difficult to carry, so why bother? Gran'father also said most of our clothes are in shreds and we'll soon be without them, too, because we never learned to make new ones. I don't know why we can't make new ones but unless it gets very cold, we really don't need them. Whenever I tell that to Gran'father, he shakes his head like he's exasperated and looks disgusted.

Now, the children here in the bunker are different from the old ones like Gran'father–we have tougher skin with back scales, more fingers, and rotating feet to accommodate the rubble. Gran'father says the children today are much heartier than in his day and the body changes will either save the human race or end it. Why would they end it? Sometimes I just don't understand him. Then he'll shake his head and mumble something about radioactivity and get lost in his memories again. He always does that…gets lost in his memories. All the old people do that. They like to sit by the fire and talk about the days before the war. I like to listen to them, but sometimes they get all crazy with their stories and don't make any sense.

Sometimes they do say good things, though. Gran'father told me a trick he used to find his way back when he went on his Walking, only I don't know that he really went on a Walking. I think he lived on the surface before the wars, and came down here after they started so he wouldn't have had a Walking. But then I think that maybe he had a Walking while he lived on the surface. Why couldn't they have had them then, too?

"You make a mark on the ground with rocks," he said, "and when you need to come home, you simply follow the rocks." Sometimes he says funny things like that. I tried to visualize a rock moving and Gran'father following the rock, and I laughed, but now I think I know what he meant–to follow the *trail* of the rocks, and I thought it might be a smart thing to do. I'd make several piles on the ground, a big pile behind me and a small pile in the direction I was heading toward the Zone, and the reverse would point the way to go home. That made sense. I smiled knowing that Gran'father probably did the same during his Walking. Maybe he wasn't so crazy after all–at least about this.

"Tell me again how the Zone become the Zone, Gran'father."

Before he spoke, Gran'father always shook his head. Now, he looked lost in thought and just when I thought he forgot my question, he spoke. "The Zone is where a blast happened long ago. There were many people in different countries before the blast and they began to argue. Soon the arguments got mean and the people began using weapons against each other."

"Like the missile behind the door in the gray room?" I asked.

"Yes, that's right." He looked away, lost in his memories, again. "That's also when people used to fly in the air," he told me.

How can I believe such a crazy thing? "I know beetles have wings and can fly, Gran'father, but I don't understand how people can."

He smiled. "The people didn't fly by themselves, boy. They'd sit in long metal tubes and the tubes would do the flying," he

Coming Of Age

said. "The tubes carried bombs and dropped them on the people they were fighting. That made the blasts and created the Zones all over the world. There were also rockets." He paused. "Those are tubes that zoom through the air without people, like the one in the gray room."

I noticed Gran'father fingered the key, again. He always did that when he talked about his memories.

"They'd smash into a target and explode," he said.

I'd laugh at these silly stories of flying tubes that had people in them.

"That's how your father and mother were killed," he said, and shook his head. "They blasted the other people, but the others blasted them too. You were only a little baby when they died." He looked up at the ceiling like there was something there, but I couldn't see anything special. Then he put his arms in front of him like he was carrying something. "This is how I held you in my arms when you were a baby and I took you down here into the bunker."

I smiled at that. We don't have many babies here, but I had seen some little ones. Some of them died, but a few grew up like me. It's mostly the girls who do the baby caring, not the boys. The girls stay in a separate part of the bunker and don't get to go outside much. Something about protecting their inside parts. I don't really know what that means but Gran'father said I'll find out after I get back from my Walking. Then, after the Walking ceremony, I have to stay with one of them for a while.

"There were many blasts," said Gran'father. "They were radioactive."

"What's radioactive?"

"If you went near it you could get sick and die. The radioactivity made you sick. Sometimes it would even change the way people looked."

"What does radioactivity look like?"

"You can't see it," he said. "You just can't stay near it for long."

"How did you know it was there if you can't see it?"

"It's like poisoned air. You know that some water holes have bad water? Well, some air is also bad and it'll kill you if you stay near it too long. Everyone had instruments to measure if we were near it." He held out his hand like he was holding something in it, moved it slowly from side to side, and clicked his tongue.

I shook my head. I can see bad water, but I can't see radioactive air. I didn't say anything.

"That's why we don't see any birds or other animals," he said. "The radioactivity killed them. Thank heaven there's not much of it anymore, especially in the Zone."

I'd heard stories and seen pictures of birds flying in the sky.

"Birds are like beetles," he explained. "They have wings and can fly, but the birds were friendly and there were a lot of them. The beetles are the only things that survived the blast besides us, and we survived only because we hid underground for many years. Some animals survived for a while because they were underground, but eventually they, too, died from radioactivity or starvation."

"How would they get radioactivity if they lived underground?"

"They got their food from the surface, so they'd have to go up and try and find some."

He shook his head slowly like he was thinking of his memories, and I looked at his beard, wondering if any bits of dirt would fall out.

"So in order to find food," he continued, "they'd have to stay out longer and longer. Remember, the blasts killed everything, including the food they needed."

Gran'father has so many great stories. Sometimes they'd make me laugh, but I learned not to laugh too much when he was telling them. He didn't seem to like it when I didn't believe his stories.

When the darkness came I laid down and slept. It wasn't a good sleep because I was anxious and excited about my Walking in the morning. When I dozed, I had a dream where a beetle found me and I had to fight it and it cut me up into little pieces.

In the morning I woke early and swallowed my breakfast pill. I put one water container and one food bar in my pack. The food

Coming Of Age

bar had three food pills in it–enough for one full day. That was all I was allowed to take.

Gran'father was sitting there and watched me when I woke up and took the pill. He wasn't smiling…none of the old men did when one of us young ones went on a Walking.

I left at the first opening of the doors after hugging Gran'father and walked through the long tunnel into the open. The sun wasn't very hot yet and I was comfortable. I walked down the hill for about two times until I came to the Zone's outer limit. By now the bright sun blasted down, and the Zone landscape looked the same everywhere–white powder, like ash from a fire, covered everything. It was a scene of total devastation as far as I could see. White rocks littered the white earth. After I walked for another time in the Zone I came upon a large mass of rubble and decided to explore it. This was what Gran'father said to look for: an a-part-ment. I pulled rocks off a large pile, digging deep into it. I enjoyed the cool ground under the rocks and found a long piece of shiny metal about an arm's length long. It was hollow with a flat end and a short groove along one edge. I stuck it in my pack. Maybe Gran'father could tell me what it was.

Pulling more rocks away, I found two small, shiny pieces of metal. Brushing the dirt away I stared at them, trying to understand what they were. One said "cold," but it wasn't cold; the other said "hot," but it wasn't hot. They were both only cool from being buried. I put them into my pack. Maybe Gran'father would know what these were. They were probably in his memories, somewhere.

I continued to pull rocks away when I saw movement to my left and glimpsed a black beetle slowly walking. It was huge, just like I had been told. It had a clumsy walk, more like a stumble, but I knew they were dangerous. I bent low hoping he didn't see me.

I waited until he walked past me, then hurried further into the Zone to avoid him. I thought about how many times I had been there. The sun was high overhead and very hot, and I wondered if I would ever understand Gran'father. "You put the sun on your wrist to tell how long you were out," he said. Jeez.

Young Adventurers

I walked on the rubble heap for about one more time and stopped at another large pile of rubble. The sun beat down on me but my back scales fanned me to keep me cool. Gran'father didn't have scales, but I guess that was because he was so old and he lost his. I supposed I'd lose mine, too, when I got that old.

I stopped and swallowed some water. The water was in an unusual container. Gran'father said you press the top and it goes "foof." That tells you that the water is fresh and the top is open so you could drink. I laughed at that. I did it now and it went "foof." It was so funny, but I was glad the water was cool.

I continued rummaging through the rocks, looking for something new to take back in addition to what I already had. I found a larger piece of glass–a mirror–that showed my eyes and face and put it in my pack. Then I saw it off to the side: mostly buried in the dirt, one corner sticking out. It looked like the big white box that Gran'father had talked about.

I dug around it for a while so I could get it free. It was just like Gran'father had said; a box that keeps food cold. I got some more of the box free and dropped to my knees to dig all of it out. I worked at freeing it for at least one sun time. I was getting really warm. My scales could only do so much to keep me cool, but soon the box stood in front of me. A pull was on the front. I grasped it and it swung open just like a door. I wanted to see the food in it. There were two compartments: a big one on top and a smaller one below it, but I couldn't see how either one kept food cold. Gran'father said that insulation kept the cold inside and you could even get ice from it, but I couldn't find any place in it that kept cold inside and there wasn't any ice. And there wasn't any food in it.

I know about ice. My friend, who did his Walking to the Mountain, told me that ice was all over. "Ice was like a very cold rock that changes to water when it gets warm, but it happens slowly." I couldn't think why Gran'father would want to put rocks that change to water in a box like this. Since I was doing my Walking in the Zone, I had to wait two seasons before I could go on a Mountain Walking.

I had finished the digging when I heard a noise and turned. Two black beetles, their shiny, black armor-plated bodies

Coming Of Age

trimmed with red, were walking toward me. I became scared and backed away. I didn't want to fight two of them.

Their brightly grouped eyes followed me, and their long legs clicked on the hard rocks as they moved, their pincers opening and closing. I watched their mouths move like they were talking. It was bad enough having to fight one beetle, but now I had two of them. I picked up a rock and held it over my head to threaten them, but they continued coming.

I aimed carefully at the nearest one and threw. The rock glanced off him but all he did was unfluff his body plate and refold it. I picked up another rock, this time a larger one, and climbed higher on the rubble. Using two hands, I held the rock over my head and smashed it down onto one, hitting him directly on top. He collapsed, then slowly stood on his rear legs and smoothed himself out. One of his legs was broken and he left it behind. I noticed that he now leaned to his right and his top body armor plate dragged as he clicked along toward me, but he was moving a little slower.

"The beetles move slowly," Gran'father had said, "because their armor is so heavy, but don't be fooled, they are very strong and when they decide to fly they are even more dangerous than when they crawl."

Another rock and another smash. The beetles were tough, I gave them that, but I didn't want to be shredded by two stupid beetles. At least I hoped I wouldn't be. They slowly scratched their way up the rubble pile I was on. As soon as one reached the top of a flat rock I smashed a large rock down hard on him. Green matter oozed from him. He was hurt but he still came, dragging several body plates. I leapt from pile to pile but they continued to come after me, the wounded one moving much slower, leaving a trail of green slime.

I'd hit the other beetle several times but now he flexed his wings, probably getting ready to fly when he thought I was unable to defend myself. They didn't fly much because they are so heavy, and they didn't stay in the air for very long, but once in the air they were very dangerous. I threw more rocks, hitting each of them but not stopping them. The mostly unhurt one again flexed his wings again, and with a buzz of noise, leapt at me. He came so close I could hear a *swoosh* as he flew by. I ducked, but I was really worried. Even though he was wounded, the beetle on the ground continued toward me. I ducked to avoid the flying beetle, knowing eventually he'd catch me and his slicers would cut deep.

I jumped down from the pile I was on, ran behind the slow-moving wounded beetle, picked up a large rock and smashed it hard on him before he could turn around. More green matter spluttered out and he struggled to free himself from under the rock. I dodged as the flying beetle spun by my head and came close enough to slice my cheek, just missing my eye. His slicer was so sharp I didn't feel the cut for several seconds. I could hear him screech, enjoying the taste of my blood as he prepared to fly at me again.

Beetle, beetle, is outside. Hurry away, you can't hide.

I took the metal rod out of my pack, thinking I'd use it as a club. When the beetle flew by I swung at him, but missed. He cut me again as he flew by, this time on my head. It hurt so much I fell to one knee. I was really worried. He circled for another attack. This time he flew straight at me, heading directly toward my face, his pincers and slicers sticking straight out ready for the kill.

I held the metal rod out in front of me, pointing it directly at the beetle's open mouth. If I missed, I would be sliced again and much deeper. It screeched as it came close and flew onto the metal and impaled itself. The force almost knocked me down. I heard it screech as it flapped its armored wings trying to remove itself from the metal rod. I set the beetle down on its back. Its legs waved as it struggled to right itself. I quickly hefted a large rock and smashed it onto his lightly armored underside. Green matter squished from him. I let him die before I pulled my metal spear out. It took me a minute to rip off his armored shell and put it into my pack to show Gran'father. I did it with the other one, too. I was breathing heavy and still very scared, but although I won the fight, I didn't feel so confident anymore. My blood dripped all over me.

My heart almost stopped when a third beetle appeared and stared at me, but decided to head to the dead beetles and devour them. I could hear him sloshing up the remains. I thought about fighting it but decided it was better to get away because the scent from my blood would only attract more beetles.

I hurried back to the white box and ran my fingers over it, letting the long fingers on top of my wrists feel it also. These fingers were very sensitive. Gran'father would want to know what it felt like. Smooth and cool, although now, where the sun hit it, it was warm.

I'd accomplished my Walking goal: to kill a beetle. I got two of them and had their armor as proof, so I thought I'd better head back. I was bloody and tired. I wiped the blood from my face before it ran into my eyes. I lost track of how many times had passed and also lost my direction. Gran'father said if I got lost to criss-cross the path I was on, not continue along it. That way it would be easier to find the right path I needed to find my way home. Gran'father had said to watch the sun. It would be behind me going to the Zone and behind me coming back. I turned to the right and walked for about a half time, then turned and walked in the other direction. My scales expanded and fanned to their limit to protect me from the heat of the sun. Even though the sun was setting, soon it would be dark and then the cold would come. My scales couldn't protect me from the cold. Without protection from the cold, I could die.

I saw hills and headed for them only to be disappointed by their barrenness. Everything was coated with white dust: the rocks, the rubble, and the ground. My eyes hurt from so much white. Gran'father said it was because of the blasts. The blasts killed everything, burned everything. He used the word "desolate." I began to understand what that meant.

I headed toward a large pile of rubble that might be able to shield me from the cold wind of night and keep the beetles from finding me. The temperature was dropping fast and a chill had set in. My scales were closed tight now to keep in what heat I had but I began to shiver. I was afraid I would die if it got too cold.

I moved rocks to make a lying place, hoping the rocks had stored enough heat to see me through the night, when off to the left I saw what looked like another white box. I ran over and hurriedly dug it out. This one had a moveable front like the other one, just like Gran'father said, but it was larger than the other one. I pulled it open and looked in. There wasn't any food in this one either. Gran'father said food would be put inside and when the door was closed the food would be kept cold. Why didn't they just leave the food outside in the cold?

I went back to my lying place and began to cover myself with warm rocks when I heard clicking noises. Sometimes the beetles prowled at night. They probably sensed my dried blood and would try to dig me out. I couldn't stay awake all night fighting them and the cold. The only thing I could think of was the white box. Maybe if I hid in it the beetles wouldn't get me and I could outlast the cold.

I climbed inside, curled up, and pulled the door closed. It was a tight fit and very uncomfortable because I had to curl my tail, which didn't like being curled and ached all the time in the box. I thought it would get cold inside but it didn't. I couldn't understand why Gran'father said it got cold inside when you closed the door, but I was glad this one wasn't cold.

I could hear beetles scratching on the box and I was very scared because they might open the door, but they never figured out how to do it. After a while, they gave up and went away. I ate one of my food pills, and as uncomfortable as I was, it made me feel better. I think I dozed during the night. Finally, when I thought about twelve times had passed, I peeked out and saw the sun and felt its early warmth. Maybe someday I could come back and take this white box back for Gran'father. It had saved my life.

I was tired and hungry and swallowed my breakfast pill. My muscles ached from the cramped position I was in all night. I had to be careful now, because I only had one food pill left. It wouldn't be long before I'd be hungry again. Once my food bar was gone my tail would start to shrink as my stored food supply got used up and my stored water would be gone. I had to get back to the bunker. Blood had caked on my face and I needed to wash it off so it wouldn't attract the beetles.

I spent several times searching for the path home. I was becoming exhausted from the effort and getting depressed that

I'd never find my way back and the sun was beginning to set again. I wasn't supposed to stay out in the Zone this long. I'd walked so far that there were no more piles with white boxes I could crawl into and no protection from the cold or the beetles. Desolate.

Then I saw one of my rock piles. It gave me new energy and lifted my spirits. All I had to do was follow it back to the bunker.

I'd been walking for many times and the darkness came quickly. It brought with it a quick drop in temperature. I had to hurry or I would die. I was getting weaker and approaching exhaustion, but I kept walking. I had to get back to the bunker...there was no other alternative.

In the distance I saw a small yellow light flickering–a fire. They had kept a fire for me. I yelled for Gran'father and ran, finally seeing the bunker. I could see Gran'father waving to me, his arms outstretched, reaching for me.

He held me close. "You had me worried, boy. When you didn't return yesterday, I thought you were lost or killed by the beetles."

"I got lost, Gran'father."

"Didn't you make marks on the ground like I told you?"

"I made some, but forgot to make more and got lost, but I did what you said and crossed back and forth until I found the markers"

"Good for you. I'm glad you're back, boy. You're all bloody." He looked me over. "What happened to your cheek and your head?"

"I got sliced by a flying beetle."

"A flying one, eh? What did you do?"

I shrugged and told him how I fought them off. I tried to make it seem like it was no big deal.

Gran'father nodded. "Two of them. Hmm. You don't seem so cocky anymore. Well, I guess you're growing up. You finished the Walking. Almost a man, now."

I smiled. "I got some things for you Gran'father." I reached to get them out of my pack but he stopped me.

"Tomorrow, boy. Tomorrow at the ceremony you can tell everyone about your great adventure. And then you get to go to the girl's side. You'll like that."

I wasn't so sure about that. I'd heard stories about what happens on the girl's side after the Walking ceremony, but it confused me. The old men snickered when they talked about it.

"Gran'father, when I was in the Zone and saw all the rubble and how desolate it was and only the beetles survived the wars, I got to thinking about the launch tube in the gray room and what it meant."

He gave me a questioning look. "What about it, boy?"

"I think I understand what you meant when you said, 'After all these years, we've never learned.'"

Gran'father grasped the key around his neck, looked at me, and smiled. "Well, I guess you really have grown up." He put his arm around my shoulders and we walked into the long tunnel to the bunker.

It was the first time I'd ever seen him smile.

Growing up in the future can be even harder if the world has been changed by science gone wrong, and you're a girl who is part of that change.

WOLF DAWN

A. L. Kaplan

Cramps gnawed at Kara's legs as she crouched behind a rock at the edge of the village. All day she'd skirted the area, spiraling closer from shadow to shadow as she studied the people and landscape. It wasn't much different from other places she'd seen. Buildings clustered along one main road with a few side streets running along a small river. People moved about, some laden with packages, and others hauling small carts. Farmers tended crops and cattle, fishermen worked as their boats bobbed at the dock. A few motor vehicles sat parked in the street. Every person moved with a purpose, like a well-rehearsed dance.

To anyone else the village would have looked normal, but to Kara, it seemed alien. If she'd been a wolf instead of a sixteen-year-old girl, her ears would have been laid flush against her head, her tail well curled down. This place pulled at forgotten memories, drew them out like a bird tugging a stubborn worm. She had to find out why.

Basic survival skills, like fire starting, gathering roots, and tanning hides, comprised her earliest memories. The rest was a patch-worked mess with huge moth-eaten holes. All she had from her old life was a small scar behind her left ear and a necklace. Jagged edges surrounded a cylindrical core on the odd medallion. Someone had entrusted her with it, but she had no idea who or why.

Her new life had begun when Hunt-leader's warm tongue nuzzled her awake eight years ago, and she'd lived with the pack ever since. For years she'd been content, but she had grown restless since her first hunt two years ago.

Kara swallowed through a sudden tightness in her throat. It was easier to face a five-hundred pound elk than other humans. Each step she'd taken today had made her hands shake more than her first hunt. In her mind, she was wolf, part of the pack, and humans killed wolves. The urge to flee was strong, but not as intense as the need for answers.

As human chatter reached Kara's ears, she flattened herself on the ground. The words felt lifeless, without the telepathic overlay that the wolves used. It was Kara's ability to wolf-talk, to understand their silent language, which had drawn Hunt-leader to her.

Memories tickled her mind, just enough to make her curious, but not enough to answer her questions. She held her breath until the people passed, then peered over the rock at them. Their woven clothes were impractical for life with the pack. Wolves played rough and could tear them to shreds in seconds. So would briars and branches.

Bands of hardened leather circled Kara's forearms and neck, armor against sharp wolf teeth. Softer leather chaps covered her legs. Her snug vest laced closed in front. A pair of hunting knives, scavenged from a burned out city, hung from her belt. The only other item of clothing she wore was a short, rabbit-fur skirt.

One house in particular drew her attention. It didn't look much different from the others, with the same weatherworn siding and ramshackle fenced yard. Not far from the back steps stood a small shed. Chickens scratched in a fenced pen nearby. Their soft clucking made her mouth water. It had been a day since her last hunt. Berries and roots weren't as filling as meat.

Something about the house felt familiar. Careful to keep out of sight, she crept toward it and wriggled under the fence. Threads from her tattered tapestry wove back into place as she touched the wood of the shed. Her heartbeat quickened. She knew this place.

Laughter filled her ears as she chased a boy through the grass. A woman called and held out a tray. Her green eyes studied Kara and the boy as they ran and selected cookies. Kara smiled at the boy, then sat on the cool grass next to the steps. Best friends. Their hands intertwined as they ate. His mom made the best cookies. The sweet flavor melted in Kara's mouth.

"Better get those rabbits cleaned before dad gets home, baby brother."

"How about you take care of your own kills for a change?"

Kara crouched down as a young man exited the house and walked toward the shed. About her age, he was slender and moved with the wiry confidence of a hunter. Despite the scowl he wore, his face was pleasant to look at, smooth with a delicate oval shape. Light-brown hair hung in a braid halfway down his back. There was something vaguely familiar about his face, but it seemed out of place with his body.

A pair of hares hung from one hand, and slung across his back was a crossbow. He stopped at a block of wood, eight feet away, and skinned the animals in a few deft strokes. The skill with which he completed the task impressed Kara. Of course, he didn't have to fight off a pack of wolves while cleaning his furs.

Intrigued, she moved closer. Usually she was extremely careful of where she stepped when stalking prey. Even the slightest sound could mean an empty belly. So the crack of a twig under her foot caught her off guard. Panic choked her breath. For half a second she glanced at the offending stick. When she looked back, a crossbow bolt was aimed at her head. A pair of blue eyes stared down at her from only a few feet away. At five foot ten, he towered over her. Kara sucked in her breath, struggling to control her racing heartbeat. Crossbows killed. They killed wolves. The impulse to flee almost overwhelmed her. She growled and inched away from the deadly weapon.

"Who are you?" he asked. "Stand up where I can see you."

Slowly Kara rose, poised to flee. His eyes widened. The tip of the crossbow dropped to the ground.

"You're dead," he whispered. The sound barely made it out his mouth. "They said you were dead."

Images race through Kara's mind. She could hardly breathe. *Deep-set brown eyes under a pair of bushy brows and a thick brown mustache. Screams, gunfire, a woman with flowing brown hair. Pain.* Her hands began to shake. Someone attacked her, stole her memories. She bared her teeth and backed away. This wasn't her pack, her home.

"Kara, wait. It's me, Ethan. We used to play together." He held his hand out.

Laughter. She ran through a grassy field with a boy. A silver-gray wolf romped at her side. She was happy. Gunfire and screams overlaid the pleasant memory. The brown-haired woman placed a necklace over her head. The wolf snarled, hackles raised.

Tears stung Kara's eyes. She grasped the medallion that hung around her neck and struggled to hold onto the nice memories. Something bad happened, but the images were confused. Only the boy was clear.

"Kara, Mist, come play."
Sunshine streamed down as she ran to Ethan's yard. Beside her loped the silver-gray wolf. The three of them slipped under the fence and ran through the fields toward the woods. Sitting in the shade of a large oak, she handed him a small package.

"Remember you," she whispered. The words felt awkward, thick around her tongue, but her mind echoed with wolf-talk.

He smiled and pointed to his neck. "I still have the necklace you made me for my eighth birthday."

A small seashell hung from a leather band at the base of Ethan's neck. Kara wiped a tear from her face. The memory of that day played in her mind. Her dad had helped her drill the hole in the shell and her mom showed her how to sew it to the leather band. Nothing had felt better than the smile on Ethan's face when he saw it. He smiled at her now, his blue eyes watery, cheeks rounded.

Wolf Dawn

There was a way humans usually greeted friends, but the action escaped her. Too long with the pack, only wolf greetings came to her. She leaned forward and licked his cheek, then rubbed her face against him. For a second he stiffened, then his arms wrapped around her and he pressed his cheek to hers. As soon as his grip loosened, she jumped back and danced around him, then dove in for another hug. If she'd had a tail it would have been wagging. Ethan laughed, then did his own version of a tail wag. They ran around the yard just like they had as children, giggling with joy. Memories continued to trickle in. Finally, they collapsed on the grass, staring up at the darkening sky.

"I can't believe it's really you," said Ethan. "I wished, prayed, but...I don't understand. Dad said you were killed by that wolf. He found your parents, torn..." A worried look filled his face. "I...I'm sorry."

"Lies." Her voice came out like a growl and she rolled into a crouch.

Doubt gnawed at her. So much of her memory was a blank. The wolves had sheltered her, protected her, made her part of the pack. *Hunt gives life. Life is land. Land feeds pack. Pack is one. Defend the land. Protect the pack.* But the image of Mist's snarl remained.

A shiver ran down her spine, and she looked away. An empty lot stood next door. There had been a house there, her house. Now all that remained were a few chimney stones. It reminded her of the skeletal remains of cities she'd passed. Leftovers from the pandemic fifty years earlier that killed billions.

Ethan didn't seem to notice her unease. He grabbed her hand and pulled her toward the door. "Mom and Dad are going to be thrilled you're alive, Kara."

Kara snatched her hand back, teeth bared, head low, growling as strongly as any cornered wolf. Ethan's Adam's apple bobbed. Slowly, he extended his hand.

"No one's going to hurt you Kara. I promise," he said, in a voice deeper than she remembered.

It was the pleading in his eyes that finally eased the fear in her gut. She sank into their deep-blue depth. She'd trusted him once. Her hand shook as she placed it in his. Ethan's soothing voice drew her up the creaky wooden steps. Eight years in the wild. Eight years running with the pack, living only in small dens or curled up with wolves. She'd always shied away from human dwellings.

Lamps flickered inside the house, giving it a warm, cheery feel. Painted yellow flowers decorated the walls. Black-eyed susans. She'd seen them growing wild. No wonder she felt so drawn to them. Ethan put the rabbits near the sink while Kara darted around the room. Every sight and smell reminded her of time playing with Ethan and visiting his family. These were friends, neighbors, people who cared about her.

"What's taking so long with those rabbits, Ethan? Did they run away from you?" said the same voice she had heard earlier.

The annoyed tone reminded her of hunt-leader when the yearlings got out of hand. A slightly older looking version of Ethan, with broader shoulders but the same light-brown hair, walked in and stared at her. While similar to Ethan's the newcomer's face was more chiseled, with a square chin. She darted behind Ethan and growled.

"What the…"

"Don't yell, Michael," said Ethan, just as the man sucked in breath to bellow. "She's a bit skittish."

"A bit…" His mouth opened and closed several times before he whispered through tightly clenched teeth. "She's also filthy and half-naked."

"Oh, real smooth, Michael," said Ethan. "It's Kara, Kara Angelharp, from next door."

Michael's brow furrowed and he shook his head. "You mean the girl you've been pining about for the past eight years? Sorry kid, but Kara is dead. She died with her parents. The wolf that slaughtered them is hanging in the living room."

No. Kara swallowed a lump in her throat. A wolf couldn't have killed her parents. She was wolf, part of the pack. They wouldn't have hurt her parents. Sweat began to drip down her back, and her stomach churned. Images whipped through her. *Screams, someone called her name. A blurred figure came toward her.* Ethan's arm slipped around her, as if sensing her confusion.

Wolf Dawn

"Just go get Mom and Dad. Tell them to move slowly and speak softly."

Michael looked at him with one raised eyebrow. "Whatever you say, baby brother.'

"Don't pay Michael any mind, Kara," said Ethan, as soon as Michael was out of earshot. "I'm glad you're back."

Tension rippled through her as Michael returned with a man and a woman, both in their mid-forties. They stared at her like one would eye a rabid animal. Scars covered the neck and arms of the man, an older-looking version of Michael. She'd seen scars like that before, on an old buck the pack hadn't quite been able to take down. The hairs on Kara's neck prickled. Humans killed wolves. Yet, many pleasant memories of people danced through her mind. Those thoughts were what kept her from fleeing out the door. That and Ethan.

The woman's green eyes studied her. It was like looking at a feminine, brown-haired version of Ethan. Kara's mind whirled, trying to remember. Mr. and Mrs. Ericson were Ethan's parents, his family, his pack.

"Poor child, it really is you," said Mrs. Ericson. "What happened to you that night? Where have you been?"

A soft puppyish whimper slipped from Kara's mouth. Try as she might, the entire night was a blank. Tears stung her eyes, and she lowered her gaze, struggling to recall the right words.

"Bad," she said, shifting her feet back and forth. Her thoughts came truncated, like wolf-talk. "No remember. Hurt. Hunt-leader find. Pack is family."

Mr. Ericson's face wrinkled. He didn't snarl, but an edge of displeasure showed. Around him, the others exchanged glances.

"No dear," said Mrs. Ericson. "You belong here, with people." She took several steps toward Kara, then crouched down, arms open wide. "Come, Kara. You're safe now."

With wolves, baring one's neck and belly meant submission, but for humans it was an embrace, a welcome back to a pack she had once been a part of. She remembered that now, and curled into the woman's arms. Safe.

Young Adventurers

Washed and dressed in more civilized clothes, as Mrs. Ericson called them, Kara fidgeted. The coarse cotton shirt hung on her small frame and the pants chafed. They covered much more skin than her leathers, yet offered less protection. She sniffed at a sleeve, then wrinkled her nose at the caustic smell of soap. Hot bathwater after years of cold dunks had felt nice, but she could have done without the scouring. Hunt-leader's tongue was much gentler.

Being treated like a pup still rankled on her, but part of her enjoyed the attention. It brought back bits and pieces of her past, like long unused human words. The grooming wasn't without its aggravations. Mrs. Ericson had been just as foiled by Kara's mass of curly brown hair as her own mother had been. After hours of detangling and trimming, she finally wrangled it with a ribbon. Kara smiled and pulled at a stray curl.

Few things had changed in the Ericson's living room. The couch was a little more faded and threadbare, making the black-eyed susans difficult to see. So was the oilcloth on the floor. There was comfort in each worn image, a feeble attempt to bring the outside world in.

Everything in the house looked familiar, even the wolf hide hanging over the couch. Emotions tightened Kara's throat and chest. Mist had been her friend. Seeing her hung out as decoration didn't feel right. Every time she looked at it her stomach twisted in a knot. *Bared teeth, a snarl. A blur of silver-gray fur. Shooting pain in her head.*

Kara bit her lip, frustrated and confused. More of her memories had returned, but not the ones that had sent her running for the forest. She continued to fidget, missing the comforting protection of her leathers. At least she had managed to sneak her knives into the socks under the pants when Mrs. Ericson wasn't looking. She doubted the older woman would approve. Despite the pleasant welcome, this family didn't feel like home.

"Yup, that's the one that killed your folks," said Michael. His light-blue eyes regarded her as he leaned on the doorframe. "Surprised they didn't gobble you up, too." He tilted his head to the side and nodded. "You're kind of pretty all cleaned up. I'm beginning to see Ethan's attraction."

Kara felt her face flush and turned away. Six feet tall and muscular, Michael was a physically attractive man, but his look was more like a predator examining a piece of meat than a pack member greeting. She perched on the balls of her feet and pulled at another escaped curl. Mrs. Ericson had called her hair impossible to tame. Could she be tamed? It was difficult to remember all the human rules, but she was determined to behave more like a human and less wolfish. That meant using spoken words instead of growls. These people didn't hear wolf-talk.

"Leave me, Michael."

A muscle twitched in his cheek and his eyes narrowed "Or what? You going to go all wolf on me? I hunt wolves."

"What are you doing, Michael?" said Ethan.

Some of her tension eased as he stepped close to her side. His shoulder brushed against her and she shifted closer. This place was familiar, yet only Ethan felt solid. The rest was like walking through a dream.

"Just having a chat with your wolf girl," said Michael. He glanced at the wolf hide. "She doesn't know a killer when she sees one."

Tears burned Kara's eyes. "Mist did not kill parents. She was a friend."

"I know you believe that, Kara," said Ethan, "But my dad was there. Mist and the others turned on them. That's why he's so adamant about hunting wolves. He doesn't want anyone else to get hurt."

"Good luck convincing her, Ethan," said Michael, before he stalked out the door.

Doubt churned in Kara as she watched him go. The thought of wolves attacking her parents or her didn't make sense. The pack wouldn't turn on one of its own like that unless there was a challenge to leadership. But a pup, never. She'd grown up with new litters each year. A young pup could steal food from the stomach of any pack member. Pups were the future. Everyone protected them. She'd always assumed humans had attacked her family. How could everything she had believed be a lie? Her hand brushed the fur on the wall. The image of running at the wolf's side with Ethan was so vivid, but was it a memory, or a fantasy?

A woman placed a necklace over her head. There was fear in the woman's eyes and a red stain on her shirt. Fire billowed in the distance. Heat radiated toward them with growing intensity.
"Keep it safe, Kara. Run!"
Confusion, panic, and pain.

"There was a fire," whispered Kara. Her head rested against Ethan's chest. "Wolves don't make fire."

Kara lay on the grass next to Ethan and nibbled on a cookie, savoring the flavor. She hadn't realized how much she's missed sweets in her time with the pack.

"This brings back memories," she said, licking her fingers.

"Good ones, I hope."

"And new ones."

She rolled over until her shoulder pressed against Ethan. The touch made her breath catch. Even as children she'd felt closer to him than anyone else. Around him she didn't have to pretend she was like other kids. She was a wolf-talker. His acceptance of her wildness only strengthened that bond. Ethan reached over to ruffle her hair but she turned her head at the last second and licked his hand.

"Down girl," he said, with a laugh. His cheeks rounded like a pair of dumplings.

"You had a crumb on your finger," she said with an impish grin.

"I'll bet I did. Hm. Looks like you have one on the tip of your nose."

He leaned in but stopped, inches from her face. Something other than fear made her heart quicken, and her breath picked up. It felt new, different. Every other thought vanished. All that mattered was Ethan. Urges she'd never felt pulled her into his

Wolf Dawn

gaze. When their lips touched, it felt like a thousand sparks going off at once. It felt so right. Breathless, they drew apart.

"You're eyes are the color of caramel," he whispered.

She felt her face flush. Part of her wanted to dance around the yard. The other part wanted to sink into another kiss. There was a bright twinkle in his eyes, then suddenly he jumped to his feet.

"Follow me," he said.

Ethan slipped behind a rhododendron bush on the side of the house. Just under the window was a small hinged panel. She smiled as Ethan opened the panel and wriggled under the house. This was their hideout, their den. Darkness, broken only by stray streaks of light filled the crawl space. It seemed so much bigger when they were young. A spark broke the darkness as Ethan struck flint to steel, then a small oil lamp began to glow. Treasures adorned the space, things only a child would admire, like bits of string, scrap metal, and old glass pieces. All of them lay under a thick coat of dust.

"I can't believe this place is still here," she said, picking up a recorder that Ethan used to play.

"Mom and dad never found it. After you were killed…I mean, disappeared, I didn't have the heart to visit." He paused, and she saw him swallow. "I missed you, Kara. I missed talking to you and Mist. Things haven't been the same."

"I know," she sighed. "I wish I remembered what happened."

Memories continued to dance just out of reach. It was more frustrating than seeing game leap to safety only inches from your grasp. But right now, sitting here with Ethan, there were other things on her mind. She pressed her lips to his, and for a while they both forgot about the past. Eventually they came up for air and Kara gazed around their little den.

"What's this?" she asked, pulling an oil skin wrapped package from under a pile of knick-knacks.

"I don't know. Open it up."

Under multiple layers of protection they found a journal. The worn leather cover felt cool under her fingers. Without thinking she grasped the chain hidden under her shirt. Tears welled in her eyes.

"Kara, what's wrong?"

"My mother's journal," she choked out. "How did it get here?"

"She must have hid it before...you know. But how did she know about this place? I never told anyone."

"Mist knew," she said, leaving unspoken her mother's ability to wolf-talk.

She stared at the words scrawled on the first page and shook her head. "I don't remember how to read."

Ethan took the book and flipped through it. "Most of this stuff is science notes and equations. Here's a formula." He turned some more pages. "And these look like logs. Some kind of experiment, I think. The handwriting changes several times, as if different people wrote in it." Turning to the end of the book, he pointed. "Look here, it's a note from your mom.

"The pandemic that nearly wiped out mankind wasn't a random mutation," he read aloud. "It was a manufactured virus intended to boost the telepathic abilities of wolves and humans. The original test subjects showed promising results with only mild flu-like side effects. A month into the experiment, vandals broke into the lab. Several vials of a more virulent strain were broken. The disease spread rapidly, mutating and contaminating everything.

"Some of the survivors and their descendants gained the ability to wolf-talk. Many would call the experiment a success, but the price paid in life wasn't worth the cost. The only benefit now is a bridge between the surviving humans, like myself, and the growing wolf population.

"Mist and her pack are descendants of the original test subjects, as am I. They have become dear friends and care for my daughter, Kara, as their own.

"I will continue to document this growing bond between our species. It is my belief that working together will strengthen our chances for survival. I will never allow the other virus these scientists created to be released."

Shivers ran down Kara's spine. *Hide it. Keep it safe.* They were the last words her mom had said. She fingered the object that hung from the chain. It looked exactly like the picture sketched in the book, the one marked *key*.

"We can't tell anyone else about this, Ethan. Promise me, you won't tell."

Nothing brightened her spirit more than a run. After reading her mother's journal, Kara needed it. Sharing it with Ethan was beyond pleasurable. Shoulder to shoulder they ran deep into the surrounding woods, farther than they had gone as children. It wasn't far enough to dispel thoughts of rampant viruses. Nor could it erase the knowledge that she was descended from an experiment. The last line they had read was the most disturbing. Somewhere there was another virus, one more dangerous than the killer fifty years ago. And she had the key.

Trees whizzed by, but Kara didn't stop. Wolf-talk echoed in her head, questioning, concerned, but she didn't answer. Finally, near a rocky outcropping miles from town, she halted, chest heaving. Ethan skidded to a stop a moment later.

A dark gray, almost black wolf stepped out of the shadows. His golden eyes fixed on Ethan. *Human hurt Kara. River-Jump protect pack.* He bared his teeth, hackles raised, tail up and bent.

Ethan froze. "I don't think he likes me."

She saw Ethan's pulse throb on the side of his neck. It had been years since they romped with Mist. Playing with wolves accustomed to people was different than facing one from the wild. Kara was part of the pack, family. Ethan was a stranger, and a human stranger at that.

She jumped in front of Ethan, blocking the advancing wolf and calling out in wolf-talk. *Ethan friend.*

"River-Jump knows something is wrong," she said out loud. "Thinks you're the cause."

"But I'd never hurt you," he said keeping his eyes on River-Jump.

Kara smiled. "Don't tell me, tell them."

"Them?" Apprehension tightened his voice. "Kara?"

"The gray behind you is called Wind. They're my brothers."

Ethan grimaced. "Protective brothers." Then in wolf-talk, he said. *Kara, Ethan, pack.*

Wind moved in first, tentatively sniffing Ethan. *Smart human. Knows wolf-talk.*

Kara find mate? said River-Jump. His head tilted as he eyed Ethan.

Kara felt her face flush. Before she could respond Ethan moved closer to River-Jump. Holding his head high, he growled at the wolf. It wasn't a mean or aggressive kind of voice, more of an assertive, dominant sound. Backed by wolf-talk, it had the desired effect. Both River-Jump and Wind crawled up to Ethan, licking, and rolling on their backs.

Kara, Ethan, come hunt? asked Wind, once all the greetings were done. *Hunt gives life. Life is land.*

Land feeds pack, said River-Jump. *Pack is one.*

Kara felt the call to hunt stir in her veins. Beside her, Ethan joined the cry. *Defend the land. Protect the pack.*

It felt good to run with the pack, her pack.

The smell and sound of the forest still filled Kara's senses as she entered the house. She and Ethan had slipped into the woods every day this week. It was a necessary escape for Kara. Well-wishing neighbors had clamored to greet her, but there was only so much she could take from strangers.

Today was her one week anniversary since returning to humanity. She, Ethan, and the two young wolves celebrated by taking down a small deer. It was their first big kill since they'd begun to run together. They'd left most of the kill with the wolves. It was one thing to spend time with the pack, explaining fang marks in a carcass to Ethan's parents was something else. Instead, they'd roasted only what they could eat in one sitting. On their way back to the house, Ethan shot a goose for his family. He was outside cleaning it and stashing their leather guards in the den.

Mr. Ericson met her in the hallway just outside of the kitchen. "Where have you been, Kara?"

"Ethan and I went for a run, Mr. Ericson," she said, lowering her gaze.

"In the woods." His voice was flat, expressionless. "Again."

"Yes."

Wolf Dawn

His chest rose and sank with a sigh. Some indiscernible emotion flashed in his eyes, then hardened. His smile looked friendly, but something made Kara uneasy.

"Give me the key, the one hanging around your neck."

Her heart skipped a beat. The key, the one thing she had to keep safe, especially with what she now knew. Mr. Ericson was a friend, Ethan's family. Why would he want her mother's key?

"I'm sorry." She sounded like a winey pup. "I can't."

Creases drew across his forehead. "Kara. Give. Me. The. Key."

The intensity of his words made her cringe. Years of living with the pack told her to obey the leader, but a voice in her head whispered rebellion. *Hide it. Keep it safe.* Kara inched back. Someone grabbed her arms in a vise-like grip. Instinctively, her feet lashed out and struck something soft. Michael cursed, and then slammed her to the floor near the kitchen. Air rushed out of her lungs. She was used to wrestling with wolves, but they didn't have hands. Rope tightened on her wrists.

A hand reached for the chain and Kara bit down, hard. Blood, warm and metallic, oozed onto her tongue. More curses poured from Michael's mouth, and then his hand hit her head hard enough to make the room spin. A shooting pain lanced her ribs as he kicked her. Cotton filled her mouth, silencing her growls and snarls.

Michael landed another kick, then yanked the necklace off her neck, breaking the chain. "That'll teach you not to bite me."

"What are you doing?" yelled Ethan, as he entered the house. "Let her go. Give that back."

Ethan dove at Michael, grappling for the necklace. Although his brother outweighed him, the intensity of his attack drove the older boy back. Michael tripped over Kara's prone figure and Ethan snatched the necklace from his grasp. So focused on his brother, Ethan didn't spot his father until the man grabbed the back of his shirt collar. Ethan dangled in the air like a pup.

"Stupid boy," said Mr. Ericson, as he pinned Ethan against the wall. "She's nothing but an animal, like her parents. Now give me that key."

Ethan's eyes widened. "No." Even suspended in the air, Ethan continued to struggle, holding the key as far from his dad as he could.

"Sorry, Ethan. We're doing this for you." Mrs. Ericson's face looked drawn, strained, as she pried the key from Ethan's hand. "We have to protect the family. It's only a matter of time before she remembers what happened."

It was as if someone had opened a floodgate. Kara gasped, nearly choking on the gag in her mouth, as her past rushed in.

Angry voices yelled, waking her from sleep. A gun fired. Her parents screamed. Mom pulled her out of bed, gave her the necklace, then dropped her out the window.

"Kara, protect it. Keep it safe. Don't let him get it, ever. He'll kill all of us, all the wolves. Run."

Mist ran at her side. Chest heaving, she gulped for air. Sharp pain jabbed the side of her head and she tripped. Blood ran down her neck. Rough hands grabbed. Terrified, Kara dug at the ground, nails raked across the grass. Ethan's dad pulled at the key, strangling. Then Mist's silver-gray form leaped over her, teeth bared. Kara scrambled to her feet and ran until she collapsed.

The memory of that night hit harder than Michael's fist. Betrayed, by their friends. Murdered. Hate burned inside her. Mist didn't kill her parents. Mr. Ericson did. And Mrs. Ericson knew. Kara strained against the narrow cords on her wrists.

Killed them, screamed Kara. *My parents.*

Ethan's face drained of color. "It was you," he stammered. "You killed them, her parents. How could you? I don't understand."

Mr. Ericson shook his head. "Of course you don't. You're too full of that cur's scent. I'm only going to explain this once, so listen up good. Her parents found the lab that created the pandemic. It changed some of the survivors and it changed those killing beasts she runs with. Wolf-talkers," he snorted. "Animals themselves. See how she acts. There's another virus locked away

Wolf Dawn

in there that'll get rid of all those wolves and wolf-talkers, but won't harm true humans like us. A counter measure created by the original scientists. The fools were too scared to use it. But now, we have the key. It's time to purify the human race, retake our world."

Still jammed against the wall by Mr. Ericson's iron grip, Ethan continued to writhe. "No, Dad, you can't do this. Please. It'll kill her. Kill her pack."

Smack. Ethan crumpled to the floor, barely conscious. Bound as she was, there was little Kara could do. Somehow she squirmed around and thrust her feet at Mr. Ericson's calves. He lurched into the wall, then whipped around and glared at her, hands clenched. Kara returned the look, waiting for him to strike. Instead he turned back to Ethan.

"Once the girl and her kind are out of the way you'll see more clearly," said his father. "Lock them in the storage room."

The door banged shut with a crash and the lock clicked. For a moment pain sank behind despair. Her parent's murderer had the key to slaughter everything she held dear. Ethan, her pack, they were all in danger. All because she trusted the man who tried to kill her, who killed her parents. The cords cut into her wrists and ankles, and the corners of her mouth were already raw from the gag. She had to save them.

Ethan! Wake up!

It was a thought, nothing more, wolf-talk. Simple, but efficient. Ethan groaned. Their eyes met.

"I'm sorry, Kara," he said. His voice sounded tight, pained. "I didn't know. I..."

Not now.

There was no more time for despair. Too many lives depended on them. It took some maneuvering, but she finally reached the knife tucked into her sock. No one had thought to check either of them for weapons. Freeing her hands was tricky. By the time she finished, her hands were coated with bloody nicks. Finally loose, she spit the gag out and moved to Ethan. His arms wrapped around her and she felt his body shake with emotion.

"I'm sorry," he said again.

"I know," she said. "Why didn't you tell them?"

"About me wolf-talking?" he shook his head. "You saw them. It wouldn't have made a difference."

She yanked on the door knob, but it wouldn't budge. The walls seemed to close in. "We have to stop them."

"Give me your knife," said Ethan. "And stay calm. This door was meant to keep people out, not in."

Using the knife as a lever, Ethan pried out the hinge pins and removed the door. Together they slipped out of their prison only to find the house deserted. It hadn't taken long to free themselves from the storeroom, but it was enough to give his parents a good head start.

"We have to stop them." It wasn't a whimper, or a cry. It was a deep-throated, protective growl. "Get your crossbow."

"We will," said Ethan. "There's a map in the back of the journal. Grab it and the leathers."

Kara howled as soon as they stepped outside. It was more than a call to hunt, it was a battle cry. Life and death hung in the balance. She didn't care if the sound startled the neighbors. *Defend the land. Protect the pack.* The cry was hurried, without the power behind it she would have liked. Even wolf-talk had its distance limits. All she could do was pray that the wolves responded.

After a quick look at the map, they raced from the town, garnering a few puzzled looks. Sunset was a few hours away and most humans didn't leave town after dark. According to the map, the lab wasn't far away. But would they get there in time?

One thought pounded in Kara's head as she ran. *Hunt gives life, life is land. Land feeds pack. Pack is one. Defend the land. Protect the pack.* This new plague threatened all packs. Beside her, Ethan struggled to keep up with the pace she set, but she could hear his mind, wolf-talking, keeping up the chant. *Hunt gives life. Life is land. Land feeds pack. Pack is one. Protect the pack. Protect the pack.*

This hunt was for more than their lives. It was for all life, all packs, for survival.

Wolf Dawn

A gray shadow detached from the underbrush and raced beside them. Footsteps almost silent. River-Jump paused, sniffing the air, then turned to the left. *Prey runs this way.*

Scout only, answered Kara as she changed directions.

Found prey. Wind sounded distant. *Female guards old den.*

Kara put on a new burst of speed. *Protect the pack.*

Remnants of a chained enclosure came into view. A half-collapsed building leaned against one of the remaining posts. Poking through the roof stood a tulip poplar. Nature was taking back its space.

In the dimming light, Kara saw Mrs. Ericson pace beside their car near a doorway. The woman held a crossbow in her hands like a rotting fish, clearly uncomfortable with the weapon. There was no sign of the men. Shivers ran up Kara's spine. She choked back a growl before it could escape, but couldn't stop her lips from curling back.

Ethan put a hand on her shoulder. *Me talk.*

She nodded, but fear gnawed at her like an old bone. There was no telling how the woman would react. *Careful*.

"Let us by, Mom." said Ethan as they slipped out of hiding. The tip of his crossbow pointed down, but he held it ready to aim. Tension etched his face.

"Kara. Ethan." Panic crept into her voice and she raised her weapon, but didn't call out. "You don't need her, Ethan."

"Don't need her? Mom. I've spent the last eight years mourning her, my best friend. Her mom was your friend as well. Or was that a lie, too?"

"I...we were friends once. But then she started that wolf-talk nonsense. I mean, really. Wolves can't talk."

Kara glared at her, unable to keep silent. They needed to get past her, quickly. "Wolves talk, Mrs. Ericson. But they don't lie like humans, or kill their young."

"I'm protecting my children," said Mrs. Ericson. She stood taller, eyes defiant and aloof. "From freaks like you. Those wolves of yours killed the game we should have taken. I'm not letting my son get sucked back into your world again. This will save Ethan and other human children."

Kara shook her head and tried to inch her way around, but Mrs. Ericson kept her weapon on her. The woman just didn't understand. "That virus will kill wolf-talkers as well as wolves."

"Oh, yes, child. You and your kind will be destroyed forever."

Emotion tightened Kara's throat. "Ethan will die from that virus."

"No he won't, he..." Her voice trailed off and she looked at Ethan. Color drained from her face as understanding dawned. Her head shook back and forth. "You can't...that's impossible."

"No, Mom. I never told you about talking to Mist because I didn't think you'd understand. I've always been a wolf-talker. There were simply no wolves to talk to after you and dad murdered Mist and her pack."

She crumpled to the ground, dropping the crossbow. "Oh god. You've got to stop them. My baby. I was just trying to protect you."

Kara dashed into the building, drawing her knives as she did. Every hair on the back of her neck stood on end. This was where it all started, the pandemic, the wolf-talking, the end of the old civilization. It was also the reason her parents were murdered. And if they didn't hurry, more would die.

Dried leaves crunched under Kara's feet. Beside her, Ethan peered into the semi-darkened space. Dim light filtered down through the broken roof, illuminating several hallways. Most ended in darkness, but a soft glow emanated from one of them. Carefully, they followed the hallway. The weight of the structure seemed to press down on Kara. If it weren't for the urgent need to find the two men, she would have bolted. As it was, each step sent her heart leaping.

Mr. Ericson's voice echoed in the hallway. "Damnit. Why isn't it opening?"

"It's been fifty years, Dad. Maybe it's stuck.

"No, no." The irritation in his voice was clear. "The girl's mother put it in here eight years ago. I saw it. She must have changed the damned password."

Kara peered into the room. Michael and Mr. Ericson hovered around a wall safe. Gouges covered the concrete around it, but

Wolf Dawn

none deep enough to free the safe. A dust covered pickax leaned against the wall just below it. Wires stretched from a car battery to a key pad. Next to the pad, embedded in a small hole, hung Kara's necklace. A faint beeping sound rang out every time Mr. Ericson pressed a button. He tugged at the safe door again and uttered more curses.

Beside her, Ethan's wolf-talk voice laughed in her mind. *Key pad lock. Needs password.*

Hope flared in Kara. There was still time. The two were so intent on the safe, they didn't notice her slink into the room with Ethan. Michael saw them first, but Ethan's arrow struck his crossbow before he could raise it, snapping the string. Wood and metal whipped back, leaving a bloody line across his face. A second weapon rested on the floor near his father's feet. Mr. Ericson had reflexes honed from years of hunting. His arrow shot off within seconds of grasping the handle.

"No!" Ethan shoved Kara out of its path, then lurched back, grunting in pain.

He stumbled to the ground. Feather fletching protruded from his left shoulder. Blood began to soak his shirt. Other pack members had fallen over the years, part of the risk hunting large prey. But nothing twisted Kara's heart as much as seeing Ethan hurt. She stood over him, lips curled back. Protecting, guarding.

Her sight narrowed to the two men by the wall. They would slaughter what remained of her family, her pack. *Defend the land. Protect the pack.* Like the crows who steal a kill, these murderers needed to be run off or destroyed. A growl burst from her throat, deep and full of anger and pain.

"You will never open that safe," she snarled.

"You're outnumbered, wolf girl," Mr. Ericson said, reaching for the pickaxe.

Kara leaped, just barely nicking his hand as he raised the weapon. A line of red glistened where her blade struck, but it did nothing to slow him down. He swung the axe in a wide arc, driving her back. Her first kill had been a bull elk with a rack more deadly than the weapon she faced now. But she had had a pack to help take that beast. Adrenaline surged through her veins, driving her on. Out of the corner of her eye she saw

Michael reloading his father's crossbow. Two foes, one of her. It was a losing battle. In her mind she heard the wolves howl, sensed them circle the building. She also knew they wouldn't enter a human building…for any reason.

Defend the land. Protect the pack. All her focus went to battling the man with the axe. It was the only way to save Ethan. An arrow whizzed by her left ear just as she darted right. Sparks brightened the room where it struck the concrete wall, drawing her attention. She hastily dodged Mr. Ericson's swing, but not fast enough to miss the flat edge. It hit with bone crushing force. Pain lanced her arm and she dropped her blade. The axe swung again, this time aimed at her head. Instead of running back, she dove closer, and sank her other knife deep into his thigh. He yelled in pain then grabbed her before she could dart away. Fingers, heavy with calluses, tightened around her throat, lifting her off the ground.

"Let her go, Dad." Ethan sat propped against the wall by the door, his crossbow loaded and aimed at his father. There was steel in his voice. "Let her go or I'll shoot."

Mr. Ericson laughed, but it wasn't a humorous sound. "And risk hitting your pet? I don't think so, Ethan. I'm doing this for your own good."

Kara's chest began to burn and she struggled to free herself, kicking and hitting with her uninjured hand. It was like fighting a bear. His grip didn't budge. A coppery haze clouded her vision. The twang of a crossbow and a dull thump barely registered. The fingers loosened their grip. Kara sucked in air as he fell back, an arrow protruding from his neck.

"You've murdered enough, Dad," whispered Ethan. Tears stained his face.

"What have you done?" Michael stared, mouth open in shock, hands shaking.

Ethan looked at his mother, who sobbed in the doorway, then back to Michael. "Protected my family."

There was no moon tonight, which suited Kara just fine. A single lamp flickered outside the house. She had promised to wait here while Ethan said goodbye to his mother and Michael,

Wolf Dawn

but it was taking longer than expected. For a few panicked moments she imagined him bound and locked in a room, or bleeding to death. But he would have wolf-talked if something like that had happened again. Too many bad memories haunted this place, and she longed to leave it far behind.

Two months of restricted activity had made recovery difficult for Kara. Broken bones were no laughing matter to a hunter. Twinges of pain still ached her arm. Ethan's injury had been more serious. He'd lost a lot of blood before they got him to the town physician.

Footsteps approached and Kara jumped, as skittish as a young wolf. Relief flooded her when she saw him. She looked up into his blue eyes, longing for his touch. Shivers ran up her spine as he brushed a hand across her cheek. Her heart fluttered. She nuzzled against his chest and felt his love telegraph through his beating heart.

"Ethan" she said. A wolfish whimper slipped into her voice.

"Ready to go?" he said with a smile.

"For days. Are you sure you're healed enough?"

Ethan answered by lifting his arm over his head, something he had been unable to do for a while. Two gray shadows greeted them as they entered the woods, tails swishing low. The beginnings of a new pack.

"Do you think my dad could have figured out the password eventually?" Ethan asked.

Kara fingered the key that once again hung from her neck. It was merely an ornament now, with no other purpose. The virus it once guarded, destroyed, the ashes buried.

Kara shook her head and smiled. "Only a wolf."

"Only a wolf."

In the distance a wolf howled, Hunt-leader saying her farewell. They answered back, joining in a cacophony of sound. The song rang out, echoing in her mind. *Defend the land. Protect the pack.*

How would you fare on another planet, if it was a home you did not choose? Neve faces many challenges, armed only with her courage, her heart, and her humanity.

SISTER GRASS

Deborah Walker

"Don't trust the aliens, that's all I'm saying," said Myra. Myra had been a good friend to Neve and Penny. She lived next door, in the prefabricated huts that were the refugees' accommodation. Neve had only been thirteen when they had first come to this Kristrall refugee world. Thirteen years old with a two year old sister to care for, she'd been grateful for Myra's advice. But now, two years later, she found Myra's attitude tiring.

"You know how hard I've saved for this, Myra. I've worked every day running errands, doing odd jobs in the camp."

The refugees were given an allowance, call it pin money, to buy small luxuries. Neve had saved every cent. She had begged for small jobs, earning a few cents, here and there. There were always small jobs to be done. It was curious how restrained and lethargic the people in the refugee camp seemed to be. They had little to do all day, but still the small tasks, that should have been easily achieved, were left undone. There was weariness in the refugee camp; it hung in the air, the miasma of a confined people.

"I've been working and saving for a year to get the entrance fee for the games. Now I've finally got enough, are you saying that I should give up?" Neve couldn't understand Myra's attitude. Myra had helped her, caring for her sister, while Neve had worked to earn the money she needed.

"I'm saying that you should think about Penny."

"I think about my sister all the time. It's Penny I'm doing this for."

Sister Grass

"Is it?"

Am I doing this for Penny? Or am I doing it for myself? Neve wondered. *No, Myra's wrong. I'm doing this for both of us.* She *was* sure of that. Myra was just like the rest of the people in this camp. She meant well, but she'd been worn out by camp life.

After the war, the Kristralls had been magnanimous in victory-offering a home to those displaced by war. Perhaps they were a benevolent species, giving aid to all those who asked. But they were paternal hosts, limiting and confining their charges.

Neve looked at Myra then, really looked at her: a small woman dressed in the refugees' uniform. Had she always looked so tired? Had she always worn that fragrance of overwhelming defeat? Neve remembered her differently.

"I need the money, Myra. There's no other way to get it. I don't want to be a refugee all of my life. The Kristralls won't allow us to work, not until they believe that we are fully integrated into their society."

When the Kristralls believed that the refugees accepted their status, accepted the Kristralls' authority, things might change. The refugees would have more freedom, be allowed to work and to take on more responsibilities. But that process would take many generations, the administrators had made that quite plain. There was only one way for Neve to acquire money, real money, and that was to participate in one of the Kristralls' games. Winning the game would mean prize-money and Neve needed money.

"What exactly did they say?" asked Myra.

"They told me about the games, described them to me and gave me a choice. I chose the lost game." In fact, the game administrators had been rather vague. There'd been many games to choose from - all ill-defined. When Never had asked for more explanation, and administrator had said, "The games are defined by the players."

What was that supposed to mean?

"Think about it," said Myra, grasping Neve's hand. "We're protected here. We have food, a safe home, more than we had on Earth."

"Can't you understand that I want more than all this?" Neve gestured to the sterile surroundings, an alien take on basic accommodation. Everything neutral-colored and functional, everything standardized, the same furnishing in a million refugee homes. She noticed the camera in the corner of the room watching them both. She stopped talking. It was easy to forget that you were constantly monitored. It wasn't wise to criticize the Kristralls' generosity.

"I know you've been working for this, and it was good, good that you've had something to aim for. But now that you're going to do it, I'm frightened, Neve, about what they might do to you. They're not like us Neve. They know things that we don't."

"They said that the game was fair. They said that I could win the game. I believe them, Myra. Whatever else they've done to us, they've never lied to us."

"Don't forget who you are, where you came from, and who bought you here."

"I'm going to do it, Myra, no matter what you say. Wish me luck, it's important that you believe in me."

"I believe in you," said Myra, but she looked away, and Neve saw the doubt in her eyes.

The technicians took out their instruments and placed a silver cap of wires over her sister's head. *She looks so small,* thought Neve.

The technicians connected the cap to a monitor, talking all the time in their fluttering language. Neve didn't recognize their species–there were hundreds of species on this refugee world. Two of the technicians laughed, they might have been sharing a joke–this was all in day's work for them.

"Please pay attention," said Neve. "She's very young. She's only four." If anything went wrong Neve would never forgive herself.

Neve looked over to Berka, the technician who spoke English. She explained the technical procedures to Neve. Neve didn't know if she had been assigned by the Kristralls as a translator, but she was grateful for the explanations. Watching

Sister Grass

her sister undergoing these long procedures would have been more difficult without Berka's calm explanations.

"We will scan her memories now, and then they will be transferred to the storage file. When her mind is empty, we will put her body into in stasis, until you claim her."

Two of the technicians exchanged glances.

"How will I do that?" asked Neve.

"Part of the lost game is not knowing. You must find your own way."

"Neve," said Penny, "I can see Mummy. She's pushing me on a swing." Neve was surprised, in the two years that they had been on this world, her sister's memories had faded. She rarely talked about their mother. She'd adapted well to life in the refugee camp. Too well, perhaps, the life of a perpetual refugee was not the life Neve wanted for her sister, nor for herself. Neve remembered her old life so well, but she pushed away those thoughts.

"The process sometimes activates old memories," said Berka. "There is no need for concern."

Neve watched until her sister's expressions started to fade. Penny's face and body grew still, her personality draining away into the alien technology.

"Almost complete now," said Berka.

Neve took her sister's hand. "I'll see you soon Penny, really soon. Remember, this is just a game."

Berka took a glass slide from the machine. "Look, these are your sister's patterns transferred onto this storage file." Neve looked at the slide. Holographic patterns moved in the glass.

"Kristrall technology is wonderfully advanced," said Berka.

"Wonderful," said Neve, staring at the changing patterns.

"My people started as refugees, too," said Berka. "In a few generations we have worked our way up to technician class. There is hope, you know."

Neve said nothing and Berka resumed her professional demeanor. "The files will be transferred to the gaming field now. You will have five hours to find your sister's pattern. Good luck."

Young Adventurers

There were a thousand patterns in the grass, the personalities of a thousand individuals scanned and transferred to this field. Neve needed to find her sister's pattern before the time ran out, one blade of grass in a field, one pattern amongst a thousand.

The cameras embedded in the glass dome, transmitted her actions to a watching audience. The lost game was very popular in this sector. But Neve had never seen it. The refugee class were not allowed access to entertainment media. The refugee class were not allowed lots of things. They weren't allowed to leave the confines of their camp. They weren't allowed to meet in large groups. They weren't allowed access to information about the world they lived on. This Kristrall refugee world was a mystery to Neve. She knew that it housed hundreds of species, but she knew little else about it. She didn't even know how far it was from Earth.

The lost game had seemed to offer her the strongest chance of success. All she had to do was find her sister, and she knew her sister so well, she'd been a mother to Penny for two years now, ever since they had left Mother behind on Earth, lost in the disarray of war.

Neve had been searching the field too long, time was slipping by. She had started the game calmly, methodically, examining the grass, staring at one corner of the field, searching for clues. But as the game progressed she became erratic, running from one side of the field to the other. Until now, she stood in the middle of field and screamed, "Penny, Penny," over and over again.

Neve smelled smoke. Part of the grass verge was smoldering. Was that a clue? She often told her sister not to touch the open fires that burnt in the homes and in the streets of the camp. It must be a clue. The fire was gathering air, sucking in the hot perfumed air of the dome. Neve ran to the verge and waved her arms in the burning grass. But her hand slipped through the holographic flames.

They had told her that she could recognize her sister's pattern. They had told her she could win the game. They had assured her that the game was fair. There must be some way of identifying her sister, but she felt overwhelmed. She was playing a game whose rules she really didn't understand. She feared that her sister would be lost in the field forever.

"You have one hour left," said a voice over the games system. Only one hour! She had been in the game four hours now, and it was almost finished. Fear threw a grey cloak over Neve, and she stood immobile, but only for a few moments. No! Not now, she thought. Save the fear for later.

"Another player wishes to join. Accepting another player will lower the prize-money. Will you accept?"

"Yes, I accept." The prize money seemed irrelevant now. Neve was fighting the fear of losing Penny. The administrators had explained that rule quite explicitly.

A figure materialized in the corner of the field. It was a member of the Kristrall race. Was this some sort of trick?

Bone white and elegant, he stood for a moment, possibly to allow the audience to admire his manifestation. When he moved it was with a fluid grace, muscles working under skin in a supple sufficiency. He was at home here, in the waving grasslands, at home with the advanced technology that had taken her sister, and in tune with the conventions of the game. But those thoughts didn't bring hope, they bought fear. *He knows all. And I know nothing. My ignorance is his foil, he'll use me to his advantage. No!* Neve pushed away the insidious thoughts of failure. She had to find Penny. This Kristrall is in the dome. She must use him to find her sister.

She ran to the alien "I need help. My sister is missing, a pattern in the grass. I've just got one hour to find her."

"My name is Greenstem, and I am honoured to meet you. Yes. Where shall we start?" He was unhurried.

His presence, his elegance made Neve feel small and dirty and insignificant. He magnified her flaws. It wasn't just his physical splendour. He had an aura of coherence and purpose that was overwhelming.

No wonder they won the war, they are so much better than us.

The Kristralls always created this response in Neve, in all the human refugees, perhaps in other species too. She had seen the Kristralls many times. They visited the human camp. Neve had seen them, chatting as they walked, taking in the sights, offering a word or two to the conquered peoples. They created this sense of wonder, as they passed.

No! Would those thoughts never be still? She was here now. She needed to find Penny. That was all that mattered. Neve subsumed her awe, ignoring the hypnotic admiration he created. She would find Penny.

"Can you show me how to find her?"

"And your name is?" Greenstem was leisurely.

"Neve. Please help me. My sister, she's here somewhere in the grass. They said she was a type eight pattern. Probably with an overlay of butterflies or hearts. They are her favorite things. She's only four."

"I am also four years."

"Four Earth years I mean."

"Ah, that is young. We measure time differently, you know."

"Right, of course. But, can you help me find her?"

Greenstem looked towards the cameras. "I will do it," he said. He walked over to a section of the grass and extended his arm, stretching and stretching the flesh, until it lost its cohesion and became a protrusion of cytoplasm stretching into the waving grass fronds. This was the first time Neve had seen this transformation. She knew Kristralls could mutate their flesh, there was endless discussion about the Kristralls in the camps, but she had never seen it done. To Neve's eyes the spectacle of his changing hands was disturbing, and it diminished him, removed some of his glamour. *He is truly alien,* she thought as she saw his body shape to his mind. With their humanoid appearance it was sometimes easy to forget how different these creatures were.

"There is an old creature here. I have met him before," said Greenstem. "I think no-one searchers for him, but he is content to be here."

He moved his arm with its web of cytoplasm over another section of grass. He was searching the grass, reading the memories of the individuals hidden within. But he was using his alien body. Is this what she needed to do to find Penny? It was impossible, but they said that the game was fair.

"Is your sister a relative?" asked Greenstem.

Sister Grass

"Yes, yes. We share parents, two parents."
"With equal chance of genetic exchange?"
"I guess."

He was moving quickly now, waving his strange hands in the grass. He would help her, he would find her sister.

"Then she may not be genetically close to you. There is a high variation in your species, I believe."

"That is not the point," said Neve. "She's my sister. She's only four. I want her back." She stared over Greenstem's shoulder as he continued his graceful movement, waving his hand through the grass. "What can you sense? Do you see her?" asked Neve.

"There is a colony. You might call them ants. The old queen guards them well. Did you say that you sister likes ants?"

"No. Butterflies, she likes butterflies."

"Ah, I will continue, then."

He moved away from the colony to another part of the field.

"Do you like this world, Neve?"

Neve stared at Greenstem. Was he making polite conversation? But she needed his help. She thought about the question. She was a refugee on an alien world. Her Father was dead. Her mother was on Earth, light years distant. Did she like being fifteen and mother to her sister? Did she like the feeling of dependence, the fact that she must be eternally grateful for the Kristralls for every mouth of food, for every breath of air? "Yes," said Neve. "This is a very beautiful world. You are a gracious and generous people." Neve knew what he wanted to hear.

She moved away from Greenstem. She knelt in the soft grass. I will do as he does. She stretched out, not her body, but her mind, trying to read meaning into the impenetrable grass. Extending her mind, outwards, outwards. *Penny, Penny, where are you darling?* And then she touched a soft place. She reached another mind. It was not her sister. She wanted to move away but it was immeasurably compelling. She didn't know the species. It was old and it spoke directly into her bones. "I will tell you a thousand secrets, stories buried in a shell and hidden in the wreath of stars. There is a particular treasure that will help your people. I lost it many years ago and it is well armed, but I will tell you a mystery..."

Neve felt a touch on her arm. The touch of alien skin brought her to her senses.

"You've been lying there for many minutes. Have you found her?" It was Greenstem, standing over her.

"No." Neve was confused. "It was a voice telling me about a treasure. It was telling me secrets." She got to her feet.

"It was probably one of the game traps."

"You have fifteen minutes left," a voice announced over the dome tannoy. "Failure to find the pattern will mean that the personality will stay within the dome."

"I've got to find her."

"Does she mean so much to you?"

"Yes."

"Then why did you allow her to enter the game?"

"We need the money."

"But refugees are provided with food, housing and limited education all at our expense."

"I know," said Neve. "But we still need money, and Penny is too young to find me. This is our best chance."

"You need money to buy *things*?"

"Yes, all right, don't judge me." There was no need to tell Greenstem, and the watching audience what she really wanted the money for. There were always opportunities for people with money–on any world. Perhaps she could even acquire enough wealth to buy an illegal passage back to Earth, maybe even find her mother again.

"I do not judge," said Greenstem. "I simply observe. And offer a bargain, if you agree. I will find her. If not she will remain here until you get enough money to play again. Perhaps you never will. Perhaps you will choose to spend your money on things. I do not judge."

Neve thought of her sister's body remaining frozen, never growing older, while her mind grew in strange directions in this alien dome. Even one day was too long. "I'll do anything," she said.

"Merge with me. Then I'll have the information to find her."

"I don't merge." Neve had seen men and women who had merged with the Kristralls. They were forlorn relics, their minds tuned to alien thoughts, unable to function. Neve needed to care for Penny. She couldn't do that if she merged with Greenstem.

"It's your only opportunity to find your sister at this point. Then you will have the money you desire."

"I just want her back."

"It can be a difficult game, for those who don't understand the consequences." Greenstem stretched out his strange hands towards her. "That is why the game always seeks new players, new species. The audience like the fresh emotions you younger species generate."

"And you?" said Neve. "What do you like?"

"I am a collector. If you merge with me, I will find your sister. Your memories will remain with me and I will gift you with my memories."

The Kristralls set a trap for me and I've walked into it, like an idiot. Was this all designed to trap me? They're watching me now, on their cameras. Watching me.

She had no choice, she must do it. She must save her sister. Someone else would become a mother to Penny. Penny would be fine. Myra would look after her. Neve extended a trembling hand to Greenstem, knowing that she would be changed forever by this merging. He would flood her with a lifetime of memories, the sea of his experiences passing through the eye of her mind. She would swim in his alien memories. Greenstem's hopes, dreams, experiences would inundate her soul. For a moment she would be him, then their memories would bind together, merging and re-creating. And she would be forever changed, while the audience watched.

Her only consolation was that her mother wasn't here, wouldn't know that she had been changed. She missed her mother so much. She's tried not to think about her, since she'd lost her. Neve had tried to be a mother to Penny. But Neve missed her mother so much.

Her mother! That's who Penny would seek. That's where she would be. Ignoring Greenstem's outstretched hand, Neve ran over to the area where Greenstem said he'd encountered the colony of ants.

There is a hive, with a Queen guarding her children. That is what Penny will seek- the mother figure.

Yes! She was here. Neve could feel the patterns of her sister's mind.

"I have found her," She shouted triumphantly to the cameras. "I have won your game, now let us go."

Greenstem came over to her. "You will achieve your acquisition of money."

"Yes, now leave us." She would have the money, but the price had been too high. The hazard to her sister had been too great. She'd been naïve. She hadn't understood the game. In her overwhelming desire to escape this world, Neve had risked too much. But even so a voice spoke inside her: *I won. I won the game. I escaped Greenstem and his machinations.*

Her sister materialized in the grass sheltered for a moment, by a huge shape with a small triangular head, which merged back into the grass. Neve ran to hug her, but her hands slipped through.

"She's a holograph," said Greenstem. "Your sister's body is in stasis–where you left it. You can collect her soon enough"

Her sister was free! That's all that mattered to Neve.

"You could have had my memories," said Greenstem sadly, "and I could have had yours. I have lived a very long time. You could have shared my experiences."

"Is this what you bought us here for? To eat our memories?"

Greenstem shrugged. "You are a new species, and your value to the game is high. But there are many of you and you breed quickly. I suggest that you play as often as you can if you wish to gain money. The value of the human mind will soon diminish." With an elegant parting gesture, Greenstem dematerialized.

Neve would never play this game again, nor any other Kristrall games. She would find new ways to make her way back to Earth. And, somehow, Neve felt sure that there *would* be other ways.

Penny's holographic image shimmered. "I like it here, Neve."

Sister Grass

Neve laughed. "You do? There are good people in this game, Penny." She bowed to the patch of grass where the alien queen's mind resided. "Thank you for looking after my sister," she said.

"Did we win, Neve?" asked Penny.

"Yes, we won their game. Let's go back to the camp."

And they had won something else as well, the knowledge that the Kristralls were not infallible and that games could be won by humans. That message would spread through the refugee camp like fire through grass.

As we have seen, space is the final frontier where a young woman can prove herself a heroine and an explorer capable of great discoveries.

TOORI'S CONSTELLATION

Anne E. Johnson

The planet Orpa had a pale purple atmosphere. "I wish all of space was purple," Toori said to Mama one night. "It would make our trip even more interesting."

"Oh, there will be plenty to hold our interest." Mama spoke through her lower mouth, which had a softer, gentler voice than the upper one. Toori loved that about Mama. Her other mother, Mimi, often used both mouths at once.

"Mimi is almost done building the spaceship, right?" Toori's leafy fingers quivered excitedly. "She said I could come on the last test run."

"That's right." Mama's center eye squinted with worry and she rubbed her bare brown sides.

"It'll be fun!" Toori assured her. But even she had a slight sense of dread. That feeling was very familiar to her, and she was sick of it. "It'll be fun," she repeated with less enthusiasm. "Six months, just the three of us in space. Imagine it: the first people to leave Orpa."

"I imagine it constantly," Mama murmured. Her skin quivered with stress.

"Mama? Why are we Lemps so scared?"

Mama got up and folded the blanket they'd been stargazing on. "It's just how we're made, sweetie. You know that. Our brains are built to emphasize fear."

It wasn't enough of an answer. "If our species is always afraid, then why do we have to be so curious? I wish we'd just

Toori's Constellation

be happy knowing what we know, so we wouldn't have to get scared by what we might find."

Mama turned an unusually stern face to Toori. "Never regret your curiosity. Never. It's a blessing. Imagine if I had never been curious."

Toori nodded, lowering all three eyes. "You wouldn't have invented Infinity wire. And without unbreakable wire, buildings would fall down during quakes. And bridges would fall apart over time. I know."

"Not only that. Don't forget that we also wouldn't have enough money to send you to that nice school." Mama winked her outer eyes playfully. "All I'm saying is, our curiosity is our best feature. And every species has a balance of traits. So we have extra fear."

"Yes, Mama." So only the sky could hear, Toori whispered, "This time we won't be scared." She wished she believed it.

The days crawled by like cooling lava. Toori tried to think about other things. It helped that she loved her school. In life science class, they built an oversized model of a flying insect called a frib.

"I've never seen one of these," Toori whispered to her friend Nere.

Their teacher, Emto, heard her. He gave all four sets of his leafy fingers a mischievous wiggle. "Nor will you see one around here, Toori. Fribs live on the opposite side of the planet from us." Smiling with his lower mouth, he spoke with the upper one. "Soon our very own Toori will be able to tell us all about flying beyond our planet. Right? Promise to give us a full report when you and your parents return?"

Without thinking, Toori blurted out what she wanted to be true. "We're not coming back. We'll just keep on flying, farther and farther into space."

The other kids burst out laughing, honking through their lips in two tones. Even Emto laughed, but more politely, through only his lower mouth. "To quote my grandfather's favorite expression," he said, "it is a Lemp's nature to be brown and slick, curious and creative, cautious and safe."

"Can't we change?" Toori argued. "Couldn't at least one of us be brave?"

Her classmates settled down and listened, as if they had secretly thought about this question. Both of Emto's jaws hung slack for a moment before he answered. "There is a difference between bravery and recklessness. Of course, an individual Lemp can act bravely for a time. But the need to feel safe is built into our brains. Think of it as a good thing. We have a strong wish to stay alive." He indicated the frib model. "What would you expect this creature to do if a jagged-fanged metzon bird tried to catch it?"

"It would get scared."

"It would fly away."

"That's right," their teacher said. He grabbed the fake frib's synthetic wings and flapped them. "That's its natural survival sense. That's what we Lemps have, too: the instinct to avoid danger."

"I have an instinct to fall asleep," a boy named Mepro whispered double-voiced from the back of the room. Raising his wide, round feet in front of him, he pretended to snore through his upper mouth.

When the students stopped giggling, Emto sighed. "I know looking at models in the classroom is not very interesting. Next week we'll take a field trip to the Reppin Meadows."

"To see the diamond bugs?" Toori asked excitedly. When a bunch of kids turned to her, she explained. "My moms took me to see them last year. It's so *fun*. The whole field sparkles."

"Well, good," said Emto. "You can give us pointers when we're there." With two smiles he added, "And maybe you'll even discover something you didn't know."

Toori hopped and skipped all the way home. It wasn't just the diamond bugs field trip that had her energized. As she expected, Mimi was waiting in front of their dwelling, leaning out of a private transport pod. "Ready for the test run?" she called.

"I am *ready*!" Toori squealed.

Mama stepped out from behind the big red pod. "And you're sure it's safe?"

Toori's Constellation

Toori could tell by the way Mimi rolled her center eye that Mama had already asked that a hundred times.

"It's safe, it's safe!" Toori giggled. "And we're even staying pretty near the ground, right, Mimi?"

"Yup. We'll stay just inside Orpa's atmosphere."

"Which means you can stay in *contact*." Mama emphasized the word with her louder, lower mouth. "*Constant* contact."

Mimi gave Mama a four-armed hug. "Except for a short time. We have to practice being off comms."

"That will feel like forever," Mama admitted.

"Just keep busy," Toori advised. "You're so amazing at planning things. Work on organizing the trip. The time will fly by."

Mimi burst out laughing. "You assume there's a single micro-detail she hasn't already planned."

Toori's slick skin rippled with excitement as she climbed onto the ship. "Why did you name it *The Reach*?" she asked Mimi. "Is it because we're reaching out into space?" As Mimi helped Toori strap herself in, Toori could tell she was stalling. "What are we reaching for?" she prodded.

"Ourselves." Mimi's answer came out in two strident voices. Abruptly she turned away and hunched over the controls.

The engine buzzed to life, but Toori couldn't think about the takeoff until she had a proper answer. "What do you mean, reaching for ourselves?" She patted her chest with her upper fingers and her belly with her lower fingers. "We're right here, aren't we?"

Mimi just smiled and turned back to her work.

Once *The Reach* left Orpa's surface, Toori's mind drifted from the conversation. She'd been on smaller air ships many times—Mimi was an aeronautics engineer, after all—but riding in this giant vessel was a whole new thrill. She gasped as the lavender clouds swallowed them up. "This is amazing!" she called out. "Why does everyone think we're going to be too scared to do this mission?"

Noticing how busy Mimi was at the controls, Toori didn't worry that she wasn't answering. *The Reach* rose higher.

A serious voice came through the intercom. "*Reach,* come in."

"*Reach* here," replied Mimi.

"All systems online?"

"Affirmative."

"Attaining orbital velocity?"

"Nearly there." Mimi paused, peering at the digital numbers blurring past on a monitor. "Aaand...orbital velocity attained."

The Reach pulled upward, challenging Orpa's gravity. Out the windows Toori watched swirls of purple and gray clouds drop away like fragments of spun sugar. She pictured the openness of space and swallowed down a lump of fear. "I can't wait to see Raya City from up there," she said, determined to stay more curious than scared.

Mimi and the command center talked back and forth. They never said anything interesting, but the sound of contact with life on the ground gave solace like a warm blanket. Toori had almost been lulled to sleep when a surprising sentence jolted her awake.

"Leaving comms range," said the voice on the intercom. "Are you sure about this, *Reach*?"

Even scarier was how Mimi didn't answer right away. Toori could see her mother's flesh vibrate.

"Um...I..." Mimi stammered.

A battle started up inside Toori's brain. Part of her was thrilled. She ached to find out what it was like to cut the tether with Orpa. But the part that was curious quickly got swallowed up. "Mimi! I'm scared! I want to go home!"

Mimi turned around, all three of her eyes yellow with panic. "Okay, yeah. We should go back down," she said through clenched upper teeth. At the same time, her lower mouth spoke into the communicator: "*Reach* returning to base."

"Good idea," said ground control. He sounded relieved, too.

"Oh, thank you, Mimi," Toori whimpered. Her relief almost drowned out that little voice in her head, but it still insisted, "Keep going. Find something new."

The ride back to the air base was awkwardly silent. They didn't even look at each other the whole way back. The closer they came to the surface of Orpa, the worse Toori felt. By the time they landed, she hated herself and the entire Lemp species.

Mama ran toward them when they disembarked. She wrapped her arms around the two of them and wailed. Toori let the hug go on too long.

"Oh, sweethearts," Mama gushed, "I'm so glad you turned around." She pulled Mimi closer and whispered, although Toori could still hear. "Let's just cancel the whole trip. I'm sure there's some other family who could go. Why do *we* have to be the ones who experiment?"

When Mama bent forward, Mimi pressed the top of her head to Mama's. "Maybe you're right," Mimi whispered in a shaky voice.

"No!" Suddenly the brave voice in Toori's head wasn't so quiet. It grew to boiling, making her shout out its rage. "No! What's wrong with us? We both were dying to leave comms range. But as soon as we were about to, we lost our nerve."

"What could we do?" Mimi asked. "It's who we are."

Toori felt betrayed. "You've been working on this since I was little. But you always knew it wouldn't work?!"

"Because we become afraid," Mama finished for her. "According to our nature."

"Then what's the point of even trying anything?" Toori sobbed. She wanted to run away, but the cocoon Mama and Mimi had formed around her was too comforting.

"Come on, my explorer," Mimi said in two voices, as if a nickname could lift the mood. "Let's go home."

For the next few days, Toori's spirit drooped. Mama made her favorite foods, Mimi sang her favorite songs. Still she moped, wondering if it was worth doing anything, knowing she'd always get too scared to finish.

The school days dragged on and nothing interested her.

"Well, *this* day should improve your mood," Mama said much too brightly one morning.

"Why?" Toori asked, poking at her breakfast pudding.

"Well, for one thing, Mimi's at the spaceport, planning modifications for *The Reach*."

Young Adventurers

Toori's anger flared. "Why bother?" She shoved her bowl away.

Mama wrapped her many flat fingers around Toori's arm. "Just because we have this...this *thing* in our nature—" she tapped her head— "it doesn't mean we should give up. We have to keep pushing, finding out what we're capable of."

Toori pictured the spaceship Mimi had designed. "*The Reach,*" she whispered, finally understanding its name. Feeling a little more hopeful, she stood up. "I'd better go to school."

"Okay, sweetheart. Enjoy your field trip."

"My what?"

"To see the diamond bugs."

"Oh, hey!" Toori had completely forgotten. "Maybe this *will* be a nice day!"

When her class transpod reached the Reppin Meadows, the ground already sparkled here and there. The students tossed out crumbled, dried millasti bark, the diamond bugs' favorite food. Soon the meadow glowed like the sky on a cloudless night.

Mepro, the troublemaker, raised two arms. "Teacher?"

Emto called on him with a nervous squint. "What's your question, Mepro?"

"Teacher, where do the diamond bugs live? They don't hang out in the grass all day, right? Do they have apartments, or what?"

Most of the other kids laughed, but Toori could tell Emto wanted to take the question seriously. "Follow me," he said with a mysterious air, "and I'll show you." He addressed Toori, who walked next to him across the field. "I'll bet you didn't know about this when you were here before." Emto paused to point at a tree.

Bursting with curiosity, Toori peered into a knot in the trunk.

"Tell the class what you see," Emto instructed her.

But she couldn't speak. She was completely mesmerized by the hundreds—maybe thousands—of gleaming diamond bugs filling the tree.

"Amazing, isn't it?" Emto laughed with his upper mouth while saying with his lower, "They never stop shining. No matter what. And the shells are unbreakable. Scientists have tried crushing them, burning them, dissolving them. But they can't be destroyed or dimmed."

"What makes them shiny?" asked another girl peeking into the tree.

"No one knows."

"Ha. You're the teacher," cracked Mepro. "You're supposed to know stuff we ask about. You're gonna get fired." Toori wished he'd be quiet, but he pushed his way through to the front of the line and said more idiotic things while he looked at the bugs. "We could catch 'em, use 'em for decorations. Cool live crawling jewelry!" He reached one hand into the crevice.

Emto rushed toward him. "Mepro, I don't think you'd better..."

Before Emto could finish, Mepro's chest and face were covered in diamond bugs. "Agh! Get them off me!" He scurried backward, swatting at himself with all four arms. Toori and a few other kids tried to help, but he moved so violently they couldn't get near him.

"Try to calm down and stay still," Emto urged.

Instead, Mepro took off across the field, flailing and screaming. Most of the diamond bugs had jumped off, but he didn't seem to notice.

"I'll go see if he's all right," Emto said grimly. "you guys stay here. And don't touch those shells."

"Nobody has to tell me twice," cracked Toori's friend Nere. The kids huddled together nervously. "Hey, Toori? Toori?"

Toori became aware of Nere calling her name and everybody staring at her. "Yeah?"

"You zoned out," Nere informed her. "You didn't get bitten, did you?"

Toori shook herself to wake up. "No, no. I was just...thinking." The thought she'd been mulling was vague, but it fascinated her. It was just an image at this point: thousands and thousands of diamond bug shells twinkling in the sky. She wasn't sure what it meant, but the vision made her feel safe.

"Hey, dreamer!" Nere poked her with a large toe. "We're leaving. Emto has to take big dummy Mepro to the Health

Center." She curled up her upper set of lips. "He's got gross bites all over."

Nodding numbly, saying something sympathetic, Toori followed Nere across the field toward the transpod. She could not erase the image of glittering diamond bugs splashed across the night sky.

Dinner was tense.

"I'm just not sure this is a good idea after all," Mama admitted, swishing her double straw through the soup. "Maybe we should just stay home."

"We've been over this and over this," Mimi growled. Toori squirmed in her seat, trying to block out her mothers' arguing. Pinching her straw between her upper teeth, Mimi added with her lower mouth, "It's my job to keep trying. Would you prefer I leave the atmosphere and go out of comms range by myself?"

"How dare you even *joke* about that."

"I'm not joking." Mimi pushed her soup away. "We have to learn about space and space travel somehow. So we have to try this."

"No. *Someone* has to try," Mama objected. "It doesn't have to be you. Why does it even have to be a Lemp at all? Why not listen to our nature and stay safe?"

Toori couldn't take any more. "Just stop it!" She wailed with both voices, "Either go or don't go, but stop fighting!" She hurried to her corner of the dwelling, lay down, and rolled toward the wall. Hearing Mimi approach, she grumbled, "I'm fine. Leave me alone, please."

Toori pressed two hands against her central eye and squeezed her outer eyes shut. It was a trick she'd figured out when she was little to make her imagination more vivid and help her organize her thoughts. As sadness made her sleepy, Toori's head filled with a surreal dream.

She saw Mimi and Mama, flying through the blackness of space in *The Reach*. She was there, too, opening a tiny door in the back of the ship. Through this opening she tossed handful after handful of diamond bugs. Catching the light of nearby stars and the sun, the multifaceted shells gleamed brightly. The bugs scurried across the vacuum as if it were a field. With all of space illuminated, the stars seemed to fade and the planet Orpa came clearly into view. Even the clouds around it burned up in the diamond bugs' fiery glow. And Toori, leaning out of *The Reach*, could see everyone on Orpa looking up and waving. Every Lemp, every giant Ganst, even the eyeless little Tegros knew where she was.

After this happy, reassuring dream, Toori woke with a burst of energy, sure she'd found a way to solve their conundrum. It was the middle of the night. Mama and Mimi lay sprawled on their pallet in the far corner. "I'll have to pass them to get to the door," Toori calculated as she stood in the purplish darkness. Their big round feet made Lemps very stable when they stood, but made creeping quite a challenge.

Toori grabbed a large satchel and clutched it in her two right arms. She splayed her fingers on the wall, letting the surface guide and steady her in the dark. Although she stepped as quietly as she could, at one point both her moms snorted and rolled over. Panicked, Toori stayed absolutely still until she heard Mama's rhythmic breathing and the soft sleep-whistle from Mimi's lower mouth. Then, giving up caution for speed, she rushed out of their dwelling.

The night stretched out huge and silent. Toori felt smaller than a diamond bug, hugging her satchel and trying to remember what she was doing outside at that hour. The big idea from her dream was fading. Pressing on her central eye, Toori tried to refocus her goal. "Collect diamond bugs," she told herself. "Use them to light our way through space." But how? She didn't know, but she still felt compelled to go to that field.

Knowing the transpods ran all night, she trotted to the nearest station and waited. She'd been on the pods too many times to be afraid. At Center station she changed to a pod running west out of the city. It didn't take long before the computer voice announced the Reppin Meadows stop.

Toori stepped off the pod and peered toward the meadow. It seemed to roll off the edges of the Allera Hills rising blacker than black beyond it. Countless lights pricked the dark ground.

"There you are," said Toori, opening the top of her satchel and setting one giant foot onto the diamond bugs' territory. During her daytime visits she hadn't been able to tell just how many bugs there were. "Millions," she gasped, watching the field pulse with more points of light than there were stars in all the universe.

Looking down, she warned, "I don't want to step on you."

The bugs must have sensed her foot coming toward them, since dozens of tiny lights hurried out of the way.

"You're smart, aren't you?" Toori laughed. It became a game, watching the bugs hustle away to make room for her foot, step after step. When she did a few twirls, the bugs moved in a big shiny spiral around her. "Is this what it feels like to be the center of the galaxy?" she called out, spinning joyously. It seemed that the stars spun too, mirroring the field of sparkly shells.

Toori danced. The diamond bugs danced. The stars danced. It was a glorious, glamorous ball. But suddenly Toori's mood sank and she stopped twirling. "I can't capture you," she told the jittery white polka dots around her feet. "What am I doing? You're living things. You'd die if I tossed you out into space."

Her dream seemed more and more ridiculous. "And how did I plan to toss you out? We have to keep the spaceship sealed up, or we'll die!" Toori sat down hard on the scrubby ground, sending the bugs dashing out of harm's way. "And what did I think you would *do* out there in space? Just float around randomly until the end of time?" She grasped at the dirt with all four sets of fingers. "It was just a silly dream."

She looked around desperately at the bugs backing away from her frantic energy. All but one. A single diamond bug shone all alone near Toori's lower left hand. She leaned over it, concerned. "What's wrong with you, little guy? Go play with your friends."

The bug started to limp away. "No, wait!" Toori begged. "Maybe I can help you." She reached to pick up the sickly creature, but stopped herself. "No. Don't want to end up in the Health Center with Mepro the dope."

Toori's Constellation

She followed the bug. The others cleared a path for it through the nubby grasses. Haltingly the loner made its way to a sharp rock jutting from the ground. A glowing horizontal light showed Toori a wide crevice under the rock. That's where the bug headed, dropping down and out of sight.

"Where's it going?" Toori asked the others. They stayed away, leaving a wide swath of empty ground in front of the crevice. "What are you afraid of?" Curiosity gripped Toori. After pushing the stone out of the way, she flopped onto her belly to take a look.

Diamond bugs. Thousands. Maybe even millions. The shells lit an underground cave with a blinding glare. It hurt her central eye, which she covered with one hand. By half-shutting her other two eyes she could just make out a surprising fact about the mountain of diamond bugs:

"They're not moving." The words came through her upper mouth, muted and somber. She poked in two fingers. The bugs in the cavern did not scatter. She reached farther in, stretching so she could grab a single shell. With great excitement she pulled it out. But then she let her fist clamp shut and with both mouths she shrieked, "Dead! They're all dead!"

Fear bubbled up like the ocean, filling her lungs and throat with the salty tang of terror. Even her brain felt like it was drowning. All that mattered was fleeing.

So Toori ran. Her big feet slapped painfully against the ground. The living diamond bugs drew zig-zagging blurs all around her. Fortunately the transpod was just arriving. Panting as she took a seat, Toori realized she'd left her satchel in the field.

"Scared again. Not fair," she grumbled into her lower hands while her upper hands covered her central eye. A hard lump touched her face. Pulling her hand back, she found that she was still clutching the dead diamond bug. She stared into its glow until the pod pulled up at her neighborhood stop.

A surprise waited on the platform: both her mothers, faces frantic, leafy fingers splayed and shaking. They lurched toward her as she stepped off the pod.

"Oh, you're safe!" wailed Mama.

Mimi wrapped all her arms around Toori. "We didn't know where you were. We were so *afraid*."

The word was like poison on Toori's skin. She squirmed away, shuddering. "Of course you were afraid," she growled bitterly. "What else could we ever be?"

Even knowing it would hurt their feelings, she didn't wait for her moms, but ran ahead and let herself into their dwelling. The metal door slammed behind her, crashing against its metal frame. Toori rushed to her pallet and lay face down. Her skin quivered with stress when she heard her moms enter.

"Don't want to talk about it," she called out preemptively.

She recognized Mama's footfalls, lighter than Mimi's. "What's wrong, sweetheart?" Mama asked. Gently, through only her top mouth. "How can we help?"

The sound of Mama's voice was so soothing that Toori rolled to face her. Mama squatted next to the pallet. Near the dinner table stood Mimi, wringing all her leafy fingers and shifting her weight back and forth.

Behind Mimi was a string lamp, one of Mama's old inventions. It captured and agitated light photons near it, making them glow in a trail up to the ceiling.

Toori looked from Mama to Mimi to the string lamp. Her brain raced.

"Please, sweetheart, answer me," Mama urged.

"Huh?" Toori started at the sensation of Mama's fingers on her head. "What did you ask me?"

Mimi stepped up and spoke sharply. "We wanted to know where you were, of course. And why you left."

"Let's ask one question at a time," said Mama.

But Toori didn't care how many questions they asked. The string lamp had given her all the answers. She sat up, talking excitedly. "I went back to the Reppin Meadows, where our class went earlier today. See, I had this dream." She moved her hands before her eyes, wiping away the dream. "No, never mind that part. The main thing is, I figured out how to make it work."

"How to make what work?" Mimi asked.

"Us going into space. Without getting scared." Toori smiled at her astonished parents. "We just need a string of lights, so

Toori's Constellation

everyone here on Orpa knows where we are, even when we're out of comms range."

Mama and Mimi exchanged the type of glance that said, "How do we break it to her?"

"No, it'll work," Toori insisted.

But Mimi bowed her head sadly. "There are no lights for that job," said her top mouth, while her bottom mouth explained, "We can't generate power along a wire for thousands of miles. And anyway, all the lights would break. Space is a harsh environment."

"What if we had lights that don't break and don't need electricity?"

"That sounds more like magic than astrophysics."

"Let our daughter explain," Mama ordered.

Mimi took a breath. "Okay. Tell us what you mean, Toori."

Toori opened her hand to show them the diamond bug shell. It gleamed, lighting the corner near her pillow. "They're indestructible. And they always glow, no matter what."

"It's beautiful," sighed Mama.

When Mimi unfurled the fingers of one hand, Toori placed the shell in her palm. "It's got an amazing construction," she admitted, squinting into the glow. "But even if it could withstand space, we'd need millions of these for them to be seen. We'd have to slaughter every single diamond bug on Orpa. Kind of cruel and irresponsible, don't you think?"

Toori tried to swallow her impatience. "I don't mean we'd *kill* them. *Ob*viously."

"Then tell us what you *do* mean," Mama encouraged her, taking the shell from Mimi's hand. "What do you have in mind?"

Toori told them about the gleaming underground cave beneath the Reppin Meadows. "It's where they go to die. I bet they always have, since the very first diamond bug."

Mimi pursed the lips of her lower mouth, the way she did when she was hopeful but skeptical. "Okay. Say there really are a million shells. Say they really will glow forever in space. How would we use them? Attach them to the ship?"

Young Adventurers

Toori pictured it clearly. She looked at Mama, not Mimi, and answered. "We could make a string of them with your Infinity wire."

For a few seconds, nobody spoke. Then Mimi put one arm around Mama and another around Toori. "I sometimes don't even know which of you two is smarter. All I can do is build things that fly. My darling ladies get all the amazing, creative ideas!"

Six big smiles beamed at each other like diamond bugs in a field at night.

The project took half a year. It seemed that every person in Raya City, from kids to senior citizens, helped in some way.

"Exploring without Fear" became the space program's new slogan.

Backhoes plunged into the hoards of diamond shells, piling them onto transpo-flats to cart away. Since every shell was vital, children helped gather up the ones that fell out and scattered on the ground.

And then there was the unbreakable Infinity wire. The city built a factory at the foot of Mount Gil, just to make the wire. Although she'd been retired for years, Mama returned to oversee the factory. The biggest challenge was figuring out where to coil the wire as it was created. Mile after mile after mile piled up, first on the factory floor, then in its yard, then in the valley below the mountain.

The entire army gathered to tie shells to the wire. Soldiers donned goggles to protect their eyes—one, two, or three lenses, depending on the species—from the blinding sheen. The wire ties had to be made in a newly-designed machine, since there was no way to cut a longer piece into bits.

"This could circle Orpa a hundred times," Toori heard a soldier say.

"Try two hundred," said another.

Toori knew the number was more like a thousand.

One day the factory manager said to Mama, "I know we're drilling one end of the wire through the base of Mount Gil. But how will we get all the rest of the wire into the rocket?"

Toori's Constellation

Toori, working nearby organizing the shell-tying teams, knew the answer. "We'll attach it to *The Reach*. That way, when we fly, we'll uncoil it behind us." Looking at Mama she admitted, "I don't know how we get the wire to the rocket."

Mama's lower mouth frowned as her upper responded. "Maybe we leave the pile here, but pull one end to the launch field."

When Toori pictured that she saw the problem right away. "We'd end up with miles and miles of the world's strongest wire stretching across the city. We'd wreck whole buildings."

"True enough," sighed Mama. "Then I guess we'll bring the rocket here.

Launch day drew the biggest crowds anyone in Raya City could remember. People of every species stood together, waving hands (or in some cases, claws or flippers) to cheer on Toori's family. Calls of encouragement wafted through the air to the platform where Toori and her moms waited to board.

"You're so brave!"

"Learn lots for all of us!"

"Wish I could go with you, but I'd never have the nerve!"

Toori spotted Emto, her teacher, waving at her. She waved back, then turned north, toward the Reppin Meadows. "Thank you," she said to all the diamond bugs that ever were.

The Reach blasted up through the clouds. They took half an orbit around Orpa before rising just beyond the atmosphere. "We'll go out of comms range soon," Mimi warned.

"Oh, my," said Mama.

Toori fought back against the panic building inside her. "They'll be able to see us, right?"

"That's the plan," replied Mimi, "as you know."

No one had anything else to say. The broadcast voice from Orpa kept on chattering. That voice was such a comfort! Toori saw in her parents' faces and in the way their skin quivered that the fear had them just like it had her. The curse of their species.

The Reach roared as they pulled away from Orpa's gravity. "Central, this is *Reach*". Mimi's double voice shook. "Leaving comms range, Central."

"No, you're really not, *Reach*," said the voice on comms.

Toori sat up.

Gasping, Mama gripped her armrests. "What does that mean? What's wrong with the ship?"

"Please explain, Central." Toori could tell that Mimi struggled to keep her voice even. "Readouts say we're going out of range."

There was a pause before Central answered. "We can see the shells glowing, *Reach*. It's working. We'll be able to track you along that wire, even when we can no longer hear you."

"That's wonderful news, Central!" Mimi cried. "Keep an eye out for us."

"We've already named it, *Reach*."

"Named what, Central?"

"Your wire. It looks like a sweeping line of sparkles in the night sky. We're calling it Toori's Constellation. Good luck, *Reach*. Central out."

Mama stretched from her harnessed seat to touch Toori's arm. "Oh, we're so proud of you."

Toori was proud, too. And eager to have an adventure, any kind of adventure, even if it only lasted the length of a wire. But mostly she was grateful not to feel afraid.

Young Adventurers

A dark future overrun with aliens drives a courageous girl into a futuristic retelling of an old fairy tale…but will she survive it?

THE HACK-JACK PROSPECT

Chantal Boudreau

Jaq couldn't remember a time when the city hadn't been overshadowed by the platforms. She couldn't recall a life without poverty either, perpetually in dirt and darkness. Only those turncoats who worked for the sky-giants, sacrificing their own kind to the invaders to save their hides and live a slightly better life, ever saw the light. While she might not be a full-on warrior, she had been raised better than that. She fought the sky-giants in her own way, from the shadows.

Not that she had had much opportunity to do them any damage in her short life, only a teen, but she dreamed of finding a way to avenge her parents someday. The sky-giants had taken her father when she had been hardly old enough to understand what was happening and her mother had struggled to keep herself and Jaq alive from that moment on. The brave woman had done everything but sell herself on the street, taking graveyards shifts that no one else would work in order to keep a roof over their heads and put food on the table. She had been on her way home from one of her late-night toils when a hack-jack addict had mugged her for what little she had on her, killing her in the process.

That had left poor little Jacqueline on her own. She likely would have either starved or been dragged into the kiddie porn trade had it not been for "Mom". That was what all of the hack-jackers in her ring called their matron, a broad woman with shoulders like a quarterback, slicked back graying hair, steely gray eyes and a jaw set in a permanent scowl. Nobody messed with Mom if they knew what was good for them. Even the rebellious ones like Jaq did what Mom told them to do for the sake of avoiding her wrath.

The first thing Mom had done after taking Jacqueline in was shorten her name. All the runners had to have a tag and Mom kept them to a single syllable, so they'd be easier to shout. Considering Jacqueline's actual name and the fact she was a jacker, Jaq made perfect sense as a moniker.

Along with the new tag had come her jack port implant, since she couldn't run the network without it, as well as the wrist monitor that would keep her from overstaying her time spent jacked in. Those who uplinked for too long became addicts like the man who had killed Jaq's mother, techno zombies who would do anything to get their next net fix. Mom didn't want any of her runners lost to addiction and Jaq didn't want that either, so she always kept within the advisable limits and jacked out when the alarm went off on her monitor.

Jaq hardly spent any time on the legit network anymore, but mainly ran on the underground one Mom had set up. Most of her work was done online, carrying code from one place to another, but there were exceptions. When Mom needed to set up a new client on her network, it wasn't safe to send the key code over the legit net. There were too many scouts watching for that type of illegal fare there.

Cow, short for Cash Cow, was what Mom called her key code, one that gave security clearance for a new client to establish themselves as a vendor or buyer in her underground network. Once there, a jacker could do anything that wasn't allowed on the legit network, without having to worry about getting caught by the sky-giant scouts. It was almost like living old-world when they still had a free net.

The problem was getting the code to a new add in the first place. In order to do that, Mom would have to send out one of her runners real-world. That presented a whole new range of dangers, everything from street criminals and hack-jack addicts to policing agents of the sky-giants. Mom saved this task for her stealthiest runners and Jaq was one of her best.

Jaq woke one morning hungrier than usual. It was no surprise considering the civic rations they were given were barely enough

The Hack-Jack Prospect

to stave off starvation and their delivery of that month's rations were already two days late. Jaq's hack-jack friend, Queue, had told her the sky-giants did that on purpose, to keep them weak and docile and to remind them who was boss. Jaq wouldn't have put that past them, considering what they had done to her family.

Mom had decided she would have to resort to buying some black market MREs to tide them over, but she needed cash to do that, and that meant picking up a new client. She startled Jaq from sleep with her usual bark, shrill and resonating.

"Jaq!"

The thin girl scrambled to her feet, brushing her mop of tangled black hair away from her eyes. Mom gestured at her with one of the carrier bags they used for safe transport of a Cow.

"I need you to bust your ass over to Lower Market Square. There's a money launderer there willing to pay for access to my network. He needs a Cow. Goes by the name of Remi. If you want to guarantee you eat tonight, you better hop to it. I've heard the monthly rations might be delayed for up to another two days."

That was longer than the sky-giants had ever starved them to date. Mom's crew had finished the last scraps in the house the night before, leftovers of leftovers that hadn't made much of a dent in their hunger. Jaq had awoken to a grumbling belly and couldn't bear the thought that she might have to wait two more days to be fed. She didn't like seeing the rest of the crew suffer either.

"I'll go," Jaq acknowledged, taking the Cow carrier from Mom. "But I want the biggest share of supper tonight. Running on an empty stomach when you're hack-jacking the network is hard enough, running like that real-world sucks the life out of you."

"As long as there's no slacking" Mom conceded. "Now get out there."

Jaq grabbed the carrier and lit off through the slum they called home. The door the runners used to slip out the back was little more than a cat-flap, but if they were caught, Mom didn't want it to be easy for the sky-giant agents to trace their prisoner back to her rat-hole.

Jaq didn't fear the outside like some of the hack-jackers did. She was agile and could deftly skirt the shadows until she reached her destination. Her dark hair and complexion made for good camouflage. Hiding was a synch.

Racing through the smog-choked alleyways, Jaq made her way to the Lower Market Square. She was all set to root out this Remi, hand off the Cow and retrieve the pay-off, but fate had other plans for her. She came to a sudden stop as she rounded the corner to the square in question, scenes of chaos meeting her startled gaze. A building was on fire, demolished in places, and the road beneath it was swarming with sky-giant agents.

"Hey–kid! Over here."

A loud whisper from beside a dumpster drew her attention. She slipped over to it quietly, hoping the stranger who had called to her might be the Remi she had been sent to find.

It wasn't.

Remi was a businessman, of sorts, but the person who had appealed to her was clearly a hack-jacker like her. He looked to be a couple of years older than she was, half again as big and more street worn, his hair spiked and his skin littered with piercings and tattoos. He bore a port similar to her own.

"I wouldn't go near that mess if I were you. They'll drag you in for questioning as a possible 'eye-witness' and then they'll find reasons to hold you indefinitely."

Jaq hadn't intended on getting any closer. She knew better. The stranger continued.

"Someone snitched on a member of the resistance–a local money launderer. They raided his apartment. I don't think there was much left of him when they were done."

Jaq's heart sank and her belly rumbled. "Money launderer? He wouldn't happen to be named Remi?"

The hack-jacker nodded.

"Damn," she groaned.

"You were here to see Remi too?"

Jaq didn't answer, but that confirmed she was.

"What was he buying?" he asked.

The Hack-Jack Prospect

She wasn't about to admit to someone she didn't know from Adam that she was running illegal code. He happened to open up to her first.

"The name's Click. I was here to drop some code that only someone like Remi would want. I was looking for hard cash, but right now I'll take anything. I'm not a seller. I'm just a freelance runner. I don't have the right connections, but if someone did, this would be worth wads."

Jaq's eyes lit up at the prospect. Mom would be upset that she hadn't been able to offload the Cow to Remi and even though it wasn't Jaq's fault, Mom might just shoot the messenger. If Jaq could work a better deal with someone else, all would be forgiven.

"Whatchya got? Maybe we can arrange a trade?" Click offered.

"I got Mom's Cow."

"Oh–sweet! I could use that. It would make running online a hell of a lot safer. I can only make quick runs right now, but one of these days the scouts are going to catch up to me. I'd give my left nut for a Cow."

Jaq snorted, but shook her head nevertheless.

"I can't give this to you without Mom's permission," she insisted. "She doesn't want freelance runners on her own personal net. You'll be robbing her of her cut for the jobs you get instead of her crew of runners. She won't like that one bit."

She turned to go, but Click grabbed her arm.

"Not so fast. The code I have here could earn her ten to twenty times what she'd lose in her cut because of you giving me Cow. There are several folks in the resistance with deep pockets who would pay a pretty penny for what I've got." He held up a chip like no other Jaq had ever seen, sealed in a jeweled-finish case. "You're looking at Magic Bean."

Jaq scrunched up her nose. She had never heard of it.

"It's some sort of sky-giant key code," Click told her. "It'll let you get through their security. I don't know exactly how, Remi did, but what matters is the people who want it will know how to use it. The Magic Bean is an underground goldmine. All

I'm asking for is a straight up trade, just so I can cover my losses. What do you say?"

Jaq was torn. They wouldn't be able to eat this Magic Bean code, which meant unless Mom could come up with another new client, they'd go hungry again that night. But she couldn't go home empty-handed and if this Magic Bean was as lucrative as Click suggested, Mom might be grateful for the trade.

"Alright...I'm in - my Cow for your Magic Bean. But if you're screwing me over, I'll find you on Mom's net and you'll pay. I mean it."

Click shrugged and handed her the chip. "No worries."

She pulled the Cow out of her carrier bag and made the exchange. Then they both made themselves scarce.

When Jaq arrived home she crept in quietly, hesitant to reveal her deal to Mom. On the way back, Jaq had decided that it might not have been such a good idea after all, but it was too late to change her mind. Hiding it from Mom was only postponing the inevitable.

Mom could sense something wrong the moment she laid eyes on Jaq.

"Where are my credits?" the stern woman demanded.

"Remi wasn't available. He had been raided by sky-giant agents. They had already razed his place by the time I got there."

Mom sighed and gestured for Jaq to hand over the carrier bag. She did so reluctantly. Without pause, Mom opened the flap. A frown settled over her face. She yanked out the jewelled-finish case.

"What the hell is this? Where's my Cow?"

"That's what I needed to tell you. The opportunity presented itself for profit. I traded for something better than Cow. That's sky-giant code...Magic Bean. It can get you past their security. You can pawn that off to the resistance for a hell of a lot more than Remi would have given you for Cow. I know it won't buy us supplies as is, but on the black market ..."

"You do know the sky-giants have moles in the resistance? They'll ignore things like Cow for bigger things, but they won't ignore something like this. If I try to sell this, I may as well paint a target on my back that screams 'I'm helping the resistance.' No

The Hack-Jack Prospect

way. Mom and her crew stay neutral. Taking on the sky-giants, as much as I would like to take them down and reclaim our world, is too much of a risk for little folk like us. Let's just stick to the underground." Mom dropped the jeweled-finish case into a wastebasket and pointed at the door. "I don't want to see your face for a few hours. Who knows how much money you just cost us by putting Cow into unvetted hands. You better hope I can find a replacement for Remi and get a new copy of Cow to them. More than likely, we're going hungry tonight."

"But...!" Jaq protested, but Mom raised a hand to silence the girl, shaking her head with the opposite hand on her hip.

"No 'but's. End of discussion. Make yourself scarce."

Jaq knew better than to argue with Mom when she assumed that pose, her already grim perma-scowl darkening even more. The hack-jacker skulked around the alleyways until nightfall and then quietly slipped into bed, the grumbling ache of her empty belly now just a persistent numbness that made her realize she had gone beyond basic hunger to the beginnings of starvation. She hoped a good night's sleep would help her shake some of the accompanying weakness.

She did not, however, manage to sleep in the next morning, awoken by a violent glare piercing the darkness of her room in the wee hours of dawn. It had entered the gloom of her tiny space through the tiny hole in her wall she liked to consider her window, and she wondered at first if Mom and her crew were to be the next victims of a sky-giant raid. The light was too blindingly bright to be the product of a sky-giant light stick, or even several, and it also glowed oddly opalescent. Since she couldn't gauge the source from her room, she scrambled into the hallway beyond her door to investigate from some other viewpoint, almost colliding with Queue in the process. His face was white with fear.

"Did you see that?!" Jaq gasped.

"Yeah–I was coming to get you because of it. You'll never believe what that is," the ginger-haired boy said as he pointed up the hallway towards their running exit route.

The pair piled out of their cat-flap door and stood in the alleyway which had been invaded by an enormous tubular beam of light, ascending into the sky. Jaq gazed up at it with wide eyes, awestruck.

"A beam? Here? How?"

The beams were part of the sky-giant beam-stock, their transportation system allowing them to travel between their sky platforms and the human cities below them.

"Mom asked me to run a job for her online, but it was a quick jog and drop and then I had some extra time left on my monitor while I was jacked in. I noticed a chip in a fancy case in the trash and it had me curious, so I plugged it in. I wondered why Mom would be throwing anything like that away. The next thing I know I'm facing a complex key code that needed just a little manipulating to open an unknown pathway into the net. I hacked it like a pro, and then suddenly there's a 'flash!' This beam opens up. I don't know about you, but I think it calls for some exploring."

Jaq smiled a wicked grin. She couldn't agree more. Then she noticed Queue's wrist monitor flickering.

"Queue, how long were you jacked in?"

He glanced down at his wrist, his face falling immediately. "I guess it was longer than I thought. I got so caught up in the hack, I lost track of time. Jeez, Jaq, I can't go back in right now..."

"No kidding." Jaq grabbed his arm and jostled him towards the direction of his room. "You're going to need to stay offline for a couple of days. Go get some rest. I'll have to handle this by myself."

"By yourself?"

She shrugged the idea off and waved him towards his room again. Reluctantly, her friend did as he was told and left her to explore the beam on her own.

"Wow," she murmured, once alone. "I never thought I'd see the day when I'd be running the beam-stock."

Mom would be fit to be tied if she knew one of her hack-jackers was about to take such a risk, but Jaq didn't care. As far as she knew, only the sky-giants and their agents ever used the beams for transport. She would be a first.

She stepped tentatively into the beam and waited.

The Hack-Jack Prospect

Two things that followed took her by surprise. The first was her sudden ascent, carried rapidly upwards by unseen forces. The second was an instant connection with the sky-giant network, online without being physically jacked in. Jaq hoped this wouldn't be a problem. If she didn't manage to go offline when she needed to, no longer a matter of simply jacking-out again, it could result in some negative long-term effects. She would have to watch her monitor closely.

Before she knew it, she was standing on a sky platform, surrounded by sky-giant structures of varying heights and widths. The sight took her breath away, seeing the sun for the very first time where it peeked in through the buildings looming over her. She also noticed the air was unusually clean, drawing in deep, satisfying breaths that left her feeling light-headed.

"Now that I'm here, what do I do?" she asked.

"What do you require?" a voice said in her head. It was a network guide. Jaq had heard of those. She immediately thought of her numb and empty belly.

"Food, I need food," she responded.

"I'll provide you with co-ordinates to the closest replicator," the guide told her.

A map appeared before her online, directing her to one of the sky-giant structures. Jaq followed it, noting at how clean the streets were compared to those of the city below. The sky platform was a paradise in comparison.

As she approached the huge door, Jaq wondered how she would ever get through it, but the doors sensors had been reprogrammed to recognize humans to allow free passage for the servants they had claimed from below. Their ability to ride the beams had been restricted, so that only trusted sky-giant agents with security clearance could travel freely back and forth, but other than specifically sky-giant only areas, that was the extent of human limitation.

Thanks to the Magic Bean, Jaq had the desired clearance. The sky-giant network viewed her as a trusted agent, with the same freedoms and privileges. Mom really had missed the true potential of her trade. But Jaq wasn't about to.

Once inside, she made her way to the replicator. When it requested her order, she decided on bacon and eggs along with a serving of juice. They rarely got those things as part of her rations and she craved protein and fat more than anything else. The smell of it, when the replicator opened, made her feel faint, her hunger then truly hitting home.

Jaq tried to pace herself, knowing if she ate too quickly, she would likely make herself sick. As she was eating, it occurred to her that she wasn't well-groomed nor dressed in the neutral-colored clothing common to the human servants the sky-giants had taken to their lairs. That was why Jaq started when an actual servant came in behind her. The mousy looking woman jumped too.

"Before you call out the alarm, would you like to get back down to the city?" Jaq asked.

The woman nodded, but she still looked frightened.

"I have the code that can get you home, but only if you help me," Jaq told her.

"I wasn't planning on exposing you. There's a sky-giant on his way, following behind me. If you don't hide right away, he'll catch you for sure...and you don't want to know what he'll do to you." The servant glanced over her shoulder, trembling.

"Hide where?"

"Get in the replicator. I'll keep him away from you. The sky-giants rarely use the replicators; they just order us to fetch things for them. They are three times our size, but they still expect us to do their heavy lifting."

Jaq scurried into the replicator, peeking out under the bottom of the cover so she could get a glimpse of the sky-giant. She had never seen one before and her curiosity was too strong to ignore. The servant stood in front of the replicator to prevent detection but Jaq's view wasn't completely obscured by this gesture. She didn't have to wait long.

Seconds after she had squeezed her way into the replicator, the door into the chamber opened and what Jaq could only assume was a sky-giant clicked in. It reminded her of some sort of bizarre splicing of a ridiculously huge praying mantis and a puffer fish. Despite its intimidatingly-large size it moved with

The Hack-Jack Prospect

grace and purpose, its elongated spiny limbs tasting the air as it went. When it spoke, breathy sounds passed into the translator it wore, aspirated noises sounding like "fee"s, "fi"s, "fo"s and the odd "fum". The robotic voice of the translator shared the sky-giant's thoughts with his servant so she could understand.

"I smell human food. Why? I did not give you leave to eat, slave."

"You know I can't access the replicator without your permission. One of the agents passed through here when I arrived. He had fabricated a meal. Some of the smell lingers," she lied.

"Hmph–must have just come back from earth-side. There's a stink like human city here too. I want you to get rid of the stench while I go cleanup for supper. I have another slave on his way with fresh meat. We caught ourselves a member of the resistance yesterday, so the meal's going to be extra special."

Jaq wondered if that meant what she thought it meant. She had heard rumors that if the humans the sky-giants took weren't deemed suitable for servants, they became food for the invaders. Were they to catch her running around a lair uninvited, they might consider her fresh meat too–hence the servant's warning.

As soon as he had clicked away again the servant who had hidden Jaq dragged her out of the replicator.

"You can't stay. We'll have to get you out the back way. If you're here when he gets back, you're done for. Whatever code you have won't do you any good then."

The servant grabbed Jaq by the hand and ran with her down the hallway. They hadn't gotten very far when she stopped abruptly. A familiar clicking sound resonated from around the corner.

"He must have circled around," she gasped. "We'll have to hide in here."

The frightened woman dove through an adjacent door, pulling Jaq along after her. It took the combined strength of two of them to swing it closed, it was that large and unwieldy, and unlike the main door, it did not open automatically at her prompting. While the servant caught her breath, Jaq scanned the room, accustomed

Young Adventurers

to making quick breaks for sanctuary and unfazed by the whole ordeal.

"Where are we?" she asked. Although alien-looking in design, she recognized what was likely a computer in the room, but none of the other items scattered about seemed familiar in any way.

"We're in my master's tech room. This is where he does some of his work and communicates with others of his kind. He also stores his more valuable tech devices here. I'm not supposed to be in here. He won't venture here until he's done with his meal, so it's safe for now."

Jaq eyed the computer. It was far larger than anything she had jacked into before, but as long as she could access the port and had her key code, she could probably figure her way around the system, given enough time. Unfortunately, time was one thing that was limited.

"Slave!"

The sky-giant bellowed upon reaching his dining area and discovering his servant was no longer there.

"I have to go," she insisted, a quaver in her voice.

"But the key code. I need to share it with you..." Jaq didn't want to leave her savior without the promised Magic Bean.

The woman pushed her hair back to reveal a port. "You could transfer it, if you have a person to person jack."

"You're a jacker too?" Jaq's face fell. "I don't have one on me. Damn–why can't I have something like that around when I need one?"

"Perhaps I can be of service," a robotic voice spoke from behind them, almost making Jaq jump out of her skin.

"What's that?" she asked.

"A mobile replicator," her new friend replied. "They are rare and extremely valuable because of their AI programming. That's why my master stores his in here, for safe keeping."

"I am the AU-G00Z model, specifically," it said with a beep. "Do you need me to replicate said person to person jack? I've accessed the schematics from the network." It directed its question at Jaq, since the servant did not have the authority to use its functions.

The Hack-Jack Prospect

"Yes...sure. If you can. Make me one of those."

The robot shuddered for a few seconds and then spit up the double jacked cord requested. Jaq gaped at it for a moment before snatching up its offering. She looked over at the servant, her face betraying her amazement.

"What else can it make?" Jaq asked.

"Almost anything that already exists, as long as the schematics are available via the network." the woman told her. "Can we hurry this up? If I don't get back to my master, he'll come looking for me and chances are he'll find you this time."

Jaq obliged her, jacking into her port as quickly as she could and sharing the code before jacking out again.

"This means you're free," Jaq said. "Do whatever you need to do to distract that sky-giant and then get this code to as many of the other humans on this platform as you can before you get lost." She pressed the jack cord into the startled woman's hand. "Then I suggest you scram from this platform while you still can. I have a plan, and if it works, this place is going to end up dangerously unstable before this day is through. You'll be safer back in the city."

"Be careful," was the last thing the servant had to say before abandoning Jaq to her proposed work. She eyed the lofty computer, wondering how she was going to reach the jack for full access. She looked over at AU-G00Z as it beeped and whirred.

"Can you give me a boost?"

"Physical, financial, chemical..." it began to prattle before Jaq interrupted.

"Up to the jack on this terminal. I want to get online." She assumed the network accessed via the terminal required higher security clearance than the general sky platform network available without being wired in, otherwise there wasn't much point to it. She hoped the Magic Bean would be enough to grant her access.

AU-G00Z hoisted Jaq up to within reach of the port and perched from this precarious position, she jacked in. A security matrix confronted her upon entry but fortunately, the code she possessed was able to decrypt and negate it.

The sky giant network was as large as the invaders were, so big Jaq feared losing herself in it. She had never run anything that size before, usually keeping to Mom's much smaller illegitimate series of servers. She wasn't even sure what she was looking for, although it would primarily be the means of support for the sky platform over her city and some way of hacking into it.

Her search eventually led her to the beam-stock system which was tied to the energy sources fuelling the anti-gravity generators. Those generators kept the sky-platform suspended over the city. If she could find a way to disrupt either the energy flow or the general function of the anti-gravity platforms, she could cause the sky platform to topple and its sky-giant residents along with it.

The system had the most complex and intricate coding Jaq had ever encountered and she almost gave up the hack without even really trying. But she reminded herself that she had never turned away from a challenge in her life and she motivated herself further by imagining Queue taunting her for being such a chicken. With a little more enthusiasm, she dove into the code and started to work at unweaving it, searching for ways to sever links and weaken the code's basic structure. If her hacking attempts did enough damage, there would be no correcting it before the platform destabilized. That was her hope, anyway.

About three-quarters of her way through deciphering the code in order to scramble it, a shrill beeping disrupted her concentration. Her wrist monitor–it warned her that she was approaching the time advisable to remain jacked in. Normally, she would have dumped her hack and made a hasty escape, but this was no ordinary situation. Besides, until she could return to the earth's surface, jacking out might not help her situation any.

"Damn! I know you'd kill me Mom, for doing this, but I have to risk staying. I have to finish up. This is too important."

Adrenaline pumping, Jaq chose to ignore the insistent warning and continued her hack, fairly certain it was nearing completion. The buzzy high from staying jacked in as long as she had made her woozy and euphoric, but it also made her work seem easier. Before long, not only had she figured out the code, but she believed she had broken it beyond compare. Now she had scant minutes to evacuate before disaster would surely strike the sky platform.

It took all her willpower to jack-out again, the departure from the network leaving her emptier and unsatisfied, but Jaq managed to do it only because she was aware of the dangers if she didn't. She still had access to the wireless general network, however so she wasn't secure just yet. She had to get back down to the city. She knew, however, that she was too disoriented to find her way out on her own.

"Take me to the nearest beam," she ordered AU-G00Z. "We're getting out of here."

"Out of here...this room?"

"Not just this room. We're going earth-side, as fast as we possibly can."

Things were already going wonky on the platform by the time they reached the beam, the entire floating structure beginning to shimmy and rock. Jaq clung to AU-G00Z as they both stumbled into the beam. She heard a sky-giant roar behind her as they leapt, the invader having spotted them and recognizing that Jaq did not belong there. It advanced on the beam as they descended and Jaq feared that it would catch up to them before they could reach safety.

Jaq and AU-G00Z had just touched ground when the beam flickered and disappeared, releasing the sky-giant in midair. Not wanting to be beneath the invader as he fell, she sprinted for the nearest basement window and forcing the mobile replicator in through it before her, took cover within.

The sky-giant hit the street with a thunderous crash, its chitin cracking and splitting as a result of the collision with the pavement, spilling out some of its liquid contents. Then the already shadowy sky darkened and Jaq knew other consequences were about to follow thanks to her interference. She crouched and cowered next to AU-G00Z, covering her head, waiting for the worst.

The sky platform above broke free of its malfunctioning stabilizers. It wobbled and veered before it finally struck earth. Jaq covered her ears and closed her eyes, praying her rebellious efforts would not end in her death along with many others. A suffocating cloud of dirt and dust blew into her basement hideout through the broken window and for a moment she believed it would spell her end, unable to breathe despite her desperate attempts to seek air. Had it not been for AU-G00Z, she surely would have died.

Fortunately, the replicator was able to produce a facsimile of clean air. It enveloped Jaq in a breathable layer just in time, countering the effects of the dust cloud. It took her several minutes of coughing and gagging to recover, her voice raspy and her lungs rattling from its residue, but at least she had survived. She dragged herself over to the broken window to look out.

Her eyes were met with a glaring sight, which would have been worse had there not been a blanket of dust and smog hanging in the air. But even filtered by these things, she now knew sunlight when she saw it. The city was no longer contained within shadow. The sky platform was gone.

Jaq had to assume it had crashed a fair distance from where she had hidden because she saw no rubble or debris remaining from the structure, but the body of the fallen sky-giant still lay sprawled in the streets not far from her. She pulled herself out through the window, hoisting AU-G00Z out after her, and then approached the body to investigate.

She prodded a part of its shattered chitin with her toe and then stepped back.

"Is it dead?" she asked.

After some examination, the mobile replicator confirmed that yes, indeed, it was dead.

"Time to take you back to Mom then" she sighed.

Glancing skyward and shielding her eyes, Jaq wondered how the city would function now that the overlords were gone. Did the resistance have a contingency plan in place? Would the sky-giants replace their fallen platform as quickly as possible? Would they try to punish the residents of the city for this act of rebellion?

Jaq didn't have the answers, but what she did know is that she would be returning to Mom with AU-G00Z to offer her. That would no doubt please the stern woman. Perhaps Jaq would be able to convince her they should share Magic Bean with other cities and elevate their efforts from resistance to revolution. Either way, they would be eating that night.

Directing the mobile replicator to follow her, Jaq started towards home.

Young Adventurers

FANTASY

ADVENTURES

Young Adventurers

What could be more exciting…and more dangerous…than chasing dragons on an airborne steamer?

THE WRECK OF THE BLUE PLOVER

David Turnbull

Angus watched as Captain Zachariah lowered his telescope. Deep in thought, the captain tapped his fingers absently against the brass rim that encased the lens. Angus felt a knot of excitement tighten in his belly. He drew in measured inhalation of breath. It didn't do anything to calm his beating heart.

A flock of black dragons had been spied toward the western horizon and Angus wasn't the only one nervously waiting for the captain to reach a decision. The airship's entire compliment was gathered on the gondola deck in hushed silence.

At sixteen Angus was the youngest person onboard the *Drunken Molly*. He felt a bit like an intruder. Unlike the rest of the crew, who mostly hailed from Tennanbrau City, he had been born in the rolling vista of green hills that encompassed the rural communities of the Low Counties.

The men of Tennanbrau tended to be broad and brawny, whereas Low county folk were small and often softly spoken. Angus sported a distinctive shock of red hair. It hung down lankly around his ears, augmenting the explosion of freckles that splattered his nose and cheeks. Many of the crew had taken to calling him *Ginger* and he was becoming increasingly convinced that hardly any of them knew his real name.

Maybe this will be my day, he thought. *Maybe today the name of Angus Stonedyke will be on everyone's lips.*

He kept his eyes fixed on Captain Zachariah. The airship captain stroked the narrow ribbon of beard that traced the line of his jaw. The only sound to be heard was the creaking of the timbers as the gondola swayed on the silver wires that hung down from its crimson balloon and rocked against the constant pummeling of the sky winds.

The captain looked up and narrowed his eyes. Angus felt the tensing of his muscles pull tighter. Everyone seemed to recognize the grin that spread on the captain's face for what it meant. But still they waited for the final confirmation. At last he gave a single nod of his head.

A loud cheer exploded from the assembled crew.

The hunt was on!

As the cheer echoed skyward Angus hurriedly donned his rope loader's helmet and rushed to his station beside his designated cannon emplacement. Brinsley, one of the rope gunners, climbed into his cockpit and, with practiced precision, checked the cannon's spring loaded trigger mechanism. Angus felt a twinge of jealously. Brinsley wasn't that much older that himself. He longed for the day that he'd be given the chance to operate a rope cannon.

The *Molly* tacked hard left and a blustering gust of icy air washed a vaporous mist across his face. He gasped from the shock of it. Trepidation began to tempter his excitement. Treacleshells, as black dragons were more commonly known, were said to be the most pernicious of all the airborne serpents. Angus had heard that tackling them was fraught with danger. Ill-tempered and notoriously difficult to capture they were a species that most dragon hunters tended to avoid.

But Captain Zachariah is not like most dragon hunters, he reminded himself.

The captain was famed for an unshakable confidence in the infallibility of his airship. The *Drunken Molly* may have been named after an inebriate Aunt that the captain had a deep affection for-but she soundly defied the unfortunate implications of her name with the velocity of her speed and the ease of her maneuverability. With the *Molly* to rely upon the captain had become renowned for taking risks that others did not even dare consider. If any airship captain could lead his crew to a

The Wreck of the Blue Plover

successful *harvesting* of a savage flock of Treacleshells it was Nathaniel Zachariah.

Checking that the beaded lead weights on the loop of the cannon's lasso were evenly spaced, and making sure the knot of the noose was sound, Angus carefully loaded the rope into the mouth of the cannon. With a tap of his fingers on his helmet he signified to Brinsley that the lasso was in place. The rope cannon gunner pulled his goggles over his eyes and swung the stubby barrel skyward.

Duty performed, Angus studied the captain as he climbed onto the raised iron gantry from where he would direct the hunt. Despite being browned and weather worn from the constant attentions of the harsh conditions endured at high altitude his features remained deceptively youthful. The pencil thin moustache that crested his upper lip was as neatly trimmed as the dark slither of beard on his jaw. Gazing unflinchingly ahead his resolute blue eyes seemed oblivious to the braided ponytail of his long black hair as it danced in the crosswind and whipped against the scaled sheen of his dragon skin jerkin.

"Steady as she goes," he called to the coxswain. "We want to be right in amongst them before the first lasso is fired."

Coxswain Grisling tightened his oil stained hand on the navigation wheel. With the other he pulled a lever to lower the rotation of the turbines. High above the gondola the crimson balloon swayed a little to this alteration in the airship's momentum.

Pushing the rim of his helmet up onto his forehead Angus glanced up at the magnificent balloon above him. It was filled with a compound that consisted mainly of refined *Dragon Breath*. Lighter than air, *Dragon Breath* was also the core component of the energy source for all of Tennanbrau City's vast factories. It was the power upon which the Emperor Julian drove his burgeoning empire ever forward.

The harvesting of *Dragon Breath* was a lucrative business and since childhood Angus had yearned for the romance and adventure of a life above the billowing cloudbank. Back home in the Low Counties he had practiced roping sheep with a long length of frayed chord that had been disposed of by the vicar when the village church installed a new bell in the belfry.

Imagining that the rugged hill sheep were dragons he had developed, through a considerable amount of trial and error, an excellent and accurate aim with his makeshift lasso. As a consequence he longed to be seated where Brinsley sat, in the cockpit behind a rope cannon, ready let loose a lasso to snare a dragon.

"Lower the bait," ordered the captain.

Immediately several lengths of rope were cast over the sides of the gondola. The ropes yanked tight. Hunks of salted meat on the hooks attached to the ends of the ropes spun with the relentless forward motion of the *Molly*.

Through the oncoming swirl of cloud Angus could see that the Treacleshells were viciously attacking a flock of geese that had been passing over the tundra in tight formation. They were hunting in pairs - the midnight hued sows swooping in to snap the necks of the geese between razor sharp teeth, while the larger boars followed swiftly through to clamp their powerful jaws around the plummeting corpses.

Then, with a grotesquely synchronized symmetry, the two would share the prize, tearing and clawing at the limp carcass, as a blizzard of bloody white feathers fluttered a macabre dance in the sky around them.

Angus felt a quickening of his pulse as Grisling steered the *Molly* straight into the midst of the flock's savage feeding frenzy. Several of them turned and let out high-pitched screeches, their tongues starkly red against the licorice tones of their scaly muzzles. The surviving geese thrust their wings, long necks outstretched, honking noisily as they made a desperate bid to escape. For a moment it seemed to Angus that the dark assembly of dragons would follow them and that the *Molly,* in turn, would be forced to give chase.

Then, almost as one, the gleaming slits of their quivering nostrils appeared to scent the salted meat dangling below the gondola. Keening noisily-three, four, five of them dipped their ferocious heads and swooped down, barbed tails slashing the air as they fell from view.

The Wreck of the Blue Plover

"Steady men," cautioned Captain Zachariah.

No sooner had he spoken these words than a rancorous looking boar rose immediately in front of Angus, hunk of meat clamped in its slavering black jaw. Brinsley traced its progress with his cannon. Beating down on its wings the boar climbed till it was almost level with the crimson balloon, gnawing at the hunk of meat and raking it with its scimitar claws. One of the gunners released his lasso and spat out a foul curse when it missed its mark.

I wouldn't have missed so easily, Angus whispered under his breath.

The Treacleshell boar dipped low once more. Following it with his sight Brinsley triggered the coiled spring on his cannon. The rope shot from the barrel and went singing through the air, the lead beads helping it maintain a rounded circumference. With an almost improbably perfect trajectory the loop of the lasso whipped around the hoary ankle of the Treacleshell's hind leg. When it dived in panic the noose pulled instantly tighter.

"First catch to Mister Brinsley!" cried Captain Zachariah. "Haul the beast in, Angus. Haul the beast in!"

Heart swelling with pride at being given such a direct order Angus made a grab for the rope. But no sooner had he started to heave back against the frantic struggle of boar than several burly crewmen snatched the rope from him and barged him out of the way. "You're too skinny, *Ginger*," goaded one of them. "Watch out you don't get dragged overboard."

Whilst they were doing this the gunner who had previously missed his mark fired off his re-loaded lasso. The rope dropped over the Treacleshell's thrashing head and pulled tight around its neck, effectively preventing it from retaliating against its capture with blistering inferno of its fiery breath.

Before Angus had the chance to do anything another crewmember grabbed the second rope and began to help the first group to heave the dragon in. Starved of oxygen, it was easily overwhelmed. The hunk of meat fell hopelessly from its slackening jaw as it slashed out with its claws. Its wings folded back to its ridged spine. It dropped like a stone. A wide net was tossed over the edge of the gondola to catch it and in no time at all it was yanked over the side and tipped onto the deck.

It came awake in an instant.

Two crewmen pinned down its jerking hind legs and stilled the whipping of its tail with their feet. Another wrestled one of its flailing black wings and held it tight. Angus was about to make a grab for the second wing but someone bustled him out of the way and took his place. Relegated to the sidelines all that was left for him was to watch as Crowhurst, one of the ship's professional dragon-wranglers, straddled the boar's scaly neck and forced its head into an upright position.

Angus heard the telltale click-click friction of the two flint-like organs that sat half way down the throat of all dragons. Despite the rope around its neck the Treacleshell was desperately trying to produce the spark that would ignite its powerful gaseous breath. Crowhurst reached down and pressed his index finger expertly against the visibly fidgeting bulge on the dragon's dark, scaly neck.

The clicking ceased.

"Fetch the *Breath Extractor*!" yelled Captain Zachariah.

A spry crewman dashed along the deck. He was carrying a piece of apparatus with a leather muzzle at one end and a long length of rubber tubing trailing from the other. He barged past Angus and yanked the muzzle over the dragon's snout. No sooner was the muzzle in place than Crowhurst swiftly buckled the straps behind the Treacleshell's head. Seconds later the cook came lurching from the galley, his skinny, tattooed arms wrapped around a narrow rimmed clay vessel. He placed the vessel on the deck and stuffed the tubing running from the end of the muzzle into its slender neck.

"Ready!" he yelled.

Crowhurst began to unloosen the knot of the noose around the Treacleshell's throat. As soon as the pressure was released there came an ominous click-click-click, followed by a furious roar. The muzzle sparked blue as a powerful burst of fiery *Dragon Breath* was forced through the insulated tube and into the clay vessel. After no more than a few seconds the cook pulled the tube away and corked the sizzling neck. It sat there

The Wreck of the Blue Plover

hissing and steaming, till someone wearing thick gantlets stepped in to drag it back to the hold.

"She'll be good for one more!" cried Captain Zachariah.

Another clay vessel was rapidly transported from the galley.

Meanwhile two more Treacleshells, duly roped and netted, were being unceremoniously deposited onto the gondola deck. Seizing his chance to finally get some hands on experience Angus rushed to help pin one of them down. The Treacleshell seemed to sense his approach. Its head snapped round and the wrangler who was straddling its ridged back lost the pressure point his fingers had on its neck.

Angus found himself staring directly into a pair of angry red eyes. Unsettled he stumbled and almost lost his footing. Above the blustering din of the wind he clearly heard the click-click-click that emanated from within her scaly throat. She let forth a howl of rage and Angus was instantaneously engulfed in a ball of blistering white fire. Blinding flames clawed all around him. He felt the sleeves of his jerkin tighten around his upper arms as fire seized hold of them. He could smell the dreadful stench of his hair singing beneath his helmet.

Crying out in terror he rolled across the deck, trying to extinguish the flames in the manner he had been previously shown. Then suddenly he was drenched by the freezing cold contents of a pail of water that came at him from the left. As he gasped for breath and tried to struggle back to his feet another bucket load came at him from the right.

"Damn near washed the freckles right off your face," said one of the bucket-wielding crewmen who'd come to his aid. Angus crouched there smoldering and dripping, cringing with embarrassment at the mocking laughter that rose all around him.

To celebrate the successful *harvesting* of Treacleshell *Breath* the crew assembled on deck and engaged in a boisterous rendition of the famous Dragon Hunter's Sky Shanty. Shivering in his wet clothing, Angus couldn't help feeling that he had still not fully earned the right to participate. So he simply stood there, swaying a little unsteadily, as he listened. Having made the first catch Brinsley got to sing the main lines, while the crew responded with the noisy rejoinder.

"Now I was born in Tennanbrau
Haul away above the clouds
And grew as tall as I am now
Haul away above the clouds
I signed on with my Captain bold
Haul away above the clouds
We traveled north to where it's cold
Haul away above the clouds
And there I swore on pain of death
Haul away above the clouds
To take the precious Dragon Breath"

Down in the hold three dozen corked vessels of said *Dragon Breath* lay cooling on the shelves. They would fetch an excellent price at auction back in Tennanbrau City. The captain had promised everyone a handsome bonus. Once their *Breath* had been taken the Treacleshells had been released back into the open skies. It would take weeks for the buildup of the natural gases in their lungs to reach sufficient levels for them to be able to breathe fire once more. Even then Angus thought that it would be a long time before anyone else dared to tackle them.

"Airship, ho!"

The singing of his crewmates was suddenly interrupted by the loud shout that went up from the watchman's station to the rear of the gondola.

Captain Zachariah rose to his feet and snapped his fingers at the grimy faced boy employed as the ship's fetcher. "Telescope! Sharp as you like!"

Boots still squelching from their drenching, the stink of fire still in his hair, Angus squeezed in behind the rest of the crew as they assembled at the rear deck railing. Dread washed over him as an airship came listing lopsided and wraithlike through the cloud mist. Something wasn't right. He could feel it in his bones.

She was a commercial vessel. Not the type of airship that would normally venture this far north. The type used for

The Wreck of the Blue Plover

transporting goods or passengers...Angus could see that her main balloon was gone, the silver wires that had lashed it to her gondola whipping erratically and dangerously loose in the wind. Only three of her smaller emergency balloons were inflated. All that remained of the section of her deck where the fourth should have been situated was a jagged chasm, exposing her guts all the way through to the gloomy interior of her hold.

The damaged airship drew close enough for Angus to see the name ornately painted onto the hull of her gondola–*The Blue Plover*. Angus had heard of her. Her captain was Finneus Watling, a former officer in the Imperial Sky Constabulary, who had used a lump sum from his retirement pension to set himself up as a merchantman.

On Captain Zachariah's order Grisling maneuvered the *Molly* alongside the wounded craft. This close the damage looked even worse that it had on her approach. Several areas of her deck were blackened and trails of smoke were still hovering near areas where it seemed as if fires had only recently fizzled out.

Angus looked at the jagged section of wood where the deck had been torn away. Perhaps the Treacleshell flock had attacked the merchant ship. If it had they would have been defenseless. This was one of the main reasons merchantmen did not often venture into the wintry skies above the tundra.

"Ho!" Captain Zachariah called across the swirling blue gap between the two airships. "Finneus Watling! Bring your crew on deck and greet my dragon hunters in the proper manner."

Silently the *Plover's* gondola listed and rocked to the asymmetrical sway of its trio of emergency balloons. "Ho!" cried the Captain again. "Can we be of assistance?"

Not a sound.

Coxswain Grisling looked sideways at Captain Zachariah.

The mood of the crew grew noticeably darker.

Angus overheard their superstitious exchanges.

"Cursed."

"Jinxed."

Then something darted across the deck of the *Plover's* gondola. Something small and swift. Before anyone had a chance to make out exactly what it was it had disappeared once more amongst the smoldering wreckage.

"Ghost," said someone, in a quiet voice.

Beside him Angus saw that Brinsley's face had turned pale. His hands were trembling as they gripped tightly to the rails of the gondola. Angus felt a cold shiver shudder down his own spine. Somehow he was unable to draw his eyes away from the swirls of smoke that danced around the *Plover's* eerily silent deck.

Just then a fierce updraft, drawn from the cold air rising from the tundra below, howled through the gap between the two airships. The *Molly* rocked back, sending several members of the crew stumbling across the deck. By the time it righted itself once more the *Plover* had been sent into an unpredictable spin that caused it to tilt and yaw as the three emergency balloons struggled against the uneven weight of the gondola.

"In again, Mister Grisling," cried Captain Zachariah. "Fetch the *longpoles* to pull her closer."

Longpoles were twelve foot in length and were mainly used by the crew on the approach to the terminus at Tennanbrau City, to ensure that an airship didn't drift too close to the walls of tall buildings. They could also be used to pull airships alongside each other.

Four crewmembers stood ready with the tall poles resting against their shoulders. The drone of the turbines vibrated through the deck as Grisling once more steered the *Molly* as close to the *Plover* as he could manage. The *longpoles* were then utilized to hook and secure the dancing wires. Finally ropes were lashed to the *Plover's* damaged decking rails to slow her glide.

"We need to tow her back to the reclamation yard at Forgsnur's Footprint," said the captain. "She'll be a risk to other airship if we leave her adrift like this. However, if there is a survivor over there, they need to be brought onboard the *Molly* for their own safety."

"There's no survivor over there," said one of the crew. "What we saw was a ghost."

"There's no such thing as ghosts," snapped Captain Zachariah.

He turned to coxswain Grisling.

The Wreck of the Blue Plover

"A volunteer," he said. "We need a volunteer to investigate."

"You heard," said Grisling. "Who's got the guts to go over for a gander?"

Most of the crew bowed their heads and studied their feet, shuffling cautiously backwards. Angus could sense their fear. No matter what the captain said they still believed there was something supernatural prowling the charred decks of the *Plover*.

Grunting in obvious disgust Crowhurst stepped forward and jutted his chest out.

"Takes a wrangler to do a job like this."

He scowled darkly at the others.

Stroking his narrow beard Captain Zachariah looked him up and down.

"Someone lighter," he said. "We don't know how stable those balloons are–or how much more weight they'll hold. Once the gondola starts to fall she'll pick up momentum and she won't stop till she smashes onto the tundra."

Angus saw the young fetcher drop to his knees and crawl rapidly back between the legs of the men. Clearly he wasn't taking any chances of being nabbed for the task. Brinsley was small–but he too had pushed himself some way back into the crowd.

Angus felt several eyes looking down at him.

He thought of the ethereal figure they had seen darting across the *Plover's* deck.

His pulse quickened. Cold sweat broke out in needle-pricks all over his body. Now Captain Zachariah looked at him. This was the moment he'd been waiting for. He couldn't be found wanting. Swallowing against the dryness that suddenly filled his mouth he stepped forward.

"I'll go," he said.

More ropes were lashed to the *Plover's* broken and scorched gondola. Slowly and cautiously she was pulled close enough to the side of the *Molly* that a wooden gangplank could be placed to span the narrow gap between the two airships. Grisling held the navigation wheel steady and cut the *Molly's* engines so that she floated freely on her crimson balloon.

Captain Zachariah squeezed Angus on the shoulder.

"Don't dally too long over there, lad."

Angus drew in a deep breath and tightened the strap of his helmet under his chin.

"That won't help you none if you fall to the tundra," said the little fetcher, who had re-emerged, cheekily confident now that at least *he* wasn't going to be expected to *volunteer*.

"This will though," said Brinsley.

Smiling sympathetically at Angus he tied a rope tightly around his waist.

"Just give it a tug when you want us to let out a little more slack," he said.

Forcing himself to smile back Angus climbed up onto the gangplank and spread his arms wide to try and gain his balance. Down below the clouds had thinned enough for him to be able to see the bleak scrub of the tundra far below, stretching flatly and monotonously for miles in every direction. Despite Grisling's best effort the gondola was still rocking slightly and the yowling squall of the wind was making it impossible for him to maintain an upright stance.

"Hands and knees, lad," said Captain Zachariah, his long ponytail slapping against dragon scales on his jerkin. "Down on your hands and knees. This is not a circus."

Heaving a sigh of relief Angus dropped to all fours and crawled rapidly across the gangplank, eyes fixed straight ahead so that he wouldn't be tempted to look down again.

The desolate deck of the *Plover* reeked with the tainted stench of ignited *Dragon Breath* and the charcoal bite of scorched wood. He had gone half way across the deck when he came upon a set of three deeply ragged furrows torn into the flooring boards. He imagined one of the Treacleshells swooping down here and raking the timbers with its talons. He imagined another sinking its powerful jaws into the side of the deck and tearing it to splinters. He could almost hear the terrified screams of the crew as they'd been mercilessly attacked with tooth and claw and fire.

Crouching low he inserted a finger into the splintery groove

The Wreck of the Blue Plover

of one of the furrows and tried to estimate the size of the talon that had clawed through the wood. It was difficult to judge. Standing back up he turned and called back a description of what he'd discovered to Captain Zachariah.

"Search below deck, lad," urged the captain. "See if you can find the poor soul who survived."

Somewhat warily Angus eyed the three emergency balloons. He didn't like the look of the one to the stern. It seemed oddly wrinkled, as if it might be slowly leaking *Breath*. He remembered what the captain had said about how the gondola would drop if her balloons gave out. The thought of that happening while he was down in the hold traced a cold shiver down his spine.

But when he looked at the expectant faces staring across at him from the *Molly* it became patently clear that there could be no turning back. If he was going to win the acceptance of his crewmates he simply had to do as the captain asked. Staggering against the erratic keeling of the gondola, he tugged at the rope. Once he had been given sufficient slack he lurched his way to the entrance of the hold.

As a consequence of the gaping hole torn into to the side of the airship the hold did not look as gloomy as it might otherwise have. Angus cautiously eased his way down the wooden stepladder. He began to feel the pull of the wind that was whipping around the confines of the *Plover's* belly in a frosty, swirling vortex.

Glad now of the protection afforded by his helmet he dismounted the ladder and turned his head sideways against the blustering barrage, squinting as he surveyed the remains of the interior. The shelves, where goods for commercial transportation might normally sit, lay entirely empty. But to the far end of the hold he could see some of the airship's supplies still piled there - sacks of potatoes and onions, a pallet bearing slabs of salted meat, two spare coils of rope, stacked in the corner.

Other than that the hold seemed as deserted as the deck had been. He was about to turn back to the ladder when he spied something crouching low beside one of the splintered beams. His pulse started to thrum as his mouth turned dry once more.

"If you are human, come out and show yourself," he said. "If you're a ghost I apologize for disturbing you. Just let me return to the deck unmolested."

"Are y-you a p-pirate?" asked a timid voice.

"A pirate?" said Angus. "Absolutely not. I'm a rope cannon loader on the finest dragon hunting airship ever to fly out of Tennanbrau City."

"And you're not going to hurt me?" asked the voice.

"I'm here to help you," said Angus. "To rescue you, if you'll let me."

The figure stepped cautiously out from behind the beam. It was a child - a girl of around ten or eleven years old. The cloak she was wearing was covered in scorch marks. Her face was grimy with soot, the outline white tear tracks tracing zigzags down her filthy cheeks.

"I'm Finneus Watling's niece," she told him. "My uncle took me on a trip to see the green hills of the Low Counties. But there was a storm and we got terribly lost. And my uncle got confused. We went north instead of south. And then the dragons came…"

She started to sob.

Angus reached out and took her by the hand.

"I'm going to get you over to the *Drunken Molly*," he said. "My captain will take care of you. He'll get you safely home."

With the wind whipping furiously around them he led the girl back to the ladder. It was then that he saw something else on the floor, just beyond the storage area, near the hole that had been torn from the side of the deck. It looked somehow too bulky to be simply the pile of rags it appeared at first to be. Another survivor?

"Wait there," he said to the girl, wrapping her hand around the first rung of the ladder.

Ducking beneath the wooden beams he dropped down onto his hands and knees and crawled towards the object. As he did so the gondola tipped a little and the object slid precariously closer to the ragged hole. The wind was blowing so fiercely into his face now that it was making his eyes water, blurring his vision.

"Hello?" he called out, inching closer. "Can you hear me?"

An eyelid trembled and blinked open.

The Wreck of the Blue Plover

A red eye stared back at him.

Angus froze.

It wasn't a human eye.

The object seemed to unfurl and rise unsteadily on clawed feet, revealing itself as a Treacleshell Sow. She was badly dazed. She shook her head, momentarily lost her footing and then rose up again. She turned to Angus, snarling through the rows of razor sharp teeth.

Then a dreadful sound rose from her throat, chilling Angus to the bone.

Click-click-click.

If she ignited her *Breath* the entire hold would be engulfed in a ball of fire. This time there would be no one to step in with a pail of water to douse the flames. Angus turned to the girl. "Run!" he yelled. Her eyes went wide. She turned and scrambled up the ladder. A chill traced his spine when he heard the padding of the dragon's feet creeping stealthily up behind him.

He swung around.

The Treacleshell sow snarled again and flapped her wings menacingly at him. The organs in her throat clacked rapidly against each other–click-click-click. She let out a roar–hot, steamy smoke belched out. But her *Breath* did not ignite. Angus dodged to the left. She still seemed a little unsteady on her feet, her head sluggish when it followed him.

It was clear though that she was fast regaining her strength. The clicking in her throat was become more rapid and forceful. Taking the risk to turn and flee after the girl could prove to be a fatal error of judgment.

In that instant he decided he only had one alternative.

With a yell he ran at the sow and dived onto her ridged back. She was so surprised by this sudden and unexpected turn of events that she fell flat on her belly. Angus reached round and pressed his fingers against the rough scales on her neck. She rose to her feet, arching her spine to try and buck him off. He dug in with his knees.

Click-click-click came the dreadful sound from her throat.

It was what Angus had been hoping for. He felt the vibrations in his fingers and quickly located the correct spot. Pressing down hard he pushed his index and middle finger so that they effectively created a barrier between the two organs. He had no idea whether this was the same technique that dragon wranglers applied.

But somehow it worked.

The clicking ceased.

Angus let forth a triumphal whoop.

The sow jerked her head left and right, trying to dislodge his fingers from their position. She arched her spine again, so sharply that his knees almost lost their hold. She whipped her tail around, thumping him hard on the shoulder as its barbed tip sliced at his cheek. He began to realize what a terrible mistake he might have made. He wasn't half as strong as a wrangler like Crowhurst and he didn't have other crewmembers to help pin down the dragon's legs.

The tail came at him again, this time from the right. He saw it from the corner of his eye and ducked low. The tail clattered against his helmet, jarring his neck and causing little silvery stars to tumble before him. The wind was howling around him, making it even more difficult keep his balance.

The sow started to throw itself around the hold, trying to use the wooden beams to knock him off. He ducked and dodged. But he was rapidly becoming exhausted. It wouldn't be long before she succeeded. Then he would be at her mercy.

Icy cold wind gushed against his face.

Suddenly the two of them were out in the open sky–falling rapidly.

Somehow in her frantic struggle the dragon must have stumbled too close the gap torn into the side of the gondola. Down they dropped. Then Angus felt the rope around waist pull painfully tight, digging into his lower ribs. He lost his grip on the dragon's back and she tumbled away from him, leaving him dangling precariously beneath the *Plover's* tarred hull.

The wind beat about him, sending the rope into a dizzying spin. Nevertheless he could see the dragon below him. She glided around in a wide arc. She caught his eye and, with an ear-piercing shriek, beat her wings and rose.

Angus tugged desperately at the rope. He looked up and saw

The Wreck of the Blue Plover

some of the *Molly's* crew looking down at him. He heard them yelling to the others. When he looked back down the dragon was rising at a terrifying speed, teeth bared in a vicious snarl.

Then, just as she was almost upon him, he felt a powerful yank on the rope and he was instantly hauled back into the hold. Scrambling frantically back across the floorboards he caught a glimpse of gleaming black scales as the sow appeared just beyond the hole.

She roared, and this time her *Breath* ignited with a fury. A dazzling ball of flame illuminated the hold. The heat of it knocked Angus flat onto his back. A fierce maelstrom of fire raged within the swirling wind just above him. It lasted only a moment before the cold air seemed to suck the life out of the fire.

Angus didn't hesitate or look back. He jumped to his feet and took the ladder rungs two at a time. The girl was waiting at the top, trembling and terrified

"I thought the dragon got you."

"Come on," said Angus, gabbing her hand. "We have to get across to the *Drunken Molly.*"

She pulled against him.

"No, the dragon will come. We'll be killed - like my uncle. Like all of his crew."

"What's your name?" asked Angus.

For a moment she seemed surprised by the question.

"Your name?" pressed Angus.

"Sonia," she said, sniffing back her tears.

"I'm Angus," he said. "Do you know who my captain is? Do you know who the captain of the *Drunken Molly* is?"

Sonia shrugged her skinny shoulders.

"Nathaniel Zachariah," said Angus.

Sonia gasped.

She had clearly heard of him.

Who hadn't?

"Really?" she said.

Angus nodded.

"You know that Captain Zachariah is the greatest dragon hunter ever to fly out of Tennanbrau City, don't you?"

Now it was Sonia who nodded.

"Do you really think that a bad tempered old Treacleshell sow is any match for Nathaniel Zachariah?"

He took her hand again. This time she didn't pull back. They both rushed headlong along the deck. "Look!" he cried when he saw that the crew had utilized the rope cannons to capture the sow. "I told you. She'll be hauled on deck and they'll take her *Breath*. She won't trouble us anymore." Sonia managed to smile, the white of her teeth contrasting sharply with the black, sooty mess of her face.

"Her name is Sonia!" Angus called over to the *Molly*. "She's Finneus Watling's niece."

"No one else alive?" asked Captain Zachariah; his face for once had lost most of its usual composure.

Angus shook his head.

Beside him Sonia let out a loud sob. But somehow she stopped herself from crying. Angus could see that she was nervously watching the Treacleshell sow, now hauled onto the *Molly's* deck and being straddled by Crowhurst while others pinned down her wings and tail.

"Once they take her *Breath* she'll be no threat to us," Angus reminded her.

She squeezed his hand–seemingly not convinced.

Angus stepped to the plank and mentally steeled himself, ready to crawl back over.

He looked down at Sonia.

"Go down on your hands and knees," he told her. "Go slowly. Don't look down. It's only a few feet across. Someone will help you at the other side."

Her lip trembled.

"I'm scared," she said.

"I'll be right behind you," promised Angus. "I won't let anything happen."

Without warning there came a sharp crack from behind them both.

When Angus looked around the emergency balloon to the stern of the gondola had finally given out. It hissed and

The Wreck of the Blue Plover

spluttered, flapping wildly as the last of the *Dragon Breath* gushed out of a ragged tear. The gondola became unbalanced and tipped so abruptly that the plank fell and spun away into the blue void. One of the ropes lashed to the side of the *Plover* snapped. The wires broke loose from the longpoles. The rope around his waist was next to go and Angus found himself sliding helter-skelter down the deck of the gondola as it keeled further into an acute dip.

He lost his grip on Sonia's hand.

She went tumbling away from him.

The dead weight of the *Plover* pulled the *Molly* with it. Angus wedged himself against the railings and found himself swallowed up by the great looming shadow of the *Molly's* balloon as she capsized and swung her gondola almost horizontal. He saw Sonia clinging to the railing at the far end of the gondola. If the *Plover* dipped any more she might be thrown out into the open skies.

He heard the captain barking a desperate order to the crew to cut the other ropes in order to save his beloved airship. Angus felt his heart sink. Cut loose the *Plover* immediately drifted a good seven or eight feet from the *Molly,* dropping ever lower in the sky as the remaining balloons struggled to keep her aloft.

Looking up at the curved belly of the *Molly's* gondola Angus could easily tell that the distance between the two airships was already growing greater by the moment. If Captain Zachariah intended to do anything at all to save him he would have to act now.

Sonia let out a scream as another of the emergency balloons burst to ragged shreds.

Hand over hand he pulled himself back along the railings till he was beside her.

"We'll be fine," he tried to assure her.

But all the time the distance between the two airships was growing even wider.

Then, just as he was about to give up hope, he saw that two of the rope cannons were being aimed in a downward trajectory. He let out cry of joy as the lassos came racing through the air towards him. One was clearly going to go wide.

But the other!

The other was his one last hope.

Grabbing Sonia and pulling her close to his chest with his left arm he punched his right fist into the air and leapt into the path of the spinning rope. His clenched fist passed cleanly through the lasso. Fingers wrapping around the knot he pulled back and yanked the noose tightly around his wrist. The lead beads bit into his flesh. The rope gnawed at him. Sonia was clinging so tightly to his neck he could hardly breathe.

The wreck of the *Blue Plover* fell away, hurtling toward the tundra, bits of her hull breaking up. In the open sky the rope began twisting and untwisting, spinning him around and back around at such a terrifying speed he felt sure his shoulder would be yanked out of its socket. Nevertheless he was being hauled up, slowly but surely. Back to his airship, his captain and his crewmates-and perhaps the chance, at last, to man a rope cannon?

Feeling drunk with elation he held onto Sonia with all the available strength he could muster. His voice hoarse against the roar of the wind he began singing-singing and laughing at the same time. At last he felt that he had the right. His voice echoed joyously to the open sky

Now I was born in Tennanbrau

Haul away above the clouds!

Young Adventurers

Fantasy tales are filled with swords and sorcery, and dashing swashbucklers can be kings or knaves, male or female…

RETURN OF THE KNAVE

Milo James Fowler

The sword sang as it left its sheath, blade gleaming in the light of the rising sun.

"Defend yourself!" cried the portly sword-bearer, gripping his weapon in both hands and brandishing it high. "You'll pay for what you've done!"

"What have I done?" The teenaged boy scampered backwards across the farmyard, his unkempt, straw-like hair falling into his eyes.

"You've taken liberties that weren't yours to take!" the man roared.

"Liberties? What liberties?" The boy's voice squeaked as he shook his hair aside. "I haven't taken any liberties!"

"Aye, you have! And now you'll pay for it."

The boy let out a squeal as the sword-bearer advanced. Scampering was no good now; the boy had to run for his life. With a quick gulp of air, he whirled and launched himself into a sprint across the barnyard, his bare feet skimming across dirt, rock, and manure alike.

"You cannot escape, blackguard!" The blade struck the ground an inch from the boy's heel. "Rogue! Villain! Scoundrel! Judgment is upon you, scurvy knave!"

The boy halted and turned about-face. "Now that's going too far."

The man chuckled, red in the face, his bulky frame bouncing. Then he swept the sword into ready position. "Defend yourself!"

The boy released another squeal and lunged aside. "You don't really have to kill me, do you?"

The sword caught the ragged hem of his trousers.

"You have transgressed. Judgment is upon you!"

"Can't we work this out a little more...civilly?" The boy leapt over a stray pig. "Like gentlemen?"

"No." The pig shrieked as it was kicked aside. "I'm not a gentleman!"

"Well, neither am I, but–" The boy grunted, clambering over a stray cow. "Can't we pretend? For my sake?"

"Your sake? You have no sake!" The cow bawled as it was knocked down. "The barbaric way we're handling this situation suits me just fine!"

"But–" The boy hesitated a moment before throwing himself onto the stray horse in his path. "You're going to end up killing me!"

"Aye, that's the idea." The man took a moment to wipe his arm across a profusely perspiring brow. "You know, it's been a while since I've experienced the heat of battle. Forgotten how much fun it can be." A stray sheep bumped against his leg, and he turned sharply.

Then he stared.

The yard had filled with animals: pigs, cows, horses, sheep, chickens, ducks, geese, dogs, cats, goats, rats, mice, llamas, all milling about, mingled and meandering. Soon there wouldn't be enough room for him to stand.

"Hey–boy–" The man cursed as two large cows pinned him between their flabby flanks. "What's going on here?"

The boy frowned. "I must've forgotten to close the gate after tending the stock this morning. I guess your barbarism kind of scared my responsibilities right out of me."

"That's–understandable–" He groaned. "Aww, I can't move. Stupid, stupid cows!"

"I guess I could get them all back where they belong," the boy proposed.

"Yeah?" Only the man's upturned face remained visible amidst all the bovine flab. "Well, what's keeping you?"

"You've got to promise you won't kill me until we've discussed our differences like reasonable gentlemen." He raised an eyebrow as the man's face slowly submerged. "Deal?"

"I shpoze sho."

Return Of The Knave

"Huh?"

"YESH!"

The boy grinned.

Wasting no time, he whistled, called, barked and quacked, herding the animals into the barn from his perch atop the large work horse. In a matter of minutes, every animal was back where it belonged, with the gate shut and bolted.

"Good work," the man gasped as feeling returned to his limbs.

"Thank you?" The boy tilted his head.

"Guess I should apologize–for scaring you that way." He stretched his sword arm and massaged his shoulder. "But I'm still gonna kill you."

Just then, the door to the farmhouse (a cottage, really, with a rat-infested thatched roof) creaked open, and a teenaged girl stepped out into the morning light. She was a graceful beauty, an awe-inspiring vision to behold, with long flaxen locks and–

"PA!" she screamed at the top of her lungs. "PAAAAA!"

Dropping his sword with a grimace, the man clapped both meaty hands over his ears and bellowed, "I'm right HEEEERE!"

"Oh." The girl noticed her father standing a few feet in front of her. (She was a wee bit far-sighted.) "There you are." She giggled with a rosy blush. "Breakfast is ready." She whirled and bolted into the cottage.

The boy stared after her–until he found a sharp blade under his nose.

"Don't you dare," the man growled. "Don't you even say boo to her."

"Why would I do that?"

"You don't think I know. But I do. And that's why I'm gonna kill you. But first–" He sheathed his sword and slapped the boy's back, gesturing toward the cottage. "Your last meal!"

The three of them–father, daughter, and up-until-now-good-and-faithful-farmhand–sat in silence around the oak table. The only sounds were the slop and dribble of gruel in their bowls. The father and farmhand used wooden spoons to eat their meal, but the farmer's daughter did not. Bowl raised to drink, she slurped noisily until her portion was gone.

"Aahhhh," she sighed with satisfaction.

The boy glanced at her–then stared. The breathtaking young beauty had gruel all over her face. Catching his gaze upon her, she smiled bashfully, and a glob of the stuff dropped from her chin with a splat. The boy swallowed, his heart in his throat. She was so...amazing.

A knife thudded into the center of the table and quivered. With a start, the boy jerked back to find the girl's father scowling at him. The dark look on the farmer's face warned the boy to keep his eyes to himself.

"Daughter."

"Yeah, Pa?" She got up and floated to his side like an angel.

"Go slop the hogs."

"But they've already been–" both she and the boy said in unison.

"No talking in unison!" the man roared, pounding the table with a fist. "I forbid it!"

Mutely, the girl and boy nodded.

"And don't nod in unison either! Don't you do anything in unison!" The man growled under his breath. "Now Daughter, there are hogs to be slopped."

"Sure, Pa." Gracefully, she glided to the door, but before leaving, she turned and glanced once more at the boy. "You won't kill him before I get back, will you?"

The man's bulky shoulders sank. "No. I won't."

Another glob of gruel fell from her face as she smiled. "Thanks, Pa."

She was gone.

"Anything to make her happy," the man sighed. He shoved aside his bowl of half-eaten gruel and opened his mouth to speak.

A squeal came from the thatched ceiling as a rat plummeted downward, landing in his bowl with a splash. Squeaking and writhing, the rodent scurried away as fast as it could.

"Stupid rats," the man muttered.

"I've been meaning to fix the roof," said the boy with an apologetic shrug.

"But you got distracted, eh? By my daughter, mayhaps?" He cursed, pounding the table with both fists. "Don't just stare at me, buffoon!"

"Uh–distracted? Well, maybe a little. I mean, she's really grown up and–"

"Both of you have. But just because you've grown up together and live together and eat together doesn't mean you get the liberty of putting goo-goo eyes on her now. She deserves better than you! What are you?"

"Huh?"

"I've seen the way she looks at you. It's as though she's just seen you for the first time. It's really kind of sweet, when you think about it." He had to dab at something glistening in the corner of his eye.

"I guess so."

"You bet it is! It's the most romantic thing I've ever seen." He shook his head. "I knew it might happen sooner or later, ever since I took you in as a tiny lad. But it can't be."

The boy frowned. "How come?"

"Because, idiot, I don't want my daughter marrying no lousy, stinky farmhand!"

"Oh, right."

"See what I'm getting at? I want the world for my girl. And you've got to admit, you're...not even close."

"Yeah." The boy stared at the table. "I guess."

"Good." The father smiled. "So I'll kill you and be done with it." He slapped the table with both hands and heaved himself to his feet.

The boy glanced at the broadsword sheathed at the man's side and gulped.

"What is it boy?" The man scowled. "You afraid to die?"

"Well, no–"

"Then get a move on. I'm fond of you, lad. No reason why your death shouldn't be a quick, simple matter."

"You're sure about this?" The boy got to his feet.

"Yep. Either I kill you like the man you ought to be, or you run off like a scared little kid and never come back."

"Since you put it that way–"

"Good fellow!" The farmer clapped his farmhand on the back with the pride of a father figure. "Let's get this over with."

The pair stepped toward the door and threw it open, the farmer laughing like they were comrades, recounting old times with their arms slung about each other's shoulders.

Until it happened.

A log crashed against the farmer's skull, and he slumped to the ground. With a short gasp and a mumbled curse, he lay still. The boy could only stare.

Tossing aside the log she'd used to brain her poor father, the girl leaned close to be certain he was still breathing. Then she screamed, "CAN YOU HEAR ME, PAAAAA?" When he didn't even stir, she nodded. "Yep, he's out."

The boy found his tongue right where he'd left it. "Why'd you do that?"

"He was going to kill you, silly. I couldn't let anything like that happen to you." She stepped over her father and took the boy's arm. "C'mon, we've got to get you a horse."

"But–why?"

"Because if you don't get out of here, he'll kill you when he comes to, and then I'll lose the only boy I've ever loved."

"Oh." He nodded, pondering her words. "Oh! You mean me!" He grinned. "I love you too, you know."

She smiled. A glob of gruel dropped from her cheek. "I thought so."

They hastened to the barn and saddled up the fastest of the work horses–one that could actually trot. Then, as they led the steed outside, hand in hand, she spoke:

"Uh..."

He stared at her. She was so...amazing.

"I had something really neat I was going to say."

He squeezed her hand. "You'll remember."

She frowned and scratched at her head. The she said, "I'VE GOT IT!"

His heart nearly stopped in his chest.

She stepped in front of him. "Alfred," she began, for that was his name. "From this day forward, you are a knave–hated by many, hunted by some, loved by one. We may never meet again,

Return Of The Knave

but in the hope that we do, I will save myself for you. I will hold you in my heart, whatever that means." She gazed at him with her eyes half-closed, her voice near a whisper, her breath heavy. "I will wait for you."

He smiled at her. "Okay. Well, see you later." He climbed up into the saddle.

"ALFRED!"

He fell off the horse.

"Kiss me, you idiot!"

"Oh–right." He struggled to his feet. "Sorry."

A moment later, they were in each other's arms, kissing as passionately as if it were the first time. Truth be told, it was the first time.

"Oh Alfred," she gasped.

"Oh Gertrude," he gasped, for that was her name. She smelled of hog slop and tasted of gruel, but he didn't mind at all.

Gertrude's father stirred as he came to, so it was in Alfred's best interest to hightail it. With one last kiss and embrace, he climbed onto the horse.

"I'll be back–someday." He gripped the reins and gazed down at the young beauty. "Maybe."

Their eyes locked, and both were filled with deep, swirling emotions and unspoken flowery words. Both had gruel on their chins.

She nodded solemnly. "I'll be here."

Waving his hand in farewell, he kicked the horse into its fastest trot and rode off into the distance. Golden hair waving in the morning breeze, Gertrude watched him go for nearly an hour. She was just that far-sighted.

During the days that followed Alfred's departure, Gertrude's father fell into a dark mood. He sat at the table from morning till night, scowling, hunkered over with a jug of mead always within reach. A giant, throbbing knot swelled from the side of his head where Gertrude's log had struck him down. He did not say a word. He ignored the rats that squealed down from the thatched ceiling. He ignored everything. He was brooding, and the matter upon which he brooded held his full attention.

On the fourth day of her father's foul silence, as Gertrude entered the cottage after a hard day of completing all Alfred's chores, the brooding man at the table finally broke his silence.

He belched.

"Nice to hear your voice, Pa," she said brightly, gliding ever-so-gracefully to the kitchen where she planned to spend the next two hours fixing a fresh pot of tasty gruel.

"I have settled the matter."

She glanced over at him. The look on his face gave her pause. "Pa?" She approached him with an uneasy feeling tickling her bowels. "What have you settled?"

He stared straight ahead without a word. Then he rose from the table and boomed, "I must go to the village, fair daughter of mine."

She frowned as he buckled on his sword and pulled on a heavy cloak. "But it's late, Pa. You'll miss supper–"

"Eat without me, Daughter. I must go." He whacked her on the head affectionately, then turned to throw open the door. "Don't expect me back till morning. I'll stay the night at the inn."

The door banged shut, and the night swallowed him whole. Gertrude heard the creak of the barn gate opening, the clop of a horse, the creak of the barn door closing, the groan of her father climbing into his saddle, the wheeze of his urging the horse forward, and the slow, steady clop of the hooves ambling away. Her brow relaxed as the sound died into the distance. With a short sigh, she bolted the cottage door and collapsed.

"Ug," she grunted as her head hit the floor.

But she didn't feel the pain of it for long. The backbreaking work of the last four days had finally caught up with her, and she reaped the rewards. Instantly, a deep sleep overcame her, a sleep deeper than any sleep she had ever slept, and she dreamed sweet, amorous dreams of the wonderful boy she adored.

It was nearly midnight before Gertrude's father rode into the village. Most of the windows were as dark as the sky, but not the tavern. It glowed like a crackling hearth, inviting any weary traveler to come partake of its warmth. As Gertrude's father drew close and dismounted, he heard raucous laughter erupt within.

Any other time, the sound would have brought a smile to his lumpy face, for the men inside were his friends and neighbors. But tonight he did not smile. Tonight, he would not laugh with them.

There was someone else he had to see.

With a determined sigh, he came to the door of the tavern and shoved it open. The laughter died as all eyes turned upon the latest arrival. They all knew what had happened with his former good-and-faithful farmhand. They all had heard. They all had big ears.

Gertrude's father nodded curtly, his eyes sweeping over the men before him. Hesitantly, they nodded back. They didn't know where he'd been lately, but rumor had it he'd been brooding. Never a good thing, that.

In the back of the tavern, at a table smothered by shadows, a single eye reflected the room's lantern light. It twitched to focus on Gertrude's father. He looked back at it. Pausing a moment, he made his way straight for it.

"Sorry about what happened, Frank," said one of the farmers as he passed.

Gertrude's father nodded and remained on-course.

"You should go after the knave and decapitate him you should, Frank," another one suggested.

"We'll help you!" A cheer went up among his friends.

"Where's he going?" a more observant one whispered to the old geezer beside him.

The geezer slapped a nearby set of false teeth into his mouth. "Looks like–" He swallowed as his eyes widened. "Sheriff Bile's table."

"Sheriff Bile?" A gasp slithered through the lot of them.

Gertrude's father stood before the lone table and squinted his eyes, peering into the impenetrable shadows. "Uh–hello?" His massive frame weaved as he peered from side to side. "Anybody there?"

Silence held the moment. Then from the darkness came a resonant voice: "Sit down, Mr. Grower."

Startled, Gertrude's father instantly obeyed–forgetting to check first if there was a seat beneath him. He hit the floor with a tremendous thump. The eye watched him from the shadows. He shrugged apologetically at it as he struggled to his feet.

"Perhaps you would do better standing," the voice suggested.

"Uh–yessir, maybe so." Gertrude's father took a moment to adjust his attire. Clearing his throat, he stood at his most respectable height. "Are you Sheriff Bile, sir?"

"I am." The eye did not blink.

"Indeed? Uh-indeed, Sir Sheriff sir, indeed I have a proposition for you. Uh-thee."

"Is that so?" The voice carried an edge of humor.

"Aye–uh-yes, indeed."

"Hmm," the voice mused. "Would this proposition have anything to do with your farmhand's sudden disappearance, perchance?"

"Perchance?" Gertrude's father frowned, then nodded. "Perchance yes. Indeed it would."

"I see." Again the eye blinked. "Very well. Share your proposition."

He cleared his throat. "Sir Sheriff, I propose that you find the knave who stole my fastest workhorse and hang him by the neck until dead."

"Is that all?"

Gertrude's father frowned. "I think so."

The voice chuckled languidly. "Well, it seems you have left out a few details."

"I have?" He scratched at his head.

"Your daughter's involvement, for starters. The fact that she may have helped this knave escape, and the rumor that certain improprieties may have taken place between the knave and herself."

Gertrude's father gasped, "Where did you–?"

"News travels fast around a village this size. And I hear everything. One should in my line of work, don't you think? I've heard the entire story more than once, and it's quite a good one–something for the storybooks. An upstanding girl of high moral character seduced by an ignorant farmhand." The eye narrowed. "Boys will be boys, after all."

Gertrude's father swallowed. "But Sir Sheriff, you've heard it

Return Of The Knave

wrong–"

"Mr. Grower, I understand your desire to protect the chaste reputation of your daughter, but allow me to be frank."

"If you want to." He shrugged. "I've never much cared for the name myself."

The eye blinked at that. "You see, Mr. Grower, people are going to believe what they want to believe. No matter what you say, they will see things as they wish. The story as I heard it was a plump, juicy one, fit to satisfy the gossip-mongers of this village for generations to come."

"But–they never really did anything!"

"Then why were you going to kill him?" The eye narrowed again.

"Well, I–" He started to fidget. "It seemed like the right thing to do."

"And do you still want him dead?"

"Of course!"

"Why is that?"

"Because–!" He was bellowing, and he didn't notice until then that all of his friends were listening intently. "Because my daughter thinks she loves him! But she can't. He's NOTHING!!"

The eye bobbed in the shadows. "He is a horse-stealing knave."

"Fit to be hung!"

"Hanged," the voice corrected.

"Huh?"

A shallow chuckle emerged from the shadows. "Mr. Grower, I believe I may have some good news for you."

"Indeed?"

"You see, I have been waiting here for you these last few nights, planning to make you a proposition of my own."

The farmer's puzzled furrows deepened. "You have?"

"It is a proposition I have been hoping to make for quite some time now, from the first day I was assigned to this village. And I believe it will suit us both quite nicely."

There was a long pause, followed by an even longer one. The eye rose slowly, suspended in shadows. "But this is not a suitable environment to discuss such an important matter. Shall we adjourn to my office?"

Gertrude's father shrugged. "I guess so."

"Fine." A gloved hand of black leather emerged to grasp the big farmer by the shoulder. "This way, Mister Grower."

Gertrude's father swallowed and nodded as he was led into the dark.

To say it was the cheery whistling of her father that woke Gertrude from the floor would have been half a truth. Of course she heard him as he prepared their breakfast, and eventually she would have wondered why he was so cheerful, but at the moment it was a rat dropping from the ceiling onto her face that–

"YAAAAAA!" she screeched, lunging upward and giving the rat a kick that sent it sailing up into the thatch from whence it had come. "Stupid rats!"

Her father turned from the gruel gurgling on the stove to beam at her with pride. "Daughter. Fruit of my loins. Beloved offspring. How I love thee!"

She frowned at him and wiped a strand of hair out of her eyes. "Hangover, Pa?"

"Ho-ho!" he laughed, bouncing and reddening. "Not today, fair daughter of mine!"

"Did you sell that fat old cow you hate–the one that kicked you between the legs when you tried to milk her?"

He held his belly and laughed. "Noooooooooo!"

"Then why are you so happy?" Hands on her hips, Gertrude wondered if her poor father had grown senile overnight. Was it possible?

"I-I'm so happy–because," he wheezed, wiping tears from his eyes. "Because I–you're–well, maybe you'd better sit down."

"Okay." Folding up her legs, she dropped to the floor with a thump.

Her father did likewise. "Ug," he groaned, rocking side to side. "I think I landed on a fork or something–can't be sure."

"You'll find it later," she said.

"Right." He cleared his throat. "Daughter, I have news for you that will make your little girl's heart leap with joy! You want to know what it is? Do you?"

Return Of The Knave

She shrugged. "Sure."

"Well, here it is: the honorable Sheriff Bile wants you to be his wife!"

Her jaw dropped open. "Huh?"

He wheezed with delight, hugging himself and rocking. "My daughter–the wife of a sheriff–an officer of the king. Oh-ho! My cup overfloweth!"

She could only stare at him.

"Oh, I am so happy for you, Daughter–sooooo happy! You'll never be in want of anything, ever. You'll have food and clothes– not this stuff that rots off you every other month–and wealth. You'll be rich!"

"But Pa–"

"Oh, Daughter, what can you say to such a wonderful offer? Are you overwhelmed? What can you say? C'mon, tell your old father."

"I feel like puking."

"Oh." He frowned at her with concern. "It must be nerves. Take some deep breaths. Slow now, in through your nose, out through your mouth." He demonstrated with great gusts that tossed his daughter's hair all about. "There now. Feel better?"

"No." She wiped her hair out of her eyes and rose to her feet. "But it's okay. Illness spurs greatness." She frowned. "Or something like that." She paced with a finger to her lips, eyes focused on the floor.

Her father watched, his head tracking her sudden changes in direction, his own brow furrowed in like manner. Her reaction to the news seemed a strange one, but perhaps he didn't know about such things. Gertrude's mother (God rest her soul) had acted fairly nutty when he'd asked for her callused, leathery hand in marriage: she'd clobbered him across the jaw and collapsed in a dead faint, revived later only to clobber him again. So perhaps it was normal for Gertrude to be pacing like this. Less violent, at least.

"Pa." Gertrude knelt beside him with an earnest look in her emerald eyes. "Pa, tell me something."

"Anything, Daughter." He whacked her on the head with affection.

She grimaced slightly, then asked in a low voice, "Did you work out some kind of sinister deal with the sheriff?"

"Uh–" His eyes darted away. "What could you possibly mean?"

Her gaze searched out his honest heart (usually located just below his natural heart, but sometimes it shifted around when he was being slightly dishonest). "You know."

"Well–" He started to squirm, his lumpy face puckering. "I–"

"Tell me, Pa."

He sighed and hung his head. "Aye. That I did."

"What was the deal?"

He groaned as if he were in pain, frowning, eyes downcast. "Well, I–" He shook his head in shame. "I promised him your hand in marriage if he would find Alfred and–"

"Kill him." Her tone was flat.

He looked as if he might burst into tears. "Aye," he gasped, nodding. The realization of what he'd done fell on him so heavily that both of his hearts sank into his bowels. "I'm so sorry, Daughter." His teary eyes rose to meet her. "I wasn't thinking. I worried so much about your future that I forgot to think of your happiness."

She touched his face tenderly. "Oh Pa, you can't help it if you're stupid sometimes." She pinched his cheek with genuine fondness, then jumped to her feet.

"I don't know what I was thinking! I mean, killing that lousy, stinky farmhand is one thing–but roping you into a marriage with a guy twice your age? Oh, I'm so ashamed!" He covered his face with his hands.

"It hasn't happened yet, Pa," she said with a determined look.

"But it's a done deal, Daughter!" he wailed. "There's nothing we can do. As soon as the sheriff's deputies bring back Alfred and hang him in the village square, Bile will be here on our doorstep expecting you to marry him!"

Gertrude didn't seem to hear her distraught father. She stared at the floor, thinking the hardest she had ever thought in her life– until a sudden idea struck her.

"EurekAAAAAA!" she screamed

"What the heck does that mean, Daughter?" her father

Return Of The Knave

grimaced, ears ringing.

But she was gone.

"Hey–!" He struggled to his feet with a groan, yelping as he tugged the fork from his backside. "Where are you going?"

Bursting through the cottage door, Gertrude's father searched high and low outside, but his oddly behaving offspring was nowhere to be found. Then he noticed something peculiar. The door to Alfred's hovel, where the lad had slept after his hours of back-breaking work, hung wide open, and from inside there came the sounds of a great ruckus.

"Daughter!" Gertrude's father cried. "I shall save thee!"

Drawing his sword, he charged the hovel, prepared to dive inside and slay whatever wretched creature was attacking his beloved child. But just as he came to the open doorway–

"Mufflefrommelmummel!" A dress had landed on his head. Savagely, he fought to free himself of it, and when he had done so, he found himself facing a masked stranger. "What the–!" he started, falling backward. "Who are you?"

"I am no one to be questioned." The stranger held out his gloved hand. "Now give me your sword and belt."

Gertrude's father instantly obeyed–though, if he had taken a moment to think about it, he wouldn't have known why he was doing so. Perhaps it was the air of authority in this masked man's voice.

"What have you done with my daughter?" He clutched the ragged dress to his breast, tears springing from his eyes.

"She has been put away for the time being." The stranger struggled as he tried to buckle the wide sword belt around his narrow waist. "But fear not. She will return."

Gertrude's father narrowed his eyes at the stranger. There was something oddly familiar about this fellow. Was it his big green eyes, which peered over the rim of the mask and under the rim of the hood he wore? Was it his height? His shape? Definitely strange for a man–narrow shoulders, wide hips.

"Hey, where have I seen you before, Stranger? Is it possible our swords have crossed before?"

"I don't see how. The only sword I have is yours."

"Oh yeah, I didn't think of that." Gertrude's father was left to

257

ponder the matter.

Sheathed sword swaying at his side, the stranger left the hovel and swaggered to the barnyard gate. His gait was peculiar–graceful, seeming to float across the ground. "I hear you've made a deal with the devil, Mr. Grower."

Gertrude's father followed him, wondering how news kept spreading around so fast lately. "Aye, indeed I have. But how do you–?"

"Remember, I am no one to be questioned."

"Right. Sorry."

The stranger came to the gate and clambered over it. "I've also heard that you tried to kill your farmhand–the best boy who ever lived, the only male creature your daughter has ever shown any affection for."

Gertrude's father sighed. "That's true enough, I suppose."

"And I've heard that you worked in his murder with that devil-deal you made." The stranger's eyes bored into Gertrude's father over the gate separating them.

"Aye." He hung his head.

"Do you regret that part of the deal as much as the other part?"

"Uh–" He tried to wrap his brain around the question. "No. But I do regret it."

The green eyes seemed to soften. "There is hope for you yet."

"Huh?"

But the stranger was gone. All that could be seen was the billowing cloud of dust kicked up by his heels as he ran like the wind, heading in the direction of the village. Gertrude's father gazed after him and held onto his daughter's dress and wondered about a lot of things. Namely, who was this stranger?

From out of the distant dust cloud came a shrill cry, "I'll be back in a bit, PAAAAAAAA!"

His jaw dropped open. "Gertrude?" He looked at the dress in his hands, and a grin tugged at a corner of his face. "Why, that little stinker!"

In the village, in the tavern, in the back corner engulfed by preternatural darkness, Sheriff Bile sat with his men. Actually,

Return Of The Knave

he was the only one sitting, and his three henchmen–two of whom were not men, but rather abominations created by the sheriff's sorcery to serve his evil purposes–stood at attention. The tavern was empty this time of day as all the good men had work to do in their fields and shops, so the sheriff usurped the place to conduct his affairs, kicking out the barkeeper and bolting the doors to keep out the public.

"Now then, Weasel," came the sheriff's voice from the shadows, his single eye resting on one of the henchmen who, remarkably, resembled a man-sized weasel. "Have we made any progress with Farmer Bob?"

Weasel's nose twitched as he whined, "He refuses to pay his taxes. Says he's already paid 'em twice this season."

"So he has." The sheriff chuckled. "Oh well. Torch his place tomorrow morning. Make it look like an accident, and take any valuables you find."

"Aye, sir." Weasel's smile bared sharp yellow teeth.

The sheriff's eye rested on a big brute of a henchman who resembled an overgrown–

"Ox, what have you done about the blacksmith? Is he singing a different tune about me yet?"

"Well, uh..." Ox scratched his head. "He ain't singin' much no more since I broke his face."

"Good work. Pay him another visit tomorrow to be certain his opinion of me has improved. I will not tolerate dissension. I am the sheriff, and this village is mine."

"Hear, hear," the three henchmen applauded.

"What about you, Tim?" Sheriff Bile abruptly set his eye on the third man standing before him, a fellow who looked as much like a Tim as anything else. "What has been done about the miller?"

"Nothing yet–"

"Kill him tomorrow."

"Uh-sir?" Weasel whined. "Is there some reason you want us to put off our dastardly deeds until tomorrow? I mean, I've always heard that it's better not to put off–"

"Yes, procrastination is the lesser part of valor," the sheriff admitted. "But in this case, we can afford to do a little procrastinating, for we shall be rewarded!"

"We will?" Ox asked with a puzzled frown.

"You won't. I will. I was using the royal we."

"Okay." Ox grinned, baring multiple gaps where teeth had once lived.

"Is there some other pressing matter, my liege?" asked Tim.

"Indeed there is, Timmy Boy. And it is a matter of the highest importance."

Weasel clapped his hands together, almost salivating as he begged, "Do tell all, sir!"

"Do you fools remember the day I first set foot in this backward village?" Sheriff Bile watched them nod. "Do you remember the first sight I set my eye upon, that which made me decide, then and there, to remain here?"

They scratched their heads. Then, in unison, they remembered: "The girl!"

"The most beautiful creature I had ever seen, and the moment I saw her, I knew she would someday be mine."

Ox nodded. "So is she?"

"Is she what?" the sheriff snapped.

"Is she yours?"

"She soon will be. I have made a deal with her father. Once we–"

"Uh–we us or we you?" Ox ascertained.

"You." The sheriff's eye glared fiercely. "Once we find the knave who stole her father's horse and hang him in the village square, I shall ride out to the girl's cottage, shake hands with her father, round up a sober priest, and the most beautiful girl on the face of the earth will be mine to have and hold for the rest of my life." He came up for air. "So, what do you think?"

They hesitated, glancing sidelong at each other. Then in unison they shouted, "We think you'll make her a right fine husband, sir!"

"Of course I will. And she had better appreciate it. If she doesn't–well, what can I say?" A coldness crept into his tone. "Then there may be another job for you."

The three henchmen chuckled with slimy malevolence. "We catch your drift, sir."

Return Of The Knave

"Good. Now go catch me that knave!"

They scurried to obey, tripping over each other and their own feet as they rushed to the tavern door. Ox slid back the bolt, Weasel heaved the door open, and Tim stepped outside.

"Aww!" he groaned as something hit him upside the head. Unconscious, he slumped to the porch and lay still.

Startled, Weasel stepped outside to see what had...

"Aww!" he yelped as something also hit him upside the head. Like a floppy, furry rag doll, he fell onto his cohort.

Ox stared at the two of them and frowned. He hung his big head out the door and looked around. "Hello?" Then he looked up. "Uh-oh–"

The log hit him squarely between the eyes, and he collapsed with a groan onto his two cohorts, squishing them beneath his monstrous bulk.

"Who goes there?" he moaned, rubbing his forehead as he struggled to regain his cloven feet. "Are you the knave whom we seek?"

Another log hit him in the back of his head, and he fell forward, shaking his head sharply.

"Show yourself, scoundrel!" Again he rose to his unsteady feet, searching for the log-throwing fiend. "Where are you, knave? Are you a coward? Do you fight a man like this?"

"Yes, I do."

Ox whirled around to face...

Another log. He tipped over backwards, once again crushing his unconscious cohorts. "Give up, scoundrel. You–" he gasped, "you cannot knock out the Ox!"

"Is that your name?"

Through a haze, Ox saw a blurry shape standing over him. Did it wear a hood? A mask? "Who are you, Stranger?"

"I am no one to be questioned." The sharp blade of a sword came up under the big creature's chin. "Take me to your leader."

Ox knew better than to argue with this log-hurling, sword-wielding fiend. So with the blade trained on his back and a few choice grunts, he got to his hind hooves and gestured toward the tavern's interior. "This way."

The stranger curtsied, then followed.

"Uh–Sheriff Bile?" Ox frowned as he arrived at the dark table. "Are you there, sir?"

The eye opened. "What is it, Ox?" came the sheriff's quiet voice.

"There's-uh somebody here to see you." He swallowed as the stranger's sword dug into his back.

"Well, where is he? I see no one."

"He's behind me, sir."

"Then step aside!"

The big oaf did so, leaving the stranger in plain sight. With his sword held straight at the sheriff now, the strange figure stood confidently, hooded, masked, cloaked, gloved, and booted, with a baggy shirt and even baggier pants. He would have looked comical and, indeed, the sheriff would have laughed out loud had it not been for the wild look in the stranger's green eyes.

"What is the meaning of this?" Bile demanded. "Who the devil are you?"

"I am no one to be questioned. And I do not appreciate references to the devil."

The sheriff's eye blinked.

"Allow me to deal with you squarely," the stranger said. "I know of your sinister deal with Farmer Grower, and I am here to give you a change of heart–one you must undergo, or else you will be forced to suffer certain unpleasantries."

The sheriff's eye narrowed. "You dare to threaten me, strange one?"

"Yes, I do. I threaten your very life. Either you forget about Farmer Grower's daughter and Farmer Grower's horse-stealing knavish farmhand, or I shall hack off your head and give it to the village children. They are in need of a new soccer ball, I hear."

The sheriff sized up the weird-looking fellow before him. "You are a brave rascal. I'll give you that. But you are also a fool." He paused to let that sink in. "Do you actually believe you can kill an officer of the king and get away with it?"

"I plan to do both–if your heart does not undergo that change I mentioned. Forget about Farmer Grower's daughter. She is in love with another–"

Return Of The Knave

"HA!" A gloved hand shot out of the darkness and pounded the table. "You, perhaps?" The sheriff's eye rose as he stood. "Hear me, strange one: the girl is mine! I have waited long to have her, and I will kill anyone who stands in my way!" A sword rang against its sheath. "To the death!"

The stranger drew back sharply as Bile emerged from the shadows. Garbed from head to foot in stylish black leather, the sheriff stood near seven feet tall, his frame muscular, his face a mass of scars, lumps, pocks, bruises, and burned flesh. His left eye socket lay empty, shriveled up tight, and his right eye bulged with malice.

"Look upon me and fear!" Bile roared, throwing back his head with dramatic laughter. "Am I not a sight to behold?"

"You should be the one wearing a mask."

"I've considered it, but then I wouldn't be able to use the whole look upon me and fear bit."

"How did you get that way?"

"Oh, that's quite a story." The sheriff lowered his sword and leaned on the hilt. "As a lad, I enjoyed making fireworks, you see. I was a real feisty little fellow, full of zest and vigor, and I seldom followed directions–which often got me into heaps of trouble, but that's beside the point. So one day, I was down in the basement of our family cottage, just mixing a routine concoction of Chinese rocket fuel when–NOW, fools!"

The stranger let out a short cry as he was pounced on from all sides. Ox took away his sword, a fully recovered Weasel grabbed his arms, and a now-conscious Tim grabbed hold of his legs, pinning him to the tavern floor. The stranger struggled in vain.

Sheriff Bile laughed, his teeth crooked and brown. "Lesson number one, your strangeness: Never trust your opponent. As I entered into that riveting albeit short-lived monologue–all fictitious, of course, as my appearance is no more than a byproduct of excelling in the usage of dark magic–my men were closing in on you, just waiting for my command to strike. You didn't even hear them coming!" He clucked his tongue. "Pathetic."

"I'm kind of new at this," the stranger admitted.

"So it would appear." The sheriff's eye narrowed, fixed on the stranger's mask as he reached out a gloved hand. "I believe the time has come for your unveiling. Let's see what you look like, Strange One."

The stranger's eyes darted in a frenzy.

Gertrude's father perked up at the sound of hoof beats trotting into the barnyard.

"Gertrude?" He rose from the table and his twenty-third game of solitaire. "Could it be? Is it she?" He moved to the cottage door with a fast beating of both his hearts. "Daughter!" he boomed as he threw open the door. But he stopped short. "Oh. It's you."

"Not much of a welcome." Alfred jumped down from the exhausted work horse.

"If I had my sword, I'd greet you proper." Glowering, the farmer stepped forward to grab the reins. "Why are you back?"

"Oh, I don't know. Homesick, I guess."

"This isn't your home–not anymore. You're a knave." Farmer Grower turned away, leading the horse to the barn. "A horse-stealing highwayman!"

"But Gertrude gave it to me." He hastened to follow. "And besides, I brought it back in one piece, so how can I truly be a knave?"

Farmer Grower shook his head, refusing to look at the boy. "Once a knave, always a knave. You can't change these things. You're fit to be hung–"

"Hanged," Alfred corrected.

"You leave my grammar alone." The big man glared at him. "You've got to die, and that's all there is to it. There's naught more to be said."

"But..." Alfred caught sight of his old hovel, its door open and everything inside a mess. "Has somebody else moved into my place?"

"No. Gertrude was in there a while ago, borrowing some of your clothes."

"Why? Where'd she go?"

Farmer Grower shrugged. "To the village. Said something about the deal I made with Sheriff Bile–"

"You made a deal with Bile?" Alfred gasped.

"Mayhaps."

"How could you? Bile is pure evil–wickedness incarnate! He robs the poor to make himself richer and kills anyone who stands in his way. Why, he's the sorcerer who killed my parents!"

The farmer threw up his hands at this very unexpected backstory. "Now you tell me!"

"Huh?"

"I've always felt that you carried a dark secret. Why'd you wait so long for the big reveal?"

The boy shrugged. "I kind of just remembered."

"Daaah, you are an idiot." The farmer hauled himself aboard the work horse and glared down at his once-upon-a-time-good-and-loyal farmhand. "Well?"

"What?"

"We're going to the village, buffoon! To rescue my daughter!" One of his brawny arms shot down, grabbed hold of the boy by his shirtfront, and hoisted him up behind him on the horse. "To redeem yourself!"

Alfred nodded. "Okay, sounds good."

"HA!" Gertrude's father gave the horse a kick. "We're off!"

And they were–at a very slow trot.

Two hours later, Gertrude's father and the infamous knave entered the village in time to find a celebratory gathering in the square. Curious, they peered through the swaying banners and signs held by cheering village people to see what the heck was going on.

Then they gasped.

And they stared.

A lopsided scaffold had been hastily erected, and dangling by their necks hung four bodies: one the size of an ox, another the shape of a weasel, the next one could have been named Tim, and the fourth...

"Eww," Alfred grimaced and swallowed. "That's Bile."

"You sure?" Farmer Grower squinted. "It was too dark for me to get a good look at him whilst we were making our sinister deal."

"I'd recognize that horrid visage anywhere."

"Aye, what a horrid visage," Grower echoed. "A truly horrid visage indeed."

Alfred rose up, scanning the crowd. "I don't see Gertrude." He jumped off the horse and pressed through the crowd.

"Hey, where are you going?" Farmer Grower called after him. "Come back, boy! They'll hang you next!"

Alfred kept moving, swallowed by the cheering, sign-and-banner-waving mob as he headed toward the scaffold. Nobody seemed to notice him, but he really wouldn't have cared if they had. His only thought was that these four dangling bodies had slain Gertrude before becoming dangling bodies, and that's why they were now dangling bodies. It was a horrible, confusing thought, one that made him oblivious to his own welfare.

Finally, he broke through the crowd and stumbled into the middle of the square beneath four sets of swaying boot heels. He took a moment to catch his breath and held up his hands to hush the people. Only they didn't need him to hush them. They had already fallen silent with their eyes fixed on him.

Without pause, Alfred shouted, "Where is Gertrude Grower?"

No response.

"Have any of you seen her?" he demanded.

Deaf and dumb, they stared back at him.

"Is she all right?"

"IT'S THE KNAVE!" They were deaf but not dumb, after all. "THE KNAVE HAS RETURNED!" they roared angrily.

One fellow held up a coil of rope and yelled, "HANG THE KNAVE!"

Already in something of a hang-happy mood, everybody agreed it was a great idea–everyone except for Alfred and, strangely enough, Farmer Grower. But they were outvoted. Before he knew what was happening, the infamous knave had been seized, fitted with a noose, and was about to be hanged by the neck until dead beside the hideous Sheriff Bile.

But then something strange happened.

"YAAAAAAAAAAAAA!!" came a sudden shriek, and all eyes turned upward to see a cloaked, hooded, masked, gloved, and booted figure sailing through the air, riding a rope attached

Return Of The Knave

to something (it doesn't really matter what) like a monkey on a vine. Swooping down with gleaming sword in hand, the figure slit the noose from the knave's throat and leapt onto the top of the scaffold. "Shame on you, village people!" The figure's green eyes glared at the cowering villagers. "I'm in the privy for just a minute, and look what you do. SHAAAME!"

They shrank back mutely and hung their heads. Only the fellow with the rope dared to speak. "But he's the knave, Strange One. He stole Farmer Grower's horse–"

"No, no he didn't!" boomed a voice from the back of the mob. All eyes turned to see Farmer Grower hopping up and down aboard the horse in question and pointing down at the horse in question. "Here it is! See? It was all just a BIG misunderstanding!"

The masked figure nodded once, hands on his hips. "Satisfied?"

The fellow with the rope glowered, muttering to himself. Then he yelled, "What of the farmer's daughter? It's a known fact this knave put GOO-GOO EYES on her!" A gasp erupted amongst the crowd, and he seized Alfred by the arm, shaking him like a rag doll for a full minute. "This knave must be hung!"

"Hanged," the crowd corrected him.

"Whatever!" His grip on Alfred inched toward his throat. "The knave must die!"

"Nope." The masked figure shook his head. "I don't think so."

"Why not?" the savage fellow demanded.

"Because." In a single move, both the mask and hood fell by the wayside to reveal the stunning beauty of none other than Gertrude Grower herself. "I should know if I've had GOO-GOO EYES put on me, now shouldn't I?"

The crowd gasped, gaped, and gawked. The fellow with the rope made a quick exit because he felt stupid. Farmer Grower wept with joy. And Alfred fell to his knees.

"Oh, my love!" he cried, arms outstretched. "How I've missed you!"

"Aww." She dropped her chin and blushed. "Thanks, Alfred."

He stood and bowed slightly. "Thanks for saving my life."

She smiled down at him. "Anytime."

"Well–" He didn't know what else to say. "Guess I'd better get back to the farm. Five days of chores are probably waiting for me."

"Nope. Only one." She shrugged. "I've been kinda keeping things going around the place in your absence. Today I slacked off a little, though."

He shook his head in awe, unable to stop staring up at her. She was so...amazing. "Well, then I guess I'd better get that day's work done."

She nodded, still smiling. "Guess so."

He smiled back. "See you later then."

She watched him turn to go. "Oh–Alfred," she halted him.

He whirled around. "Yeah?"

"You'll need these." She took a moment to pull off his work gloves and toss them down.

"Thanks." He grinned as he caught them.

"And these, too." She dropped her rear end onto the scaffold with a thump that sent the dangling bodies a-wobbling. "Your boots." She grunted as she pried them off and dropped one at a time.

"Thanks again." Boots under one arm and gloves in one hand, he waved up at her and grinned, then dashed away.

As a cool breeze caught her flaxen locks and played with them, she watched him go from atop the scaffold and turned away with a radiant expression only when he had reached the barnyard of her father's distant farm.

She was just a wee bit far-sighted, after all.

That night, Farmer Grower, Gertrude, and Alfred sat around their oak table and laughed, talked, and slurped their gruel without the use of utensils. It was a good time had by all, a happy time, a joyous time. A messy time.

"Ha-HA!" Gertrude bellowed, forehead to chin covered in great gooey gruel globs.

"Ho-ho!" Farmer Grower echoed, pointing at his beloved daughter. "A new addition for your Strange One character!"

Alfred chuckled along for a while, then grew serious as he asked her, "My love…"

A sudden blow sent him to the floor. The laugher stopped.

"Listen, boy," Gertrude's father hissed at him under the table, "The deal was you go on living and working here if you put the love stuff on hold for a while. A nice, loooong while. You address my daughter as Miss Gertrude and nothing else, you got that?"

"Got it," Alfred groaned, struggling to regain his seat.

"I don't want to go back to threatening your life every other day." Clearing his throat, Farmer Grower returned to his gruel.

Gertrude watched Alfred. "Did you want to ask me something?"

"Uh–yeah. Yes, Miss Gertrude." He swallowed and glanced over at her father who nodded approvingly. "How did you manage to hang those four villainous rogues? I mean, how did you go about incapacitating them?"

She smiled at him. Then she shrugged. "A blow to the groin works wonders." She laughed at his startled expression. "Yeah, I just kicked 'em where it hurts, one by one, and they weren't really any trouble after that. Nobody in the village liked them anyway, so it didn't take much convincing to get them strung up."

"But–" He frowned. "Didn't anybody recognize you? Didn't anybody see you?"

"Bile did. He pulled off my mask and was so dumbfounded– they all were. Well, that's the moment I went into action. And once I had Pa's sword again, there was really nothing they could do to stop me."

Farmer Grower beamed with pride.

Alfred could only shake his head in awe. "You're amazing, Miss Gertrude."

She giggled. "I know."

"So what about this alter ego of yours, Daughter?" her father interjected. "Do you plan to use him again to right the wrongs of the land?"

"Oh, I don't know," she sighed. "It was fun, but I can tell it would take a lot out of me if I did it every day." She shrugged. "Maybe just now and then. You know, when the need arises."

Her father nodded solemnly. "A noble daughter, Thought–Er–

I mean, a very noble thought, Daughter. Yes indeed."

Alfred gazed into her eyes. "And if you ever need a sidekick..." he proposed.

She winked at him. "I'll know where to find you."

"That's right. Because I have returned, and I will never leave you again."

Farmer Grower cleared his throat and gave Alfred a steely-eyed look.

"That is, as long as I do my chores and address you as Miss Gertrude and speak to you only at mealtimes and treat you with all the honor, dignity, and respect that you deserve." He came up for air.

Gertrude's father whacked him on the head. "There may be hope for you yet, knave!"

Gertrude smiled happily and a glob of gruel hit the table with a loud splat. Then her entire face-full of gruel plopped onto the table. She started to laugh, hysterically, screeching, head thrown back with mouth gaping wide, her limbs flailing as she hooted like a maniac.

Alfred could only stare in wonder, his heart in his throat. She was so...amazing.

Young Adventurers

Meet Mikhaila, a young warrior girl in a world where magic can save you, if your heart is true and you have the training…

FIRST MISSION

Jack Mulcahy

Mikhaila felt as if her arms would break if she had to keep the sword in the ready position any longer. How had she got herself into so much trouble so fast? Her second day? Only yesterday Sergeant Hamish had welcomed the sixteen-year-old recruit to Company E and complimented her on her commendable record. Now she was "Blockhead," the recruit whose actions might have cost her comrade his life.

To ease the tension, she focused on the sword, instead of on her anger at Corporal Beorn, who'd sent her and Kester, her recruit partner, on the practice exercise to get a message through a thirty-five-mile stretch of mountainous, wooded terrain undetected, each carrying a fifty-pound pack. The route was full of dried leaves and dead branches, hidden roots to trip them and brambles that scratched and clawed at them. "Your worthless lives depend on absolute silence," Beorn had told them. "In combat, the slightest noise could mean death or capture."

Mikhaila had grown up in the woods of Auriga, so moving silently through such terrain was not difficult for her, despite her being taller than most boys her age and even some men. She and Kester had both traveled most of the course when Beorn sprang his trap. Her legs by this time lacked most of their springiness, and her lungs burned, yet still she managed to keep silent, not even allowing her panting to escape into the air. She could see the camp through the thinning trees; perhaps she'd begun to slow down, anticipating the sweet feeling of collapsing into her bunk. Just when she could imagine the end of the long journey, four masked figures ambushed her, provoking an involuntary cry.

That had brought Beorn out, yelling and cursing, as her

assailants removed their and masks to stand revealed as four fellow recruits. "Blockhead!" Beorn had screamed. "You just got yourself captured and your partner killed! Stupid, careless blockhead!"

"Blockhead! Blockhead! Blockhead!" the other recruits had chanted in unison.

Bastards! she thought now. *Lucky for them I didn't use my Magic and transform them into spears or something!*

So now she was "Blockhead," forced to stand this unending guard duty holding the sword that clearly weighed less than an oak tree, though not much. *Worst of all, he was right, I did fail the mission,* she thought for the thousandth time. *If it had been real combat, Kester would be dead and I'd be on my way to Rahesh as a damned slave! What kind of soldier does that make me?*

"Everybody makes mistakes, Mikhaila. Don't let it get to you." The whisper was Kester's. He stepped from the shadows into the faint light of the torches. Kester was short, with a feline face and hair almost as golden as Mikhaila's. "If we didn't fail, how'd we ever learn and improve? That's what me da' always said."

"Get out of here!" Mikhaila hissed. "If Corporal Beorn or Sergeant Hamish find you here..."

"Relax. You worry too much. They won't find me. Remember, the Corporal didn't catch *me* this afternoon, he caught *you.*"

"And now the Sergeant's caught you, recruit!" Sergeant Hamish appeared suddenly out of the darkness, a tall, ruddy-featured man with a shock of red hair that stood up like a hedge. He wore a long mustache that covered his lips and curled on the ends. Mikhaila, seeing him for the first time yesterday, had wondered how he managed to eat without getting a mouthful of mustache.

The Sergeant's blue eyes gleamed like twin stars in the dim light. "You thought your Sergeant forgot how to move quietly, eh?" he asked.

Kester had come stiffly to attention. "N-no, sir. I mean, Sergeant...I mean..."

First Mission

"As you were," Hamish sighed. "Now, make yourself scarce, recruit." Over his shoulder, he added, "And when I say scarce, that's just what I mean. I don't want to see so much as your shadow within a hundred feet of here by the time I turn back around."

Kester disappeared into the shadows. Sergeant Hamish walked around Mikhaila, who kept her eyes fixed at a point in the middle distance, though she yearned to follow his movements. *But that's part of his test, to see how disciplined I am, 'specially after my failure today. I'll show him!*

"Sword gets heavy after the first hour or so, doesn't it, recruit?" Hamish said, his voice unreadable.

Mikhaila settled for the safe answer. "I'll manage, Sergeant," she said, despite the fires of pain in her right arm.

Hamish came around to face her. "Put it down," he said. "With that answer, you might as well have hung a sign around your neck that said, 'I'm feeding you wolfshit.'" He watched her ease the sword down. She made sure to perform the task exactly as she'd been taught, until the blade slid into its scabbard with a satisfying breath of steel on felt. Then she came to attention, trying to ignore the pins and needles that washed over her right arm and shoulder.

"Hurts, I know," Hamish said. "And had I been here, Beorn would not have been allowed to inflict it on you. Still, despite what I'm sure are your angry thoughts on how unfair it all was, Beorn's test was fair. There are no rules in war, Mikhaila. The Raheshis won't allow for your being tired. That's when you're the most vulnerable, and you've just learnt a valuable lesson. I hope. The shame should have been enough. Beorn went farther than necessary. You may consider yourself confined to quarters until dawn. Dismissed."

Mikhaila found the strength to salute. "Yes, Sergeant. Thank you, Sergeant."

Three days after her test, Mikhaila was part of a ten-member team that had crossed into Rahesh through the mysterious Forest of Hærne, on a mission to observe and report enemy activity. Some said Hærne was haunted, home to all manner of mysterious spirits and creatures, most of which slept during the day. So Mikhaila hoped. After they'd entered, the Forest had closed quickly behind them, as if to hem them in and prevent their escape. Overhead, a few stray sunbeams struggled to penetrate the leafy roof, but it was mostly dank and dark. Plants with huge multihued leaves lashed at them. Networks of vines sought to trip them up. Even the trees seemed aware of them. *None too pleased with us, either,* she thought. As if the Forest had allied with their Raheshi enemies. The forests back home always seemed alive too, but clean and fresh with the scent of pine and bay and spruce. Here lurked the stench of rotting leaves, swamp gas and death. All forests were alive in some way, she had always thought. This forest was alive, too, but malevolent.

Foolish girl, she scolded herself, *stop thinking such nonsense! Focus on the mission!* Step after excruciating step she followed her comrades, careful not to place her foot on a branch or twig, keeping clear of roots that could trip and broken twigs that could snap and betray her.

When Beorn gave the signal the entire group dropped to a crouch into the brush. "Blockhead!" Beorn's whisper seemed as loud as a shout, though only three recruits separated them. He'd stopped under the branches of a huge oak tree. When she nodded, he continued, "Crawl through those brambles and see what's up there on the road. Do it without giving us all away, Blockhead."

Mikhaila flushed but did as the Corporal ordered, silent as a grave. *Bad enough he called me that, but now the whole squad calls me it now, even the other recruits.* Rapier strapped tight across her back and spear tucked under her right arm, she squirmed noiselessly through the thorns until she reached a point beside the road. What now? She glanced back, saw Beorn's signal to stay in position, and nodded acknowledgement.

Time crawled. She became aware of every drop of sweat, every itch, every scratch of the wool tunic. Nothing moved up or down the road, as far as she could see. But when she glanced back again for Corporal Beorn, not only could she not see him, but the very section of forest where he and the others had hidden

First Mission

seemed different. There was no huge oak tree, no waist-high thicket of weeds and brush. The area now seemed dominated by white-clad beeches, mingled here and there with willow and bay.

Worst yet was the troll who marched up the road in the peculiar bow-legged gait common to his race. He was larger than a man, and broader across the shoulders and midsection, though his arms and bowed legs appeared stunted in proportion. Over his hairless chest he wore a leather vest, and trews of the same material covered his legs. His head was pumpkin-shaped, with gray, wispy hair that fluttered in the breeze like gossamer. He had pointed ears that stuck out and bristled with hair, tiny, malicious eyes, a beaklike, predatory nose, and a mouth that was a narrow slash across his clay-colored face. A curved sword hung from a belt around his waist, and he wore heavy leather boots with pointed tips that looked like steel. When he aimed his vicious face in Mikhaila's direction, the Aurigan recruit froze, thinking surely he would see her, but he did not seem to. *Trolls hate daylight,* she thought. *What's this one doing out now? Maybe they don't see well in the daytime. I hope.*

Then the troll froze, and she saw its nostrils flare, heard it sniffing. *Goddess Fehtan, which way is the wind blowing? Am I upwind or down? Dare I draw my sword, and hope he doesn't see or hear the movement?*

The troll growled, *"Gjanna nog akœf!"* and charged at her, its sword pointed straight out. Mikhaila gave it no chance to reach her, springing to her feet and seizing her own weapon in a single, fluid movement. Then it was all as the drillmasters had taught her: Strike, parry, thrust. The troll would try not to kill her; not with the gold she would bring as a slave. That gave her an advantage, she hoped.

Yet, for all its size and bulk, the troll was quick and nimble. For every attack she made, it had an effective parry. It fought like a machine, and nearly as quickly. Could it tire? The way it used its sword effectively neutralized her chances of closing in to grab it and use her Weapons-Magic. Her light rapier was no match for the troll's heavier blade. The creature pressed the attack, forcing her backward, until she was stopped by the bole of a huge elm, which wrapped two of its branches around her before she could react, pinning her.

Confidently, the troll approached. Mikhaila, terrified, struggled to free herself. She tried her Weapons-Magic on the tree, but the tree was so ancient, and its will so powerful and malevolent, that her Magic was like a fly trying to kill an elephant. But as the troll reached out for her, another option occurred to her. *It may kill me, but I'll sooner be dead than a slave!* The troll grabbed her arm, and with that contact, she used her Magic, transforming it into a lightning bolt that struck the tree with a force that split it down the middle. As the elm began to fall, Mikhaila squirmed away, avoiding being crushed, though she lost her helmet. A branch struck her exposed head and the world went dark.

Was it hours or minutes before she awakened? She had no idea. She was bound hands and ankles, in a deep, narrow hole in the ground. Another rope wrapped around her chest, under her arms, attached to some point above, presumably to haul her in and out of here. Somewhere up there, voices were arguing in the harsh Raheshi language. From what she could understand of Rahesho, the argument seemed to be about her.

"And I say we *jebâc* the Aurigan now, the priests be damned," one of them growled. "Lot of us haven't *njóta pjá* in near a month, and besides, it'd teach 'er her place. Make 'er easier to bring back." Mikhaila's blood froze at the thought of how many Raheshis would be taking their pleasure with her. *Stay calm, girl,* she told herself. *Panic will only make your worst fears more likely to happen. You know what General Eurydice always taught you about learning as much about your enemy as you can first.*

"You know better'n that, Nagl," said another. "We bring 'em in *vârdvieta,* them's orders, 'cause they brings more *siolfor* that way. An' the more *siolfor* the dealers get, the more we get. Then you can buy all the girls you want."

"Are you in charge here, Helem, or am I?" Nagl answered. This last comment sent a shiver through Mikhaila she could not control. If Nagl had his way...*No, this might be a situation she could use to her advantage later.* She heard the voices of others

First Mission

muttering encouragement, either to Nagl or to Helem.

"Neither 'a yez," a third voice broke in, hushing the other two. "Fine sight this is, I must say! I leave yez alone fer a day, an' yez're arguin' over the blonde when yez know yez has orders ta leave 'em be. An' them orders, in case yez forgot, comes from all the way up top, from Magister Nejemiya hisself. So we'll have no more talk about any diddlin' the captive from here on out! Understood?" When Nagl did not answer quickly enough, the man repeated, "Understood?"

She could almost see Nagl slump as he said, "Understood, Cap'n." It was all she could do not to heave a sigh of relief, even when Nagl added, "Waste of a fine-lookin' tail, though."

"Enough!" the Captain roared. "Maybe twenty lashes'll teach you some respect for orders!"

So they're not so unified, are they? Remember that. And remember, too, that you rescued General Eurydice from scum like these when you were only fourteen.

But how to get out of here? Had they seen her use her Magic? Should she risk it now, or wait for a more advantageous time, which might or might not present itself?

It was impossible to see the sky above the ceiling of trees, but she thought she saw the flicker of fires reflected off low branches. So it was likely night. Were they waiting for day to move? In this strange forest, that might be the wisest course.

After what seemed forever, she saw signs that the fires were starting to diminish, suggesting that most of her enemies would be sleeping. *Now or never,* she thought. She squirmed in her bonds, constantly listening for any sign of anyone approaching. Then she used her Magic on the ropes around her hands, turning them into a pair of short gauntlets. Her hands free, she transformed the bindings on her ankles into greaves. The rope around her chest she left in place; it must be tied to a tree or a post above. If she tampered with it, someone would surely notice.

She tried digging out a bit of the side of the pit. That would take too long. She gave a tentative tug on the rope that disappeared somewhere above, and felt resistance. Nothing else to do but try climbing. *If they're going to give me a way out,* she thought, *I'm a fool if I don't try it.* She spit on each hand and levered herself up the rope with hands and feet. Her hands burned, despite the sword-calluses, and she could not move too quickly, lest her captors notice the rope tautening or moving up top. Finally, she was peering over the rim of the hole as far as she could in all directions. She saw nothing, heard nothing. She hauled herself out of the hole, untied the rope around her waist, and dropped to all fours.

Keep moving. She crept to the shadow of a nearby tent. From within, she heard the sounds of snoring.

The camp occupied the closest to a clearing Hærne offered, and the tents were arranged around and beside trees, which stood like giant sentinels. She smelled the remains of a roasted boar amid the odor of decay that overlay the forest. Here and there, banked fires still glowed faintly. She had just dashed across an open space for the shadow of a tall tree when she heard two sets of footsteps approaching.

"I don't care what the captain says. That was the voice she recognized as belonging to Nagl. "I'm going to have some fun with that Aurigan wench."

"Just be careful we don't damage 'er," another voice said.

"You worry too much, Brandir," Nagl snarled. "Besides, who's going to believe a slave, even if she does complain? Now let's haul 'er out of that hole an'–"

Mikhaila was on them like a tigress Before Nagl could react, she leapt and kicked him in the chin. The blow snapped his head back and sent him into the pit. In a single movement, Mikhaila was back on her feet. "Ready to die, 'master'?" she sneered at the second Raheshi. When she stabbed at his eyes with her stiffened fingers, he ducked and tried to head-butt her in the belly, but the boiled leather cuirass she'd created with her Magic took most of the force, and she rolled with the blow. She kicked him over her head, where he landed with a snap on his neck and did not move again. Then she turned her attention to Nagl, in the pit, who was struggling without success to clamber up the smooth sides. She had to finish this quickly, she knew, before someone heard and raised the alarm, so she found a large flat rock and dropped it on him, dashing his brains out. Then she

First Mission

fled, not looking back.

She had just reached the camp perimeter when she encountered the guard. "Who goes there?" he called, just loudly enough to awaken anybody nearby. She charged him, even as he raised his spear defensively, and took him down, twisting his head until she heard the bones snap. But now others in the camp were starting to stir. She plunged into the bushes surrounding the camp, praying she did not smash into a tree or break an ankle over a hidden root. Through tall grasses and around huge trees, she fled, ducking low branches and narrowly avoiding vines that sought to catch her and brambles that snatched at her like claws. Behind her, she could see torches through the woods. She must put distance between herself and pursuit, quickly. She had no fear of exhaustion, nor of betraying herself by making noise, despite the results of Corporal Beorn's test, but she had no real idea where she was or which way the border lay. She might blunder on like this for hours and make no real forward progress. She had to go to ground somewhere until daylight, when she would have a better chance of finding her way out.

Suddenly, the terrain sank, and she tumbled down a long hill, landing at the bottom of a dry stream bed, littered with rocks and broken branches. This might be good luck, for she could follow it for a time and at least feel certain of not running into a tree. As she scrambled along the rocky crevasse, however, she became aware of something watching her, a malevolent presence more felt than seen. She paused for a few heartbeats, aware that the sounds of pursuit had disappeared, and it occurred to her to wonder whether she had been directed this way, either by her pursuers or by something else.

Eventually she came to the mouth of a cave. Before entering, she paused, listened, smelled. She heard nothing; but the scent of rot and death was overpowering, and she decided against seeking shelter there. But when she turned away, she found her path blocked by a solid wall of thick brush that had not been there a moment ago, leaving her no choice but to enter the void. With a prayer to Goddess Fehtan the Warrior, she ducked into the darkness.

The stink was even worse inside the cavern, and she nearly

gagged, but there was no other way but forward. All her fears of the dark arose, prickling her skin and wracking her with shivers. With an effort of will, she forced the fear down, but it did not vanish, merely subsided, waiting beneath the surface of her mind as a hidden lion waits for the gazelle. *You saved General Eurydice from the Raheshis,* she chided herself. *Just keep your wits about you.* But that was so hard when she could not see her hand in front of her face. *Light,* she thought, *what I wouldn't give now for a light of some kind!* She paused a moment, considering, then felt around under her feet until her toe struck a fair-sized rock. She bent down and hefted it, found it was about the right size for her needs, then focused her Weapons-Magic. What better weapon against the darkness than light? And the rock began to glow from within, illuminating the chamber with a white brilliance that dazzled her eyes at first, after the darkness. When her vision cleared, she nearly dropped the rock at the sight of the five manacled skeletons that lined the wall on her right side. A rat poked its nose out of an otherwise empty eye socket, and snakes crawled around the shins and arms of the shackled figures.

Then, beyond the skeletons, she saw the glint of eyes, watching her. The hairs on the back of her neck prickled, and her every muscle stiffened. Swallowing hard, she grabbed a long bone that had fallen to the floor of the cave and transformed it into a gladius. "Who's there?" she asked.

A sharp hissing answered her. A snake? What kind of–?

"Goddess!" she cried, nearly dropping the sword as a rat the size of a lion emerged into the light. It snarled, revealing teeth like swords. Hooked claws seemed to leap from its forepaws.

A chill raced down Mikhaila's spine. All the primeval fears of rats and monsters raced through her. Uncle Luc had once been bitten on the hand by a rat, Mama had told her, a rat that only let go after they'd killed it.

She swallowed and backed away. The rat followed. *Courage isn't the absence of fear*, Fehtan said. *It's when you don't let that fear cloud your thinking.* As she backed away, she noticed the rat's nose and ears twitching, but there seemed no movement in its eyes. *It lives here in the dark. And I come in with this light. I* *wonder...*she poured a little more of the Magic into the rock, brightening the glare, and saw the rat's eyes begin to blink and water. So it was sniffing and listening for her, rather than using its sight! Eyeing her surroundings, she silently slipped to her right. The monster's ears twitched, but it did not follow her movement. It crept closer. She remained where she stood until the creature's eye was nearly opposite her. Then she leapt, swordpoint first, jabbing straight into the rat's exposed left eye. It roared and lashed out with its claws, which raked Mikhaila's arm, forcing her to drop the sword, which reverted to a bone. The intrepid Aurigan shifted toward the thing's blinded left side. Her arm bled where the rat's claws had torn it; only Fehtan's mercy had saved her from losing the arm. But she had damaged the rat, too, more than she'd realized, for its right front paw hung limp and useless. Now she heard the creature's heavy, labored breathing. *It may be dying,* she thought. But wounded animals were the most dangerous.

The rat growled again, and pushed off its left legs toward her, snapping. Mikhaila's agility kept her from falling prey to the beast. The change in position put her within reach of another bone. But her wounded right arm would not obey her, so she would have to set down the rock she'd been using for light if she was to reach for the bone.

But then she caught a faint glimmer of light at the end of the cave, beyond the rat.

Without a moment's hesitation, she dropped the rock and grabbed the bone with her left hand in the same movement, transforming it into a torch. She jabbed at the rat, forcing it away from her, then raced around the huge form toward the source of the light. As she ran, the light seemed to grow no larger, however, and she wondered if it were not merely another malevolent trick of Hærne. Behind her, she could hear the roaring, growling rat dragging its huge body on two legs.

Finally, though, she saw that she was indeed approaching the mouth of the cave, and that the passage narrowed the closer to the surface it led.

Then she stumbled over a crevice in the cave floor. The rat closed in. Mikhaila smelled its blood, heard the growls from its throat, saw its laboring effort to haul itself after her. She scrambled to her feet, dizzy from the fall, narrowly missing the bite of the rat's teeth. The girl was sure she could not continue further, wounded and exhausted as she was, but she dragged herself on, certain that at any moment she would fall prey to the giant beast.

And then the rat was no longer behind her. It had wedged itself into the narrow passage, unable to pursue further or turn back. With a sigh of relief, she clambered free of the cave and collapsed onto the soft grass of a meadow, Hærne behind her, looming like a nightmare, yet powerless to harm her further.

She dragged herself to her feet. The camp! She must find the Aurigan camp and tell them where the Raheshis were! She looked to her left, saw the sun rising over the snow-covered peak of Mount Kjamrha, the highest of the Sassaine Mountains. *At least I didn't end up in Rahesh,* she thought.

To find her comrades, she must venture into Hærne again.

She turned north, keeping the sun on her right, and began her trek, paralleling the forest for as long as possible. If she could find the place where they'd entered, she knew she could find the Aurigans.

For defense, she found a fallen branch to transform into a sword again. Before long, she encountered a stream, and she took a moment to scoop some water into her mouth. But cleaning her wound would have to wait until...

A twig snapped. She spun, sword at the ready.

"You look like hell, Blockhead." It was Corporal Beorn, alone. She snapped to attention and tried to salute, but could not raise her right arm. "We thought you ran away."

"No, Corporal," she answered. "But I did find the Raheshi camp."

Beorn lifted an eyebrow. "Did you now?" he said. "And could you show your comrades where this camp might be?"

She thought a moment, wondering if she could find the dry stream bed again without leading her fellows through the cave. "I believe I could," she said. "I got a good look at it. See, they–"

"They captured you," Beorn finished. He gave a whistle, and a man in the uniform of a Raheshi sergeant stepped from the

First Mission

forest. "Sergeant Nijl, is this the Aurigan you captured?"

"Yes, sir," came the voice she remembered from captivity.

"We'll have to make certain she doesn't warn her comrades, now, won't we?" Beorn said. "Do you think you can hold onto her this time?"

Beorne reached for the sword Mikhaila still held, but the Aurigan girl charged, knocking him off his feet as she had the Raheshi from the night before. *Damn them, they are not going to make me a slave!* was her furious thought.

Unlike last night's foe, however, Beorn was more sturdily built, so Mikhaila's charge only knocked him down and did not disable him. He leapt to his feet as Sergeant Nijl approached, and each foe seized one of Mikhaila's arms. The Aurigan girl cried out from the pain in her wounded right arm, but she struggled nonetheless, planting her feet and exerting pressure so her enemies could not capitalize on their grip. With all her strength, Mikhaila pulled, and Nijl lost his footing and his grip on her, which left her free to focus her magic on Beorn, turning him into a ball of flame that quickly flickered and died. But when she turned to face Nijl, she found herself staring down a dirk.

"I should–"

Suddenly an arrow quivered in Nijl's neck. Amid a gout of blood, he gave a gurgling noise and collapsed.

Mikhaila turned, and there stood Kester, lowering a bow that was almost as tall as he was.

"You took your own sweet time finding me," she said.

A young man's life can change in one day, once he learns what he can, and cannot, do.

THE POWER

Nathan Hystad

Grand Master Haz closed his eyes and everything went silent. The birds stopped chirping, the villagers stopped talking, and the wind even stopped howling - all for a moment.

Power thrummed from his finger-tips as he pointed them at the four candidates standing on display. Tal felt his pulse quicken as the fingers passed by him; the grizzled mage didn't give him so much as a glance. Karry, beside him, stood tall and proud as the Mage's hand glowed blue, the power spreading over her body. She twitched and convulsed as she lifted from the ground. As if a string holding her snapped, she fell to the ground with a thump. Tal moved to help her but the Grand Master shook his head in a warning. He stood firm, worrying his friend had been hurt, but knowing she'd be alright...they always were.

The Mage strode in front of them, and each of Tal's other companions fell to the ground in heaps as the magic raged through them. Tal worried as Haz stood before him, hand blazing blue. Would he find out he could throw fireballs? Or would he have a more functional Power unleashed? Maybe he would be able to make water from air! That would help his family and their farmer neighbors bring in great crops.

"I'm sorry my son. You have no Power." The Grand Master turned to the crowd of people, "Until next year. Thank you all for witnessing this great day."

No Power! What was he going to do? No one had *no* Power! It was unheard of. Sure some had mundane things they could do. Heating water a couple of degrees with a touch, or turning a

The Power

mushroom green with a thought, but never had there been someone with no Power! Tal slowly walked away from the main-stage and down the stairs behind it. He knew his parents were in the front row waiting to congratulate him, but he'd failed them. He'd seen the disappointment in his father's eyes as the Mage had spoken, and he just couldn't face them quite yet. He wasn't quite old enough to live on his own but he would be of marrying age in another two years.

The celebration had begun already and the whole town was set up for the grand festival. Naming day was a festival like no other. He was sure his friends up on the stage would have a great night, and for a moment he felt guilty for not staying with them to find out what Power they had. He knew they would forgive him. Life without magic? How could it be?

The sun was setting and Mistress Ging was busy lighting lanterns and candles around the feasting tables. There would be drink, and food, and dancing. But who was going to want to dance with a *nothing* like him now? He grabbed a pastry from a table and kept walking until he was well away from the busyness of the town. Rarely was the whole town together in one place, and at the moment it was too much for Tal to handle. He had to figure out what he was going to do with himself. Would he just work the fields his whole life, doing back-breaking work while there were people who use their Power to do it in a fraction of the time?

The evening turned into night as he sat on a hill a couple of miles from town. Stars shone brightly in the dark sky, and he pulled his tunic closer as he wrapped his arms around himself. It was getting cold and he knew it was time to go back and face his parents. Maybe life wouldn't be so bad, just different than everyone else's. Hell, it's not like he had an ability before and lost it. He just would never know what it's like. Surely that was better.

His heart jumped into his throat when he saw lightning repeatedly flash towards the centre of town. Bright green strikes that certainly didn't look natural rained down from the sky. Tal had no idea what was happening but he figured it could have been one of his friends testing their new ability. Some Powers were hard to control at first. At least that was what he'd been told. He sauntered towards home, aware that he would be reprimanded for disappearing without telling anyone where he was off too. His pace was brisk and soon the strange lightning ceased. Tal's stomach growled when he thought of the suckling pig roasting over the fires, and the buttered bread, so soft it would melt in your mouth. He sniffed and swore he could smell the roasting pig…then he saw the flames.

The whole town must be ablaze to have that much fire! He ran the last mile, lungs burning by the time he rounded the corner to the edge of the village. There was heavy smoke in the air, and the festival area had been demolished. Shards of trees and tables littered the ground, and he could see what he'd smelled before. It wasn't pig; the burned people were blackened to a crisp. There was no sign of anyone living until he heard a scream. He took the long way around the town's centre, worrying he would see his parents and friends dead on the ground. He shook with fear, but adrenaline kept his body moving.

Behind the stage they'd stood on earlier were the survivors. Many of them were sprawled on the ground, some with injuries, but most looked to be breathing. Tal hid behind a thick oak and peered around the side of it, hoping to get a better view without compromising his position. A hulking man stood with guards on either side. *Not a lot of back-up if you're going to invade a whole village.* The thought was cut short when he saw the dark green glow surround the large man. He was wearing a flowing green robe; his long black hair hung to his waist. One of the guards turned to the side, away from his master and Tal cringed when he saw the blank face. *They are real! What are we dealing with here?*

The *faceless* were monsters parents told their children about to get them to stay in bed when they were little. It was said that if a child was caught out of bed past the witching hour, the faceless would come and devour them. Some like Tal had challenged the theory and had survived to question their existence. He didn't question it anymore.

Every instinct told him to run away and hide, but he couldn't do that to his family. For the first time he saw the people tied

The Power

together in a line beside the roaring fire. The sky was dark and it was hard to see their faces between the night sky and the smoke but he was sure one of them was his mother, and one was the Grand Master.

The Green Mage's voice sounded calm but it carried far and Tal could hear every word from behind the tree.

"Haz, the great Blue Mage, here in a backwater dump, and dancing with peasants! What a sight."

The Grand Master shifted uncomfortably but even from this distance, Tal could see his eyes burn blue with rage. Then Tal saw what was holding them together and keeping their Power at bay. The rope tethering his friends together glowed a soft green. He'd heard of powerful magic objects that would counter someone's use of the Power. This must be one of those. But to stop the ten people from using their abilities must have taken a lot of strength. The Green Mage must have been a very powerful man to have this much control, and to have tamed two of the faceless.

"How did you find me, Lar, when I had every ward possible up against you?" the Grand Master asked, his voice hardly more than a growl.

"Just as always, the student becomes the Master. It was inevitable that I become more powerful than you. I only had to convince my friends here to let me out of the cage you put me in." The large man looked at the faceless beside him. They stayed motionless. "Once they realized that I could help them more than an old man, sending them a pittance every few moons to keep me imprisoned, they quickly became amicable to my cause."

Tal tried to understand what he was hearing. He called the Grand Master Haz the Blue Mage. Well that was impossible. The Blue Mage was just a character from the storybooks; the King's right hand man from hundreds of years ago. The books said he trained all of the Mages of the Spectrum until they started to turn on him. Orange and Green revolted and they disappeared. No one knew where they had gone. Could it be? He did glow blue, and he always seemed to know more than a village Mage should.

"So what do you want? You come here and kill innocent people? *My* innocent people! I always knew you were bad news, but there were many nights I couldn't sleep at night, wondering if I'd done the wrong thing having you and Zin locked away. Now at least my conscience is clear," Haz said.

"It's simple. I want your amulet, and I want you dead. Like I said, it's simple. Then I will free Zin, take an army of the faceless and overthrow the throne. With me in power, I will bring back the Spectrum and we will rule this world as we should have centuries ago. You will die because of your ego and morals old man. It could have been different, if you were willing to bend a knee to me so many years ago."

The Blue Mage looked defeated, his shoulders slumped and his head fell forward in resignation. "Take me, but leave the villagers. They have done nothing to you. They didn't even know who I was." His voice carried, though it was no more than a whisper.

"I can't leave witnesses. They have to die." He said the words with no affliction. Tal knew this man had no heart. He had to find a way to stop this. But how? He scanned area for a weapon. Maybe he could sneak up and kill the Green Mage. Once dead, the Power would return to the captured. It sounded so easy, until Tal realized he had no skills with weapons and could scarcely imagine killing someone. But he knew he had to try. He couldn't let the man kill all his family and friends.

A wood-splitting axe leaned against a tree between him and the intruders. He had to get it, it was the only way.

Tal could hear nothing but his own heart beat as he crept towards the axe. Leaves and twigs crunched under his feet but when he looked up, no one had turned in his direction. As he approached his heart beat so loud that he was sure they would hear it too. The tree was thinner than the last one, and he had to shrug his shoulders in to make sure he was hidden behind it. He gripped the wooded axe tight in his hands, the grain of it pressed hard into his sweating palms.

He was only about ten paces from Lar's back…he would just have to be extra quiet. As he crept towards the group, he saw the Grand Master lift his head, eyes blazing blue. He screamed with

The Power

a ferocity Tal couldn't have imagined from the grizzled, old man. He raised his arms and his fingers crackled with blue Power. The Green Mage laughed and Tal knew this was the time to strike, while he was distracted.

Axe raised, he ran at the huge man, he saw his mother's eyes go wide at the sight and as he swung the axe down for a killing strike, one of the faceless stepped to the side. The axe plunged into its chest, blood pumped out of the creature. Lar turned; a smile spread over his handsome face.

"What is this? A young man with more guts than you it appears, Haz," He looked back at the Blue Mage to see his blue energy fade to nothing. "Did you really think I didn't tune that specifically for you old man? Enough of these games!" He raised his huge green-glowing fist and shot Power from it at Tal. He covered his face and felt tears falling down his face as the green surrounded him. Was he dead? He didn't feel dead. Looking up, he saw Lar's eyes go wide as he let his arm fall to his side.

"Impossible! No one is immune to my Power. I am the Great Green Mage!" He flung more magic at Tal and other than his vision turning green, nothing happened.

Tal grabbed the axe, and pulled it from the faceless' chest. The other one came for him, knife drawn. Suddenly they didn't seem so scary. They didn't even have eyes to see him! The creature thrust the knife at him and he spun to the side, axe wildly swinging away. It connected with something and he realized he'd missed and hit a tree. He tugged hard and the blade came free, splinters of wood fell to the ground. The faceless thrust again and this time Tal took a less wild swing. It cleaved part of the thing's arm off; the hand fell with the knife still gripped tight.

The Green Mage stood with his mouth wide open and he stopped firing his magic at Tal who was running for the tied up villagers.

"Tal, that's your Power, don't you see? Magic doesn't affect you. That's why my magic couldn't sense anything in you!" The Grand Master shouted at him.

The only way any of them were going to make it out of this alive was if he could get the Blue Mage free of the bonds cancelling out his Power. Tal grabbed the glowing green rope at both ends on either side of the Mage's hands. The glow faded to nothing between his grip, and soon the rope was on the ground in front of them, smoldering with Blue Power.

Now that Haz the Blue was free, he urged the other villagers back. They dashed behind him and away from the ensuing battle. The large Green Mage had already begun throwing green fireballs at his old mentor. Blue and Green explosions lit up the smoky, dark night sky as the two fought fiercely.

Soon Tal could tell the Green was winning, and he knew he would have to do something to turn the tide. Since the magic wouldn't harm him, he had to incapacitate the man who was three times his size. Just because his Power wouldn't do anything didn't mean his massive fist wouldn't. He spotted the burnt rope and grabbed it judging it just long enough to do the job. In the midst of fireballs, he crouched and crawled over behind the Green Mage. He tied the rope into a large loop so it could be pulled and tightened, like the ones he used to catch loose cattle. *This could work; he's about the same size as a cow.*

He swung the rope around in circles and let it fly as the Grand Master distracted him with a new tactic–running. Lar started forward but soon found himself with a rope around his body; arms held tight to his sides. Tal struggled to keep the rope tight around the man while waiting for the Haz to come and help him. The Blue Mage shot Power into the rope and soon it glowed bright blue. The Green Mage was captured!

"My boy, you did it! By the hair of a dog, you did it!" Haz's blue eyes burnt bright.

The rest of the villagers freed themselves from their now loose bonds and went to help those who were injured. Tal smiled as Karry came over and gave him a hug. "Thank you for saving us," she said.

"So the Power can't sense me hey? This could be good. So what do we do with him?" He pointed at the raging man in the blue rope.

"I figure I've been hiding long enough. It's time I get the Spectrum back together." Haz fumbled in his robe and pulled out a dark stone on a leather rope. He tossed it at Tal and the rock

The Power

burned bright Red. "For starters, I need a Red," he said with a wink.

Tal flushed with excitement at the thought of being one of the legendary Mages. From across the fire, he saw his mother hugging his father and though he felt happy that his family was safe, he remembered the burned bodies as he entered the town. The Green Mage would have to pay for what he did.

"I know what you're thinking, son, but I have something better planned. We leave tomorrow. I have some friends I want you to meet. We will take care of this one and find someone worthy of the Green." Haz looked like the Grand Master he had grown up around once again.

Lar glared at Tal, and he was sure it wasn't going to be as easy as Haz made it sound. Life had changed so much in just one day, and he was excited to see where it took him.

A sword may be some girls' best friend, but all others may need is their wits, an attitude and a little magic.

THE BLUE ORB
H.L. Pauff

"For the love of the gods, can you try and avoid the bumps? Are you purposefully trying to hit each one?" Talip said.

The driver of the carriage turned his head and snarled at the young girl sitting in the back. "Quit your bellyaching, girly. You've done nothing but complain this whole trip. It's a road, you brat! It's bound to be bumpy."

Talip crossed her arms and lowered her voice. "There might be nothing you can do about the bumps, but you could do something about your stench."

The driver pulled the horses to a halt. "Excuse me? What did you say? I thought you said something dumb, but you cannot possibly be that foolish."

"I said you stink worse than a latrine!" Talip shouted at the man.

"That's it! Get off, girly. You're done."

"What?"

"You heard me. The ride's over. Off."

Talip look around. Only the small dirt road twisting and turning broke the hold the forest had on the area. "We're not close to the village yet."

"Off."

She peered over the side of the carriage. "But it's all muddy. I am going to get all muddy."

The driver lurched to his feet which sent Talip scrambling. She hopped off the carriage and into a puddle of mud and shrieked when it splashed into her face. With a flick of the wrist

The Blue Orb

and a laughing snort, the driver snapped his reins and the horses started to pull the carriage away. Talip wiped the mud from her eyes just in time to snatch her traveling case off the back of the carriage.

"You big dolt!" She watched the carriage get smaller and smaller until it vanished and she was left only with the dense forest for company. Cold, dirty water seeped through her shoes and the fabric of her socks and chills shot through her body.

"I hate this stupid village," she said. Towering trees lined the twisty road and she knew that following the road would lead her to the village, but she decided that taking the long way was for suckers. Cutting a path through the forest would get her home quicker and out of her ruined socks faster.

Only in the presence of the dense forest did it dawn on her that she was truly heading home. She had gone months without seeing trees during her stay in Haver City. There were so many things to see and do that she hardly even thought about the forest or the village or even her parents. Every day, her cousin took her to see someplace new and exciting. When every day started with a stroll through the markets to devour delicious pastries and flirt with boys, how could every day not be exciting?

There would not be any delicious pastries in the village. She'd be lucky to even get a piece of black, stale bread. There were no majestic stone buildings or paved roads. And there were, of course, no boys. The blacksmith's son sometimes looked okay, with his mouth closed. When he opened it, it looked like his two front teeth were fighting each other.

"I hate this place," she said with a grunt as she carried her heavy bag through the forest. "If I ever see that driver again, I'll kill him."

She knew she was close to the village when she saw the old hag's shack and the nearby pond in the small clearing among the trees. Its thatched roof was damp from the rain and its walls looked ready to crumble from rot. The windows were dark, but Talip always imagined that the old hag liked to sit in the dark. Her shack stood far from the village, but still close enough to be the stuff of any child's nightmares. Talip was always scared that if she wandered too far into the forest the old hag would turn her into a rock. Now that she was older she came to realize that the old hag was just a crazy old woman. But that didn't mean she was going to go near the shack. She could smell the cat pee from where she stood. Instead, she made sure to take a wide route to avoid getting too close to it.

As she drew nearer to the village and could start to see some of the homes through the trees, she did her best to get her mind in a good place. She needed to start planting the seeds in the minds of her parents to let her move out to the city permanently.

She found her parents standing over the fire and a boiling pot of stew. "I'm home. Hello, hello. Mmmm...smells wonderful," she said, walking past them. "Doesn't smell as good as some of the food in the city. You wouldn't believe the variety. Wait until I tell you everything."

Talip walked down the hall and went straight into her room. She plopped down on her lumpy and dirty mattress and tried to suppress the happy feelings bubbling inside of her at the thought of being home. Home was home no matter how grimy, but she couldn't let home be home forever. She didn't want to be like the sad people who never escaped. She listened for the footsteps of her parents coming to ask her all about the trip, but they never came. She went down the hallway toward the kitchen where she found the two of them sitting at the table slurping their stew.

"You didn't call me to tell me it was ready?" Talip grabbed a wooden bowl from the cupboard and went over to the cauldron. It was empty.

"You didn't save me any?" She looked at her parents. "You knew I was coming home today." Her mother and father looked at each other and shrugged. "What am I going to eat now?" Talip dropped her bowl on the table and slumped in her chair. She looked at both of them. "Well? Aren't you going to ask me about the trip? What's wrong with the two of you?"

Her parents looked at each other again and shrugged. Talip was about to start screaming at them when a blue light from outside pierced the windows. Her parents rose to their feet and started for the door.

"Where are you going? Hello? I just got home. Pay attention to me!" She followed them outside and saw all of the villagers

The Blue Orb

leaving their homes and walking towards the blue light in the center of the village.

"What are you doing?" Talip chased her parents and followed them until they reached the edge of the village square and stood in a line with all of the other villagers. Seated on a pedestal in the middle of the square stood a pulsating and glowing blue orb. The crowd stood around it, their eyes transfixed on it, their mouths hanging open.

Talip tugged on her father's sleeve and looked at her mother. Their eyes stayed fixed on the orb as if she wasn't even there. "Nice decoration. What is this?" she asked. "Is this some sort of joke? Har...har...okay, I'm home now. You can knock it off."

Through the crowd she spotted a few of the village kids that were her own age. Their eyes, too, were glued to the glowing orb. "Ginon, what are you doing?" she asked the boy with the bowl haircut. The boy shrugged without looking at her.

"This isn't funny," she shouted. "Not funny at all. What is that thing?" She turned to look at the glowing orb. Each wave of light hit her like an ocean wave. She wanted to get back to her parents to kick her mother in the shin and slap her father, but she found herself taking a spot around the village square where she could see the orb unobstructed. "This is ridiculous," she told herself and then shrugged and continued watching the orb.

The sun began to set and only when the orb ceased glowing did Talip turn her gaze away from it. "What is going on?" she asked. The crowd around her began to disperse and return to their homes. Talip chased after her parents who were walking into their house. "Mother, Father, the orb...I don't understand. The words to describe it are not there. I...I..."

Her father set a pot of water over the fire while her mother began to chop up some meat and vegetables. "Answer me," Talip said. She screamed when she saw the shoulders of her parents go up in a shrug. She grabbed her mom by the shoulders and shook the woman as hard and as fast as she could. When she let go and the woman went right back to chopping a beet, tears welled up in Talip's eyes.

She rushed through the door and took another look at the dormant orb before she ran down the dirt path. She had to get to the main road and find help before the sun completely set. There had to be some traders still on the road that could help her, that could make sense of what was going on.

Her mud caked shoes thudded against the dirt road as she ran. All those months of fine pastries had made running difficult and left her breathing like an overworked animal. She stopped for a moment to chase away the dizziness that threatened to drop her.

From the edge of the forest, a robed figure in a black hood emerged. On the other side of the road, another figure emerged and then five more figures appeared to block her way. In the shadows of the setting sun, their black robes made them appear part of the shadows.

"Hello?" Talip said, feeling her stomach churning at the sight of the figures. Their hoods shrouded their faces in darkness. "What are you doing?"

The figures looked at each other. "She appears to be outside of the influence," one of them said.

"Influence? What is this? What are you talking about?" Talip started to back away from them. Every step she took backwards, the hooded figures took one step forward in unison to match her.

"Stop," she shouted at them.

"We cannot allow this," one of them said. Their hands came up, palms facing forward. A blue light began to swirl in each of their palms, growing larger and larger until the swirling balls shot forward at Talip. She dropped to the ground and pressed her face against the dirt a moment before the balls screamed past her with intense heat.

Talip jumped to her feet and ran for the woods. She could feel the heat behind her as the robed figures launched more of the swirling blue fireballs at her. They crashed into trees, scorching the bark and bringing down branches all around her. They slammed into the mud at her heels and sent scores of mud balls into the air. Talip kept running and screamed and cried for help in the empty forest. She kept her focus forward and refused to look back for fear of catching one of the fireballs in the face. If she was going to go out, she didn't want to see it coming.

She ducked behind a cluster of rocks and tried to breathe. Her breath was ragged and shallow and she felt like she couldn't get

The Blue Orb

enough air into her lungs no matter how hard she tried. She strained her ears, listening for more of the fireballs but she heard none. Instead, she heard the sounds of twigs snapping and leaves crunching, sounds that increasingly crept towards her.

Ahead of her she could see the dirty, old shack that belonged to the hag and she knew she had to just get past the shack and past the pond and she would be close to the village. Whatever trance had fallen upon the villagers, she hoped the sight of strangers throwing blue fire would snap them out of it.

With her body pressed against the rock, she peered over the side. She could see the hooded figures in the distance wandering through the forest looking for her. Talip took a deep breath and then started to tip toe towards the shack. If she could just get behind it, she figured she would have enough cover to make it back to the village.

As she approached the shack, a storm of fireballs rained down in front of her and lit the wet leaves and twigs as if they had been baking in the summer sun for weeks. A fire spread and engulfed the nearby trees, blocking her escape. Burning bark and branches and leaves fell from the sky in a fury of blue flame.

Talip covered her head and ran towards the shack, bursting through the front door and closing it behind her. The inside of the shack had been destroyed. Tables and chairs and bookcases had been overturned, spilling their contents all over the dirt floor. Vases had been smashed and picture frames had been broken, but there was no sign of the old hag. Talip crouched in the corner and hoped beyond reason that they hadn't seen her come inside or that they would forget about her.

What little hope she had disappeared when one of the hooded figures appeared in the window. When it disappeared, a column of blue fire appeared on the wall of the shack and spread quickly. Every inch of her body poured out sweat from the heat. Before long, all four walls of the shack and the ceiling came alive with blue flame. Talip cried and moaned hoping to awake from this nightmare back at the city with her relatives.

There was a loud crack at the back wall. The ceiling would collapse at any moment. Two more cracks followed, each louder than the last. An armored fist jutted through the back wall and ripped a hole open. An old woman clad in rusted armor stood in the opening amidst the swirling blue fire.

"This way," the old woman yelled.

Talip jumped through the hole and followed the old woman past the pond and through the forest, running as fast as her tired legs would carry her. She heard shouts and could feel the heat at her back, but did not stop running. If the old woman in all that armor could keep running, then so could she.

Only when the burning shack disappeared into the forest behind them and the shouts faded did Talip stop to catch her breath. "I think we lost…"

"Quiet," the old woman said. The two of them listened to the sounds of leaves rustling and ancient trees groaning. Satisfied, the old woman leaned her sword and shield against the base of a tree. The latter's surface had been previously charred black.

Talip watched the old woman remove her helm and let her grey hair fall down to her shoulders. She could see her long nose and the warts all over her face.

"You...you..." Talip started to back away. "You're...You're the old hag." Talip tried to run, but the old hag grabbed her arm and before Talip could scream, an armored hand clamped down over her mouth.

"Would you be quiet?" the old hag said. "You are going to get us killed. If I let go, will you promise not to scream?"

Her hand smelled like an old foot, but Talip nodded. The old hag removed her hand and Talip proceeded to scream.

"What did I just say?" The old hag clamped her hand over Talip's mouth again, muffling her screams. "My name is not "old hag". My name is Milta and if you want to survive out here you will start trusting me and you will stop screaming. Do you understand, girl?"

Talip nodded and this time she did not scream when Milta removed her hand. "What did you do to everyone in the village? You've made everyone lose their minds."

"Do you see that shield? Do you see this armor? It has been a long time since I've had to carry these. They are trying to kill me as well. I do not know what is going on. Did you not come from the village?"

The Blue Orb

"Yes, I did," Talip said, "But I just returned today. I was in Haver City for the last few months visiting relatives."

"Then you are not under the orb's influence." Milta managed a dry-skinned smile.

"Neither are you."

Milta picked up her shield and sheathed her dull sword. "My home is far from the village, presumably outside of the orb's influence. I noticed the men in the black hoods months ago. They crept around the woods and on the outskirts of the village, but I thought them to be just curious travelers. Had I known what they were, I would have done something. I would have said something. I only knew when they came for me and I had to flee my home."

"Where are you hiding out now?"

Milta jerked her head towards the forest. "I will show you. We should not stay out in the open any longer."

Talip followed Milta deeper into the woods, staying well behind her in case the old hag tried any of the tricks she was known for in the stories.

"You're not going to turn me into a rock or something, are you?" Talip asked.

Milta sighed. "If I wanted to turn you into a rock, I would have done so already. Besides, I only turn people into leaves." Talip gasped, but Milta let out a giggle that unfroze her.

The older woman led Talip to the base of the mountains and to a cave that contained a fire pit and a few scant possessions. The entrance to the cave was barely a slit in the rock that both of them could barely fit through. Inside, a terrible stench filled the cave and Talip could feel the dampness of the cave crawling over her skin. In the corner of the room sat a tremendous pile of dead rats. Some of them had been skinned, but more of them sat soaking wet with matted fur. Talip pretended to ignore the rats and said nothing about them. "You live here now?"

"It is only temporary until I take my home back," Milta said.

"You saw those hooded people. Your home is destroyed. Look at your shield!" Talip looked at the burn marks on the shield and shivers ran through her body.

"My home is not destroyed. My house is destroyed. My home is there, occupied by intruders. My house can be rebuilt."

"What are you going to do?"

"It is a good thing you are here. Two are better than one if we are going to save the village."

Talip's eyes went wide. "Me? I can't help! I don't even know how I could help. We need to get onto the main road and call for help."

Milta took a seat on a rock and slouched against the cave wall. A heavy wind funneled through the tiny opening and blasted them with cold air. Leaves rode the wind and filled the cave, but so did other visitors. A blue and yellow butterfly touched down on Milta's knee. She scooped it up with a finger to examine it closely.

"So pretty. So complex. Look at all of the colors. Extraordinary creatures."

Talip waved her hand in front of Milta's face and sent the butterfly scurrying to the air. "Hey. Focus. How are we going to get to the road?"

"We are not going to the road. We will never make it. I have tried. They guard the road in all directions. They do not want anyone leaving. They want the orb to continue to do whatever it is doing."

"So then what? We sit in this cave and die? I'd rather you turn me into a rock."

"No. We armor you and arm you and we storm the village. The orb came first and destabilized the village. It was only after the orb sat in the village square that these strangers came. We remove the orb and perhaps everything will return to normal."

"I don't know how to fight," Talip said. Milta did not answer her. Instead, she got to her feet and went deeper into the cave. She returned with a few flat pieces of rock and a branch that had been sharpened at one end.

"These will make no blacksmith jealous, but they should suffice." She handed Talip the sharpened stick. "Now we just need to fasten these to your body."

The Blue Orb

With some vines and stray pieces of rope, Milta secured the slabs against Talip's chest and back as a makeshift breast plate. "It's heavy," Talip complained.

Milta pressed the tip of her sword against the front rock. "And it will protect you from stabbings and hopefully it will offer some protection against blue flame as well. Let us waste no more time."

The two women trudged through the forest towards the village. With heavy rock strapped to her, Talip struggled to navigate the terrain and often stopped to catch her breath. Talip had no idea where she was and Milta refused to stop.

"Please wait. Two seconds," Talip said. She wanted to put her hands on her knees and rest, but bending over was not an option at the moment. "Why are you doing this?" Talip asked. "Why do you even care? You can just run from here."

"What do you mean?"

"Most of the village hates you. They think you trick children and harm them. They don't consider you part of the village."

"Perhaps I do things more unconventionally than most, but this is still my home. I will protect it. Just like everyone in the village would protect it if they were able."

By the time the village came into view, night had chased away the light. The blue light ebbed and flowed over the trees and brush and it seemed to have grown in intensity from the last time that Talip had seen it. Even from a distance she could feel its pull.

"No matter what," Milta whispered, "We must destroy the orb. We must–"

"They are outside the influence," a voice shouted. A group of hooded figures appeared behind them, their black robes and hoods cloaking them in the darkness. A blue fireball raced past Talip's face. She dove behind a tree while Milta charged straight at the invaders with her dull sword.

Talip crawled on her belly and searched for a safe place to hide, but the grunts and screams of Milta stopped her. "I need to help her," Talip said out loud. Her heart beat loud enough that she could feel its vibrations in the back of her throat. She rushed out from behind the tree in time to see Milta stick one of the strangers with her sword. The figure moaned and collapsed into a pile of ash.

Talip ran towards the nearest stranger and aimed her sharpened stick at its back. A fireball exploded the ground in front of her and sent her stumbling. She could still feel the heat from the blue flame as a figure stood above her. Its hands came together and the swirling genesis of a fireball appeared. Talip closed her eyes and screamed until she felt the heavy metal footsteps of Milta rush across the forest floor to cut into the figure. The blue flame died and a shower of ash covered Talip.

Milta deflected a fireball with her shield and went after another figure. A second one appeared behind her, conspiring to blast her from behind. Talip jumped to her feet and ran the stick through the stranger's back before it could harm Milta. As soon as the tip pierced the skin, it erupted into a plume of ash.

"There are too many," Milta said, her face darkened by soot and ash. Despite the number of strangers she dispatched, more and more of them continued to emerge from the darkness of the forest. "We have to run. Go, girl!"

With enemies closing all around, the two women swung their weapons wildly to create space before they turned and ran towards the village. Fireballs sailed overhead, smacking treetops and thatched rooftops. In the center of the village, they found the entire village gathered in the square, mesmerized by the orb. Talip spotted her mother and father among the crowd, their faces even more gaunt and lifeless than before.

The two women edged their way through the crowd and stood before the orb, its glow too bright to look at directly. "What is it?" Talip asked.

"Does it matter?"

"Where did it come from?"

"Does it matter?"

Milta raised her sword and brought it down atop the orb with all of her fury. The sword clanged against the orb and bounced off. She tried it again. The orb continued its steady pulsating glow uninterrupted. For good measure, Talip smacked it with her stick which did nothing except shatter her stick.

"What do we do?" Talip asked.

The Blue Orb

Milta looked behind them. A group of hooded men appeared at the back of the crowd and began weaving their way towards them. "We will have to figure it out later." Milta reached down and plucked the orb from its pedestal. "This way." She clutched the orb against her side and sprinted through the crowd towards the forest. The eyes of everyone in the village followed her and when she reached the edge of the village a great cry rose up amongst the villagers

"Run," Talip screamed as the villagers, including her mother and father, came rushing after them with eyes hungry for the orb. Milta let her shield drop to the ground and secured the orb with both hands as she ran. Talip tried to ask what the plan was, but she couldn't find the words or the courage to open her mouth.

There was a surge of blue light and a scream and Milta crumbled to the ground. Her helm had been knocked off and smoke rose from the back of her head. "Milta!"

Milta looked up at Talip and rolled the orb towards her before the villagers descended upon her like a pack of wild animals. "Get it far from here!" she heard Milta yell before she started screaming.

Talip grabbed the orb and ran with tears streaming down her face. In her hands she held the orb and its blue light flashed directly in her face. It made her feel slow and sluggish and temped to stop and stare into its gaze. "I must keep going," she said out loud over and over again to keep herself from falling into the orb.

She came to a stop. "I must keep going." She tried to close her eyes, but they forced themselves open to peer down at the orb. "I really need to keep going." Talip shrugged and stared into the glowing ball. A fireball whizzed past her.

"No!" she screamed and raced forward and found herself in the clearing surrounding the smoldering ruins of Milta's house. Every step was difficult and it felt like there was an invisible rope around her waist pulling her backwards. She dropped to her knees and tried to inch her way forward through the mud. A group of hooded figures emerged in the forest behind her. Somewhere far away, she could hear the howls of the villagers.

"I must keep going. I must cover the light." She dug her fingernails into the ground and pulled herself forward towards the nearby pond, the one place no one in the village would come near. She could feel the hooded figures on her heels stalking her and hear the crackling sounds of blue fire. Clawing forward, she came to the edge of the pond and dangled the orb over the water, but it would not leave her hands. She tried to throw it, but it stuck to her skin as if a permanent adhesive had been applied.

She staggered to her feet and took one last look at the hooded figures before falling backwards into the pond. The scum and dirty water rushed into her mouth and her nostrils as she rocketed towards the bottom of the pond. Her face hit its sandy bottom first. The orb continued to glow, lighting up the murky water. Talip dug with what little energy she had left and buried the orb, smothering its light with a layer of mud. Talip floated towards the surface, hoping that was enough, but she prepared herself to face a volley of blue fire if it wasn't.

She reached the surface and crawled out of the pond, sucking in as much air as she could. There was no sign of the hooded figures and the noise from the village had died down. When she returned to the village as the sun was rising, she found the square quiet and empty.

Her mother was the first to greet her when she walked through the door. "When did you get back, sweetheart?"

Talip looked at her mother's kind eyes. Her face looked cheerful and full of life. "You don't know? You don't remember?"

Her mother gave her a confused look. "Why are you soaking wet? I didn't hear any rain." She wanted to tell her mother everything, but the words wouldn't leave her mouth. Instead, she sat down at the table and her mother began preparing a dish for her. "I can't wait to hear all about your trip."

Her father appeared in the doorway with a rag he was using to wipe blood off his hands. "What did you do to yourself?" her mother asked him.

He shrugged. "I don't know what I did. Must have cut myself on something." He came over to Talip and gave her a kiss on the forehead before going outside.

The Blue Orb

After a few days of watching everyone in the town go about their business as if nothing had happened, Talip stood in the middle of the town square. She dropped her paintbrush and looked at the blue and yellow butterfly she had painted. "There," she whispered, "You'll always be a part of this town."

CONTRIBUTORS

F. Paul Wilson is the award-winning, New York Times bestselling author of the Repairman Jack series and more than 40 books spanning science fiction, horror thrillers, contemporary thrillers, young adult books and some novels that defy categorization. *The Tomb*, the book that introduced his popular antihero, Repairman Jack, is in development by Beacon Films. Wilson has peeked into Jack's teenage life in three young adult novels: *Secret Histories, Secret Circles* and *Secret Vengeance*.

Wilson has also edited two anthologies - *Freak Show* and *Diagnosis: Terminal* - and written for stage, screen, and interactive media. Among his many awards: *Wheels Within Wheels* won the first Prometheus Award in 1979; *Sims* won another, *The Tomb* received the Porgie Award from The West Coast Review of Books and his novelette *Aftershock* won the 1999 Bram Stoker Award for short fiction.

Jeffrey Westhoff has served as a film critic, feature writer, reporter and copy editor in his career as a journalist. Westhoff wrote his first novel, *The Boy Who Knew Too Much*, while working as a freelance writer.

Westhoff grew up in Erie, Pa. where he spent his Saturday mornings at the library and his Saturday nights at the movies. His love of reading and films prepared him for his future as a movie critic. During his 25 years as a film critic Westhoff interviewed every actor to play James Bond except Sean Connery. He has contributed to RogerEbert.com and written book reviews for the Chicago Sun-Times. Westhoff lives in Chicago's Northwest suburbs with his wife Jeannette and is hard at work on his second novel. *The Boy Who Knew Too Much* is an action-charged YA adventure that blends the suspense of Alfred Hitchcock with the thrills of James Bond.

Jeff Ayers and Kevin Lauderdale write cross-country between Washington state and Virginia. Jeff is the author of *Voyages of Imagination: The Star Trek Fiction Companion* and the novel *Long Overdue*, and is a regular contributor to multiple newspapers and magazines with several short stories to his credit. Kevin's short fiction has appeared in numerous genre anthologies, raging from the worlds of Star Trek to Lovecraftian mythos. Jake and Kayla's adventures continue in the YA novel, *The Fourth Lion*.

Victoria Pitts Caine is a native Californian and lives in the San Joaquin Valley with her husband and two daughters. Her interests include genealogy and exotic gemstone collecting, both of which she's incorporated into her novels. While her genre is inspirational, she likes to refer to herself as a Romance Adventure Novelist.

Caine's three novels-*Alvarado Gold, Cairo*, and *The Tempering Agent*-form a mystery/suspense trilogy spanning two continents. She also has two novellas, *Like a Lily* and *Not Bound by Time*. All of her current works have been on the genre best seller's list on Amazon.

Caine has received recognition in both fiction and nonfiction from: Enduring Romance top 10 picks, William Saroyan Writing Conference, Byline Magazine, Writer's Journal Magazine and The Southern California Genealogical Society.

Caine is a former staff technician for the environmental sector working in air pollution control.

Kevin Singer is an army veteran and former journalist who has covered stories ranging from murder trials to cancer breakthroughs. His suspense fiction combines his interests in the supernatural, psychology, and the generally offbeat.

His short stories: *Road to Magdalena, Always Mine, Left Among the Mutants* and *Demon's Reach*–are available on Amazon.com, as is his full length novel *The Last Conquistador*.

Singer lives in Jersey City, New Jersey.

C.A. Verstraete enjoys writing stories with a scare or two. Her short fiction has appeared online and in anthologies including Timeshares and Steampunk'd from DAW Books, *Athena's Daughters* from Silence in the Library, and coming in the Baby Shoes Flash Fiction anthology.

Girl Z: My Life As A Teenage Zombie, received a 2014 Lovey Award for Best Paranormal and Sci-Fi book at the Love is Murder Mystery Conference; and was the 2013 Halloween Book Festival Young Adult Winner.

Verstraete has also written a nonfiction book on miniatures collecting, In *Miniature Style II*, and a children's book, *Searching For A Starry Night, A Miniature Art Mystery*.

Visit her at http://cverstraete.com or see her blog, http://girlzombieauthors.blogspot.com.

David Perlmutter is a freelance writer based in Winnipeg, Manitoba, Canada. The holder of an MA degree from the Universities of Manitoba and Winnipeg, and a lifelong animation fan, he has published short fiction in a variety of genres for various magazines and anthologies, as well as essays on his favorite topics for similar publishers. He is the author of *America Toons In: A History of Television Animation* (McFarland and Co.), *The Singular Adventures Of Jefferson Ball* (Chupa Cabra House), *The Pups* (Booklocker.com), *Certain Private Conversations and Other Stories* (Aurora Publishing), and *Orthicon; or, the History of a Bad Idea* (Linkville Press, forthcoming).

Morton M. Rumberg is a retired U.S. Air Force Officer who served as a Rescue and Survival technician teaching escape and evasion and survival techniques to air crew members; he survived a tour in Vietnam and barely survived two hardship tours in the Pentagon as a computer systems action officer. Mort was also an information technology consultant and a manager with a large international health care insurance company designing computer business systems. He has a Bachelor of Science degree in Business Administration, a Master of Arts in Teaching, and a Doctorate in Education. He was an adjunct professor of computer sciences for several universities in the Washington, DC area. He was also a volunteer with Alexandria Police Department and the Animal Welfare League of Alexandria, and active in the Northern Virginia chapter of the

Association of Information Technology Professionals. Visit his website at mmrumberg.com.

Amy Kaplan holds an MFA in sculpture from the Maryland Institute College of Art and spent several years teaching art in the public school system. Her work has been included in the anthology, *Suppose: Drabbles, Flash Fiction, and Short Stories*, and *Dragonfly Arts Magazine 2014*. She is also the current president of the Maryland Writers Association's Howard County Chapter. You can read more of her short works and poems at ALKaplan.wordpress.com. When she is not writing or indulging in her fascination with wolves, Amy manages props for a local dinner theatre. She lives and writes in Laurel, MD.

Deborah Walker grew up in the most English town in the country, but she soon high-tailed it down to London, where she now lives with her partner, Chris, and her two young children. You can find Deborah in the British Museum trawling the past for future inspiration or on her blog: Deborah Walker's Bibliography. Her stories have appeared in Nature's Futures, Cosmos, Daily Science Fiction and The Year's Best SF 18 and have been translated into a dozen languages and dialects.

Anne E. Johnson–Drawing on an eclectic background that includes degrees in classical languages and musicology, Johnson has published in a wide variety of topics and genres.

Her tween paranormal mystery, *Ebenezer's Locker*, is available as an e-book from MuseItUp Publishing. *Green Light Delivery* and *Blue Diamond Delivery*, noir-inspired science fiction novels for adults, are now available as print and e-book from Candlemark & Gleam. *Trouble at the Scriptorium*, a medieval mystery novel for tweens, is available from Royal Fireworks Press. Her speculative fiction has been published in *FrostFire Worlds, Young Explorer's Adventure Guide 2015, Rainbow Riot*, Slink Chunk Press, and elsewhere. She's written feature articles about music for The New York Times and Stagebill Magazine, and seven non-fiction books for kids with the Rosen Group. She's published dozens of short stories in a variety of genres, for both children and adults. Anne lives in Brooklyn, NY.

Chantal Boudreau is an accountant by day and an author/illustrator during evenings and weekends who lives by the ocean in beautiful Nova Scotia, Canada with her husband and two children. In addition to being a CMA-MBA, she has a BA with a major in English from Dalhousie University. A member of the Horror Writers Association, she writes and illustrates predominantly horror, dark fantasy and fantasy and has had several of her short stories published in anthologies. *Fervor*, her debut novel, a dystopian science fantasy tale, was released in March of 2011, followed by its sequels, *Elevation, Transcendence and Providence*. Other books published include her Masters & Renegades fantasy series (*Magic University, Casualties of War, Prisoners of Fate*) and The Snowy Barrens Trilogy, her YA tribal dark fantasy trilogy.

David Turnbull is a writer of fantasy living in London. Sometimes this includes a 'Sci-Fi' or a' Horror' slant. *The Wreck of the Blue Plover* is set in the same world featured in his Middle Grade fantasy *The Tale Of Euan Redeap* published by Wyvern Publications, due to be re-released Springbok Publications as book one of a three part trilogy. Two other stand-alone stories also set in this world have been published in 'The White Sail' (*Knowonder*) and *Different Dragons II* (Wolfsinger Publications).

Milo James Fowler is a teacher by day, speculative fiction writer by night, and an active SFWA member. When he's not grading papers, he's imagining what the world might be like in a dozen alternate realities.

His short fiction has appeared in more than 100 publications, including AE SciFi,Cosmos, Daily Science Fiction, Nature, Shimmer, and the Wastelands 2 anthology. His novel *Captain Bartholomew Quasar and the Space-Time Displacement Conundrum* will be available later this year.

Jack Mulcahy has been published in a number of markets, including Flashing Swords, Abandoned Towers, and Pulp Empire. In his secret identity, he is a resume writer.

Nathan Hystad is a writer from Alberta, Canada. He's had flash fiction published in both Kraxon Magazine, and Saturday Night Reader. *A Haunting Past* can be found in the anthology, Malevolence: Tales from Beyond the Veil. *The Attic* was included in Whispers from the Past: Fright and Fear, and *The Garden* can be seen in 9 Tales Told in the Dark 4. He also has stories slated to be in the upcoming anthologies: The Secret life of Ghosts, and The Ghost Papers Volume 1.

H.L. Pauff is a science fiction, fantasy, horror, and anything-else-he-want-to-be writer living in Baltimore. He has written a handful of novels, none of which he is ready to share with the world. Some of his favorite authors include: George R.R. Martin, Neil Gaiman, Peter Watts, and Jack McDevitt. He tries to write as much as possible, but when he's not writing he's reading, playing basketball, traveling, or making blood sacrifices to this thing that lives in his room and meows at him all day.

Made in the USA
Middletown, DE
10 June 2018